Kalandaka

The New York Squirrel

By

Peter Gallina

Kalandaka

The New York Squirrel

First published in 2006

©Peter Gallina 2006

ISBN : 978-1-84728-131-9

Peter Gallina asserts the moral right to be identified as the author of this work.

All rights reserved. No part of this publication may be reproduced, stored in a retrieval system, or transmitted, in any form or by any means, electronic, mechanical, photocopying, recording or otherwise, without the prior permission of the author.

for Matty James
and Taz

Contents

Forward

The events detailed in this story take place in a nondescript year, but in any case, it was not very long ago.

The areas and locations described herein all exist and can easily be visited by the curious reader wishing to retrace the steps of Kalandaka and his friends.

Gray squirrels have become one of the planets most successful and popular mammals and they have a great deal of self-esteem. As a result, the modern names they have given to each other tend to reflect this positive outlook on life and themselves in particular. Therefore all squirrel first names mean in fact 'squirrel' in some human language or dialect.

Rats take their names generally from the areas of New York where they were born, pigeons use names handed down to them from a legendary group of pigeon settlers who arrived from France with the Statue of Liberty, while most of the domestic animals in the city simply accept the names assigned to them by humans.

Maps and drawings, photographs and lots more to accompany the adventures of Kalandaka can be downloaded for free at:

www.kalandaka.com.

The Scramble

'Oh come on Skudzo, do something'

'No, No, got to wait 'til she's distracted'

Two squirrels were sitting side by side on a long branch of an elm tree. It hung ever so slightly over the pathway that led from Clinton Castle to State Street. It was a freezing cold January morning and all around everything was covered in a slippery gray-white frost. The few people that were about were all trying to hurry out of the cold and wind in the park. Below them, about twenty yards in front, was a small five-year-old girl walking slowly down the path with her mother. She was wrapped up warm in a fluffy white coat after a gruesomely cold trip to the statue. The girl was carrying a small white paper bag filled with honey-glazed peanuts. They were still warm.

'She's opened the bag! Come on, Come on!!'

'Timing, Mokus, timing. She has to be holding the bag just right'

The two squirrels sat motionless, their eyes fixed on the little girl and her every move.

Skudzo was, by squirrel standards, not the best-looking specimen you could imagine. He was twice as big as the others, had a bushy tail the size of a pineapple, and a large dark circular birthmark on his gray chest. Mokus on the other hand was a much smaller gray squirrel, with chubbier cheeks, who was along to see what he could learn from a scramble master. For a second he took his gaze off the girl as a sparrow landed on the edge of their branch, and at that moment the little girl offered up the open bag of nuts to her mother...

'NOW!!' cried Skudzo as he dived down from the branch and landed with an almost audible thud a foot or so in front of the girl. As he hit the ground he raised his tail over his head, stretched out his arms and wiggled around in front of her in a very funky fashion.

'Do Wappy do wap do do do' he sang as he wiggled.

The effect was instant, the little girl screamed with shock and the bag dropped to the floor scattering nuts all over the path in front of Skudzo.

'SCRAMBLE!' shouted Mokus and he too bounded down to the action. On hearing his cry around twenty other squirrels, who had been laying in wait behind various other bushes, benches and trees ran across to the nut bounty. These were joined seconds later by several dive-bombing sparrows. The frenzy lasted only a few moments and before the girl's mother could calm her daughter down, the crowd had gone. Even the pigeons that swooped in were too late. All that remained was a lonely looking empty white paper bag, and the wind soon had that away.

'Don't worry Carol honey, mommy will get you some more nuts' said the woman as she hurried her still shocked daughter onto the tourist bus. As the bus pulled off, little Carol gazed out of the window onto the park but could not see a single squirrel.

The squirrels of Battery Park are, by and large, a friendly bunch. They, like many other New Yorkers, prey on the streams of tourists that pass through on their way to the ferries for Ellis Island and the Statue of Liberty. Most people, tourists and locals alike, find them cute enough and are always happy to offer them tidbits or just smile and point when they see them running up the trees to their little homes high in the branches. The squirrels themselves are happy with the free chow, but are even happier to let folks believe in the tree house theory. It might just work for their country cousins, but these are city squirrels, more so, New York squirrels, and ask any New Yorker if they think it is a good idea to live in a tree in Manhattan and they will tell you that you are crazy.

The holes in the trees are fakes, follies if you like, used to fool the locals (humans, cats and dogs alike). The ones the Parks Department of the city built for them are used as gambling houses for nuts, or high stakes like dry fruit. They are sometimes used to stash food, or as look out posts, but most New York squirrels live in large secret warrens, known as Dreys, underground. The Battery Park residents have their home under the east side of Clinton Castle, and it was here – about six feet down – that an argument was breaking out.

In a large burrowed out room were packed many squirrels of all shapes and sizes. The floor, like most in the den, was covered in a mixture of fur and used paper. There was even the odd nut or two lying around, but no one was interested in food at this moment. All eyes were on the center where two females were standing in front of a much older, larger male squirrel. He seemed to be smiling.

'You really can't go you know'

The old gray squirrel was talking in a severe tone to the females, though they did not seem too intimidated by him. He had a slight tick that made him appear to be smiling strangely every now and again, but he was at this moment very serious.

14

'I don't want to have to hear this every year' he continued, 'it's dangerous, it's too cold and to be quite frank I don't see the point'

'We all need more space, and the smell in here is getting out of hand' said one of the female squirrels, her large eyes batting quickly

'And if you think we are going to mate with the same beatniks as last year you had better think again' said the other female.

An indignant silence fell over the crowd in the room that was interrupted by Mokus, 'Just what is so wrong with us?' he sounded almost as if he was pleading, 'myself and the rest of the guys are organizing the rumble... err... sorry I mean acrobatic display.... for you girls in a few days, and we have been practicing for weeks'

'Yeah, right' answered the first female sarcastically, 'Well Lana and I remember last year's pitiful display of squirrel prowess. Two ground hops and a miserable belly jump from a tree on the corner of State Street to the bench below it...at least four of you losers fell in the trash can and never even made it to the bench'

'That's the leap of death!' replied a wide-eyed small gray squirrel. He knew how much the acrobatic displays meant during the mating season. The girls were only interested in the best of the best. 'It's not so easy' he continued solemnly, 'remember what happened to Bilka last year'

A couple of squirrels bowed and shook their heads, but it sounded as if they were trying to muffle laughter.

'Well he had been at those cherry liquor chocolates I had found in the waste bin earlier' interrupted Skudzo 'He was a little tipsy'

'This year' continued Mokus, 'we are going to have a triple leap tree course followed by two double spin falls and *then* the leap of death'

As he finished he puffed up his chest and waited for gasps of astonishment from the girls, he did not get any. The old squirrel looked pleased though, 'That's the spirit Mokus' he said smiling, or maybe it was his tick you never could tell.

'Thank you Olmaxon' replied Mokus, 'it's going to be the most exciting one yet'

'Guys, guys' interrupted Lana, 'I've heard that in Central Park the real males hold acrobatic shows that last for days leaping from hundreds of trees, some as high as the moon. They train all year round and don't even get sweaty feet'

(Squirrels sweat glands are found in the soles their feet, so whenever they get nervous or exhausted they leave little sweaty footprints on the ground.)

Most of the squirrels in the room looked around awkwardly and shuffled their feet a bit, they had all heard of how wonderful Central Park was and how brave the squirrels were from there, so on this point no one could argue. Everyone present had heard how the squirrels in Central Park were bigger and braver even than Skudzo, who, weighing in at 2lbs and nearly 30 inches in length, was already twice the size of anyone else.

They had heard the tales of the Central Park squirrel that saved his litter from a cat or the one who had got a taxi to visit his cousins in another park uptown. Not forgetting the famous family of Central Park squirrels that adopted a magic mouse who conjured up dry fruit for them every night, and of course all knew of the legendary acrobatic displays of February. No one had ever met a Central Park squirrel, or ever been there for that matter, but everyone had heard the stories.

It was down to old Olmaxon to try and break the mood of inferiority that was rapidly descending on the males present. 'Come on ladies' he said 'they are just tales told by traveling rats to make us jealous'

In New York rats are the grapevine for all news, true or not. They don't necessarily lie, but news always gets distorted the further it travels. If one rat sees a man give a squirrel a nut, and a friendly pat in Central Park, he tells another rat. That rat in turn tells another and another, by the time the news hits the squirrels in, say, Union Square, you will hear that the same man had become four men who had caught the squirrel, stolen his nuts, burnt his home and then set him lose with a radio transmitter in his brain. You can imagine the type of stories the Battery Park Squirrels get to hear by the time the story reaches them at the very end of Manhattan.

'And your cubs' Olmaxon continued, trying to change tact a little 'who is going to keep an eye on the little ones?'

The general mood of the room was behind Olmaxon, hardly surprising since they were all males and Lana and Veverita were considered 'top branch' females. Mokus in particular had had his eye on Lana since last year. In fact he was just about to try to reinstate the general level of male pride with more plans for the upcoming acrobatic display but was interrupted by a small but clear voice from the back of the room.

'If the ladies want to leave, why should we try and stop them?'

Skudzo gave a startled jump since the small dark headed squirrel that he hardly had noticed sitting next to him was speaking, and now every face in the room was looking in his direction.

'Err, well look..Er young Koona isn't it?' fumbled Olmaxon looking over at the little squirrel.

'My name is Kalandaka, Sir' he said with a slightly bolder tone as he had caught what he thought was a warm glance from Lana's eyes.

'Yes, that's it, Kalan' continued Olmaxon, 'As I have been trying to impress upon everyone for ages now it really is far too dangerous'

He felt it was time to wrap the argument up with his trump card. He hadn't wanted to stoop this low, but if little male squirrels started taking the girls side, things could turn nasty. He put on his deepest most somber voice. 'Well I for one still have sleepless nights thinking about poor old Otan and Simolak'

It had the desired effect, everyone – even Lana and Veverita – looked nervously at each other. They all remembered last summer, the two young squirrels so much in love, so rebellious, so adventurous, so totally flattened by a massive Double Decker tour bus as they tried to cross over State Street on their way to a better place.

'Let's hear no more about it tonight' he concluded as everyone started nodding their heads and began shuffling out of the room. Olmaxon bowed his head solemnly for maximum effect, but as the last squirrels were leaving the room, he looked up, 'Skudzo and young Koona come over here please' Olmaxon knew he had to nip this one in the bud.

'Its Kalandaka sir' said the small squirrel, politely but firmly.

'Yes, of course it is', said Olmaxon 'Now tell me young Kalan, have you ever been border dousing?'

Skudzo sighed and looked upwards, he knew what was coming

'No, not yet' replied Kalan eagerly

'Well I'd like you to go with Skudzo tomorrow. I think it's time you learnt how to douse well, and it's also the best way I can think for you to see for yourself just how dangerous it is outside this park' Olmaxon looked up to Skudzo, 'If that's ok with you Skudzo?' he inquired his tick almost gone and a real smile came across his face.

'Yeah, no problem' replied Skudzo, 'I'll look after him, but I'm not so sure he'll last more than a few trees and the odd street light' he laughed then paused to think for a second, 'I'd like to take Bilka along as well. You know, as back up in case we run out'

Olmaxon nodded his agreement at Skudzo then turned and looked down to Kalandaka, who seemed to be happily excited by the plan for tomorrow. 'Young Kalan, you make sure that you do as Skudzo and Bilka tell you, and make sure you drink a lot tonight and again tomorrow morning. We don't want you drying out too fast on your first Border Douse'

Kalandaka smiled as he eagerly nodded to Olmaxon and with Skudzo patting him on the back they both left the meeting room.

'I know a good place where we can start drinking right now' boomed Skudzo as they walked down the corridor.

The old squirrel looked down on the floor - tired but happy that he had kept things all under control. If Olmaxon had been able to understand English, he might have read the headlines on an old piece of newspaper that was lining the floor directly under him. It would certainly have confirmed to him just how dangerous it was outside Battery Park:

'CHINATOWN TABBY'S CAT CRUSADE'

Hester Street Resident Ms Soo Lee is justly proud of her record-beating cat, Shokobaba, who must surely be the most prolific rat catcher New York has ever seen. Over the past year Shokobaba has dispatched over a hundred rats, as Ms Lee told our reporter 'Her tally last week alone was four rats, two pigeons and a squirrel'

The Douse

Squirrels rarely travel too far from their homes. Even New York squirrels generally stay within a 200 feet radius of their Dreys. However being so territorial it is important that other animals know whose patch of land they are on and regular douse patrols achieve that aim. A normal douse patrol involves two or three male squirrels, and their job is to urinate over everything they can on the borders of the squirrel territory. Trees, park benches, parking meters, fire hydrants, streetlights, people standing still for too long, you name it they pee on it. A good douser needs to be quite adventurous, since the borders are the most dangerous areas of the squirrels' home. He needs to have a good memory and organization skills, since there is no point peeing on the same tree twice in one day, and he must use his liquid assets sparingly if he is going to be able to complete the tour of duty. He also needs to have a large bladder.

The largest squirrel bladder in Battery Park belonged to Bilka. He was quite an old squirrel, but unlike Olmaxon, who preferred to spend most of his time underground, Bilka was always out and about. This was because he had always found the outside world interesting. Every day brought with it new colors, smells and surprises. Home in the dark dank corridors of the central drey was safe and warm, but Bilka felt that you could only really appreciate your abode by enjoying every aspect and exploring every corner of what was ouitside your home. For Bilka home was where he felt happy, and running around discovering was when he felt the most content.

He was up and out early this morning looking for something good to drink, since the night before Skudzo had asked him to accompany a young squirrel on his first douse. He ran from trashcan to trashcan searching for his favorite tipple – the remains of soft drinks from cans or plastic cups. He ran with a slight limp, the result of a nasty fall a while back. Unkind folks back at the central drey said that is what you got from always wanting to scurry about outside. However, Bilka argued that adventure by definition involves risk otherwise there is no thrill. The truth was that he fell while trying to impress Veverita with the 'leap of death'. The chocolate liquors he had found, and polished off earlier, had given him the courage to try a backward triple leap, but had taken away his coordination. He did not get involved with the mating acrobatics any more.

The sun had risen, but the clear skies it brought with it just seemed to make the whole day colder.

'Hey Bilka!'

He stuck his head out from under the trash he was shifting through

'Come on you scavenger, this young lad can't keep it in forever, if we don't start soon he's going to explode!'

Bilka saw the familiar bulk of Skudzo and a smaller, darker squirrel who seemed to be dancing around with a worried looked on his face. They were wrapped in their tails under the bench by his trashcan.

'Yeah alright, I'm ready, just looking for a last minute top up' he shouted across to them. In a flash he dived over to where there were. 'Feeling the cold ladies?' he scoffed, as he looked at Skudzo and Kalan still half hidden by their tails. 'Well Skudzo' he continued, 'who's the little guy?'

'This is Kalandaka,' replied Skudzo patting the young squirrel on his shoulder. This was too much for poor Kalan, who had drunk more than he had ever believed possible over the past few hours and he lost bladder control.

'Whoa! Not here' laughed Skudzo as he sidestepped to avoid getting wet, 'come on, let's start running, that should hold it off for a bit longer'

Kalan felt embarrassed, but started to run with the others nonetheless, and was relived to find that Skudzo had been right. They ran darting around the trees, scurrying across several paths until they arrived at the furthest end of the park, near Battery Place. They all sat down together, a little out of breath. With Bilka keeping lookout, Skudzo started to explain the basic rules of dousing to Kalan.

'Now then' began Skudzo, 'before we go spraying willy-nilly we have to make sure it's really necessary. Smell the base of this tree' He had bounced over to the base of a nearby tree, Kalan followed and sniffed the air around.

'Smells like home,' answered Kalan

'Right! Doused yesterday by yours truly and still going strong' replied Skudzo full of pride 'no need to waste time here' He jumped over to a nearby bush

'And here?'

Kalan followed, 'Errg' he said with a slightly disgusted tone in his voice 'Dog'

'And here?' Skudzo had jumped over to the leg of a park bench

'Man' said Kalan as he sniffed, 'Sweaty man' he added.

'Well would you like to put things right and start the douse?' asked Skudzo smiling at the little squirrel. Kalan needed no further encouragement and started to take the strain off his tiny stretched bladder. Small wisps of vapor curled upwards into the freezing air.

'That's good,' said Skudzo as he watched Kalan, 'but don't waste it all, just a few squirts on each spot, we've got a lot to do yet'

'OK' replied Kalan, who was feeling a lot better 'I'll try and make it last'

Just as Kalan had finished dousing the area, they heard a familiar 'WHACK-WHACK' sound. Bilka had spotted danger and was furiously banging his tail on the ground. 'KENNY!' he cried, and all three shot up the nearest tree.

A few seconds later, a small white-brown Jack Russell terrier came bounding up to where they had been sitting. Dangling his red leash behind him. He sniffed around the base of the tree, moved over to the bush and then the park bench.

'Oooh squirrels!' he said to himself with glee and promptly lifted his leg up and sprayed in turn all three places.

'*Kenny!*' A man's voice boomed out across the park. 'Here boy, come on!'

Kenny sniffed around to make sure all trace of squirrel smell had been replaced by his own 'Eau du Kenny' and ran off towards his balding owner.

'You are such a naughty boy, pulling on the leash, come on get back inside, let's go' The balding owner tightened the leash around Kenny's collar and they both started to walk towards the castle.

'I bet I could make sure that mutt stays on his leash' mumbled Skudzo angrily, 'that's the third time this week'

'He seems to have done it deliberately' Kalan caught himself thinking out loud

'Oh he does' assured Skudzo, 'That mutt will sniff around until he finds our scent, he won't pee on anything else'

'I suppose you'll want me to douse the place again, Skudzo?' asked Kalan

'No, no that's ok, leave it to Bilka, let's move on, we are behind schedule already' answered Skudzo.

Kenny turned around and started to tug on his leash. He saw the three squirrels hopping down from the tree and run around putting an end to his handiwork. 'Calm down Kenny!' The balding owner had no intention of letting Kenny escape again and tightened his grip on the leash. 'You can chase the squirrels another day'

Kenny whined under his breath, and as the balding man dragged him away, he eyed the squirrels as they darted off in a wavy line, pausing for a second by each tree or trashcan, as they moved quickly along the edge of the park.

Squirrels can move very quickly for their size. Some have been recorded moving at speeds of over 20 miles per hour, but no one had ever speed clocked

Kalandaka. Skudzo watched, amazed at the speed and agility of his new young friend.

'He's a natural' he said to Bilka as they both watched Kalan spray the base of a street light, make two hops and a spin twist over to the leg of a bench. He then made a large leap over to a trashcan followed by a half twist-flying leap up into a nearby tree.

Kalan was dousing a little every time he landed and found that, having got rid of most of the extra liquid weight he had been carrying, he could coordinate his speed and balance better. 'This is great!' he said as he jumped over to where Bilka and Skudzo were sitting watching him. 'I've never felt so invigorated'

Bilka smiled, 'that's really good Kalan, but where we are off to now it's a little more dangerous, so you just watch ok?'

Skudzo pointed to the road with his tail, 'Bilka's right, over there is the outer boundary and we have to douse it. Everything there is a danger to us, men, dogs, cars, bikes, you have to keep your wits about you boy'

'What's beyond the road?' asked Kalan

'The rest of the world' said Bilka

'Well yes,' interrupted Skudzo, 'but the road is like a natural boundary for us'

'Central Park' Bilka carried on talking, Kalan could sense an almost enchanted tone in his voice 'Lot's of adventures, different types of food, squirrels, answers' Skudzo seemed a little irritated and nudged Bilka with his tail.

'Wow' Kalan peered closer at the distant road, 'has no one ever crossed it?'

'No they haven't' replied Skudzo a little angrily, 'and when we get there you will see why!' He turned to Bilka who seem to have drifted off, 'You stop daydreaming and keep your eye on him'

Skudzo looked at Kalan who was wide eyed with excitement. 'You watch us closely' said Skudzo, Kalan nodded, 'and don't leave the park boundary' Kalan continued nodding and the three of them set off.

By now, Battery Place was getting quite busy. Morning commuters were beginning to bustle around, even the first tour buses had arrived. Kalan had often seen the buses and cars, but never this close. The noise was intense, and the smells were changing constantly. There was a flurry of sounds and colors. 'What do you think Kalan?' Skudzo had to shout to make himself heard, 'the outer boundary, ours to douse!'

The douse boundary of Battery Park was quite big by squirrel standards. It started along the park fencing near Battery Place, following it along State Street, down to almost opposite the South ferry metro stop. It then stretched and waved its way along the riverside walk from Minuit Plaza back up towards

Battery Place by way of the castle and the ferry booth. To be honest it was such a large area that the boundaries changed quite often, depending on who was doing the dousing. It generally took three groups of squirrels two days to make a complete douse, and of course it was one of those never-ending jobs like cleaning the windows on the Empire State building, once you had finished it was time to start again.

Skudzo, Kalan and Bilka were doing the most hazardous area today the State Street side of Battery Place. Some squirrels kept their dousing to the park limits, Skudzo liked to douse the area between the sidewalk and the road. Kalan jumped up into a nearby tree so he could get a better look. He saw Bilka and Skudzo dodging backwards and forwards over the sidewalk and into the gutter. People passed by, but didn't seem to be paying any attention to them. All of a sudden Kalan noticed that Bilka had stopped. He was sitting on the edge of the sidewalk with his back to Kalan, facing more or less the direction of the customhouse. A car drove by so close that the wind rush it created blew Bilka's tail back. However the squirrel didn't move as if he were transfixed, or hurt thought Kalan. He dived down from the safety of his tree and ran the twenty yards or so to where Bilka was sitting motionless.

'What's up Bilka? Are you OK?' asked Kalan concerned as he sat next to the still squirrel.

Bilka didn't reply, he just kept staring ahead. Kalan began to feel too exposed and turned around looking in every direction for trouble and for Skudzo. People were walking by, but none of them were aware of the squirrels, and Skudzo was nowhere to be seen. Kalan found the noise coming from the road deafening. He brushed Bilka with his tail. Bilka turned and looked at Kalan. He spoke with a warm smile.

'Don't let them tell you life's only about what you can see' Kalan looked up to Bilka who had a strangely peaceful look in his eyes, 'Life is also about what you dream, what you can't see, what you can only imagine' He gazed back across the road, 'Maybe Kalan, it's not worth seeing after all, maybe your imagination is better than mine' he smiled again 'but you'll only know if you go and take a look for yourself'

Bilka, sensing that Kalan was very nervous placed a comforting tail over the younger squirrels shoulder, 'Better to know the answers – good or bad – and sleep peacefully, instead of lying awake each night wondering'.

As Kalan looked at Bilka his tail suddenly hit the ground and thumped hard. 'KENNY!' he shouted, 'RUN!'

Kalan wheeled around to see the familiar brown-white form of Kenny running directly towards them, he had managed to break loose again from his balding owner who was screaming

'STOP KENNY! COME BACK HERE!'

Kalan felt Bilka move, not towards the park, but across the road. 'Bilka!!' he cried. Some cars honked and one big white one seemed to screech to a halt suddenly, but Bilka had disappeared. In an instant Kalan regained control of himself and turned to run, but it was too late, standing in front of him was Kenny panting and drooling while looking down at the tiny squirrel. His owner was still some hundred yards away. Kalan froze, normally his instincts would have gone into automatic and bounced him back into the trees, but he found he couldn't move.

Kenny froze as well. This isn't what normally happens. Normally squirrels scatter at the first sight of him and then he could have fun chasing them up the trees, then spraying all over their turf. What should he do now? Kenny thought for a moment while looking down at the obviously terrified squirrel. He decided to break the ice.

'Hello' but before he could finish another word he felt something heavy jump on his back.

'RUN KALAN!'

It was Skudzo, he had dived up onto Kenny's back and dug his claws in.

'OWWWW!!' screamed Kenny as he was forced to suddenly shift his attention. In a split second Kalan moved and ran as fast as he could, dodging between the legs of Kenny's owner, and leapt into the nearest tree. He was followed seconds later by Skudzo and a barking Kenny.

'You all right?' panted Skudzo, as they jumped up into the highest branches.

'Yes I'm ok…. But Bilka?' he replied.

Below them they could hear Kenny barking madly. 'Hey! That hurt!' he moaned then went on to furiously pee all over the tree before his owner got him back on the lead.

'No evening walk for you! Bad boy!' puffed Kenny's balding owner. He started to drag the still complaining Kenny away.

'Ahh shut up Baldy, this is my park, and this is my tree, damn smelly squirrels, hey!! Get off me you big brute, put me down I got legs!' The squirrels couldn't hear the rest of Kenny's wailings as his owner had picked him up and was walking away out of earshot.

'Didn't you see Bilka?' asked Kalan, still shaking a little. He noticed that Skudzo too seemed shocked.

'I saw you both by the curb" said Skudzo, 'then as Kenny came I saw Bilka leap out into the road, and you just freezing in front of that dog' he said having finally got his breath back.

'But is he…..?' Kalan didn't want to finish the sentence afraid of what the answer might be.

'No, no don't worry, I think he made it' replied Skudzo as he wrapped his tail around Kalan. 'Generally there is much more noise from the road if something had hit him', but even as he spoke deep down Skudzo wasn't sure. His mind was also turning over something else 'That dog' he said, 'I thought it was going to rip you into tiny little pieces'

Kalan thought for a second about Kenny as the the dog's smell wafted up the tree. 'I don't think he wanted to hurt anybody, but he's ruined all our efforts here today,' he told Skudzo, but his mind was still on Bilka. 'Shouldn't we go looking for him Skudzo, he might be in trouble'

'We can't cross the road Kalan' replied Skudzo, 'and besides, where would we start to look?'

The two squirrels sat silently for a few moments looking at each other, both of them a little uncertain in their thoughts and also as to what to do next. 'He had been acting strange for some time now' said Skudzo after a while, 'all melancholy and soulful. Did he say anything to you Kalan?'

Kalan told Skudzo what he had heard. Skudzo listened intently and thought about it in silence for a few moments after Kalan had finished. However before he could speak another squirrel leapt over from the branch of another tree.

'Hey! Guys, Mokus and the rest of the Fellas are practicing, you coming to watch?' It was a small fluffy white-gray squirrel around Kalan's age. 'They've got this new routine see and......' he paused and sniffed the air 'Errg! What a stink! That smell it's...'

'Yeah yeah! We know' interrupted Skudzo

'But I thought you were supposed to be dousing?' replied the new arrival

As Skudzo started to argue with the little squirrel, Kalan looked out across in the direction of the old customhouse. He felt pretty certain that Bilka was all right, and started to think about what Bilka had said before he had run off. Maybe he had already started to find the answers.

'Come on!' Skudzo's barking voice broke Kalan's thoughts, 'We've got to tell Olmaxon, this little devil here is going to sort out Kenny's mess downstairs'

Leaving the newcomer to douse the base of the tree Kalan and Skudzo raced towards the castle, paying little attention to the small crowd of people that Mokus and his acrobatic training squirrels had attracted to several trees in the middle of the park.

Over the next few days douse patrols were doubled and the Battery Park boundaries reduced in size, the area where Bilka had disappeared was made out of bounds. All squirrels were on the look out for any sign of Bilka, and the rats were tapped for any information they could provide. Little Kenny had also doubled his efforts 'he must be giving old Baldy hell at home,' thought Olmaxon, as he seemed to be in the park morning, noon and night.

Kalan spent most of the time dousing and thinking. Mokus had tried to get him involved in his February 14th display acrobatic team, but Kalan had politely turned him down. He instead had been planning on using the 14th of February as the day to put a stop to Kenny's troublemaking.

The Hanky Panky Rumble

'You've got to be kidding me' said Skudzo as he looked incredulously at Kalan, 'Who in their right mind is going to want to get that close?'

The two squirrels sat under their favorite park bench by the south entrance to Clinton castle. The sun had just risen and the light frost than had developed on the surface of the previous nights snowfall started to glisten and sparkle. All around them there was a flurry of activity as literally dozens of squirrels were bustling about preparing for the big show. Some were practicing last minute twist jump turns from the ends of benches, others trying small run jumps into the nearby trees. One squirrel, Sincab, was talking bets in his Parks Department drey in the tree directly above where Skudzo and Kalan were sitting. There was a constant to-ing and fro-in up and down the tree as squirrels were racing up with nuts and dry fruit placing bets on the event, some even on themselves. Sincab was giving good odds on a lot of things. On who could make the leap of death successfully and not end up in the trashcan below, who could make the most double twists in a single jump, even who would be mating with who. Below Sincab's drey, two other large squirrels bounced down to where Skudzo and Kalan were still talking. One of them had his cheeks and paws full of nuts.

'Hi Fellas, we're ready for ya, just let Risu here unload his savings with Sincab'. As Risu raced up to Sincab's drey, Skudzo gave a welcoming smile to the other squirrel.

'Hey Ardilla, you know what this little tyke wants to do on today's douse?' he said pushing Kalan playfully with his tail. Ardilla twitched his nose in the direction of Kalan and shook his head, as Skudzo explained Kalan's plan, Ardilla started to laugh and tap his tail on the floor excitedly.

'Hey' said Kalan indignantly, 'it will work, I'm certain. We have to stop Kenny and his one dog vendetta, or we may as well be dousing into thin air'

'Kalan' laughed Ardilla, 'I love it. It's a great plan!'

'You do?' said Skudzo, a little surprised.

'Yeah' replied Ardilla, 'he's right. Kenny ruins every douse, but I'm not so sure I want the job of luring him into Kalan's trap. That's pretty dangerous'

'Don't worry' said Kalan, 'I'm going to do that, I'll douse around till I'm empty then I can move faster'

'But Kalan, I...' interrupted Skudzo, but Kalan looked him in the eyes and carried on talking,

'Besides, it won't be the first time I've been face to face with that dog'

Skudzo nodded quietly to himself, and at that moment a nutless Risu arrived, 'That crook Sincab is only giving evens on Mokus' He stopped and saw that something was up. 'What?' he asked.

'Risu my pal' said Ardilla, 'We are going dog hunting'

'Great' Risu replied with everything but enthusiasm. The four squirrels set off towards the park boundary at Battery Place, for it was there that Kenny generally made his morning appearance. A wind had started to blow in from the South-West as the heatless sun moved higher into the cloudless light blue sky, it was going to be a very cold day.

'They normally come out from over there,' said Kalan indicating with his tail the corner of Broadway, 'If I spray along here' he continued 'and then around the fence perimeter he should follow pretty soon enough'

'What if Baldy has him on that red lead of his?' asked Skudzo

'Well, we'll think of something, I'm going to run near Kenny, that should make him want to escape from Baldy badly enough'

Skudzo still had his doubts, Ardilla saw this and spoke directly, 'Kalan, what if Kenny breaks free? He's done it before'

'I'm counting on that! ' replied Kalan confidently, 'I'm going to douse the area now, then when Kenny is on my tail I'll just pretend, so I'll be too quick for him to catch me'

'And us?' inquired Risu, 'I'm fit to burst'

'You've gotta hold it in' sighed Skudzo, resigning himself to the fact that Kalan's plan was going ahead regardless of his misgivings.

'That's right' said Kalan, 'I want you all sitting up there' He pointed to the first branch of the maple tree under which they were sitting. Then patting Skudzo on the back he jumped and started to run along the park fence.

'Will someone fill me in, please' asked Risu.

As Ardilla and Skudzo explained the plan to Risu, Kalan was busy darting from one trashcan to another, spraying a little here and there. He dived under a bench, then turned and jumped into a path. He felt a little tense. What if Kenny didn't show? What if Kenny couldn't break loose from Baldy? What would happen if Kenny caught him? His thoughts moved through his mind as quickly as he was running. He leaped up onto the perimeter fence and scurried along the top back towards the Maple tree, and in one jump he was sitting with the others.

'Nice leap' said Ardilla admiringly.

'Hope that dog can't jump as high,' said Skudzo.

'Speaking of jumping' Risu was rocking back and forth to keep his mind of his full bladder, 'Are we going to be alive to catch the show? I gotta lot of nuts riding on Mokus'

'Yeah, Yeah don't worry Risu,' replied Kalan

'You're going to lose those nuts anyhow' Skudzo moved over to Risu, 'Mokus is never going to make two double spin falls during the leap of death, that trashcan is going to eat him up'

Risu was about to argue when Kalan interrupted to try and get their minds back to the matter in hand, 'We'll all be back in time. Kenny and Baldy are creatures of habit. I've been watching them for days'

He looked around to make sure he had their attention then continued, 'I reckon Kenny will pick up my scent around the third tree, then he should spray his way all the way here'. He looked down to the base of the maple tree in which the four squirrels were sitting 'Then we have him' he smiled triumphantly.

'And what if he doesn't follow' asked Ardilla

'Well then I'll race down and get him to chase me here' replied Kalan in a very confident tone.

And so they waited around ten feet up the tree on a very small branch that sagged slightly under their weight. Their fur and tails blowing lazily in the freezing breeze. Down below a few other dogs and their owners were passing by. A large obedient Alsatian was walking step for step with his elderly owner. A young woman, her face almost hidden by a large black woolen scarf, was calling to her Dalmatian. Her dog was tugging on his lead trying to stay a few precious seconds longer near the curb where he had found something interesting, a squashed chocolate bar as it happened. None of these dogs seemed too concerned with where Kalan had doused, to them it was just another of New York many smells. Only Kenny seemed to take a great delight in covering up squirrel scent, it was like a hobby.

'Why do you think he does it?' Risu broke the silence, partly to get his mind off wanting to pee.

'Dunno!!' replied Skudzo, 'Maybe a squirrel bit him when he was a puppy'

Ardilla smiled at Skudzo, but Kalan spoke without turning away from the road, 'I just think he's bored'

'You could have a point there' said Skudzo, 'Baldy doesn't look as if he's much fun to hang out with' he then put on a deeper, mimicking voice, 'Here Kenny! Come Kenny! Good boy! Bad dog! NO MORE Kenny!!'

The other squirrels, including Kalan, started to giggle at Skudzo's impersonation. Then all of a sudden their ears pricked up as their heard in the distance the real thing.

'NO! KENNY!'

Down below the squirrels a familiar couple had turned the corner. The balding owner had a dark black woolen jacket with the collar turned up. He was shouting to his dog, who was, as usual, tugging hard on his leash. Kenny whined back miserably at his owner.

'See what I mean!' laughed Skudzo, 'You always know a relationship is on the rocks when the conversation dries up'

Ardilla turned to Kalan, 'Hey! Even if Kenny wants to follow, Baldy has got a tight grip on him this morning. That dog is going to have difficulty lifting his leg, let alone chasing after squirrels'

Kalan saw that Ardilla was right. Kenny had smelt the squirrels' trail, but Baldy had sat down on a park bench and had a firm hold on Kenny's leash. The little terrier couldn't move more than a few feet in any direction.

'Well that's that,' said Risu

Kalan's mind was racing, 'No wait!' he said, and turned to Skudzo who could see that his little friend was about to come up with a dangerous solution. 'Skudzo, could you do a tickler for me on Baldy?'

Skudzo didn't have time to reply as Kalan was speaking as quickly as he was thinking.

'Look, leave me to grab Kenny's attention, while you get Baldy to loosen his grip. Then I'll make Kenny chase me around a bit, while you dash back here and wait with the others'

Skudzo sighed as he saw that both Ardilla and Risu were looking at him as intensely as Kalan.

'Come on Skudzo, you are the best tickler in Battery Park' pleaded Kalan.

'Go on Skudzo' said Risu, 'Make the man's hair stand on end'

Skudzo smiled at Risu and thought for a second, then nodded his agreement to Kalan. In an instant both he and Kalan jumped down to the ground.

Skudzo was indeed Battery Park's best tickler. This is the curious and unique New York squirrel technique of surprising humans while they throw the odd nut, by running up their leg. Since ticklers have a fearless reputation to maintain he had felt obliged to agree.

Both squirrels ran towards the bench, but Skudzo took a wider semi-circular route to avoid being seen by the dog, while Kalan made a beeline directly towards Kenny, who spotted him straight away. Kalan started to hop about around ten yards away from the terrier, but pretended not to notice him. Kenny started to bark.

'Shut up Kenny! Calm down will ya!' The balding owner turned to look at his dog and pulled hard on the leash. As he glared angrily at Kenny, he felt that weird tingling sensation you get when you know you are being watched. He slowly turned his gaze forward to the ground below him, and was slightly shocked to see a very large squirrel staring him straight in the face. It was almost as if the little animal had his hands on his hips.

'Nothing!' shouted Baldy his voice a little shaky. 'I ain't got nothing for you little fella' he paused then added almost as an afterthought, 'sorry'

Baldy then felt another heavy tug on the lead and he turned his head angrily back to Kenny.

'KENNY!!' he cried 'NO MO.......'

The balding owner's voice shuddered to a halt as he felt a surprising sensation of fast moving tickles working their way like lightning up his left leg, onto his chest and up onto his shoulder. He turned his head and found himself face to face with Skudzo. He could even feel the squirrel's warm breath on his nose.

'Wappy do,' said Skudzo casually

'AAAARRRRGGGHH' Baldy screamed, let go of the lead, and leapt up into the air. Skudzo bounced down onto the bench and was already on his way back to the tree by the time Baldy's feet touched the ground.

Kenny – already tugging hard on his leash – felt himself propelled forward and raced towards Kalan, free at last. The little squirrel was ready though, and started to dart left and right, pausing for a millisecond to make sure Kenny was following.

'KENNY *NO!*' Baldy was still shaking with shock, but slowly pulled himself together and started to chase after the little tear away.

Kenny started to get distracted as he chased after Kalan. Chasing the squirrel was great fun, but he still had to stop here and there to spray over the squirrel's scent. He made sure however that he kept a good distance between himself and Baldy, though it wasn't easy chasing a squirrel, keeping away from Baldy and spraying. Kenny had never peed so fast in his life.

Skudzo jumped up into the tree a few seconds before Kalan arrived. 'Come on! Jump up' Risu shouted down,

Kalan didn't answer, he was looking down the path to make sure Kenny was still on his tail. The Jack Russell had stopped to sniff a bench about thirty yards away, Baldy was closing in fast, if he grabbed Kenny now it was all over. Kalan started to bang his tail furiously on the ground to attract the dog's attention, but Kenny had lost interest in the chase. He started to pee on the side of the bench and didn't even look towards Kalan.

'What now?'

Kalan heard Skudzo shout down from the tree, and in a flash knew what he had to do. He took a deep breath and ran over to tickle Kenny. He ran as fast as he could, Kenny had his head under the bench as Kalan took a running jump onto Kenny's shoulders. He then made a half twist turn back to the ground, and carried on running back towards the tree, he didn't need to turn around to hear that Kenny was, at last, in hot pursuit. Kalan reached the base of the tree and gave it one last quick spray as he leapt to safety. Kenny bounded up to the base of the tree a split second after and smelt the ground. 'Whoa! What a squirrelly stink' he laughed. He turned his head and saw Baldy closing the gap. 'Time for one last pee' he said smugly and lifted his leg.

'Same here!' came a tiny voice from above, and Kenny felt an odd, warm and wet sensation all over his back.

'What the....' then the overpowering odor hit his senses. He was being doused. 'ERRG, ARRG Noooo' he started to spin around in circles, then tried desperately rolling about on the ground, the smell was overpowering.

'Come here you crazy mutt! Cut that out. Bad dog!' Baldy had arrived, a little out of breath, and grabbed his dog who was still writhing around on the ground, as if gripped by electric shocks. 'What's wrong with you?'

'No, leave me alone, get off..... nooo the smell!' Baldy reached down and picked up his dog. He couldn't hear the squirrels laughing, but Kenny could. 'You rotten rodents! Oooh POOH! You lousy.... HEY!! Get off me will ya? Put me down!'

'Calm down Kenny! What the devil are you playing at?' As much as Baldy tried, he couldn't hold the writhing Kenny in his arms. In the end he decided to just tighten the leash around his collar and drag his wailing dog away. Baldy didn't even notice the four squirrels sitting in the branch directly over his head.

'Now we don't have to douse at all, just let Kenny walk around the park for half an hour' Ardilla laughed out loud as he and the others watched Kenny being hauled away back towards Broadway. All the other dogs started to growl and bark as they caught a whiff of Kenny as he went by, some even tried to attack him. Kenny moved as close to Baldy as he could and with his tail between his legs turned the corner and was gone.

'Poor dog' said Kalan, 'You don't think we went too far do you?' He turned to look at the others who were still laughing.

'He had it coming' replied Skudzo, ' I was half tempted to douse Baldy as well when he came over, that would have extended our boundary this week into his apartment'

'I'm glad you didn't' smiled Kalan as the laughter started to die down, but deep down he couldn't help feeling a little bit sorry for Kenny.

'Come on then squirrel with a conscience,' said Skudzo who could tell what his friend was thinking, 'Let's go see those second raters down at the show'

'Hey!! Too right' cried out Risu, who had completely forgotten during all the excitement that he had his entire winter savings riding on Mokus in today's acrobatic display. 'It's probably already started'

Risu was right. Towards the center of the park at the end of the Hope Garden most of the Battery Park squirrels had clustered around a couple of trees above the benches. The sight had even attracted a small crowd of people. The group of tourists, from Nebraska, had been on their way to the ferry for Ellis Island but had stopped halfway because no one had ever seen so many squirrels in one place at one time. They had no idea of course that they were merely guests at the: 'Annual Battery Park Squirrel Acrobatic Display of Speed, Agility and Courage To Promote Positive Mating' The Battery Park residents had shortened this very long-winded title over the years, and most young squirrels referred to it simply as the 'Hanky-Panky Rumble'.

It is the most important event on the squirrel calendar, not just in Battery Park, but all over New York citywide squirrel 'rumbles' are a regular occurrence in February. This is because it is the height of the mating season, and female squirrels are notoriously fickle. It is very rare that a female will mate with the same male twice, so the displays are a way the older male squirrels have of proving themselves worthy of a second chance. While for the younger squirrels it gives them the possibility to make a name for themselves, grab a girl, and generally show off.

The 'Hanky – Panky Rumble' is also popular with squirrels who are no longer interested in the mating game, since it is also the perfect excuse for all squirrels to indulge in one of their favorite vices – gambling.

Most New Yorkers think that squirrels save up nuts for the freezing Manhattan winter. The frenzied way in which squirrels will beg for nuts from everyone and anybody who happens to be strolling in a city park in the months leading up to February is only a way for them to increase their betting power for the rumble. The increasingly wild and frantic way in which those same squirrels will beg for nuts from everyone and anybody who happens to be strolling in a city park in the months directly after February is only a way for them to pay off the bookies.

Battery Park's biggest bookkeeper was a surly silvery gray squirrel called Sincab. He was watching over the events from his Parks Department Drey. He flicked his long tail up above his head to check the direction of the wind.

'Hmmmm' he thought to himself, 'Pretty weak south westerly, that's not going to knock him off course'

Sincab had the usual bookies worries. Most of the nuts in his drey were bets placed on one of the contestants for the leap of death, Mokus, and as much as Sincab hated to admit it to himself, the odds were in Mokus's favor.

Down below him, Kalan and his three friends had arrived and saw that the rumble was in full swing. The human crowd that had gathered was almost as excited as the squirrel one, and both parties were making a lot of noise.

'Look Mommy!' cried out one of the kids from Nebraska, 'That little squirrel just fell in the trash can'

'Awww, poor little fella, that's the third one' replied her mother. 'I don't know why they have to spin and turn like they do instead of just jumping straight'

What the woman didn't realize is that was the whole point of the leap of death. This is the highlight of the Hanky Panky Rumble, a large eight-foot jump from the elm tree on the corner of the path across the benches below. The more triple twist turns a squirrel can do, the more points he can earn. Ekom - the squirrel currently residing in the black trashcan – had been trying the triple spin, after successfully completing a back turn jump from the top of the park light. He sat, pride damaged and points lost, listening to the crowds outside.

Among the many sounds was the barking sound of a squirrel commentator, 'And Ekom fails for the second year running, and next up we have a newcomer. NOLAI!!'

Ekom sat hunched up against one side of the trashcan, he thought forlornly about Veverita – the girl he had hoped to impress, he also thought about the nuts he had lost vainly betting on his own success. Ekom puffed up his cheeks, gave a heavy sigh, and looked upwards towards the sky. For a split second he saw and heard Nolai fly past while successfully triple turning.

'Hut, Hut, quick turn'

The squirrel crowd outside cheered loudly. 'Amazing leap by Nolai!'

The human crowd outside cheered loudly. 'Hey! Wow! Did ya see that!?'

A lot of the humans were taking photographs. Nolai himself jumped down from the bench armrest and was greeted by two other squirrels who hopped along beside him. 'Well done Nolai!' said the first one 'I've never seen a triple spin twist done backwards before' Nolai smiled modestly then all three turned quickly to find themselves face to face with a Nebraskan tourist armed with a pocket point and shoot camera.

'Smile guys!'

The three squirrels stood motionless as the flash popped. A second later they were already bounding up the nearest tree. The tourist returned to his where his wife was sitting, a little perplexed, 'You know honey, if I didn't know better I'd swear those little fella were posing'

'Oh Henry' said his small but very portly wife in the cheery manner she used whenever she wasn't paying him the slightest bit of attention. She was busy offering nuts to another squirrel who was sitting on her shoe. 'Will you look at this guy?' she said 'I keep on giving him nuts, but he doesn't run away or nothing, just keeps stuffing them in his cheeks. See? See how chubby they are?'

What she didn't realize that the squirrel, was trying to raise enough capital to try another bet after losing heavily on Ekom. He was getting a little frustrated as the woman wasn't handing out the nuts fast enough, and what he really had his eye on was her little daughter's bag of assorted. The little girl was holding on to them tightly.

'Mommy, Mommy' she cried out, 'There's still a squirrel in the trashcan, it didn't come out. Do you think it's all right? Mommy?'

Her mother didn't reply as the squirrel on her shoe had her attention in a classic squirrel 'cutie stare'. 'Oh Henry! Isn't he just the cutest thing?'

The squirrel kept the eye contact going as he stuffed away another nut. 'Just give us the nuts lady' he muttered under his breath in a mantra like way 'Give us the nuts, give us the nuts, GIVE US THE NUTS'.

Kalan and his three dousing buddies had settled down to watch what was left of the rumble halfway up the tree overlooking the leap of death. It was pretty crowded as here were a lot of the females, a couple of rats under cover watching the show, and the main judge Olmaxon.

Lana, who recognized Kalan, smiled and bounced over towards him, 'Hello there' she said cheerily.

'Hi' replied Kalan a little nervously.

Both squirrels looked at each other and after a brief awkward silence Kalan, his nose twitching, spoke up, 'Great leap by Nolai'

'Oh yes' replied Lana quickly, 'I think Veverita is very interested in him. Why aren't you doing anything today?'

'Nah!' said Kalan, 'I'm not interested'

This was not entirely true. Kalan loved jumping and running, but he preferred doing these things for his own enjoyment and to perfect his skills rather then just showing off in front of others. 'And besides' continued Kalan, 'I thought you and the other girls weren't interested either. Last month you were all for leaving'

Lana looked a little puzzled for a moment, and then gave a little giggle. 'Oh that' she laughed, 'Oh Kalan, we complain to Olmaxon every year. We don't want you guys getting all complacent' She smiled at Kalan, who felt his stomach float down to his feet. 'We girls moan a little every year, it's our way of getting things done around here. We aren't going anywhere stupid'

Kalan said nothing, he felt too foolish to speak.

'Hey Lana!', Lana turned her head to see who was calling her

'Come on! Mokus is about to go for it' the unseen voice continued,

Kalan spoke quickly his thoughts and frustrations pouring out of his mouth. 'I think about leaving all the time, I thought that you would......' Lana was already hopping away.

'Later Kalan' she shouted as she jumped up a couple of branches to get a better view.

'But Central Park, the rest of New York?' Kalan called out after her. He didn't move, he felt angry with himself. Angry for being so naïve, and also annoyed at feeling so nervous around Lana. He just looked down at his feet.

'Hey Kalan' It was Skudzo who had come up beside him, 'Better to be a fool for a moment, than to be foolish all your life'. Skudzo moved his large tail over Kalan's feet and smiled. 'Let's go watch Risu's face as he loses all his winter savings on Mokus!'

Kalan looked up and saw Ardilla and a very nervous looking Risu bouncing down to the bench underneath the leap of death with Skudzo close behind. He took a deep breath, then jumped down and followed. All four squirrels joined the others sitting on and around the bench. Ekom was still sulking at the bottom of the trashcan. He didn't want to come out, this defiance being heightened as he heard cries of excitement as Mokus jumped from branch to branch above in preparation for his leap. Ekom felt miserable. Everyone had forgotten about him, nobody seemed to care if he was hurt or not. He let out a tiny wail of miserable frustration. There was however one person at the rumble who had not forgotten about Ekom.

'Mommy! Mommy! There's still a little squirrel in the trashcan' The little girl's mother wasn't listening, she was still transfixed by the squirrel sitting on her foot, 'Well I'm going to see if he's ok,' the girl said defiantly, and clutching her bag of nuts she made her way over to the trashcan. In the tree above her Mokus was ready. He milked the last barks of adulation, made another wind direction test with his tail, took two small steps backwards and leaped into the air.

'Mommy! Mommy! Look another one!' screamed out the little girl from almost directly underneath Mokus. In that spilt second his concentration left him, and instead of turning in mid-air he fell directly into the trashcan below. Ekom sidestepped out of Mokus's way as he fell onto the trash.

'You Ok? asked Ekom, who all of a sudden was feeling a little better. After all, the odds on favorite in the rumble was lying next to him at the bottom of the loser trashcan.

'I....I...' spluttered a confused Mokus, his mind in shock. 'What the .....?'

Then the light above the two squirrels began to fade and he saw the looming face of the girl looking down on the pair of them in the trash. 'Hey! Little squirrel are you OK?'

Without thinking, Mokus leaped out of the trashcan so quickly that his movement caught the girl completely by surprise. 'OOHH!' she cried in shock and dropped her bag of nuts. In a brief moment of lucidity Mokus saw his chance and barked:

'SCRAMBLE!!'

There were cheers from the watching squirrels as many of them dived down onto the scattered nuts surrounding the girl's feet. A surprise scramble at a rumble was unprecedented. So much so that even a couple of rats, who had been hiding successfully in the crowd of squirrels, forgot themselves in the excitement and joined in the nut rush.

Now whereas humans will let squirrels run around all over the place, rats have not been so successful at integrating themselves into polite New York society. The rats know the score, and the screams of horror that came from the crowd as Murray and his rat pal Delancy broke cover reminded them almost instantly of their mistake.

'OH MY GAWD!......RATS!' The Nebraskans went crazy.

'Grab the kids Audrey! Where the hell did they come from?' cried out one voice

'It's disgusting! Filthy rodents in a public park' screamed out another.

The squirrels carried on collecting nuts regardless. Murray and Delancy, experts as they were at avoiding the public gaze for too long, scurried off as fast as they could to towards the east side restaurant.

'I feel we got a little too excited there Murray,' said Delancy to his friend as they ran.

'Yeah, it's a pity we have to miss the rumble and hurry' replied Murray.

Rats always speak in Rhyme. Some Brooklyn ones have been experimenting with rap, but fads in the rat community don't generally last too long. Since rats have got such a desperate reputation, and almost everyone in town seems to be out for their blood, modern day New York rats always travel in pairs. It's a lot safer in a city full of enemies, as who better to look after your back than your best friend? This coupling up for safety has, over the generations, helped to develop this rhyming couplet language and a lot of historic rat friendships. The escapades of Rutgers and Ludlow or the poems of Lispenard and Stanton are legendary in the New York rat community.

'Sitting in this metro sewer, is very cold and wet,

But at least I'm free and happy, not somebody's pet'

The best way to get the message across is always a rhyme, and at least it's an understandable language which squirrels find easy and polite. It's certainly a lot better than the obscenities pigeons are always coming out with, and back at the scramble a few verbal fights were breaking out between pigeons and squirrels.

'Scram tree-huggers!'

Dozens of pigeons had dived over to the scramble scene and were pushing out the remaining squirrels.

'Hey! That's my nut,' moaned one small squirrel as four pigeons mobbed then robbed him of it.

'Was, loser, was. Go bury yourself!'

Most of the squirrels were leaving the area, as the scene caused by the surprise appearance of Murray and Delancy had caused Olmaxon to call off the remaining jumps. Some were making their way up to Sincab's betting drey, most of the others were hopping back to the central drey under the castle to see if Olmaxon would declare a rumble champion.

Kalan and his friends started to run over to one of the main drey entrances behind the General Booth tablet. Behind them they heard the motor of a small green buggy as it drove up to where the Nebraskans were arguing. It had the familiar maple leaf emblem of the Parks Department on the front of its engine. The two employees didn't even have time to get out before angry Nebraskans surrounded them.

'It's a disgrace, rats running around in broad daylight. We've got children here!'

'My child was attacked by a squirrel' cried out the little girl's mother who had snapped out of her squirrel cutie stare. As if on cue Ekom decided that it was time for him to exit the trashcan, and he jumped up onto the edge, then bounded off across Hope Garden.

'See! See!' cried the Nebraskan mother, 'They lay in wait in the garbage, just like the rats' She pointed a chubby finger in the general direction of Ekom as he hopped away.

Down in the main drey the chattering was intense. In the large meeting room Olmaxon and the other judges were busy weighing up the points won and lost.

'Now I know,' shouted Olmaxon above the din, 'I know…' He raised his voice again to make sure he had got some attention, 'I know that Nolai has got 100 points with his exceptional back twist triple turn and successful leap'

Some cheers broke out above the whispering.

'BUT!.' Olmaxon raised his voice again, 'Even though Mokus didn't complete the leap of death, his incredible scramble success has got him also 100 points' There was more cheering from the crowd. 'So' he continued when the noise had calmed down a little. 'After talking it over with the other judges,' he nodded to the small group of elderly squirrels sitting to his left, 'We have decided to have one final test to decide the winner this year'

The packed meeting room filled with noise as everyone tried to have their say. Some didn't think it was fair on Nolai, others were excited at the prospect.

Mokus in the meantime was going around telling everyone that he had planned the scramble all along. 'After I saw that girl, I knew what I had to do' He cooed to a couple of female squirrels who started to bat their eyelids in a most flirty fashion.

'I don't believe all that guff from Mokus,' said Skudzo, who was sitting near the back of the room with Kalan. Kalan shrugged his shoulders in a very non-committal manner.

'HEY! OLMAXON!' Skudzo's booming voice made itself heard above the nattering squirrels. 'What type of test?'

Olmaxon barked loudly again to bring the attention back to himself. There were still a few whispering voices near the back, so he beat his tail firmly on the ground until he got almost complete silence. 'There will be a race between Nolai and Mokus. A simple run from the tail of the eagle to the inside of the hollow stone. The winner will be declared rumble champion'

The room stopped being quiet and everyone started shouting, barking, talking. This year's rumble had already proven to be spectacular enough, but a race had never been held in competition before. The course was simple enough, from the eagle on the edge of the East Coast Memorial westwards across the park to the Korean War Memorial (the 'hollow stone') Olmaxon wove his tail above his head to indicate that he more to say. 'Now listen to me again please everyone' he shouted, 'Since today's events have attracted a little too much human attention, and most probably the P.D will be spending the next few days rat hunting, we will hold this race a week from today at night. That should give enough time for things to blow over, and also give our two competitors a little time to look over the course'

A large squirrel tapped Olmaxon on his shoulder and started to whisper in the old squirrel's ear. Olmaxon started to smile, but as everyone in the room knew, this was just a nervous tick. The prospect of bad news that this signaled brought the room to total silence more effectively than anything else Olmaxon had done.

'Err...well now.. Everyone' Olmaxon spoke a little nervously, 'I've been asked to tell you that Sincab's drey is currently being searched by the Parks Department for rats, so anyone wanting to collect their rumble winnings will have to wait until tomorrow' There was a collective mumbling from the crowd. Olmaxon took a deep breath then continued, 'Also Sincab is not, I repeat, not paying out on Mokus since the odds stipulated the completion of the leap of death and not the points won, so ...err... sorry about that'

At this the meeting room exploded in uproar. Squirrels throwing their arms in the air in dismay, tails were flying everywhere.

'Come on Skudzo, lets find Risu' said Kalan. Skudzo smiled and started to push a path for them through the arguing squirrels. As they left the main room they could hear Olmaxon trying to keep order behind them.

'Look, he would have given you odds on a scramble if you had asked. Besides you've all got a week to raise more funds, then you can bet again on the race.........No you can't go to his drey, he's got the P.D in there!'

Indeed outside the main drey was almost as chaotic as inside. Two parks department and one police car had arrived on the pathway in front of the castle. Two Parks Department employees were up the tree planting rat poison, others were poking around the trashcans, while the police kept the Nebraskans calm. Murray and Delancy, the rat culprits of this entire furor, were long gone. Sincab, one of only a couple of squirrels still outside, was keeping a close watch over his drey. He wasn't worried about the parks employees running all around his home, since his nuts were safely stashed in a hollow part of the tree trunk directly under his drey. He was in fact incredibly happy with himself, thanks to Mokus he had made a killing today.

The Stash

Irving Miller had never been so popular. Over the past few days 'The Squirrel Guy', as he liked to be called, had found himself surrounded by his favorite animals. They had even started to wait for him outside the old Bowling Green metro entrance at the top of the park overlooking the Custom House.

'Hey Fellas! Geesh you guys must be real hungry,' he said as he walked along the path that lead to his favorite bench near the castle. Since he had retired from his 9-5 Irving had decided to dedicate his remaining mornings to feeding the squirrels in Battery Park. This pastime also proved to be a handy supplement to his miserly pension. He helped passing tourists' get a photo – op with a squirrel on their knee or shoulder, or maybe grabbing a nut from their hands. The squirrels on the whole found this all a little humiliating. Generally only the younger squirrels trying to save up, or older ones with serious debts to pay, would be hanging around Irving's bench of a morning. Normally he could count on no more than a dozen squirrels to play with, but today at least that many had been waiting for him by the metro exit. By the time he got to his bench he found another twenty or so hopping around, some were barking.

'Come on sweaty! Out with the nuts!' 'The Squirrel Guy' was known by a different name by his beloved, but highly smell sensitive squirrels.

'Come on, come on, before the others get here! Nuts!!' cried out one of them,

'Hey! Sweaty, check this out!' barked another squirrel who tried to grab Irving's attention by doing a back somersault.

'Hey! That's cute little fella', Irving smiled and offered the first nut of the day to the acrobatic squirrel. Once he had done this all the other squirrels started back somersaulting as well, barking at the old man as they jumped.

'Hey Sweaty over here!'

'Look at me! Watch this one'

'Throw the nuts, throw the nuts!'

Irving looked around at the incredible scene of some thirty squirrels jumping backwards all around him, some more successfully than others, and felt his heart race. 'OH! My goodness' he gasped and taking a deep breath he sat down and slowly opened his small backpack. Some younger squirrels stopped jumping and moved in closer, trying to catch Irving's eyes in the hope of getting him in a 'cutie stare', not knowing that he was quite immune to that old squirrel trick.

In Irving's backpack were perhaps two pounds of assorted nuts, and as he glanced to either side he started to get a funny feeling that the squirrels might just mob him for them, so he pulled out a massive handful and threw them over onto the grass behind the bench. Some squirrels dived onto the grass, but just as many stayed around the bench. 'What has gotten into you guys?' he asked loudly. He had no idea that most of them had lost their entire winter savings on Mokus, and that there were only a few days left before the race. That contest would give them the chance to win back something. Irving had arrived at 9:00am, by 9:15am his bag was empty, and by 9:16am there wasn't one squirrel within thirty yards of him.

A couple of hundred yards behind Irving sat Kalandaka. He was atop the tallest of four sightseeing telescopes overlooking the Hudson from the Promenade. This was his favorite spot to come when Kalan wanted to kick back and think things over. He sat, back towards the park, gazing out over the bay. It wasn't the view that attracted him, but more the relaxing effect he got from looking at the water. Nothing but vast stretches of gray blue water, no buildings, no people, nothing to confuse his thoughts. Here he could turn his mind off, try to block out his constant thinking. All those thoughts of leaving Battery Park, of going to look for Bilka, of Central Park. The imagining of the adventures, excitement and danger that looking out across to the buildings in the other direction brought on. Kalan had no longing for the sea, he found it just gave his mind a rest. This morning though, his mind was racing more than usual. He hadn't seen Kenny since the day of the rumble. Maybe he and the others had gone too far, maybe the poor mutt might never want to go out again.

'No, No' he said out loud to himself, 'Stop it!' and he tried to hypnotize himself with the lulling motion of the water. But what about Skudzo? Would he come along if Kalan asked? Maybe Risu? Would Olmaxon try and stop him? How long would it take to get to Central Park?

Try as he might Kalan just couldn't stop himself thinking. Each unanswered question linked itself to the next and they all danced around in his brain. They danced and danced until they found a partner, so the question, 'How long would it take to get to Central Park?' joined up with 'How would he find the way there?' Eventually these couplings gave birth to lots of little baby questions like, 'Is it big?' 'Would it be dangerous?' Kalan started to roll his head slowly under the weight of all these questions.

'Are you crazy? Is that your problem?' The deep laughing voice of Skudzo broke up the dancing instantly. He was sitting on another telescope slightly below Kalan's left. 'Planning on going for a swim?'

Kalan looked down to where Skudzo was sitting and waved his tail. He was very pleased to see his friend, and happy that his mind was free. 'Oh Skudzo' sighed Kalan, 'I'm just feeling pretty confused these days'

'Still thinking about leaving aren't you?' said Skudzo.

'Yeah' replied Kalan, 'That, and other things' He twitched his nose and carried on talking. 'Skudzo, since we doused Kenny, he hasn't been seen. You don't think we hurt him do you?'

'Only his pride' said Skudzo, 'and besides, if that's all you are worrying about turn around'

Kalan turned towards the park and saw coming down the path from the children's playground the familiar couple of Baldy and Kenny. However, this time Kenny was walking close to his owner with his head down and his tail firmly between his legs, as if he was trying to attract as little attention as possible.

'Been watching the pair of them for around ten minutes,' said Skudzo 'And Kenny hasn't peed on our scent at all. In fact when he smells us he whines, backs away, and nearly trips Baldy up'

Kalan looked closer. Kenny struck a pretty forlorn picture. Other dogs growled as they passed him.

'Anyway Kalan' continued Skudzo, I've been trying to find you all morning. Not because of Kenny, but because there might be some news about Bilka' Kalan's ears pricked up immediately and his mouth opened, but he made no sound. 'Well I was talking to Delancy last night, and he said they have got some rat friends staying over from uptown who ran into a fat squirrel who said he came from Battery Park' Skudzo carried on talking while Kalan stared at him excitedly. 'But hey, you know what rats are like, I couldn't get much out of Delancy. I thought we could pop by the rats under the restaurant and ask these new guys ourselves'

'Oh yes!' said Kalan excitedly. 'Can we go now?'

'No can do' replied Skudzo, 'I've got to rush, I'm supposed to be helping Mokus practice jumping down from the eagle. Look I'll meet you back here at sundown and we'll go together then' Without waiting for Kalan's reply, Skudzo jumped down from the telescope and hopped off up the promenade towards the East Coast Memorial.

Kalan felt a lot happier. Bilka! What had he been up too? How was he? He shook his head to stop these new questions from trying to enter his mind. They would have to wait till tonight.

A disturbing whining noise also distracted him and he turned to where it had come from. Baldy had sat down on a bench and Kenny was sitting nervously between his owner's feet. Kalan noticed that a couple of hopeful squirrels had skipped over to Baldy in the hope of a nut or two. He saw that Kenny, instead of barking, just whined a little and slunk further behind his owner's legs. Baldy shooed the squirrels away.

'I wish you would pull yourself together lad,' he shouted down to his dog. 'You can't hide forever you know! Come on out from under there!' Baldy pulled on Kenny's leash, and his Jack Russell took a few reluctant steps forward from underneath the bench.

Kalan gave a guilty sigh, then made a flying leap down from his telescope onto the ground. He darted in a large semi-circle in the direction of Baldy's bench, so that he could approach it from behind. The wind was blowing towards Kalan as he approached the bench, so Kenny couldn't smell him arrive.

'Pssst! Kenny!' said Kalan in a loud whisper. The little dog turned quickly and almost immediately started to whine. Baldy wasn't paying much attention anymore as he had noticed a beautiful woman walking along the pathway. 'Kenny. Listen, it's not a trap or a surprise, just be cool ok?' Kenny just whined slowly, and started to shuffle around nervously. 'Kenny *calm down!*' said Kalan, surprising even himself as to how similar he sounded to Baldy. Kenny stopped whining, but wouldn't keep still. Kalan continued, 'I've just come over to say sorry for what we did to you the other week. OK?' Kenny stopped shuffling his feet. 'And, well, you don't have to worry, I'll make sure it doesn't happen again'

With this Kalan dug around inside his fur pockets and found a small nut. He threw it over to Kenny who just sniffed at it. 'You don't like nuts?' asked Kalan, moving a little closer. He was now only about two yards away from the dog.

'Nah!' replied Kenny softly, 'You got any chocolate?'

While Kalan was trying to make the peace with the Jack Russell, further down the promenade, sitting on the grass near the large eagle, Skudzo had arrived and was talking to Mokus. He was explaining the best way of jumping off the end of the metal bird's tail. Both squirrels looked upwards at the massive monument. It appeared the same color as the sky above Battery Park that morning, darkest gray. 'You gotta try and push hard with your back legs' said Skudzo as Mokus watched him intently. 'If you get a good kick-off, it should help you fly over to the stone fence before gravity brings you down to land. Then you will have a few yards head start over Nolai, who is still going to have to jump the fence before he can catch up with you' Mokus nodded, but the expression on his face was one of disbelief. 'Watch' said Skudzo as he jumped up onto the eagle, and climbed to the tail. 'It's very slippery, so you've got to tiptoe out to the edge on your claws' Skudzo shouted down to Mokus, 'Or you will just keep sliding backwards'

Mokus kept on watching, but the wind was so intense that he couldn't hear Skudzo well. In fact he thought Skudzo was shouting something about red doors, but he smiled and nodded all the same. Skudzo gripped the edge of the tail with his claws, and pushed his body backwards, then flew off like an uncoiled spring. He glided through the cold air, over Mokus, landed for a second on the stone fence and then with a final bounce landed in the center of the path.

'Nice jump, Skudzo' said a strange voice. The large squirrel needed a second to get his bearings, then stood dumbfounded as he saw the owner of the voice and Baldy walk by. Kenny was smiling, with his head held high.

Mokus bounced over to where Skudzo was standing, still transfixed. 'That was some leap Skudzo, but I'll never manage it' He said with a mixture of awe and despair. He saw however that Skudzo was still in a fixed silence.'Skudzo? Are you ok?'

Skudzo replied very slowly. 'Mokus' he said while watching the man and his dog disappear around a corner 'I swear that dog knows my name' Skudzo turned to Mokus and hit him roughly around the cheeks with his tail. 'Well? What are you standing around staring at? Let's get back to the eagle'

As they moved off towards the gigantic metal bird, it started to pour down. It was the type of rain that you knew would last all day. Cold northwesterly winds blew the rain in people's faces, and made umbrellas useless, so everyone ran for cover. Most of the squirrels moved out of the rain and went underground. There were a few optimistic ones that could be seen hanging around in dry corners hoping for the rain to let up. A few others were sitting on the edges of the tree Dreys. These squirrels were waiting for something else. They were hoping that the rain and the strong winds would uncover some of the many hidden 'nut stashes' dotted around the park.

Most squirrels hide their spare nuts in the ground. First they check that no one is watching. Then they dig small holes maybe one or two inches deep, bury their bounty, then cover them with loose soil, leaves or anything else handy. On miserable days such as today, the rain softens up the ground making it easier for the wind to reveal the hidden goodies. One of the squirrels hoping to make good in the bad weather was Risu. He had lost everything at the Rumble and had spent the last few days trying to raise as many nuts as he could to stake on the forthcoming race, and try and make good his losses. Risu sat shivering with his tail wrapped tightly around his body on the edge of a small drey overlooking the largest open space of the park. He felt miserable, and not just for the cold and rain. He kept thinking of how dumb he had been to bet it all on Mokus. If only he had kept a bit to one side. Then there was 'Smelly' Irving. He had sacrificed a great deal of self-esteem over the past few days, dancing for the squirrel man and his tourist spectators. Risu shuddered slightly as he remembered the embarrassing hopping dance he had done that morning in front of some kids for a meager hazelnut from Irving.

'Never, never again' he said out loud to himself and shuddered to himself again.

The rain was beginning to let up slightly, now instead of torrential it was merely heavy. Risu looked down onto the park and noticed a squirrel dart across the grass, going from one tree to another. He saw that it was making its way towards his drey, the squirrel looked familiar.

'Hey Risu!' shouted Kalan as he jumped up the tree and literally splashed into Risu's drey. 'Whoa! It's wet out there,' he laughed as he shook the water from his tail. Risu said nothing, just smiled meekly and looked down at his own tail, which had begun to swish lazily by his feet. 'What's got into you Risu?' Kalan asked, seeing that his friend seemed a little ill at ease.

'Oh nothing much' replied Risu unconvincingly.

'Come on Risu, cheer up' said Kalan rubbing his still damp tail over Risu's. 'Listen, I've got some great news. Today I spoke to Kenny'

Risu's eyes opened wider. 'What?' he said, a little taken aback 'You mean that dog we...'

'Yes!' replied Kalan, 'He's ok really, we are friends now. He has been to Central Park you know' There was silence. Kalan's dreamy enthusiasm for Central Park had never really rubbed off onto Risu. 'I've promised to find him some chocolate, and he's going to tell me how to get there' Risu opened his mouth to reply, but Kalan continued talking. 'But that's not all!' he said excitedly, 'Some rats bumped into Bilka, and tonight me and Skudzo are going over to hear what they have to say down at their restaurant. Do you want to come along as well, to find out how he is?'

Again Risu made an attempt to reply, but this time he was interrupted by another squirrel who at that moment dived in through the mouth of the Drey.

'Hey! You two!' shouted the large newcomer. He was dripping wet and didn't seem too happy. It was an older squirrel, one of Olmaxon's friends.

With Olmaxon getting older and rarely leaving the main warren, it was thanks to squirrels like this one that he got to know everything that was happening in the park. 'Olmaxon's worried that with this bad weather, and the large number of desperate squirrels in the park...' As the squirrel spoke he looked squarely at Risu, who hung his head sheepishly. 'Some of them might be planning to use the situation to raid their colleague's stashes' Kalan and Risu looked at each other. Kalan couldn't help but notice how guilty Risu's eyes appeared. 'So you two guys' continued the squirrel, 'can keep a look out for trouble makers from up here, and sound the alarm if you see anyone about to loose their nuts' The new arrival paused and started to sniff the air inside the Drey. Risu began to back very slowly into the corner. 'But while I am here, I may as well have a check around' he said in a manner that Kalan found mildly menacing. He also noticed that Risu had backed himself into the corner and was shaking slightly.

The older squirrel started to sniff the ground and moved closer towards Risu's corner. Kalan thought quickly, and then started to shout loudly.

'Look! Look!'

The squirrel turned to see Kalan at the edge of the Drey barking madly down onto the park below. 'What is it?' he said as he moved away from Risu, 'What's got into you Kalan?'

'Down there, by the large Elm,' said Kalan excitedly, 'I just saw two squirrels fighting over a stash'

'What? Where?' said the squirrel as he tried to peer out through the rain. 'I don't see anything'

'I guess my barking must have scared them off' Kalan replied calmly. 'Do you want me to jump down there and check it out for you?'

'No, wait' said the squirrel, his eyes darting around the park below him 'Wait here and keep lookout, I'll go down'. In a bounce he was gone.

'You going to tell me what's up?' said Kalan looking over to Risu the moment the older squirrel had left.

Risu moved meekly over to one side, and Kalan could see a small pile of nuts that he had been hiding. 'I think they are his' gulped Risu. Kalan looked on, unblinkingly. 'He didn't hide them very well, they were poking out from under a leaf by the edge of the main lawn'

'Risu, you can't go stealing other squirrels nuts,' cried out Kalan, feeling a little angry.

'Hey! I'm not the only one,' replied Risu indignantly, 'I saw that really thin squirrel, and a few others rooting around'

'Just because others do it, doesn't make stealing right. How would you feel if your stash was raided?' said Kalan, noticing that Risu was almost in tears.

'Somebody already did,' blabbed out Risu. 'I don't have anything. I've lost it all' Kalan glanced out of the drey to make sure no one was coming, and then moved closer to Risu. 'I have been trying to save since the rumble,' Risu continued 'but this morning I found my nuts had gone. All I've got left is this one hazelnut from smelly this morning' He pulled out a nut from a pocket of his fur. 'And what good is that!' and threw the nut to the floor. 'So I thought, what the hell, I'll just do the same'

'And how does it feel?' asked Kalan.

'Miserable' moaned Risu, 'I already felt down 'cause I had nothing left. Now this morning I've added fear and self-loathing'

'Well I can think of one way to cheer you up straight away,' said Kalan Risu looked up, with a hopeful glint in his watery eyes, 'Let's get these nuts back in his hide hole, before he notices they are missing'

Risu smiled slowly and the two of them quickly set about stuffing their fur with the older squirrel's stash. Once they had made sure they had everything, they started to slowly climb down the tree in the rain, talking care not to drop anything.

'You lead the way!' Kalan shouted above the wind

The two squirrels made their way quickly but carefully across the lawn. The owner of the nuts had his hide hole by a bush near the edge of the grass. Kalan kept lookout while Risu put the nuts back. Risu started to cover the stash with as many soggy leaves and twigs as he could find.

'STOP THAT!' cried Kalan, the wind and the rain making normal conversation difficult

Risu looked up startled 'WHY?' he cried back.

Kalan moved closer to Risu, 'You told me he only covered it with a single leaf' he said

'Yeah, that's why I found it,' barked back Risu, 'It's got to be covered up well or someone else will steal them'

'No Risu' said Kalan sternly, 'You've got to leave it exactly as you found it. If someone else gets his nuts, then that's the way it goes. The important thing is that it isn't you'

Risu shrugged, but did as Kalan asked. He removed the extra leaves and twigs and left the stash pretty much as he had found it.

'Come on, lets get out of here and under cover,' shouted Kalan, and they both ran off towards the main warren under the castle.

The rain didn't let up for the rest of the day, and most of the Battery Park squirrels stayed underground. Kalan spent most of the day going around to see who might want to go with him later and hear what the rats had to say about Bilka. He was genuinely surprised to find that no one was in the slightest bit interested.

By late afternoon the rain was still coming down, but had turned into a light drizzle. Kalan was sitting by the east entrance, the one by the bushes next to the General Booth Memorial, and he noticed that the wind had let up completely. Behind him he heard some pattering and turned to see Risu and a very young female squirrel.

'Hey Risu, you decided to come after all' he said and nodded politely to the new face.

'Yeah' replied Risu, 'And I've found someone else. This is Funni'

Funni was a tiny squirrel, so much so she made Risu look big. Her fur was dark gray, but her tail was almost totally white. 'Hi' she said in unison with Kalan. 'Risu tells me the rats know what happened to Bilka'

'That's right, yes,' replied Kalan.

'So let's go!' she barked, and jumped straight out of the entranceway. Kalan looked at Risu, who made his trademark shoulder shrug, and the pair of them chased out after Funni. They caught up with her outside and since the rain had turned the lawn into a soggy swamp they followed the pathway towards the telescopes on the promenade. Kalan explained to the others that Skudzo should be there waiting for them.

So it came as a surprise to all squirrels, as they ran down the pathway, when they saw Skudzo waving his tail franticly at them from where he was sitting between the stone fence pillars near the eagle.

'Hey! Don't stand there!' he cried out to them from the fence. The three squirrels looked at each other in confusion, and then Risu looked upwards and cried out,

'*LOOK OUT!*'

It was too late for them to move, Mokus came hurtling down on top of them. Risu managed to push Funni out of the way, but Mokus landed squarely on top of Kalan. More dazed than hurt, they picked themselves up. Mokus had a manic grin on his face.

'Hey! I did it. I did it!' Mokus laughed and hugged Risu with his tail. 'Skudzo!' he shouted, but then lowered his voice when he turned to see that the big squirrel had already arrived on the scene. 'I made it to the path. Did you see? I made it!'

'Well done Mokus' said Skudzo, 'It took you all day, but you did it'

Mokus was turning around, looking at all the squirrels, his eyes begging for praise, but Kalan and his friends weren't really sure what he was supposed to have achieved.

'That's enough for today, we can try some more tomorrow' said Skudzo.

'I can go? Great!' Mokus turned around and looked straight at Kalan, 'I did it' he said again, this time in a manic whisper, then started to make his way down the path to the castle.

'Hey Mokus!' called out Skudzo. Mokus turned his head. 'Now don't go telling everybody you can jump to the path from the eagle. Keep it quiet, and we will keep our advantage'

Mokus waved his tail in a very non-committal fashion, and ran off down the path.

'Yeah right' said Risu under his breath, finally realizing the reason for Mokus's fall from the sky. Skudzo moved around and looked sternly at Risu for a second, then turned to Kalan.

'So where are you three off to in this rain?' he asked while looking at Funni with the type of strained expression someone gets when they think they recognize a face, but can't remember who it belongs to.

'The rats' replied Kalan, 'Skudzo, remember? To find out about Bilka'

'What?' said Skudzo, 'Oh yeah…. the rats' His voice trailed off into a strange silence. He turned his head, first to Risu, then towards the path Mokus had just run down. 'You know Kalan' he said slowly, keeping his eyes fixed on the path. 'You three go on ahead. I'll meet you at the restaurant later'

Before Kalan could reply Skudzo had already started to run down the path after Mokus.

'But, what's up with him?' said Kalan desperately.

'I think,' replied Risu, 'It's just dawned on him that Mokus has the biggest mouth in Battery Park. I figure that it will take Mokus about ten minutes before every squirrel at home knows he can jump from the eagle's tail'

Kalan laughed. 'Oh yeah! I hadn't realized. Poor old Skudzo,'

'Guys!' Funni pushed her tail between the two squirrels as she interrupted. 'Are we going to the restaurant or not?'

'Yes' replied Kalan 'Come on then'

The three of them made their way down onto the stone path leading out of the East Coast Memorial and headed east towards the 'American Park' restaurant.

Now New York may be the world's most ethnically diverse city, with people and animals from all over the world living in relative harmony. However there is one group of residents who are considered outcasts even though they outnumber everyone else ten to one. The New York rat population, like the squirrels, are social rodents, but unlike the squirrels they have to travel in pairs for mutual protection. Also for reasons of personal safety they are always on the move, never staying in one place for too long. Most parts of Manhattan have a type of rat 'hotel' where they can relax, eat, mate and catch up on the latest news before hitting the road again. The Battery Park rat residence is an underground burrow between the 'American Park' restaurant and the children's playground on the southeast border, and as Kalan and his friends arrived it was teeming.

'Hey! Squirrels down from the park,' cried out a very fat rat the moment they walked into the main room.

'Guys, listen, outside is it dark?' said another.

'Almost' replied Funni, then she turned to Kalan who was on his hind legs trying to peer over the rats looking for a familiar face. 'Whom are we supposed to be meeting?' she asked him.

'I don't know,' answered Kalan, 'but I think that's Delancy over there at the back, let's ask him'

The three squirrels pushed their way through the mass of rat bodies as politely as they could. The rats seemed to be getting agitated, and many were moving towards the entrance, waiting for someone to tell them the sun had gone down and it was safe to go out. Rats rarely travel above ground in daylight, for obvious reasons of personal security.

'Delancy!' cried out Kalan, 'Is that you?'

A large brown rat with shorter than usual whiskers turned round.

'Hello fellas! Park squirrels, well then, what are you doing here?' he asked pleasantly looking at all three of them in turn, but failing to remember anyone's name. Before Kalan could speak, an almost totally black rat sitting next to Delancy answered the question.

'Bet they want to know about that other squirrel Crosby met up town dear'

Delancy turned and glared at the black rat. 'Don't call me dear, you know I don't like it Murray,' he said in an angry whisper.

'Sorry, just slipped out. Won't happen again, don't you worry' said Murray with a sneaky grin.

At that moment a high pitched shrill came from a rat at the entrance. Eventually the strange noise developed into a voice which the squirrels could understand, 'Lights gone, it's time to go' it said and many of the rats shivered with excitement, and in twos, started to make their way out into Battery Park to forage.

'No need to push, take it slow' said the rat's partner in a much deeper toned voice as the exiting rats scurried past.

Kalan turned his attention back to Delancy. 'This Crosby fella,' he said anxiously, 'Is he around? We've all come to hear about what he saw. We think he might have met an old friend of ours'

Delancy twitched his short whiskers and moved a little closer to Kalan. 'Crosby and his friend Jackson arrived here yesterday' he started, but Murray finished off his sentence for him in typical rat style.

'And boy have those two rats got a lot to say!'

Holding a conversation with New York rats can be a little disconcerting for the uninitiated. The rhyming couplets they use to communicate are easy enough to understand, but it can get a bit confusing when they finish off each other's sentences. The real problems arrive when one of the pair leaves you alone to communicate with the other.

'I'll go and have a look and see if I can find them for you. I think they are staying near the playground' said Delancy, and without waiting for a reply was pushing his way out of the room. Kalan, Funni and Risu found themselves alone with Murray. After a short silence Murray spoke up. 'I didn't hear much of their story, only got the gist of it,' he said with a broad grin.

'Can you tell us anything at all?' said Funni. The rat looked at her inquisitively, but didn't reply. 'Is Bilka all right at least?' she tried again, but Murray said nothing. Funni was starting to get a little frustrated with the silence and elbowed Kalan.

'Err I know you must be wanting to get outside with the others Murray, and I promise we won't stay long. It's just that we are very concerned for our friend, and we really want to know if he is ok' said Kalan

Murray nodded his head, and looked kindly at Kalan and the others, but still said nothing. Kalan sighed, but Funni was beginning to loose her patience.

'Why won't you answer us?' she said angrily to Murray.

'RATSPEAK!' cried out Risu, making everybody, including Murray, jump a little.

'What are you on about?' said Funni, turning to Risu.

'He can't reply. You don't rhyme Funni,' said Risu proudly as he remembered some conversation he had had about rats with his mother a long time ago.

'Of course!' said Kalan as the penny dropped on him too. 'I remember. He can't answer unless the last word of our reply rhymes with the last word he said'

The grin returned to Murray's face, and he looked up hopefully to Kalan.

'I don't remember the last word though' said Risu and shrugged his shoulders at Murray

'Well I happened to be listening' said Funni, 'and he said that he hadn't been paying attention to the story and only got the gist of it' She paused for a moment then added, 'So what rhymes with it?'

'Sit?' said Kalan

'Hit, fit' said Risu thinking quickly 'erm..mit?'

'That's not a word!' said Funni, 'Come on! Think of one we can put at the end of a sentence!'

As Murray looked on amused, the three of them huddled together and started desperately to put a sentence together. Eventually, after convincing Risu that a mit was not something you eat, Funni turned to Murray. 'Please tell us what you know, even if it's just a little bit,' she said.

Murray gave another broad grin, and scratched behind his ear with his hind leg. 'Well I know the guys met a squirrel who had a nasty run in with a cat'

A collective shudder ran down the spines of the three squirrels. Although none of them had ever seen a cat, all of them had heard terrible stories. About how sharp a cat's teeth are, and how their claws are long and deadly. Olmaxon used to tell the story of when he was a young cub he remembered how a cat ran amok in Battery Park for weeks terrorizing the squirrels and rats alike.

'Cat's kill squirrels for fun,' Risu whispered nervously to Funni.

'Was the squirrel ok Murray? What was his name?' she said quickly turning back to Murray, who naturally made no reply. 'Oh this is hopeless!' shouted Funni slapping her tail on the ground in frustration.

'We are on the wrong end of this conversation' said Kalan, trying to concentrate on the moment rather than the images of monstrous cats with razor sharp teeth that were racing around his mind.

'What do you mean?' asked Funni.

'Well in Ratspeak we have to say things that rhyme with the last word Murray said, right?' Kalan stopped in mid sentence to make sure Risu had understood what he had said so far. Risu nodded, in a way that hinted that he hadn't. 'So let's finish this couplet and then start another before he answers!'

'Hey right!' said Funni enthusiastically, 'then he's got to find the rhyme!'

The squirrels conferred for a moment. Kalan would finish the couplet, and then before Murray could say anything Funni would ask him a question directly.

'Ready?' Kalan spoke to Funni, but kept his eyes on Murray.

'Ready'

Kalan began speaking, slowly but clearly. 'It must have been terrible with a bad vicious cat all dark and fat'

Murray nodded and opened his mouth to speak, but Funni got there first. 'This squirrel they met, did they mention a name?' She paused for a second then added, 'It's so important for me'

'Don't say too much or you will confuse him' whispered Risu in her ear.

'I don't remember a name' Murray replied, 'but you can ask them yourselves, look behind you and see'

The squirrels had been so wrapped up in their conversation with Murray that they had failed to notice the large group of figures that had entered the main rat burrow. Delancy was back, with two very tough looking but quite petite rats whom Kalan assumed correctly to be Crosby and Jackson. However what came as a real surprise to him were the squirrels who were accompanying them. Skudzo, the squirrel who's nuts Risu had almost stolen and a worried looking Olmaxon.

Skudzo ran straight over to Kalan. 'You know that nutcase Mokus has gone and told the whole burrow that he can jump the eagle's tail!'

Kalan tried to hide his concern over the presence of Olmaxon and show some for Skudzo. 'I can't believe it' Skudzo went on, 'Any advantage he had is blown, and that Nolai kid will be out there training as well tomorrow you just wait and see'

Kalan shrugged his shoulders in a very non – committal way, very typical of Risu. 'What can you do?' he said, 'He's his own worst enemy'

Kalan waved his tail over towards Delancy who was talking to Olmaxon. 'What are they doing here?' he asked, trying to sound as uninterested as possible. 'I've never seen Olmaxon out from under the castle this late'

'Well when I told him the rats may have a story about Bilka, and that you three had gone to hear it, he insisted on coming along'

Skudzo turned his attention from Kalan to Risu, who was quietly talking to Funni, and whacked him firmly on the shoulders with his tail. 'Hey you old smoothie!' Skudzo shouted then he watched as the force of the impact sent Risu flying into Funni's arms.

'Whoa! Later, later Romeo, we've got a story to hear!' Skudzo roared with laughter at his own mischief, and Risu turned bright red with embarrassment.

'Really!' muttered Funni and moved over towards Delancy, Olmaxon and the others.

'This way everyone, make yourselves comfortable, Crosby and Jackson are ready to tell their fantastic tale' said Delancy as he invited the squirrels to sit in a small corner of the room. Crosby and Jackson jumped up onto a small mound of dirt in front of the corner, almost like a small stage, and waited smiling until everyone was seated. There is nothing rats like more than a captive audience.

As Kalan took a place next to a silent Olmaxon and caught a wink from Skudzo, he couldn't help thinking who really had the biggest mouth in Battery Park. Between Mokus and Skudzo it was a tough call.

Crosby, or it may have been Jackson - Kalan had no idea who was who, cleared his throat. 'Crosby and Jackson's Manhattan Adventure, number forty – five' He said in a squeaky but forceful voice. His friend continued the sentence for him in an even more dramatic tone,

'Where we escape from Columbus Park and Shokobaba............... *ALIVE!*'

Kalan sensed that the whole story would probably be recited in this way. He wasn't going to be wrong.

The Manhattan Adventure number 45

'Folks who know us understand we fear nothing and have seen it all'

'And that day in Columbus Park, we showed our stuff, we stood tall'

'Against the evil Shokobaba, with her fur as white as her heart is black'

'With teeth like razors, and claws so sharp, always ready to attack'

'We began the day watching the old people dance'

'Yeah, they move so slowly, as if in a trance'

At this point in the show, Crosby pushed his arms forward, then raised them slowly in the air, in a rat version of Tai Chi.

'We watched them move in slow motion from the bottom of the Baxter Street fence'

Risu started to giggle as now Jackson, as well as Crosby, continued with their demonstration of carefully slow body movements.

'Hey! Don't knock it, it really does make you less tense'

Olmaxon glared at Risu who put his tail over his mouth to stop himself from getting a fit of the giggles. The rats continued,

'Then we saw halfway up the fence a large squirrel just hanging there'

'Moving his tail in time with the old folks, he didn't seem to have a care'

'But it was too early, too bright and too dangerous to say hello'

'So we just jumped down the water drain and went below'

Skudzo began to shuffle about in the corner. 'Riveting stuff' he muttered.

Olmaxon turned and put his tail over his mouth, 'Sssshh'.

By now Risu's giggling fit had spread to Funni and both of them were trying desperately to stifle their nervous laughter.

The rats, realizing that they were beginning to loose their audience, turned up the dramatic tone a notch,

'The rat home under Columbus Park was silent and almost empty'

From behind Crosby as he spoke, Delancy made a small spooky wailing sound to try and help increase the tension. 'Whoooooooaaaaa'. Jackson continued talking,

'In fact the only two rats still there were Bayard and Vesey'

'They offered us some food, asked how we were and from where we had arrived'

'When we told them we had come down the Bowery, they said we were lucky to have survived'

'This part of New York is run by Shokobaba, Bayard did say'

'If you know what's right you should hurry on your way'

'She's killed or maimed so many rats around here, we are not safe even when it's dark'

'And she's personally removed all the squirrels from Columbus Park'

' 'All?' I asked, 'but I saw one just now"

'Watching the old folks move with the Tao'

'Vesey looked worried and asked, 'Who is this stranger?"

"We must hurry and warn him that he is in danger"

'Vesey ran for the exit, then turned to us to shout'

"Shokobaba's owner always brings her here for the morning workout"

'So we ran out the hide up to the street, Vesey first with Bayard bringing up the rear'

'But as we came out we were met with a surprise that filled us with fear'

'That cat was there waiting as we came outside, and he had grabbed poor Vesey by the throat'

'The rest of us froze as we saw Vesey struggle, but the cat just laughed and started to gloat'

'Her claws squeezed tightly around Vesey's neck and she spoke with a sneer'

"Hello Vesey, who are your friends? What are you all doing here?"

'Not stopping to think I jumped on her back'

'She didn't expect his surprise attack'

'I dug my claws in, but it did no good'

'She just held on to Vesey as hard as she could'

'As I fought I saw Vesey's eyes bulge with pain'

'His life force was almost gone as Jackson struggled in vain'

'Then we heard a voice from the humans shout loud and clear'

"Shoko!' cried an old lady 'Stop fighting and get over here"

'The vile cat turned to her owner, but kept poor Vesey in her grip'

'No matter what happened she wasn't going to let that rat slip'

'As the old woman came over, Jackson jumped off the cat'

'I was worried, she seemed to be carrying a bat'

'He ran and joined Bayard and I near the drain'

'And we could still hear Vesey struggle with pain'

' 'Your friends have gone rat' said Shoko purring in Vesey's ear'

' 'Seems you are all mine at last my little dear' '

'By now the old woman had arrived at the scene'

'She had a face like her cat's, all nasty and mean'

' 'Stop playing Shoko! Kill that rat, I'm missing my Tai Chi' '

' 'Time to say goodbye" said Shoko to Vesey with evil glee'

'We watched helpless as Shoko punched Vesey......... four or more hits!'

'Then out flicked two claws, as long as chopsticks!'

' 'So long Vesey, time to meet the rat maker' said Shoko as Vesey went pale'

'But before she could strike, that bad cat let out an ungodly wail'

'We saw the squirrel from before had her tail in his jaws!'

'And the shock made her release Vesey from her deadly claws'

'Vesey slunk down and joined us, bleeding and bruised'

'As Bayard took him below, he looked back at us bemused'

'But that squirrel was hanging on to the twisting and turning cat'

'Even the old woman was trying to hit it with her bat'

'Then she spotted us, and came over wielding her stick'

'So we had to jump down the drain in haste..........I mean quick!'

'But as we fell down below through the gap'

'From the street above we heard the sound of a bone crack'

'Then the biggest scream of pain we have heard in our lives,'

'Cut through the silent drain like a thousand noisy knives'

'Then we heard the old woman crazily crying with all her might'

'But we were more concerned to check if Vesey was alright'

'So we ran to the burrow and saw Vesey was well'

'With maybe just a scar and another story to tell'

'I was curious to know what had happened after we'd left in such a hurry'

'So Bayard led us to another rat exit near the corner of Mulberry'

'At the mouth of that drain Bayard told us there was nothing he could see'

'He turned and suggested the best view point could be found up a tree'

'So without a thought and full of curiosity......'

'Crosby ran up a nearby Elm with some velocity'

'I saw a large crowd of people over on Baxter Street'

'Old folks waving their arms and stamping their feet'

'But I couldn't see Shoko or the squirrel, dead or alive'

'So he jumped back down to the drain in a single dive'

'We stayed on at Columbus and helped the injured Vesey convalesce,'

'But after a week we felt it time to move on nonetheless'

'During that time we asked everyone we could, but it was to no end'

'We never knew what happened to Shoko or the squirrel who helped save our friend'

With this last line, Crosby and Jackson both bowed. The squirrels all sat in silence, Risu's giggling fit long gone. Delancy made everyone jump as he started clapping. 'Well done, really well done Fellas!'

Murray joined in the applause, 'Yeah! More, more, come on tell us!'

'Goodness me no!' Olmaxon whispered as he and the other squirrels slowly joined in with the clapping. He raised his voice and spoke towards the rats on the stage. 'Thank you both so much for a very interesting story, but it's getting late and we must be leaving'

'Oh but you should stay and hear about the trouble we had afterwards by Rector Street' pleaded Crosby.

'Yes, yes,' said Olmaxon as he and the older squirrel began ushering the others towards the exit, 'I'll contact Delancy so another day we can meet'

'But...' began Funni before the older squirrel silenced her with a scowl.

'We'll talk outside' whispered Olmaxon.

Despite protests and pleas from the rats to stop and listen to more tales and even with the younger squirrels dragging their feet, Olmaxon managed to hurry and fuss all of the squirrels out of the rat place and outside into the children's playground.

It had become a freezing cold evening, but Kalan was fuming inside too much to feel it. Even though he felt annoyed at being forced to leave the rats, he saw that Olmaxon looked quite angry, and even worse, very worried. For this reason Kalan felt it best to keep quiet for the moment.

As they hurried back to the castle in silence Kalan looked closely at the other squirrels. The older squirrel had his usual deadly serious expression, but it certainly held no air of "worried" like the one currently residing on the face of his boss Olmaxon. Funni looked as angry and upset as Kalan felt, while Risu just appeared to be cold. Skudzo, on the other hand, was trying to avoid Kalan's gaze altogether. After a few minutes they arrived at the General Booth entrance to the main drey under Castle Clinton.

With Olmaxon leading the way, and his colleague bringing up the rear, the group of silent squirrels jumped down into the main corridor and eventually made their way to the main meeting hall.

When they were all inside Olmaxon turned to face the others with his nervous smile very evident. Kalan noticed that his expression was much more worried than angry now. He started to speak in a loud whisper,

'Now everybody, I know that you are all curious about Bilka and what may or may not have happened to him......'

'Concerned!' cried out Funni, 'Concerned not curious'

Olmaxon twitched but carried on in the same tone of voice.

'That's as maybe, but the bottom line is that we can't believe rats. We all know that they will say anything to get attention in front of a captive gullible audience' A nervous smile moved across his face and the top right of his mouth twitched twice, 'So I don't want you going near their place again. Is that clear?'

'But what if that was Bilka those rats met?' Kalan spoke up, trying to keep the tone of his voice as reasonably sounding as possible. This only seemed to make Olmaxon worse and he lost all pretence of whispering,

'But what?' he shouted, 'What difference would it possibly make?'

His outburst startled the squirrels, and on seeing this he lowered his voice a little. 'You shouldn't have listened to those silly rats. I know that they will have put ideas in your head. Well forget them. No one is going out from here to find him'

Olmaxon waved his tail above his head as a chorus of 'buts' and indignation came out from the three squirrels. 'But nothing!' he shouted again, 'I don't want to hear it. Battery Park is your home, and if Bilka chose to leave it, then that's his own lookout and no concern of yours' Olmaxon started to make his way to the exit as he was in no mood for a debate. 'And just to make sure you all have time to reflect on this, I've decided to ground the three of you in the drey until after the race'

By the time he had got to the exit he turned back towards Kalan and the others, his voice returning back to a whisper, 'Trust me, it's for your own good'

He nodded to the other squirrel, and then went off down the corridor. The older squirrel now turned towards the other three,

'I'll assign someone to keep an eye on you lot each day' he said with a just the tiniest hint of menace. 'Skudzo, you keep your eye on them until I can draw up a schedule with some other elders'

Then he too was gone down the corridor without even a second look at Kalan, Risu and Funni.

Skudzo came forward from the shadowy part of the corner where he had been trying to hide himself during Olmaxon's rant. 'I'm sorry Kalan,' he said looking genuinely apologetic. 'I had no idea he was going to hit the roof like that when I told him you guys had gone to meet the rats'

'Don't worry Skudzo, its ok' said Kalan, but stopped and turned around as he heard Funni starting to cry.

'Hey!' said Risu, 'Come on Funni, it's not that bad being grounded. It was getting too cold outside anyway' He put his tail around her shoulders. She looked up with her eyes full of tears.

'But I ....' she sobbed quietly, 'I can't just stay here not knowing what's happened to Bilka. He's my father'

Risu and Kalan gave each other an understanding glance, and then Kalan moved closer and whispered softly in her ear. 'We'll find out Funni, we'll find out I promise'

The Race Night

Olmaxon had been true to his word and Kalan, Funni and Risu had all been closely watched to make sure they didn't leave the drey in the days leading up to the race. Each day a different, older squirrel had been assigned to keep an eye on them, some more willingly than others. One had spent his day following the squirrels talking all the time about how Bilka had been such a strange character, but at the end of the day always a fool. He eventually reduced Funni to tears.

Skudzo divided his time during his watch from apologizing to everyone and then complaining about Mokus's training for the race. 'The only way he's going to win is if Nolai starts running backwards!' he had said to Kalan a few days earlier. By race night the entire drey was of the same opinion and the odds were stacked against Mokus.

Today Ardilla was reluctantly looking after the three and he too had put all his nuts on Nolai to win.

'He can't loose' he said to Risu. Risu shrugged. He would have loved to place a bet, but since he hadn't a nut in the world there was nothing doing. There was also the small matter of not being around to collect any eventual winnings, since he had agreed with Kalan and Funni that tonight they would be leaving Battery Park.

'Of course I've put a couple of nuts on old Mokus as well' continued Ardilla, 'I mean you've got to hedge your bets, nothing is certain'

Risu shrugged and nodded at the same time. This is a difficult action for most, but Risu could pull it off quite naturally. He was really only half listening to Ardilla. His mind was on the plan. They were going to leave the park tonight while everyone was wrapped up watching the race and make their way up to Central Park, looking for Bilka on the way. Risu nodded slowly to himself as he pondered the whole business. Sounds simple enough. Why on earth had he agreed? Maybe because he had nothing left to loose? He shrugged. Maybe it really would be a 'great adventure' as Kalan had said. He lifted his shoulders up past his neck, then another thought hit him mid-shrug. Maybe he just wanted to stay near Funni? His shoulders stayed up around his ears, this idea made him more nervous than all the others.

'Hey! Are you ok?' interrupted Ardilla, 'Is there something wrong with your neck?'

'Sorry, it's nothing,' said Risu as he straightened himself out. 'I reckon it's just that I don't want her to get into any trouble'

'What? Who?' said Ardilla who didn't realize that Risu had just been thinking out loud.

'Erm…' Risu thought quickly, 'Er Funni of course. I told her not to bet tonight since…' his mind raced back to something he thought he had heard Ardilla say earlier, 'Since nothing is certain these days'

Ardilla laughed out loud. 'Too right!' he said and slapped Risu on the back with his tail.

In a corner out of earshot, but still in sight of Ardilla, Kalan and Funni were sitting closely together whispering. 'I'll need at least an hour Funni' said Kalan, 'I'll have to run along the promenade not to be noticed, so it will take me a little longer to get there and back'

Funni sighed, 'But even if the rats can tell you the best way to start on out of here, with Ratspeak it's going to take them all day'

Kalan looked back at her and smiled, 'yeah and I am sure they will want to tell me a story as well while I am in their company, but I promise to be quick' He tilted his head in the direction of Ardilla. 'You just worry about keeping Ardilla busy 'til I get back' As Kalan looked he noticed that Risu was alone. 'Hey!' shouted Kalan across the room, 'Where's he gone?'

Risu bounced over to Kalan and Funni. 'Dunno,' he said, 'mentioned something about tonight's race, then said he'd be back in a second' Risu looked about to make sure no one else was around. 'Are you really certain Kalan,' Risu lowered his voice, 'about tonight and all? Why not just wait until later when we aren't grounded?'

Kalan replied instantly. 'Risu, tonight is the only night when everybody will have something else on their minds. Even Olmaxon is going to be worrying more about the race than us lot' Risu opened his mouth to form a 'but'. 'And anyway' continued Kalan, 'Now's the time, I can feel it. I am sure we can find Bilka'

Funni moved towards the pair. 'Plus Risu, if we leave it any longer you will probably go and change your mind' She said nudging him gently in the ribs. Risu nodded slowly in agreement.

'Don't worry' he said, 'I'm in' He raised his tail and the other two slapped it lightly with their own.

'Hey! If you three have got some inside secret on the race tonight, I wanna know!' Ardilla was back. 'I've just put my whole stash down on the race. Geesh. Sincab's giving terrible odds tonight, I wish I had more nuts'

'And you can't even search for more today 'cause that old grouch Olmaxon has got you in here with us' Kalan said, successfully guessing Ardilla's train of thought.

'Yeah you said it' said Ardilla gloomily. 'You know I've got nothing against you guys, but I've never seen the old guy so tense. If he had caught me just now betting on the race I reckon he would have grounded me as well'

As Kalan looked at Ardilla's unhappy face he began thinking that maybe he wouldn't have to sneak away without Ardilla knowing, just maybe he could try a different approach. 'If I gave you my nut stash to bet with Ardilla' he said confidently, 'Would you do me a favor?'

'Hey! I can't go betting for you Kalan, it was risky enough doing it for me' Ardilla replied a little indignantly.

'No, no' said Kalan softly, 'I don't bet, you know that. I mean you use my nuts to bet for yourself. I'll give them to you' Ardilla said nothing. Risu and Funni looked nervously at Kalan, who didn't take his eyes off Ardilla as he continued talking slowly, 'I'll give you all my stash if you turn a blind eye to me leaving the drey for an hour or so'

Ardilla thought for a moment, but shook his head. 'Are you crazy? If you get caught outside Olmaxon will blow his top and I'll be grounded for certain'

Kalan was ready for this reply, 'That's as maybe' Kalan spoke quickly but softly. 'But what say I give you my stash now, so you can go bet it all straight away. So even if I do get seen outside – which I won't – and you get grounded – which you won't – you've still been able to make the biggest bet of your life. Grounded or not, no one is going to be able to stop you collecting your winnings!'

Kalan crossed his arms and looked confidently at Ardilla who was obviously weighing up the risks in his mind.

'You keep your stash here in the drey?' Ardilla said after a short while, the tone of his voice very different from before.

'Well not exactly' replied Kalan. 'It's all hidden two inches down to the left of General Booth'

'You keep your stash by the main entrance to the drey?' said Funni as she looked incredulously at Kalan, 'But everyone passes by there everyday' she carried on, turning her gaze towards an equally confused Risu.

'Everyone passes by' said Kalan with a large confident smile on his face, 'but no one ever stops! It's the safest place of all if you think about it'

Kalan turned back to Ardilla. 'It's not a fortune Ardilla, but it's all yours if you let me out for an hour' Ardilla said nothing and didn't move. 'Go and check to see its all there' said Kalan. 'In fact go and use it all now, make another bet with it'

Ardilla shook his whole body as if he had just felt a cold blast of air. 'Give me five minutes!' he said excitedly. He turned tail and was gone.

'Your whole stash Kalan! What's got into you?' said Risu.

'Oh I don't care, it's not going to be much use to us on the road is it?' Kalan moved away from his friends and stuck his head out of the room and looked down the corridor. 'No ones around. I'm off!' he said.

'Hey! But.........' began Risu, but Kalan broke him off.

'Just tell Ardilla I assumed his agreement, and that I'll be back in an hour or so' He whispered a loud bye then sped down the corridor.

It was about nine o'clock in the morning and Kalan found the drey empty. Squirrels mostly forage in the early morning, and this being race night, everyone had be out since first light vigorously searching for funds. Kalan met no – one as he scurried along the long dark corridors towards the south exit. This was the one that pops out on the south side of Castle Clinton, close to the promenade. After several days cooped up inside, the bright light of the morning hurt Kalan's eyes as he jumped up the Elm directly above the exit. It took a few moments for his eyes to adjust, but from one of the higher branches he checked to make sure the route he wanted to take to the rats was clear. He could see that most of the squirrels were rooting around in the park or near the Castle entrance, some foraging, others working the tourists. The promenade was crowded with people queuing for the ferries, but no squirrels, so without any further hesitation Kalan jumped down and started to run.

It didn't take him long to get down to the rat's place. It never seems to take long to get anywhere when your mind is racing faster than your legs, and Kalan's thoughts pushed and pulled him along Admiral Dewey Promenade.

When Kalan arrived at the rat's entrance hole, he had to wait anxiously for what seemed like an eternity as two large men were moving boxes out of the restaurant. Eventually they both went back inside, and he jumped down the rat hole and was in. He looked around but at first could not see any familiar faces amongst the rodents. He noticed that a few of them were grouped together laughing at a pink piece of paper one was holding up high. Kalan squinted in the low light, it seemed to be one of the papers the Parks Department leave on the trees whenever they have been hunting for rats.

'Bromethalin!' shouted out the one holding the pink paper, 'What are they trying to do?'

'Yeah!' laughed out another, 'Even my granddad was immune to that one back in '92' Some other rats came over to look at the paper.

'Oh that strain of toxin again, well those jokers have got to be kidding'

'I quite like it,' replied another, 'tastes a lot like fried chicken'

As the group of rats started laughing Kalan moved his way around them and eventually saw a face he recognized. 'Hey Delancy!' he called across the room as he walked closer. The rat looked over towards Kalan and gave a welcoming smile.

'Hello there,' said Kalan as he came face to face to Delancy. 'Nice to see you again, how are you?' Kalan spoke quickly since it's always best to have the first say in a rat conversation. He didn't have time to think up rhyming couplets for every sentence, and if you get to speak first you don't have too.

'Can't complain' replied Delancy, 'but poor old Murray's got a dose of flu'

'Oh I'm sorry to hear that, hope it's not contagious'

'He'll live, but when he sneezes the noise is outrageous!'

Kalan giggled softly, but then straightened himself up and tried to look serious for a moment. 'Look Delancy' he said, 'I'll be up front with you, I'm here because I really need a little advice'

'You need help in finding your way uptown to look for your friend?'

Delancy looked at Kalan with his friendly eyes wide open knowing that he had shocked the squirrel by guessing his thoughts, but then his eyes moved to one side as he realized he hadn't finished his couplet, 'And that's real nice'

'Wow!' said Kalan, genuinely surprised 'I can't believe it! Are my thoughts so transparent that they show?'

'Hey!' Delancy replied, 'When it comes to looking out for your friends us rats are the first to know'

'Well I and others want to leave tonight, but I have no idea which way to go to be honest'

'Wait here' said Delancy, 'I think Murray's got something that could help you in your squirrel quest'

He turned and ran off down one of the closer corridors. Kalan could hear some strange sniffling noises followed by an almighty sneeze that he assumed was Murray. It was so loud that even the rats having a laugh at the expense of the Parks Department looked up from their paper. Delancy reappeared at the entrance to the corridor and looked over to them. 'Murray says he's feeling better, but still a little meek' he said in an almost fatherly manner.

'Yeah well I think he'll sneeze himself into the middle of next week' cried back one of them and they all started laughing again.

Delancy ignored them and moved back over to where Kalan was waiting. He held out something heavy and round, and offered it to Kalan. Then before

Kalan could take it, Delancy pulled it back towards himself and looked at it closely. He shook his head and lifted his nose up in the air. He twitched his whiskers almost as if they were some sort of radar. Then he put the ball to his mouth and gnawed at little mark on its surface, seemingly satisfied with this last minute modification he offered it again to Kalan

Kalan took it in his hands. It was a black ball that seemed to be floating inside a plastic one. It had lots of green and white human markings on it, with one long green line in the middle. As Kalan held it the black ball floated around slowly inside its casing. 'What is this Delancy?' Kalan asked slowly in a slightly nervous tone that was mixed with anticipation.

'It's magic, you'll see' replied Delancy, with a glint in his eye.

Back at the drey Ardilla, unsurprisingly enough, wasn't very happy. 'When will he be back? How could he go off like that? What if he's spotted?'

'Keep it together Ardilla' said Risu, ignoring the long list of unanswerable questions.

'He won't be long' said Funni.

Risu's curiosity was starting to get the better of him, 'Besides, you made your extra bet with Kalan's stash' He moved closer to Ardilla, 'By the by how much did he have?'

Ardilla stopped pacing up and down and a small grin grew on his face. 'Yeah, he did have quite a bit, a lot of walnuts for some reason. Amazing hiding place, just think I practically walked over his stash every day and never knew it was there' He stopped for a moment, then fell back into his anxious questioning again, 'But why did he give it all to me like that? On a whim? What are you three really up too? Olmaxon is bound to come by any moment now, when is he coming back?'

Ardilla was interrupted by a small but clear voice from behind,

'Olmaxon's down at the hollow statue helping to decide on the finishing line for the race tonight'

'Kalan!' shouted Funni, and Kalan saw the relief on all of their faces as they turned to greet him.

'And in answer to the rest of your questions Ardilla, we are planning on finding Bilka, then heading off to Central Park. As for my stash, I gave it to you because...' Kalan dragged out the word as he thought for a moment, 'because too many possessions have a habit of tying a squirrel down'

'Ha!' Risu laughed sarcastically, 'Well that won't worry Ardilla, as I think he's bet the lot'

Ardilla's grin was broader than ever now that Kalan was back, 'Yeah only until tomorrow little Risu. After I have been to see Sincab and collected my winnings I'll have a lot to tie me down. Thanks again Kalan!'

For the rest of the day Kalan, Risu and Funni huddled themselves in a corner and went over their plan for the night. Both Risu and Funni were impressed by the 'magic nut', a name Risu had thought up, that Delancy the rat had given them. Kalan explained how it worked.

'Delancy says that this long pointed line always indicates uptown, and this tooth mark he made on it indicates the way we have to go to find Central Park. Wherever we are, we can't get lost. We ask whoever we meet for information to find Bilka, and even if they send us in another direction we will always know had to get back on course for Central Park' Kalan carried on excitedly, 'The black ball is always moving, but the line always points in the same direction' He moved around to face Risu, holding the ball with outstretched arms, 'Watch Funni, see how the line points at Risu now I am facing him?' Funni nodded and followed along as Kalan slowly turned around until he had his back to Risu. 'See? Even if I turn my back to him, the line still points back to Risu'

Risu hopped over to have a look and both he and Funni gazed at the fluorescent green markings on the small, smooth ball.

'And all those other markings and stuff?' said Funni slowly pointing at the many little white lines and green letters that were printed on the side of the black ball as it floated in its transparent casing. Delancy's tooth mark was above the letters 'NE'

'I don't know about those,' said Kalan, 'Delancy only told me about the long green line, and that we have to follow his mark' He tapped the tip of the arrow that was pointing to a large green letter N, then to Delancy's tooth mark to its right., 'And if we get out there and don't find Bilka, or just a city full of cats and dogs, I guess we just follow the other end to get back here' said Risu as he tapped the other end of the line, that was attached to a letter S.

'We *will* find Bilka!' cried out Funni angrily.

'Yes we will' said Kalan quickly, 'But Risu is right, with this magic nut we can't get lost' The three of them spent a few minutes in silence contemplating the floating ball until Risu broke the silence.

'Can we eat it?'

'Now why would you want to do that?' said Kalan exasperatedly

'Dunno,' shrugged Risu, 'I'm hungry I guess'

Above them the sky had darkened long before dusk and as night fell so did the sky. There was little wind so the rain came down in an almost straight line, and showed no intention of giving up until morning. Some squirrels were happy with this, since by around seven the rain had seen off the last of the humans, and they had the park to themselves for a change. Others thought it meant the race should be called off.

'How can they get a grip on the metal bird to start? With this rain they will slip' Skudzo was shouting out his worries to the race committee that was having a last minute meeting in the main hall of the drey.

'You mean Mokus will slip and fall' replied an unseen voice from the back of the hall.

'It's not just that' Skudzo carried on, 'With all this rain its going to be difficult to see, they may loose their direction'

'You mean Mokus will get lost' called out the heckler again.

'Hey!' Skudzo shouted across in the general direction of the voice, but turned back to the committee. 'Rain puddles are forming, they're dangerous, and what if someone falls in?'

'What you mean is Mokus can't swim!'

The whole room started to laugh as Skudzo tried to push his way over to his unseen detractor. Olmaxon called him back., 'Skudzo!' he spoke loudly enough for everyone to hear him.'The race will go ahead. I don't want to hear any excuses, and I expect to see both competitors by the metal bird shortly'

The room roared its approval, and most of the squirrels began to leave to get to the best viewing positions outside for the race. Nobody cared about whether Kalan and his friends were still obeying the curfew as they passed by their room, Olmaxon included. This was just as well since they were no longer there.

Skudzo hurried over to Mokus, who was feeling, nonetheless, very confident.

'The rain will affect Nolai as well Skudzo' he said as his burly trainer entered his burrowed out room.

'Yeah well, just remember what I said before, to keep to the paths. Don't go on the grass or you'll get bogged down, and don't even think of trying to......'

'OK, OK!' interrupted Mokus. 'I know the drill, we've been through it a hundred times already. I'll be OK'

Skudzo nodded and muttered something under his breath.

'And Skudzo,' said Mokus as he filled his chest with air, 'I intend to win this'

Skudzo smiled proudly. He had always felt a little guilty since he had never had much confidence in Mokus winning, and he was pleased to see that Mokus hadn't lost faith in himself. 'Come on champ,' he said 'Let's roll!'

The pair of them made their way out of the drey and into the pouring rain of the park, which despite being wet and cold was in fact teeming with activity. Most of the trees along the race route were full of squirrels. Many, including a few curious rats, were sitting underneath park benches. There were three very small squirrels who were sitting near the race route, but inside a trashcan close to the entrance to Castle Clinton. They had their backs to the inside walls of the trashcan to avoid the rain, and one of them held a small plastic ball in his claws.

'The moment the race passes us, we run up the main path until we get to the corner of the park. We cross the road there and are on our way'

Kalan was outlining the planned run up through Hope Garden and on to the corner of State Street and Battery Place. Even though he spoke with confidence Funni couldn't help noticing the ball in his paws shaking slightly. Maybe Kalan noticed this as he turned to her as he continued speaking, 'The rain is perfect Funni. There are no people about, and probably not much on the road either. We can be over and safe in seconds'

'Safe?' answered Risu in a very sarcastic tone.

Funni nudged him hard with her elbow, 'We will be safe and on our way!' she said trying to echo Kalan's confidence.

'Hold this' said Kalan, and he threw the ball to Funni who caught it and drew it closely towards her chest. Kalan jumped up and put his head out of the trashcan.

'Well?' said Risu from below, 'What can you see?'

'I think they are almost ready' Kalan shouted down, 'Not long now!'

What Kalan saw through the rain would have, to a human eye, appeared to be nothing more than an empty rain swept City Park. Streetlights illuminating wet empty pathways and vacant benches. Not a soul about, at first glance, but a person looking again could see what Kalan saw. Under the benches dozens of squirrels, huddled together from the rain, looking out along the pathway in expectation. Up in the trees, more squirrels. Some on the branches, some inside tree holes looking out. Some chewing nuts, some pushing for a better position, but most just talking and laughing in eager anticipation. Kalan could feel the atmosphere heavy with excited tension. As he shook the rain from his eyes he wasn't sure how much of that tension was for the race, and how much was for what he was about to do.

A few hundred yards to the left of Kalan's trashcan, under a bench near the East Coast Memorial, a small group of squirrels sat in discussion. In fact the group was divided into two.

Olmaxon, Skudzo and several others were having a heated debate to one side of the bench, and a very quiet pair of squirrels on the other side. Mokus and Nolai had nothing to say since their minds were trying to concentrate on the race. Mokus tried to look at Nolai through the corner of his eye, and caught Nolai looking back. They both turned away from each other in a slightly embarrassed way. Mokus looked down at this tail while Nolai fixed his gaze on Olmaxon's back fur, which, strangely, seemed to moving gently in the opposite direction to his body movements. Olmaxon had his back to Nolai and Mokus while he was talking to the other squirrels. Nolai couldn't quite hear what they were talking about, but this became an irrelevant point as Olmaxon turned quickly to face him and Mokus.

'Well if you two feel ready then we can begin' he said with a stern smile. 'Skudzo will accompany you both to the metal eagle and when you are in your positions, and on his command, you can begin' He paused, and then moved over towards the two nervous squirrels. 'Good luck to you both, and may the best squirrel win'

As he came closer to the squirrels Olmaxon put one arm around Nolai and another around Mokus in what, at first, appeared to be a friendly hug of encouragement, but then quickly turned into a gentle shove toward the eagle. Skudzo was already out on the path standing waiting for them, using his tail to cover himself from the rain, 'Come on guys, let's go race!' he shouted over to them, and started to run towards the eagle. Mokus and Nolai ran after him. Olmaxon and the others also ran from under the bench, but in the other direction down the path towards the Korean War Memorial. This was going to be the 'hollow statue' finishing line. Some squirrels lining the path, and bored with waiting for the action to start, broke out in halfhearted cheers as Olmaxon and the others ran along the pathway.

Back beneath the eagle Skudzo shouted up a few last minute instructions to Nolai and Mokus as they climbed up. 'Grip with your claws to stop yourself slipping', 'Use your tail to balance yourselves', 'Don't worry about the rain, you are already as wet as you are going to get'

Nolai and Mokus moved with great difficulty, but eventually reached the tail feather of the eagle. It slopped downwards so they used their tails as makeshift breaks in front of their feet to stop themselves slipping down.

Skudzo had in the meantime jumped onto the stone fence separating the East Coast Memorial from the rest of Battery Park, and from there he had a much better view of everything, and could still be heard by Nolai and Mokus. When it was clear that they had both spotted him he raised his tail high over his head. 'When you see my tail drop,' he barked as loud as he could, 'you both start'

On seeing this both squirrels allowed gravity to slowly pull them down towards the edge of the tail. Once there, they gripped the edge with their front claws and pulled up their hind legs ready to jump. Through the wall of falling rain they watched Skudzo intently. For a moment it seemed as if time had come to a complete halt, as all three squirrels remained totally motionless. They did not even blink. Only the continual pouring rain gave any indication that time moved on regardless.

All the other squirrels watching the eagle took a collective deep breath as they watched the two racers get into their starting positions.

From the tip of their trashcan Funni, Risu and Kalan all took deep breaths as they sensed the atmosphere in the park. Skudzo did likewise to clam his nerves as he noticed his tail starting to shake. Mokus was the last squirrel to take a deep breath as Skudzo's tail smashed down through the rain, and he expelled this saved oxygen as he flung himself into the air. Nolai too pushed himself into the night sky, and both squirrels were airborne before Skudzo's tail hit the stone fence.

A very strange sound rang around Battery Park in that moment, like a hundred small dogs all crying out 'ARF!' at the same time, as the tension and held in breaths of air all found a release. Risu almost started to jump off from the edge of the trashcan as the tension broke, but he was held back by Kalan, 'Wait till they go past us' he whispered.

Risu did not have to wait for long. Both Mokus and Nolai had flown straight over Skudzo and landed on the path. Cheered on by squirrels from all sides they raced neck and neck down the pathway and passed in front of Kalan's trashcan at the beginning of Hope Garden. As they turned right and headed towards the Korean War Memorial, they were followed a split second later by dozens of squirrels, and a few rats, who did not want to miss the finish.

'Now!' Kalan shouted, and the three of them jumped down from the trashcan and ran directly along the path towards the edge of the park. They failed to notice a large squirrel, who had been bringing up the rear of the race chasers, turn away from the squirrel crowd and follow them up the path to the road's edge. As Kalan and the others ran up towards the old Bowling Green metro exit, they heard another large squirrel group 'Arf' erupt from behind them.

'I wonder who won' puffed Risu as he joined the other two at the edge of the park. Kalan had stopped by the park fence, with only the sidewalk separating them from the road and beyond. As Kalan had hoped there was not a car in sight, not a human soul to be seen.

'Let's not think about it too much' he said anxiously to the others, 'Let's just go to the edge of the sidewalk and then go for it'

Risu looked across State Street at the gray stone building on the other side. The old Customs house looked very cold and unwelcoming. He shivered a bit, but as his eyes panned along he also saw, through the wall of rain, a few trees and a park like fence to the left of the Custom House. This picked him up a little.

'Ok guys' he said, and the three of them hopped slowly across the sidewalk to the edge of the road.

'This is it!' said Funni, 'One last look at home' As she turned to look back towards Battery Park she yelped out in shock. Standing behind her with his hands on his hips and rain pouring down his face was Skudzo.

'Don't you try and stop us' she shouted out in a frustrated and yet defensive tone. 'Our minds are made up'

'Skudzo,' said Kalan calmly, 'You know what we are going to do don't you?'

Skudzo, rather than angry, felt very confused. He thought about things for a minute and looked beyond the small squirrels across the road towards the Customs House. His gaze gradually turned back towards Kalan, then to Funni and finally came to rest on Risu.

Risu shrugged, 'Hey Skudzo, we're off. Can you believe it, even me?'

An uneasy silence followed broken only by the sounds of squirrels barking and yelping from inside the park. Skudzo opened his mouth to speak, but was surprised to find that no words came out. Risu moved towards Skudzo, 'Why don't you come along as well?' he said.

Skudzo still had his mouth open. 'I can't' he said slowly, 'and you shouldn't'

Kalan moved towards his big friend and placed his tail on Skudzo shoulders. 'We have to go Skudzo. Otherwise I'll never sleep peacefully again' Kalan laughed a little, 'Besides we will be fine, and I promise we'll get a message to you so you know everything's ok'

Skudzo found it difficult to look at Kalan in the eyes, and hung his head low. 'So this is goodbye?' he whispered softly.

'I think it's easier if we think of it more as just a simple 'goodnight" said Kalan as he gave Skudzo a hug.

'Goodnight Skudzo' said Funni, and she too hugged Skudzo tightly.

'Good night big boy' said Risu and he slapped Skudzo's shoulders with his tail.

Skudzo said nothing, but lifted his head and looked at the three young squirrels. Kalan jumped down from the edge of the sidewalk, checked the road in both directions and shouted out, 'Let's go guys. Goodnight Skudzo!'

The three squirrels, charged with a reserve of Adrenalin they never knew they had, rushed out onto State Street. The large squirrel stared as Kalan, Risu and Funni ran across the road to the Custom House. He watched as they arrived safely on the other side, then saw them turn right and enter the tiny Bowling Green Park. As he stood there looking the rain continued to drip down his wet face, mixing itself freely with his tears.

The Broadway

'I don't believe it! I don't believe it!'

Risu was jumping up and down with excitement. From the top branch of the highest Elm in the Bowling Green Park he could see over into Battery Park. He couldn't believe he had actually crossed the road, he couldn't believe he could see Battery Park as if he was still there. However the really mind-blowing thing, for Risu, was the fact that he couldn't believe he was actually enjoying his first real taste of adventure. He was still on a high from the adrenalin rush of earlier, even though he Kalan and Funni had now been in the Bowling Green for a couple of hours.

The rain had begun to let up a little, and the downpour and turned into a light drizzle which just bounced off the squirrels fur. It was past midnight, but all three squirrels had never felt more awake. Kalan had been running up and down each tree analyzing the green line on his 'magic nut' and trying to decide on the best route out of The Green. He wanted that everyone distance themselves from Battery Park while the streets were still empty and dark. From the edge of his branch looking down Broadway he could see where the road splits in two at the metal sculpture of the Wall Street Bull. Beyond that everything else just seemed to melt into a dark gray mix of unwelcoming buildings. Kalan took another look down at his ball and saw that Delancy's tooth mark by the arrowed line was insisting that that was the way to go.

'Are we going to stay here all night Kalan?' Funni had jumped up beside him, 'I've found a hollow in on of the trees here, we could stay there'

'Well no Funni' replied Kalan, 'If you and Risu are up to it we should go on, before the whole place starts filling up with people'

'What's the plan Cap e tan?' whispered a still exhilarated Risu as he also arrived on Kalan's branch.

Kalan moved closer to his two friends, and nudged himself between them. 'I think its best if we take it bit by bit. See that fat metal object over there?' He pointed to the bull with his tail. Risu and Funni nodded.

'Well, we jump down and run underneath that first. Then I'll jump up on top of it and find the next thing to run to. That's how we'll start out. Find a safe place and run to it. Once we get there we look for the next one'

Risu and Funni continued nodding slowly, in fact they hadn't stopped since Kalan had started talking. 'You see with the help of Delancy's nut we know more or less the way to go, but obviously we don't know what to expect. Moving on like this, stage by stage, when we run into trouble we can easily run back to the last place we came from'

Risu stopped nodding. A word Kalan had just said started to run around his mind knocking things over. 'When?' said Risu, very slowly.

Kalan turned towards Risu, his face smiling. 'When' he said and gave Risu an almost malicious wink.

'Kalan's right Risu,' said Funni, 'We would be naïve to think its going to be easy. At least thinking this way we can prepare for stuff'

Risu looked at his two friends. The 'when' in his mind had settled down in an easy chair, but was still nervously tapping its knee up and down. He sighed and shrugged.

'Come on then' said Kalan, then grabbing the trunk of the Elm started on down the tree headfirst. The others followed and within moments, they were through the Bowling Green fence and soon under the giant bull's stomach.

Tancredi had been watching the three squirrels from the moment they had arrived in his little part of New York and woken him up a few hours ago. The small but very chubby sparrow was annoyed at having been woken up, but this short lived emotion soon turned into curiosity. Why had these three wet squirrels suddenly appeared in his park? At first he had thought they were part of the race crowd that had gotten lost during all the excitement, but watching them now as they sat under the bull, he began to think they might have their own secret agenda. Then again, thought Tancredi as he ruffled his wings, if they were looking to get back to Battery Park they were going the wrong way. He really should let them know.

Tancredi took off into the air. As he flew down to the bull he saw that one of the squirrels had jumped up onto the head of the statue. Tancredi landed on the bull's left horn.

'Hey pal,' he chirped, 'If yous looking to get back to the park, yous going the wrong way'

'That's ok' said Kalan as he turned to look at the sparrow, 'We aren't going back'

'I knew it! I knew it!' Tancredi sang out loudly, 'I said to myself, Tancredi those squirrels ain't lost, theys going places' He paused as he saw that Kalan had turned away from him and was peering through the drizzle up Broadway. 'Where is yous going squirrely?'

Kalan turned back to look at Tancredi. 'Well for now we are just going across the road to that garbage can' And he pointed with his tail to what he had seen around a hundred yards further up Broadway. 'Then we plan on finding my friend, and then we are going to Central Park'

'Yous finding your friend in a trashcan?' asked Tancredi.

'No, no' smiled Kalan. 'It's just that it's the first time any of us have ever done anything like this, so we are taking it just one step at a time. We really don't know what to expect so the trashcan is just the next bit'

Tancredi gazed at Kalan fascinated by this matter of fact squirrel. 'Well squirrely' he said eventually 'Yous going to have a lot of bits before you get to Central Park'

'Hey Kalan, who are you talking to?' Risu shouted out from under the bull.

'A friend' shouted Kalan, then quickly turned his attention back towards the sparrow. 'Want to come and say hello to the others?'

'Oh sure' replied Tancredi.

'Well follow me. By the way, the name's Kalan' Before Tancredi could reply the squirrel had already jumped down onto the sidewalk. The sparrow quickly followed him down and hopped under the bull and out of the rain. He opened his wings and flapped them free of water.

'And I is Tancredi' he said proudly to all three squirrels, 'and yous guys woke me up. And......' Tancredi stopped in mid sentence and his eyes bulged as he focused them on Risu. 'And I is knowing you pal'

'Really?' said Risu a little nervously, 'I don't think so. I'm Risu' He shuffled a little backwards, his memory in overdrive, but try as he might he couldn't place the little sparrow in his mind.

'Yeah sure, I is knowing you' continued Tancredi, 'I is rememberin' yous dancin' for that smelly guy with the nuts. I is rememberin' you jumpin' backwards and hittin' that water bowl he leaves for yous guys'

Risu's memory instantly took him back to that unfortunate incident. He remembered seeing how Irving had given a nut to a young squirrel who had just done a backwards somersault. Risu, desperate as ever make good his permanent nut deficit, tried to do the same. However he totally miscalculated everything and landed head first into the small plastic bowl of water Irving always left for the squirrels by his bench. The squirrel man used to weigh the bowl down with stones, and Risu grimaced as he remembered painfully hitting a rock with his head, then swaggering from side to side shaking water all over the place. He remembered Irving shouting as the water splashed over his shoes, he remembered the laughing sparrows.

'Yes, yous was funny pal, and to think smelly man never gave you no nut, no nothing' said Tancredi remembering the moment as clearly as Risu.

Risu, very much embarrassed, moved even further backwards almost going out from under the bull. Then a car came screaming down Broadway, its headlights blaring white light under the bull. The squirrels froze in terror, as it drove past and screeched a right turn into Battery Place. This was too much for Risu. The moment the car passed, he let out a small whimper and bolted from under the bull back towards the Bowling Green.

'RISU!' cried out Kalan, but Risu heard nothing. The 'when' in his head had already jumped out from the easy chair and was using it to smash up everything in the room. Kalan looked at Funni. 'Are you Ok?' he asked.

Funni was still a little nervous from the car, but whispered that she felt fine. Tancredi had not moved an inch. He just twitched his head to one side, a little confused. 'Yous want I go see if your pal is ok?' he asked trying to sound as helpful as possible.

'We should all go,' replied Kalan.

So the two squirrels ran out from under the bull back to the green, followed by a low flying sparrow. As they ran they spotted Risu at the top of the nearest Elm wrapped up in his tail. As Kalan and Funni climbed up the tree Tancredi landed on Risu's branch. 'Sorry if I upset yous pal' he said with a genuine remorse, 'It's just that when I sees a face, I's never forget it'

'That's ok' replied Risu in an almost silent whisper. 'It's my fault' he carried on raising his voice a little as the others arrived. 'Touch of the nerves, that's all'

Kalan moved closer to Risu and put his head close to his friend's ear, 'No more sweaty guy on our adventure Risu. And you wont have to dance for nuts anymore either' Risu unwrapped himself from his tail, and used it to give Kalan a hug.

'Ahh that's nice, yous guys are good pals' said Tancredi.

'We've got to look after each other Tancredi' said Funni as she too moved over to hug Risu. 'We've got a long way to go'

'Too right pal' said Tancredi, 'Central park is long ways up town'

As Funni moved closer to Risu she could sense that he had calmed down a lot.

'Look Risu, we'll stay here tonight' said Kalan, 'Funni's found a hollow, so we can hole up there 'til you feel up to heading out'

'No way' replied Risu, 'Hey, I'm ok. I was just testing out your theory that we could run back when we get into trouble' Risu put on a smile that soon spread to everyone. 'Come on' he said, 'We've got a trashcan to visit'

Soon all three squirrels were back under the bull. It had finally stopped raining, but some water still dripped down from the bull suggesting the opposite as they looked out across the road.

'I'll go first' said Kalan, 'Check its ok, then when you see me wave my tail you two come on over'

'Yeah, no problem' replied Risu.

Kalan prepared to run, then quickly turned back as he remembered something important. 'Don't forget to check the road both ways before you run across'

'Don't worry about us' said Funni 'get going'

Kalan hurried out from under the bull and ran to the edge of the road. He saw some lights up Broadway in the distance, but they didn't seem to be moving. Convinced that nothing was coming he fixed his eyes on the trashcan and sped across Broadway towards it. He jumped directly from the street up onto its rim, and immediately looked and smelled around the outside, before jumping down inside. They were not particularly nice smells but they weren't dangerous ones either. The trashcan was full of soggy copies of the Daily News that smelt very musty and sagged a little under his weight. As Kalan emerged from the trashcan he found Tancredi had landed on its edge as well.

'Yous done this before?' asked the sparrow.

'Nope' said Kalan as he waved his tail in the direction of Funni and Risu, 'First time' Kalan felt a strong feeling of pride towards his two friends as he watched them run from the bull to the edge of Broadway, check for traffic, then run across towards him.

'That wasn't so bad' puffed Risu as he jumped up to join Kalan and Tancredi.

'Hey yeah' said Funni, 'It's a lot easier the second time'

The three of them jumped inside the trashcan, while Tancredi perched himself on the side looking down at them. He saw Kalan pull out from his fur a round ball that had green marks that glowed in the dark. He watched as they all huddled around it and excitedly discussed their next move.

'What's that?' shouted down Tancredi, Funni looked up at the sparrow,

'It helps us know which way to go next' she said helpfully. She took another glance at the green line and Delancy's mark, then jumped up to join Tancredi on the edge. 'But' she said as she looked down Broadway, 'it seems to be pointing to inside that building'

Tancredi turned his head to look where Funni was pointing. 'Yous got a key?' he asked innocently. He genuinely believed that these squirrels were about to do anything.

'No 'cause we're not going in' Kalan and Risu also jumped up onto the top of the trashcan. 'We'll stick to the road,' continued Kalan 'and wait till an opening turns up'

However, as Kalan stared down Broadway for the next place to move to, it didn't look like there were going to be any openings to run down. All he could see were dull, gray buildings and a road that, as another car passed by and made Risu and Funni jump back inside the trashcan, seemed to be getting slowly busier.

'If yous not going back to the park' said Tancredi, 'It's a long way up to the next one' Kalan looked at Tancredi. The portly sparrow smiled back at him. 'Guess yous could make it up to the church before sun up. There's another squirrel I knows who lives up there. He's ok. Talks funny though'

As Tancredi spoke it suddenly dawned on Kalandaka that he had completely overlooked something very important.

'Tancredi, have you ever met any other squirrels?' he asked.

'Are you kidding pal?' Tancredi hopped over closer to Kalan, 'I knows them all. I knows the squirrels up City Hall that think they owns the place. The one up at the church with the funny voice, he's always talking but he's really nice. I knows all you guys down here by the water. You guys are a lot of fun, always something going on in the Battery. I saws that race last night, that was cool'

'Who won?' interrupted Risu from inside the trashcan, but Kalan kept Tancredi's attention.

'No, I'm sorry Tancredi, I meant have you ever met any other squirrels in your park?'

'Oh I get you pal' said Tancredi, 'You squirrelys never leave your turf, never seen a squirrel on my bowling green'

'Ah well' Kalan sighed as thoughts of Tancredi meeting Bilka vanished from his mind.

'Hey' said Tancredi, sensing that he should try and say something positive 'I ain't on the Green a lot. I'm always out and about, only really come home when its time to put my head down. You guys woke me up'

'Yes I know I'm sorry' replied Kalan, 'We'll be on our way so you can get back to sleep'

'Ah, don't worry 'bout that pal, I'll help you guys up to the church. I'm wide awake now'

Risu and Funni remerged from the trashcan. 'It's getting too smelly down there' said Funni, 'Where's the next stop Kalan?'

'Well Tancredi, how do you want us to go about this?' said Kalan, 'Remember that we really don't want to run any further than we can see'

'Oh that's ok' replied the sparrow, 'church ain't too far up the street. I'll fly on and finds somewhere nice and safe for you guys to run to'

Kalan turned to Risu and Funni to see if this was going to be fine with them. He did not have to ask, both seemed ready to trust Tancredi. The sparrow himself was happy to, at last, be of some use to these strange new friends. He stretched his tiny wings out and flew a foot or two into the air, where he hovered for a moment, 'But listen guys, I ain't going to shout for yous, just watch me. I'll hover still like so you know it's safe to come over. Don't want to make any unnecessary noise now the rains stopped, could be all sorts of undesirables out. You get me?'

'Undesirables?' said Funni

'Yeah, cats and the like' chirped back Tancredi, 'Yous keep it down 'til we get to the church'. With that he spun around the trashcan a couple of times, and then flew off.

The squirrels on the top of the trashcan looked at each other. Each knew what the other was thinking, and each one tried to hide the fear Tancredi's words had instilled. 'Sooner or later we'll bump into one of those killers' said Funni.

'Maybe not' replied Risu trying to sound confident, 'You never know, going bit by bit like this we might avoid ever meeting any'

'Whatever we come up against we'll be fine as long as we look out for each other' said Kalan, and the other two murmured their agreement with this, more perhaps to convince themselves rather than each other. 'In fact' Kalan carried on, 'I worry for any cat that tries to break up this road trip' He slapped his tail defiantly on this side of the trashcan. This had much more effect on boosting everyone's confidence.

'Too right' said Funni as she filled her lungs with a confident breath of freezing night air, 'Now where's that little bird got to?'

About sixty yards away, hovering by a street light was Tancredi. He floated up and down a little then landed on the top edge of a parking sign that was attached to the pole. Then he flew off and hovered again for a moment, then landed again on the sign. The sparrow kept on doing this for some moments until Risu said, 'I think he wants us to run up that street light and sit on that sign'

'You both ready?' said Kalan Funni and Risu mouthed yes. 'Let's go' said Kalan and started to run down the trashcan onto the sidewalk. Risu followed, and Funni took one last look around her then jumped down after them.

As the squirrels ran up Broadway towards Tancredi's pole, the sparrow flew down to the sidewalk to wait for them. He seemed a little agitated. 'Keep to the road not the sidewalk' he said as the squirrels arrived and ran quickly up the pole.

They all sat on the edge of the parking sign and it wobbled a little under their weight. It felt precarious and Kalan started instantly looking for somewhere else to run to. Tancredi landed on the parking sign as well and even his tiny body made it shake even more. 'The road guys, stick to the edge of the road' Tancredi said again.

'You gotta be kidding' said Risu, 'The road is too dangerous'

'No, no believe me its safer' Tancredi continued adamantly, 'Sidewalk got people, got cats. Edge of the roads ok. Too close to the sidewalk for cars, people can't sees you so well, and it smells too bad for cats'

Risu thought about this for a moment. Tancredi might well have a point. He had certainly noticed the smell. New York is a city of a million and one smells, and Risu had discovered that a lot of the worst ones seemed to have congregated by the edge of the roads.

'We'll try and stick to the edge Tancredi' said Kalan, 'but our next stop is going to be those plants by that door, you see?'

Everyone looked to where Kalan's tail was pointing. There was a row of half a dozen large potted plants outside the main entrance to one of the office buildings about another hundred yards further up the street.

'I'll go first this time' said Risu as he found that the wobbling sign was beginning to make him feel a little motion sick.

'Ok then' said Kalan and Risu hurried down the pole certain that he had heard Funni whisper 'take care'. He zigzagged across the sidewalk, and was in the potted plants in no time.

'You guys can sure move quick' Tancredi had flown down and followed Risu, and hovered above as the squirrel checked around the plants.

'What do you think Tancredi?' said Risu in a very loud attempt at whispering. 'Seems safe enough, lets get the others'

Tancredi chirped in agreement, and Risu ran for a second into the middle of the sidewalk. He waved his tail above his head, then ran straight back into one of the pots. As he sat waiting for the others he smiled at Tancredi. Yet again he was feeling that warm glow of exhilarated excitement.

It took the squirrels about an hour and a half, with Tancredi's help, to make their way up Broadway in this manner. They stopped on top of post boxes, under a parked car and even inside the sign at number 55 Broadway. By the time they got to the corner of Broadway and Rector Street all four animals were feeling completely exhausted.

From their latest trashcan hideout they all gazed out in awe at the tall, elegant brown spire of Trinity Church. The diamond framed clock face on the side indicated that is had gone half past five in the morning.

'Wait here guys I'll go see if my squirrelys pals awake' said Tancredi and he flew across Rector Street and disappeared into the church grounds.

Kalan hoped that he would not take too long. They city was beginning to wake up. Cars were passing on a regular basis now, and there were even a few people walking about. The sparrow did not give Kalan time to worry much, he was back in less than a minute. 'He's not in' he said as he landed on the edge of the trashcan, 'but I guess he won't mind if yous wait for him at his place. Yous all friendly squirrelys after all'

'Some are less friendly than you might think' said Risu

'Where does he live?' said Funni softly, 'In that tall building?' she continued indicating the church spire while imagining a large regal squirrel looking out across Broadway each morning from high up in the elegant tower.

'Nah, he's got a cozy little place underground. Come on I'll show yous'

Partly out of excitement at have finally arrived at somewhere apparently safe to rest, and partly out of shear exhaustion, the squirrels crossed Rector Street together and without looking. They easily jumped through the fence and into the churchyard and followed the low flying Tancredi to a gray monument near the middle of the grounds. Tancredi started to jump up and down by the corner of the Fulton headstone. 'It's down there' he said excitedly as he hopped around.

The squirrels could see the mouth of a tiny hole covered by a small shrub. Kalan moved closer and smelt the air around the entrance to this half hidden drey. It was definately a squirrel smell, but there was something odd about it.

'Wait for me here, I won't be a moment' he said to the others without turning around and pushed his way through the shrub and into the drey. By now the unfamiliar smell had reached the noses of the others.

Risu shrugged and looked at Funni, 'Smells like my granddad' he said. Funni agreed that while it was not an unpleasant smell, it was just one she had never come across before.

'Its ok guys, a bit small but cozy enough' Kalan had reappeared at the mouth of the drey. 'Are you really sure this squirrel is going to be all right with us resting up in his home Tancredi?' Kalan asked, already too tired to care one way or the other. As he spoke Risu and Funni hurried past him and into the drey.

'Oh sure, he's a nice squirrely. He's always telling Tancredi that he never gets any visitors, well now I is bringin' him three' Tancredi made a couple of hops towards Kalan and almost pushed him into the drey with his wings. 'Now yous get down there and get some shut eye. I is bushed and I is going home. I'll come back later when yous all rested up'

Kalan need no further encouragement. He thanked Tancredi for all his help and dived back underground.

Inside the tiny drey Risu and Funni had already fallen asleep in the corner furthest from the entrance. Kalan moved over towards them and nuzzled himself between their tails. They did not wake, and in a moment Kalan too was in a deep sleep.

The Red Squirrel

The squirrels slept solidly in the drey under the Fulton memorial for most of the day. By the time Kalan poked his head outside it had already gone five in the afternoon and the light was fading fast. Funni woke as well and was surprised to find that she had been sleeping with her head on Risu's shoulders. She quickly sat up and went over to Kalan. 'How do you feel?' she said

'Fine' replied Kalan, but his stomach growled. Risu's first word as he woke up summed up the nagging sensation all three of them were feeling.

'Food!' cried Risu. 'I'm starving' He started shifting through the paper and matted fur that lined the floor of the drey. 'This squirrel who lives here must have something stashed away'

'Risu!' said Kalan firmly 'We've already assumed his hospitality, we can't go stealing his food as well'

Risu looked up at Kalan, his eyes bulging pleadingly. 'But I've never been so hungry' he whined.

'Well stop moaning and let's go out and find something to eat' said Funni.

They all agreed not to venture out of the church grounds, and to meet back at the drey before it got completely dark. As Risu and Funni hurried off in different directions, Kalan jumped up onto the Fulton memorial and looked up at the majestic church. Even though his stomach was complaining, his curiosity to see the view from atop the spire was too great. He ran over to the side of the church, and using his claws to grip the grooves of the sandstone bricks, pulled himself up the wall. He reached the roof of the southern annex and heard some fluttering noises. For a second he thought that maybe Tancredi had come back with a few friends,

'What are you doing up here you filthy furball?'

A large pigeon landed directly in front of Kalan.

'Get your smelly butt off our roof!' shouted out another that had landed on the edge of the annex.

'Sorry' said Kalan knowing too well that trying to be polite with New York pigeons was pointless.

'Sorry my aunt. Scram before you stink the whole place up with your pong'

Kalan ignored the pigeons' insults as best he could, and jumped past them onto the main wall of Trinity Church.

'Wrong way you furry freak!'

Kalan could hear them continue calling up insults as he scaled the church clock tower, but soon the rushing wind was making more noise. About two thirds up he came to a small balcony. He made himself comfortable on its ledge and turned around to view his new surroundings. He could see down Broadway the way they had come the night before, to his left the start of Wall Street. His hunger had left him, and he breathed in deeply. Dusk was falling and the street lights had already started to come on. He could see many people moving around, all seemed to be trying to walk faster than each other. They weren't the same type of humans he was used to seeing in Battery Park, these people appeared to be more stressed and less relaxed. Kalan saw that many were walking downstairs going underground, apparently there was a metro stop in front of the church. That meant rats. Maybe, thought Kalan, he could get a message back to Skudzo. Kalan peered over the ledge of the balcony and looked down onto the church grounds. He could not see Funni, but he could make out Risu moving quickly back and forth along the side of the annex. The pigeons were trying to poop on him from above.

Why were pigeons so nasty? Kalan began to ponder. Why couldn't they be friendly like sparrows? Almost as if they had been queuing up outside waiting for the right moment to barge in, an army of questions began to invade Kalan's mind.

Tancredi. Of course, Tancredi could get a message back to Skudzo, but what had happened to him? Where was the owner of the drey they had slept in? Were they going to find any food? What was Skudzo doing now? Should they leave the church tonight?

As Kalan began to make himself dizzy under the weight of all his questions he felt someone tap him gently on his shoulder. Kalan, a little startled, whirled his head around to see a large slender squirrel sitting behind him.

'I often come up here myself. It really is a wonderful way to unwind'

Kalan said nothing in reply. His eyes looked in amazement at this new figure. He was a squirrel, but he was red. He had long tufted ears and talked with a very strange accent.

'Sorry if I startled you old boy' the red squirrel continued sensing Kalan's unease. 'The name's Sciurus. Sunda Sciurus, and I am so awfully pleased to make your acquaintance' The squirrel took Kalan's paw with both of his and shook it vigorously. 'But please, let's not be slaves to formality, do call me Sunda'

Kalan regained his composure a little, 'I'm Kalan' he said softly.

'Splendid' said Sunda, and he gave Kalan's paw one last good shake. 'I saw you chaps arrive this morning, but thought it best to let you sleep. Tancredi told me you had been traveling all night'

'You know Tancredi?' said Kalan.

'Oh yes. He's such a dear. We had a good old chinwag. The portly fellow came back around lunchtime, but you three were still fast asleep at the Clermont'

'The Clermont?' asked Kalan.

'That's my home' replied Sunda. 'A home's never really complete until you give it a name I do hope you chaps didn't find it in too much of a mess. I really have been meaning to give it a jolly good spring clean, but you know how it is...... the mind is willing, but the body is just bone idle' Sunda laughed at his own humor. Kalan was already feeling more relaxed and smiled.

'So you live here?' he said

'Of course!' replied Sunda. 'Been here several years now' he paused for a second, 'Oh do excuse me, let me correct myself. I've been in this country for several years and here at Trinity for the last two. And let me tell you dear boy, I just adore the place'

'Where are you from?' said Kalan, 'I've never heard an accent like yours before, and I've never seen a squirrel as red as you either'

'I'm English' said Sunda with pride. 'I was brought over here a few years ago by some humans as part of a breeding program. We red's are remarkably rare you know' Kalan listened and watched as Sunda spoke, completely fascinated. 'There was this group of terribly snobby types down at the Battery Park City who had this awful idea of populating their local park with us reds. They were under the impression it would give their area a more exclusive feel' Sunda tutted and shook his head as he remembered, 'Well I wasn't having any of it. Besides the females they expected us to mate with were from the Canadian countryside. Perish the thought! Kissing one of those ladies is a lot like kissing a brick wall' Kalan nodded knowingly, even though he had no idea what kissing a female squirrel was like. 'Ho ho, yes indeed' continued Sunda, 'I was having none of that malarkey' He paused again for a moment as he collected his thoughts, 'Although I suppose maybe it was because I am such an awful snob myself' Sunda chuckled to himself again. 'So I ran off, spent a day trying to pluck up the courage to cross over West Street, and found my way here'

Kalan's stomach used this pause in Sunda's speech to let out such a large growl that even the red squirrel could hear it. 'But I digress too much' he said, 'I should think that you and your friends are probably quite famished. Let me offer you all dinner'

Kalan agreed eagerly to this suggestion, and the two of them started to make their way down from the Trinity Church tower, with Sunda leading the way. As Kalan followed he noticed that Sunda's color acted almost like a natural camouflage against the brown sandstone of the church. As they reached the ground Kalan saw straight away that Risu was back on top of the Fulton memorial, waving his tail around as if he were trying to swat a fly. Risu saw them coming and hid his tail behind his back. As he watched he noticed that the long svelte squirrel running alongside made Kalan look so short and stocky.

'Hello' said Risu as they both jumped up to join him.

'Risu' said Kalan, 'This is the owner of the drey we slept in last night'

'The name's Sunda Sciurus, but please call me Sunda. It's a pleasure to meet you Risu' said Sunda gracefully as he reached out to shake Risu's paw.

'Err, Hi' said Risu a little overwhelmed, 'sorry for not asking before, but we didn't know where you were' he said slowly.

'Oh think nothing of it old boy' replied Sunda.

'Sunda's from England' added Kalan as he noticed Risu's confused expression.

'Oh Where's that?' asked Risu.

'On the other side of the world' said Sunda lowering the tone of his voice for a little dramatic effect.

'New Jersey?'

'Even further than that' replied Sunda with a smile, 'but I can't help but notice that you seem to be at odds with your appendage'

Risu needed a few seconds before he understood what Sunda had asked him. 'Oh you mean my tail, hey its nothing'

'Now then, now then' said Sunda 'Come on there, lets have a look'

Risu gave a little embarrassed shrug, and lifted his tail up where Kalan and Sunda could see where the pigeons had successfully hit it. 'It's all sticky and smelly, and it won't shift' Risu cried softly.

'Oh we can soon sort that out dear boy' said Sunda and he jumped down from the monument and ran into his drey.

'He talks funny,' said Risu to Kalan as he saw Sunda disappear inside the mouth of the drey.

'He seems nice though, he didn't mind us sleeping at his place' Kalan said smiling. 'While you were playing with the pigeons did you see Funni?' he asked

'She's here!' Funni called out from behind as she jumped up and sat next to Kalan. 'I saw that Kalan found a friend,' she said looking at Risu, 'and you found the pigeons. But did anyone find anything to eat? I struck out'

Both her friends said nothing and shook their heads. At that moment Sunda reappeared carrying a couple of large pieces of paper in his paws.

'Oh hello there' he said as he saw Funni, 'Sunda Sciurus at your service madam'

He put down the papers he was carrying and rubbed his paws briskly on his thigh then held one out. Funni blushed slightly, and not really knowing what to say or do held out her paw. Sunda grasped it, bent over slightly and kissed it gently. 'Charmed to meet you I'm sure. May I enquire as to the name of the owner of this delightfully delicate paw?' Funni blushed even more but said her name softly. 'What a beautiful name for such a beautiful squirrel' Funni giggled gently.

'Now you must excuse me for one moment as I have to attend to your friend Risu' Sunda started to pick up the pieces of paper and turned to Risu. For a second he thought he caught Risu glaring at him, but as he moved closer Risu just gave a childish smile. 'Now then young man, lets get rid of this pigeon poop'

Sunda grabbed Risu's tail, and using the pieces of paper as makeshift gloves, started picking away at the pigeon droppings from the tail fur. 'Oh my word what a whiff' he said as he started to work, 'I really don't wish to know what those pigeons had for lunch'

Everybody watched as Sunda quickly picked away at the pigeon guano stuck to Risu's tail. Risu grimaced a couple of times as Sunda pulled off the occasional hair, but Sunda was finished in a couple of minutes. 'There you go, good as new' said Sunda

Risu whirled his tail above his head. 'Wow thanks a lot!' he said gratefully.

'Now' said Sunda turning to the others, 'let's have dinner, come on chaps,' and everyone followed him as he jumped down and into the drey.

With all four squirrels inside the drey felt very cramped, but the thought of food and eating helped them to easily ignore any feelings of discomfort. Sunda began digging in a corner of his drey, and pulled up some assorted nuts. He placed a few handfuls in the center of the drey. 'Please now don't be modest, help yourselves' he said. The others did not need to be asked twice. 'It's not much I know' continued Sunda, 'I live quite frugally here at the Clermont, and well to be brutally honest I don't often get many visitors'

'Clermont?' mumbled Risu with his mouth full.

'That's what he calls this place' Kalan leaned over and whispered in Risu's ear.

Sunda's tufted ears twitched to one side, and he nodded. 'Yes it's true, giving a name to your home makes it much a more comfortable place don't you think?'

While speaking Sunda noticed that Risu had already finished his first nut. He pushed another towards him with his long red tail. 'Tuck in' Risu mouthed thanks and started to devour his second hazelnut. 'In fact I recently met a lovely squirrel who told me that ones home is only really comfortable when one spends as little time as possible in it. When you are out exploring the world, coming home is so much more satisfying than staying in it all day'

Kalan dropped the nut he was holding. He knew of only one squirrel who thought like that. 'Bilka!' he shouted loud enough to make Funni and Risu jump.

'Yes that's the fellow' said Sunda, 'big burly chap came by a couple of weeks ago. Do you know him?' Sunda noticed that all three squirrels had stopped eating and were staring intently at him. He ears twitched again. 'I suppose you do' he said slowly as he looked at their faces.

Funni felt a rush of mixed feelings come over her, but the main one was relief, relief that at last she had some confirmation that her father was alive and well. She looked up over to Kalan, her eyes full of tears but a large smile on her face.

'He's ok' she whispered to Kalan.

'So, erm, are you chaps looking for Bilka?' said Sunda inquiringly.

'Yes we are' said Kalan, 'How was he? Was he ok?'

'Oh he was full of beans' replied Sunda cheerily, 'he stayed with me for a couple of days and we had some very interesting conversations. He's quite the philosopher you know' Sunda paused and made a little sigh. 'But he was full of the wanderlust, so I introduced him to a couple of rats I know down at Wall Street station. We said our goodbyes and off he went'

'Did he say where he was going?' asked Funni.

'No not really' replied Sunda, 'almost certainly uptown though. To tell the truth I don't even believe he knew himself. I think he's just letting his curiosity pull him along' He frowned for a second. 'So are you boys trying to find him and convince him to come back home with you?'

'No, we want to join him' said Risu, 'we've got a magic nut and were going to find him with it and go on up to Central Park together'

Sunda scratched his head and smiled broadly. 'Well that does sound like a cracking adventure. If I was a little younger, and somewhat less fainéant, I'd come along as well'

'Could you take us to the rats at the metro station?' asked Kalan.

'Of course dear boy, but not now' replied Sunda, 'It's the busiest time down there right now, lots of people rushing around trying to get back to their dreys. I'll certainly take you a little later when everything's died down a bit' Kalan and the others agreed. 'In the meantime what say we finish eating, and then maybe you could let me see this magic nut of yours? It sounds most intriguing' said Sunda cheerily.

The squirrels spent the next few hours devouring the best part of Sunda's stash and talking. They showed Sunda Delancy's ball which he inspected carefully with great interest, and asked him many questions. They asked him about Bilka, about himself, about Central Park. Sunda did not mind at all, in fact he loved the attention. In fact they spoke for so long that they lost all track of time. By the time Funni reminded Sunda of his promise to take them to the rats at Wall Street station, it had already gone midnight.

The Metro

'Oh yes how silly of me, I almost forgot' said Sunda as Funni reminded him of the rats. 'Come on then chaps, let's see if these rodent fellows know which direction Bilka went'

Sunda was already on his feet and heading for the exit, but the others needed a moment to stretch their legs after having been seated for so long. The freezing cold night air hit their faces ferociously as they came out of Clermont and into the grounds of Trinity Church.

'Brrrrr' shook Risu, 'I'd gotten so comfortable down there I'd forgotten it's winter. Not really the best of times to go on long journeys uptown'

'Why surely not' said Sunda, 'You boys could travel uptown using the metro lines. That's the way the rats get around town. It's warmer, you are underground, there are not so many people and those fellows would most certainly know the quickest way to Central Park'

'Hey! That doesn't sound like a bad idea' said Risu nudging Kalan with his elbow.

Kalan had been gazing up at the illuminated Spire of Trinity Church. He was almost entranced by its design. Everything pointed upwards reaching into the night sky. He found it gave him a very positive feeling.

'Onwards and upwards' he murmured to himself, then he felt Risu nudge him again. 'Travel with the rats?' Kalan said coming quickly back down to earth. 'Yes, maybe using the metro wouldn't be a bad idea, but we've never been down there before, so let's see what its like before deciding'

Sunda waved his tail gently over their heads to get their attention and everyone followed him to the edge of the church grounds on Broadway. From the church fence they could see steps leading down into the metro. As they looked down Risu noticed Funni was shaking. 'Are you ok?' he asked

'Yeah, sure. It's just the cold' she lied.

Sunda indicated to the others to stay where they were and he jumped down onto the street and went to the top stair. He looked around and smelt the air, then jumped back up to the fence. 'Well it seems fine, let's do it this way. I'll go first with Risu, then if it's all clear down there, I'll come back for you chaps'

No one disagreed, so Risu and Sunda jumped between the church fence rails and, keeping to the side, ran down the steps into the metro. At that time of night the Trinity Church exit of the Wall Street metro stop was closed, but Sunda and Risu had no difficulty getting under the gate and into the empty station.

'So where do these rats hang out Sunda?' whispered Risu.

'Oh they've got this delightful little place under the tracks on platform two'

Keeping their backs to the wall the squirrels scurried across the empty station, then certain no one was about, they ran under the ticket barriers and onto the platform.

Living all his life in Battery Park Risu was used to the sounds of metro trains running underneath him, but here actually inside the metro for the first time the noises and smells were over whelming. It did not help Risu's senses that at that same moment a train shot through on the opposite track at full speed on its way uptown. Risu almost jumped out of his fur. Sunda quickly put his paws over Risu's ears to try and help block out some of the noise.

'I know the first time I saw one of those beasts I nearly fell over' Sunda said calmingly after the train had passed.

Risu's ears were still ringing slightly. 'What?' said Risu, shouting to try and hear himself above the ringing.

'Ssssh!' said Sunda putting his paw over Risu's mouth. 'Let's go before another one comes along. If we are down on the tracks when a train passes its no joke'

Risu attempted a shrug, but Sunda was already tugging at his shoulder fur. They hopped over to the edge of the platform and then effortlessly down the quite steep drop onto the side of the track.

Back above ground both Kalan and Funni had also heard the express pass by. Kalan noticed that Funni was now shaking almost uncontrollably. 'Funni what is wrong? You're not still cold are you?' he asked concerned.

'I... I........ I can't do it' stuttered Funni almost in tears. 'I can't go down there. I'm so sorry Kalan, but, but I can't control myself. I'm too scared'

'Hey Funni,' said Kalan 'You have just run off with us from your home. You are one brave squirrel. I saw you jumping in and out of the road on our way up here, even with cars passing by'

Funni continued to shake nervously.

'Down there' continued Kalan glancing down the stairs, 'It might be noisy, but if Sunda says it's safer than traveling over ground, then I believe him'

Funni pulled her legs closer to her chest and hugged them with her arms. 'Please don't make me go down there Kalan' and she started to rock to and fro apprehensively.

Kalan edged his way closer to Funni. 'I won't make you do anything you don't want to do Funni' he said, nudging her gently with his tail. Funni looked at Kalan, and although he was smiling warmly at her she still sensed a tiny sigh of frustration from him.

Funni really could not help herself though. The metro had always scared her. For as long as she could remember the sounds of trains traveling through the night had often kept her awake back at Battery Park. Sometimes it got so bad she would leave the drey and climb an Elm to sleep in one of the Parks Departments chilly wooden efforts. The idea of going down inside the metro now completely terrified her. Kalan also felt uneasy. He had never seen Funni, or indeed any squirrel, shaking so uncontrollably. 'Look Funni, why don't you wait for me back at Sunda's place, I'll wait here for the others. Forget about the Metro' Funni didn't look at Kalan, but kept on rocking backwards and forwards. 'We'll find out if the rats here have any news about Bilka, but we'll keep on looking for him above ground. Besides we both know your father isn't the type to stay underground for too long anyhow eh? If we are going to find him, we are only going to be able to outside'

This cheered Funni up a little. It even dawned on Kalan, as he spoke, that what he was saying was probably very true. 'Ok' said Funni and she stopped rocking. 'But you take care down there'

'And you try to calm down' replied Kalan, 'In fact I'm putting you in charge of Delancy's nut'

Kalan dipped into a fur pocket in his lower chest and pulled out the large ball. He pushed it into Funni's still shaking paws, then turned around and checked the church grounds behind them. 'Go on Funni, back to the drey. See you in a little while,' and he gave her a little shove with his tail.

Grasping the ball close to her chest, Funni ran down the church pathway in the direction of the Fulton monument. Kalan gave another sigh as he watched her run off, but this time it was one of relief mixed with a little satisfaction. Of course Bilka wouldn't be underground he thought to himself, he hated being underground as much as his daughter.

Kalan turned his attention back to the stairs leading down to the station, as he did he heard the sound of another train passing by underneath. Now while for Kalan up by the church fence the sound of the train passing was loud, the same noise for Risu and Sunda was deafening.

Risu had followed Sunda down onto the train tracks, but as they were making their way towards the tunnel they had heard another train approaching. This time not on the opposite tracks, but on theirs.

'Oh dash it all, this is going to be a tad awkward' said Sunda, 'jump over the rail Risu, and keep your face and tail down in the center' The red squirrel jumped over the train rail, then turned to see that Risu was still standing by the track wall in a state of mild confusion. The growing sound of the oncoming train forced Sunda to shout.

'STOP DILLY DALLYING RISU. JUMP NOW!'

The effect of the normally mildly spoken Sunda screaming at the top of his voice slapped Risu out of his confused trance. Without any further thought he jumped over to Sunda and both of them turned and lay flat on the ground.

'KEEP YOUR TAIL DOWN' shouted Sunda

The ground beneath them began to vibrate intensely as the train approached from Courtland Street. Sunda put his arm over Risu's chest and pushed his mouth as close to Risu's ear as possible.

'I FIND IT HELPS IF YOU SHOUT!'

'WHAT?' yelled Risu

'AS THE TRAIN PASSES OVER JUST LET IT ALL OUT! HERE IT COMES!'

The train roared into the station, and like the express before it, it had no intention of stopping. The ground around the squirrels was now shaking violently and both Risu and Sunda screamed at the top of their voices as the train passed over them, blowing their fur flat on their bodies.

'AAAAAAAAAAARRRRRRRRRRHHHHHH'

Their screaming lasted longer than the passing of the train, but like a deflating balloon it began to peter out.

'AAAAAAAAAARRrrrrooooo...........oo'

The squirrels slowly lifted up their heads and turned to see two mice looking over at them a little bewildered from the side of the tracks. Risu could see that the mice were saying something to him, but the ringing in his ears would not let him hear anything else.

'I CANT HEAR YOU!' he shouted across to the mice, then turned to Sunda, who was also trying to tell him something, 'I CANT HEAR YOU EITHER!' he said trying to shake the ringing out of his ears.

'I CANT HEAR YOU' replied Sunda, 'LET'S GET TO THE RATS PLACE BEOFRE ANOTHER TRAIN COMES'

Sunda pulled Risu up from the ground and tugged at his arm. Risu understood that it was time to go. As he started to run down the tunnel behind Sunda he turned and gave a little wave at the mice. He felt an instant affinity with them since they were both shrugging.

About twenty yards into the tunnel Sunda waved his tail to the right, and jumped back over to the side. 'It's down here' he shouted back at Risu who nodded and followed despite still not being able to hear much. He caught up with Sunda as the red squirrel was using his tail to move some paper garbage to reveal a small opening in the wall. Despite his smell senses having been almost tipped off the scale by the multitude of odors he had been experiencing since arriving in the metro, as Risu ventured down the hole with Sunda the overwhelming smell of rat pushed all the others out of his nose.

Back above ground Kalan was still waiting, albeit now a little less patiently, by the church railings. Funni, in the meantime, was sitting inside Clermont analyzing Delancy's ball. Its glowing green arrow was having an almost hypnotic affect on her as it hovered lazily under the plastic covering. Funni felt a lot calmer and the shakes had left her. She did feel however that she had let Kalan and the others down. 'They are just going to treat you as a burden and not as an asset from now on, girl' she said to herself.

Funni did not want to be the one they looked out for on this journey, she wanted to help, to contribute and not to hold everybody back every time she got scared. She thought back to her uncontrollable display of fear by the metro station and almost started to cry. 'No, stop that!' she scolded herself, 'Don't mope girl, think'

She looked back at the floating arrow, and its pointed edge made her think of the church spire. It gave her an idea. 'They can talk to the rats all they like, but I'll climb to the top of the church and with this nut I can plan our route uptown'

She took a deep confident breath, 'Yes! I'll be able to see over all the buildings from up there, I'll be able to see exactly where this nut is pointing to' She hugged Delancy's ball, and full of renewed confidence in herself, jumped up out of the drey and ran over to the Trinity Church Annex. Funni's belief in her idea made climbing the Annex wall easy, but by the time she reached the roof and looked up at the brownstone tower still looming above, her confidence began to wane a little. 'It looks even higher from up here than it does from the drey' she thought to herself as she ran along the tooth shaped brick edges of the Annex. She got to the main wall of the church building and started to climb.

Kalan had not seen Funni leave Clermont, nor had he seen her climbing the church wall. He was, however, looking up into the sky around the church spire. He was musing over different things. 'What ever happened to Tancredi?' he thought to himself as he followed the majestic linear lines of the Trinity Church spire into the open sky. He missed the porky little sparrow. Kalan heard another train sound and turned his gaze back to the station. 'What is taking those two so long?' he thought as he looked back down the stairs, 'I do hope they haven't run into any trouble'

Funni, on the other hand, had. Around sixty feet up from the ground, she needed to climb just another couple to get onto the main roof of the church, but her way was blocked by a ledge with three sleeping pigeons. What to do? It was sheer wall with no place to grip on either side of her. If she ran up and over them they would wake up in a foul mood and cause trouble. If she shouted up and asked them to let her pass…….. Hell no, she reasoned, that would be even worse. 'Nothing for it girl' she thought to herself, 'You're just going to have to climb back down and find another way up'

Before she could start to make her way down the middle pigeon directly above her made a disgusting bodily sound and, although he was still fast asleep, moved his rear end to the edge of the ledge.

'Oh no' said Funni out loud, and she pushed her body as flat as she could against the stone. More repulsive noises came from above. It sounded like someone trying to pull his bare foot from a sticky pool of mud, changing his mind and then pushing it back inside again. Funni heard the pigeon guano whoosh past less than an inch from her ear. Feelings of relief that it had missed her were soon gone as she felt Delancy's ball slipping out from her fur. 'No, no' she moaned quietly to herself as she pushed her body harder against the wall to try and stop the ball from falling further. She started to inch her way back down, keeping as close to it as she could, but it was beginning to get painful and the ball was now scraping against the sandstone. To make matters worse it was now time for the Trinity Church clock to let lower Manhattan know it was two o'clock.

The sound of the first chime took Funni by surprise and she almost lost her grip on the wall. She felt the ball slip down past her legs, but on the second chime she miraculously managed to stop its fall for a moment with her tail. She desperately whacked the ball up towards the roof with it, but instead of landing on the roof as she hoped the ball hit the pooping pigeon on his rear end. The pigeon woke with a start and the ball crashed down to the ground. Funni watched helplessly as Delancy's ball fell downwards. Amazingly it did not shatter and break when it hit the ground, instead it bounced about twenty feet back into the air and under the force of its own propulsion flung itself over the railings and onto the street.

Kalan turned to look upwards as he heard the pigeons wake up startled, but he failed to notice Delancy's ball as it flew over him on its way to Broadway. He watched as the pigeons instinctively flew away from the ledge to a safer one higher up on the church tower, then thinking nothing more about it turned his attention back to the metro stairs.

'You alright Maurice?' said the larger of the three pigeons.

'It stings' moaned Maurice, 'What happened? Did any of you see anything?'

His two friends shook their heads, so Maurice peered downwards to see if he could find the reason for his painful wake up. He saw it soon enough. 'Look down there on the Annex' he shouted to the others.

'Yeah, it's a squirrel' came the reply from one of his pigeon friends.

'I bet it did it Maurice' said the other, 'remember we were playing around with one of them yesterday. Maybe it's their way of getting their own back'

The pigeons watched through gaping eyes as Funni ran along the roof of the Annex and started to make her way down the side of the wall. 'What do you want to do Maurice?'

Maurice shuffled a little. The pain in his rear had turned into a dull tingling sensation. 'Nothing' he said, twitching his head.

'What do you mean nothing?' replied one of the pigeons, 'that squirrel woke us all up and smacked you. I say let's smack it back'

'Yeah' said the other twitching his head aggressively, 'smack it!'

'No wait a minute,' said Maurice, trying to think, 'We do nothing now, we plan something out, and we wait for a better moment'

'No way Maurice. Let's smack it NOW!' The other pigeons were beginning to squawk loudly, feathers wanted to fly.

However, Maurice, for the first time in his life, was trying to think things through. In difference to thousands of years of pigeon evolution he was attempting to weigh up his options, to plan a strategy, to make an informed decision. The mighty weight of such a revolutionary diversion from standard passerine thinking was, in the end, too much for Maurice's pigeon brain. As the smarting pain returned to his rear end he bowed to peer pressure. 'Ah to hell with planning! Come on lets smack some squirrel'

Squawking loudly the three pigeons took off and dive bombed down towards Funni, who by now had reached the ground, and heard them coming. She ran as fast as she could and managed to dive head first inside the drey. The pigeons swooped down over the top of the Fulton monument just as Funni's tail disappeared down the hole.

Back over by the railings Kalan had not been paying much attention to the pigeons since he was beginning to get worried about the others in the metro. With Funni in the drey and Sunda and Risu who knows where, Kalan was starting to feel a little feeble. He was between a rock and a hard place. Go back and look after Funni and the other two might panic when they come out and find no one waiting for them. Go down and look for Risu and Sunda, and maybe get lost or worse in the metro. Kalan sighed and shuffled around nervously, but made up his mind. 'I'll wait a little longer, but then I'm going down after them'

As he thought to himself he turned to see if he could make out why the pigeons were still squawking. He was surprised to see that they were all hanging around the monument.

'We can wait all you want you wretched vermin' Maurice called down the mouth of the drey, while the other two pigeons strutted around flapping their wings provocatively and joining in with occasional 'Yeahs' and 'Too rights'.

'You can't hide in there forever furball' Maurice continued, 'and when you do get the courage to come out, ya yellow livered rodent, we'll make you wish you hadn't'

The pigeons were working themselves up into frenzy. Maurice hopped around the entrance to the drey screaming insults through the opening, while the others flew up and down from the monument.

Funni, safe inside the drey, tried to ignore the pigeons taunts as best she could. The main thing on her mind was the loss of Delancy's precious ball. Instead of helping everyone out she had lost the one thing that could help them get uptown. What would everyone think? Maybe they would send her back to Battery Park? Funni felt like crying, convinced that she had let everyone down.

'You miserable smelly fink' continued the shrill pigeon voice from above ground, 'Hide in your stinking hole, like the sleaze bucket you are'

However the more the pigeons continued to provoke her, the more Funni felt less like crying and more like asserting herself. She had freaked out at the metro, lost the magic nut on the church roof and was now cowering in a hole hiding from three foul mouthed bullies. 'Why don't you just dig another hole for yourself and go sit in it?' she said scolding herself, 'Come on, pull yourself together girl'

Up above the incessant insulting had stopped, but she could still hear the pigeons flapping around. 'Came to the end of their vocabulary I guess' she mused. She lifted herself up and started to move towards the exit. No more hiding she had decided. Time to face up to them. As she made her way upwards she heard a familiar whooshing sound followed almost instantly by a tiny splat. The pigeons had given up on their verbal offensive and moved on to a more physical one, they were now pooping on the entrance to the drey. For Funni this was the final straw.

'No NO!' she shouted and ran out of the drey. Side stepping the pigeon guano lying by the entrance she emerged from Clermont and jumped instantly up onto the monument.

Her surprising and unexpected exit took the pigeons off guard and they, instinctively, flew a few yards away. Their initial fear was short-lived and it changed to curiosity as they realized that the squirrel they had been tormenting had come out to face them. They flew down and landed on the ground blocking the entrance to the drey. They fluffed up their feathers and moved around doing their 'tough guy' swagger. Funni, still more angry then scared, glared down at the three pigeons. She did think for a moment about apologizing and explaining what had happened, but as she watched Maurice and the others twitch their heads aggressively, she remembered that trying to reason with pigeons was an exercise in futility.

Pigeons over time and across the world have been able to integrate themselves into modern day cities with effortless ease. Although many people realize that they carry diseases, erode and sometimes even destroy buildings with their never ending supply of sticky excrement, and have as such dubbed them 'rats with wings', there are just as many others who love the birds. Lots of people leave out bread and crumbs for them. Many cities have major squares or piazzas where people vie to have their photo taken with the birds. There are even some societies who proffer the theory that being pooped on by a pigeon brings the victim good luck. The single fact that they can fly has saved the modern day urban pigeon from the pyre status given to rats.

Funni knew the truth however. If a pigeon pooped on you it was never accidental, but always a vindictive act. She knew that pigeons, and the New York community was a shining example, were malicious, spiteful, ill mannered and foul mouthed. Manhattan pigeons would hurl abuse at people and animals they did not like claiming that an aggressive stance was the best way of surviving in a modern metropolis. They have no friends in the city and even view their country cousins with as much contempt as everybody else they meet. However like most loud mouthed bullies, their belligerent attitude is just covering up a deep held fear of everyone and everything.

As Funni sat defiantly above the pigeons on the edge of the Fulton monument the three pigeons found themselves unsure as to their next move. Their quarry had come out to face them. Now what? Maurice decided on the old pigeon favorite, insult and abuse.

'Filthy rat bag thinks she's so great' he sneered to the others.

'Yeah' they laughed back

'Great at being lice infested squirrel scum' Maurice squawked.

'Too right' The other squirrels nodded vigorously.

Funni said nothing, but started to whack her tail on the stone. She continued to scowl at the birds. Maurice had been expecting a verbal sound off, but Funni's stony silence made him feel uneasy.

'Mangy mammal. I can smell your rotten pong from here' he shouted up to Funni hoping for a response. 'Lost your tongue in that filthly mouth of yours?'

Funni continued to whack her tail rhythmically on the stone and fixed Maurice with an angry stare. The pigeons continued twitching their heads, but the action had become a little less aggressive and a little more agitated.

'What you going to do Maurice?' whispered one of them.

Maurice had no idea, and he began to feel the pain return to his rear end. 'Shut up!' he shouted to his colleague while looking at the ground trying to avoid Funni's stare.

The sound of her tail thumping was drilling into his brain and it dawned on him for the first time in his life that, bar insults or poop, he had nothing left to throw into the ring. He let out an aggravated squawk and flew up to Funni. He fluttered his wings hear her face and landed a few inches from her on the edge of the monument. Funni stopped banging her tail and the two of them just stared at each other for what seemed like an age. 'You just watch out for yourself' said Maurice eventually in the most macho aggressive tone he could muster, ''Cause we'll be watching out for you' He then twitched his head to one side and flew up in the air quickly followed by the others.

Funni really wanted to shout out after them, but knew better than to bait the birds at their own game and bit on her tongue. She watched them as they flew back up to the church ledge.

'What was all that about?' Funni whirled around to see Kalan, Sunda and a very dirty looking Risu sitting on the ground below her. She felt straight away very relieved to see everyone and jumped down to greet them.

'Did they hurt you? Are you ok?' asked Kalan.

'I'm fine' said Funni, 'I just ruffled their feathers a little, but their bark is worse than their bite'

Both Kalan and Risu smiled with relief and Sunda hopped over to inspect his drey entrance. Funni attempted a smile as well, but her heart started to sink as she remembered the reason for getting into trouble with the pigeons in the first place. How was she going to tell them she had lost Delancy's nut? She took a deep breath and started to speak, but was before she could utter a sound Sunda started shouting.

'Oh my giddy aunt! Those repulsive feathered fiends have gone and pooped on my door'

Sunda's outburst distracted Funni from her moment of confession, and she followed Kalan and Risu as they went over to see what the problem was.

'This really is too much!' Sunda turned towards the church and waved a tiny defiant fist up in the direction of the pigeons.

'You desecrating dropouts! How would you like me to come and do the same on your front door when you are entertaining guests?'

'Come on Sunda' said Kalan, 'Don't let them get to you, we'll help you tidy it up'

'That's awfully decent of you old boy, but you know this type of mindless vandalism really does get my pecker up' Sunda sighed and clamed down a little. Kalan and the others ran around the surrounding area grabbing pieces of paper and long grass, then they all helped Sunda wipe the guano away from the entrance to Clermont. It did not take them long and in a short while they were all back inside. Kalan was still very anxious to hear what had happened with the rats down in the station and looked at Sunda intently.

Sunda looked around his crowded drey. He noticed that Funni was sitting silently in one corner her eyes fixed on a point on the ground, while Kalan sat with a wide eyed and impatient expression on his face in another. Risu, in the middle, had a nonchalant expression and shrugged as Sunda caught his eye.

'Well there isn't that much to tell you know' began Sunda, 'The rats down in the station certainly remember Bilka and told us that he was going uptown, but that he didn't really fancy the idea of traveling on the metro'

Funni looked up at Sunda as she heard this and Sunda gave her a broad knowing smile. 'So Funni dear if you want to find Bilka quickly, traveling the rat route underground won't be very helpful'

Risu leaned over to Funni. 'And I'm not going down there again' he said and opened his arms in front of her to show off just how dirty he was. 'I mean just look at me, and I don't think I'll ever hear clearly again' He patted his ear with his paw.

'Don't exaggerate' smiled Funni and she started to help Risu pick the metro dirt from his fur.

'Yes, the first time in the metro can be a somewhat harrowing experience' said Sunda, 'But Risu conducted himself admirably, and I must say he is a dab hand when it comes to Ratspeak'

'I've had a little experience' Risu blushed and glanced over at Kalan.

'Is that all the rats told you?' asked Kalan a little despairingly.

'More or less' shrugged Risu

Kalan looked back at Sunda who shrugged in a Risu like manner. 'They did mention the fact they had heard that Bilka had been in a fight with a certain cat called Shokobaba up at Columbus Park, but Risu told me that you already knew that. The rats hadn't had any news about him since then, sorry old boy'

'Well I guess no news isn't necessarily bad news' sighed Kalan.

'I asked them to pass a message back to Skudzo to let him know we were ok' said Risu.

'That was a good idea Risu,' replied Kalan, 'I had hoped to ask Tancredi, but he seems to have disappeared'

'Oh don't you worry yourself over that porky fellow' interrupted Sunda, 'he'll pop up again sooner or later'

'Well we should get some rest guys' said Kalan, 'then later on we can check our magic nut and plan our way uptown' Funni felt her stomach drop down to her feet, but said nothing.

'I concur completely, splendid idea' said Sunda, 'but if you don't mind I'll just nip out and douse the area a bit so we don't have to sleep with the smell of pigeon poop all night'

It was not long before all the squirrels were laying curled up asleep on the drey floor. All of them except Funni of course. She stared wide eyed at the wall in an almost limbo like trance. The type when your thoughts won't let you sleep, nor do they offer any solutions to your worries. She just concentrated her mind on one mantra, she had lost the magic nut.

Sunda woke up to the sound of the Trinity church clock sounding off midday. He saw that Kalan and Risu were still fast asleep, but that Funni was no longer in the room. He stretched his tail, then moved quietly outside. His eyes took a few seconds to adjust themselves to the bright but gray glare outside. Sunda looked around and saw that Funni was sitting with her back to him by the church railings looking down over Rector Street. 'Good day to you young lady' he said cheerily. Funni turned her head slightly in his direction, but said nothing. Sunda moved closer. 'I suppose those rotten pigeons got to you last night eh? Well not to worry, if you like I can go and douse their ledge later if that would cheer you up?' Sunda chuckled but saw that Funni's eyes were filled with tears and she was staying silent. He decided to try another approach.

'Kalan told me about your worries at the metro station. I shouldn't really betray his confidence, but Funni dear it's quite a common problem and certainly nothing to be ashamed of, everybody has something that scares them. It's perfectly normal. Just think my mother was afraid of heights. Poor dear used to spend all day on the ground, used to get dizzy just sitting on a bench sometimes'

Funni turned and looked directly at Sunda, 'What scares you?' she said in a half whisper. Sunda's nose twitched as he thought for a moment.

'Thunderstorms really put the willies up me,' he said 'when one of those comes over you will find me shaking like a leaf in the corner of Clermont, and jumping with fright every time the sky lights up with the lightning.

Sunda saw that Funni had relaxed a little. 'You see' he continued, 'we all have our fears, it's perfectly normal. And real friends never hold them against you'

'That's very sweet of you Sunda' said Funni, 'but that's not it' Sunda's tufted ears twitched, 'Last night I was trying to climb the church and I lost the magic nut Delancy gave us'

Funni carried on and tearfully told Sunda everything that had happened earlier. The red squirrel listened intently but said nothing until Funni had let it all out. 'Now what am I going to say to Kalan and Risu?' She turned towards Sunda her eyes still filled with tears.

Sunda nodded thoughtfully to himself then looked at Funni and smiled. 'Pigeons do have a habit of darkening ones day don't they? No matter how good a mood one is in, they will do their utmost to bring you down'

'Maybe,' said Funni, 'I should tell them the pigeons stole it?'

'No dear' replied Sunda, 'lying only helps in eventually making you feel even guiltier' The red squirrel turned his body towards Rector Street and spoke for a moment without looking at Funni, 'Look here now Funni, tell me something. Would you and your friends have embarked on this adventure if you had never received that nut?'

'Well, yes, I guess so' said Funni, 'We had already decided to go before Kalan turned up with it'

Sunda whirled around to face Funni, 'Well there you go then dear girl' he said 'It's just a minor inconvenience, a little setback, nothing more'

'No it's not' moaned Funni, 'They'll hate me. When they find out they won't want me to carry on with them. I've let them down again, like I did at the station'

Sunda moved closer to Funni and grabbed her shoulders gently. 'Turn around and lets look at the church behind us' said Sunda calmly.

'Why?' sobbed Funni as she let Sunda turn her body around.

'Just do it, you'll see why' said Sunda.

As Funni turned herself around, she looked up at the beautiful brownstone church. Her eyes instantly narrowed as she saw and focused on a ledge with pigeons.

'Tell me what you can see' Sunda whispered in her ear.

'Good for nothing pigeons'

'No, no dear, forget the pigeons look at the church'

Funni sighed and tried to take in the edifice. She looked at the bell tower and the clock face in its diamond frame. The somber looking statues of humans on some of the ledges, the way in which all the lines of the building seemed to reach up into the sky. It was, she grudgingly admitted to herself, a magnificent site. 'It's very beautiful Sunda' she said eventually.

'And just think' replied Sunda, 'You are looking at the third one'

'The third one?' asked Funni

'Oh yes indeed. The humans needed to build it a third time because their first church here burnt down and I believe the second one just collapsed after a rather heavy snowfall' Funni continued to gaze at the church as Sunda spoke. 'What you see is an excellent example of how some people just did not give up after having a setback or a failure, in the end they built one church which was better, stronger and more majestic than all the others'

Sunda could see that his point was being understood as Funni started to nod to herself slowly. 'Everybody gets let down, or takes a wrong turn sooner or later Funni dear. Good lord I've had my share of upsets' Funni turned and looked at Sunda, 'But not everybody does as the chaps who built this church did. Learn from what went wrong and have the strength of character to change things. The problems we face and overcome today help us make solutions for tomorrow'

'You're right I guess' said Funni very gently.

'But you still need to find the courage to face up to your mistakes' continued Sunda 'and frankly Funni you have more courage than all those pigeons up there put together. Funni took a deep breath and stopped hunching. 'And secondly what happened to you yesterday, you can't even consider it as a mistake, just a silly setback. Think of it like that Funni and believe me dear it won't feel so awful'

Funni smiled and turned back towards the church. She was feeling better with herself. They both sat in silence for a few moments then Funni spoke up. 'Well when they wake up I'll tell them and get it over with' She turned her head towards Sunda who was smiling broadly.

'But they'll get over it!' she said confidently and Sunda's smile drew itself across her face as well.

They did not like it. After Funni had told Risu and Kalan how she had lost Delancy's nut an air of depression fell over Clermont. Risu went into a silent sulk in one corner and Kalan just sighed and said it was ok. It was obvious to Funni that it wasn't. The rest of the day dragged by. Sunda tried to talk some confidence back into everyone but to no avail. Risu and Kalan were upset with the loss of the magic nut, Funni was upset with herself and Sunda was upset by the miserable mood in general. 'I just hope that we all feel different in the morning' said Sunda at the end of the day as all of them were silently preparing for sleep. 'I'm sure you will all regain your confidence after a good night's repose'

No one replied, each one still gripped by their own feelings and thoughts. Sunda was only partly correct however. Whereas it is true that sleeping on your problems sometimes helps to diminish their potency, a new impetus is often needed to put folks back on track.

The return of Tancredi

'Hey! Hey! Is you guys still sleeping down there?'

A tiny voice echoed around the small drey. 'Hey! Wake up yous guys. Yous all missing a lovely morning' Risu turned in his sleep trying to block the noise from his mind, Kalan opened his eyes. 'Geesh you squirrelys are always sleeping'

'Tancredi!' cried out Kalan excitedly and in one swift movement was up and out of the drey. His outburst successfully penetrated Risu's subconscious and he too, reluctantly, woke up.

'Tancredi?' he murmured to himself as he watched through half closed eyes Funni and Sunda stretch themselves and follow Kalan out of the drey.

'Yes I is back squirrelly pal' said Tancredi as Kalan rushed out of the drey to meet him. The fat sparrow was hovering above the mouth of the drey and landed with a waddle in front of Kalan.

'Where did you get to?' Kalan said, 'we were beginning to wonder'

'Oh I is been up town to visit some friends, and I was asking if anyone's seen your pal and you know what? He's been seen just about everywheres from Columbus to Union' As Tancredi was talking about his recent trip uptown Sunda, Funni, and a very slow moving Risu, joined Kalan sitting under the Fulton monument. 'My Uncle Totti told us that this Bilko squirrel helped save the lives of some rats in Columbus Park. He took on a cat'

'Yes' said Kalan, 'We heard that too, but we don't know what happened to Bilka after'

'Oh he's ok!' said Tancredi, 'My Uncle Totti says he heard that your pal is living it up with the squirrelys in Tompkins'

'Where is Tompkins?' asked Funni, neither she nor the others were familiar with the name.

'It's a park uptown, over to the east. I've never been me, but my Uncle Totti has. He says there's good feeding there and wow..lots of squirrelys'

'And it would seem the long lost Bilka?' said Sunda

Tancredi nodded his head energetically. 'Yeah Uncle Totti he knows what's what and what's where'

'And just think' continued Sunda, 'Bilka got all the way up there without a magic nut from the rats'

As Sunda spoke he looked at Kalan and Risu and widened his eyes. Kalan looked down at the ground, then threw a sheepish gaze at Risu, then an even more sheepish one at Funni.

'Sunda's right' said Risu, 'we can do this without any silly nut' He moved over to Funni and looked at her apologetically. 'I'm sorry I got the hump with you Funni'

Funni at first stared back sternly at Risu, but soon her face melted into a forgiving grin, that widened even further as Kalan hopped over. 'We were acting like a pair of childish cubs' he said, 'I'm sorry'

Tancredi looked over at Sunda a little confused as he saw the other three squirrels wrap their tails together in a large group hug. 'They fell out with each other last night' Sunda explained quietly to the sparrow, 'But thanks to you dear boy, I think they have all learnt a valuable lesson'

'What I do?' squeaked Tancredi

'You just reminded them that hope springs eternal'

'Oh that!' said Tancredi nodding knowingly but still not understanding a word. Tancredi spent the rest of the morning keeping everyone's spirits up by telling all he had heard about Bilka, and by mid- afternoon it was decided that an introduction to Uncle Totti was needed. He lived on the way, at the top of a clock in City Hall Park.

'That's a weird place to have a home' said Risu as the five of them were talking together at the bottom of the church grounds near the fence on Trinity Place.

'Well Uncle Totti he likes to know the time' said Tancredi, 'He says a bird who knows the time knows what's what and what's where'

'And how are we going to get to his clock?' asked Funni.

'Oh that's easy squirrelly girlie' replied Tancredi, 'Uncle Totti's clock is up the road in a straight line from here. Yous stick to the Broadway and yous be there in no time'

'How do you all feel about heading off tonight?' asked Kalan and looked around at everyone. Risu shrugged and Funni nodded.

'I'm easy' said Risu.

'Are you sure you chaps wouldn't like to stay for a couple of days more?' said Sunda who was beginning to realize that he was going to miss his new friends when they left.

'You've been very kind to us' said Kalan, 'but the sooner we get back on the road the closer we get to finding Bilka' Kalan paused for a moment as he too realized that he would miss the red squirrel. 'Hey!' Kalan grabbed Sunda's arm, 'Why not come along with us? I'm sure you would enjoy yourself, and we would love to have you along'

'Oh yes Sunda' said Funni enthusiastically 'that would be great'

Sunda smiled, but shook his head, 'That's very decent of you and all' he said, 'and, you know, a while back I certainly would have jumped at the opportunity. However I have had a great deal of excitement and change in my life, and here at Trinity Church I really have found my peace of mind'

The Battery Park squirrels looked on fondly as Sunda spoke, they could sense his inner calm, 'You chaps have the wanderlust, the desire to discover and find your own center of gravity, just like I had. And I am jolly well certain that you will find what you are looking for'

'How do you know you have found what you were looking for Sunda?' asked Kalan.

'Yeah' said Risu, 'Maybe there's something else up the next tree, how can you be so sure?'

'You'll know' said Sunda, 'You'll know when your mind stops asking you questions about what you are doing with yourself and about why you do or did things' Sunda saw that he was confusing his audience, 'What I mean chaps is this. Instead of you thinking to yourself, 'Why didn't I run up that tree?' you ask yourself, 'Why is that tree?' You know you have found your place when your mind can dedicate itself to grander thoughts'

The squirrels still looked confused, and Tancredi had completely missed the point and tuned out, as sparrows often do. 'So yous coming to see Uncle Totti or no?

'No' said Sunda softly with a smile, 'But please convey to him my fondest regards, and tell him that he and his family are more than welcome to come and visit whenever they want'

'Oh sure I will' said Tancredi.

'And don't forget to tell him that my clock here at Trinity keeps perfect time' said Sunda as he pointed towards the clock tower with his tail.

'Oh yes, yes that's important, 'cause Uncle Totti's got to know the right time 'cause he says a sparrow who knows the right time ...'

All the squirrels interrupted and finished off Tancredi's sentence for him.

'Knows what's what and what's where!'

Everyone started to laugh, including Tancredi.

'Ha Ha! Yes I guess I said that before'

'Just once or twice' laughed Funni.

It was not long before the squirrels were at the other end of the Church grounds overlooking Broadway planning their way uptown. Tancredi had flown off along the route to check out places they could hide in along the way. It was getting dark, but Broadway was still very busy with lots of people hurrying around on their way home from the office. None of them noticed the four squirrels sitting behind the bars of the church railings with their heads sticking out and looking up Broadway.

'See all that construction?' asked Sunda pointing to the scaffolding surrounding the building adjacent to the church grounds, 'That's a perfect start. People construct that around buildings that need repair and at night it is completely empty. You are well away from the pavement and can move along quickly without any problems'

'And it looks like it would be a good vantage point to see where we can go next,' said Kalan noticing how high the metal construction and wooden platforms went up the side of the building.

'Of course, absolutely' nodded Sunda, 'I've seen a lot of this scaffolding up around here lately, so use it whenever you can'

'Anything that keeps us away from the road is good by me' said Risu as a taxi honked its horn at two people running across Broadway from Wall Street. The taxi driver stuck his head out of the window and shouted various obscenities to the two pedestrians as he drove past. The two people shouted back at him from the sidewalk.

'Yeah! Tell it to your mother dirt bag!' called out one of the men, then he and his colleague promptly joined the flow of others running down the stairs in the metro.

'They are a lot like pigeons you know' said Funni as she watched the scene.

'Well they are somewhat similar' said Sunda, 'in that they use verbal aggression as a form of self-defense'

'That's as maybe' said Risu, 'but at least they don't poop on their own doorstep' He winked at Funni, but she wasn't looking at him.

'Let's get back to Clermont' said Sunda, 'if you want to head off later I strongly suggest you all get some sleep. Heaven knows how long Tancredi will take'

'I think I'll stay here a little longer' said Kalan, 'I'll join you all in a bit ok?'

'Sleeps good' said Risu, 'and I don't suppose you've got a few nuts for the road eh Sunda, old boy?'

'I'll see what I can rustle up for you chaps' smiled Sunda, 'come on then if you're hungry. See you shortly Kalan'

Sunda, Risu and Funni hopped off towards the Fulton monument leaving Kalan to gaze at the people running around outside the church. He saw people smoking then throw the lighted cigarette to the ground before going down into the metro. He saw a car driver roll down his window and throw something out as he drove by. He watched as another person threw a wrapper at a trashcan and miss completely. It landed on the ground and the light wind blew it towards the church. Kalan thought about what Risu had said earlier. 'Well they might not poop on their own doorsteps' he thought to himself, 'but they still have no respect for anyone else's'

'Hey! Squirrelly!'

A small but very familiar voice broke Kalan's thought. The fat sparrow had perched himself directly above Kalan on the church railing. 'I is back!' said the bird dramatically, and then swooped excitedly to the ground behind Kalan.

'Hi Tancredi! What's it looking like out there?' asked Kalan.

'Oh you guys got a long stretch of road to follow to get up to Uncle Tottis, but I is finding lots of places for you to hide in on the way'

'Well done Tancredi that's great. Let's go and tell the others before they go to sleep'

Kalan motioned at Tancredi to follow and they both made their way over towards Clermont.
The Trinity Church clock struck seven as Tancredi settled down on the edge of the Fulton monument to address the four squirrels sitting on the ground directly below him. 'Well to start' he chirped, 'It's a longer than the one yous had from my place to here'

'How long do you think it's going to take us Tancredi?' asked Kalan.

'For yous guys two hours, maybe more, maybe less I guess' said Tancredi vaguely. Birds really have no idea how long traveling on foot along the ground takes. 'But Uncle Totti he's really looking forward to meeting yous guys' he added cheerily.

'Did you notice much scaffolding on buildings along the way?' asked Sunda.

'Oh there's plenty of that stuff' said Tancredi, 'But yous got like seven or eight roads to cross'

Risu made a very audible gulp.

'Plus the last one yous got to cross to get to Uncle Totti's is the biggest. Very wide. Uncle Totti's clock is in the middle of the road like'

'Is it busy late at night?' asked Funni.

'Uncle Totti says the best time to cross it around three or four in the morning, but yous got to have two sets of eyes 'cause cars and buses come from every direction'

'Why does Uncle Totti have to live in such a difficult place to get to?' moaned Risu.

'Ain't difficult for a bird' came Tancredi's obvious reply. Risu shrugged.

'If we leave here around midnight, we should get to this big crossing by three' Kalan found himself thinking out aloud.

'Oh sure' said Tancredi, 'and well now that's sorted I'm outta here. I'll see yous at twelve' Tancredi flapped his wings and started to take off.

'Hey wait!' cried out Risu, 'Where are you going?'

'I is pooped squirrely. Gotta go home and rest me up if I is to take you guys all the way up to Uncle Tottis. You guys should lay up some as well, it's gonna be a long night' Tancredi hovered above the squirrels for a moment and then darted off in the general direction of the Bowling Green.

'Our portly friend is quite right chaps' said Sunda, 'You boys go get some rest while I go off and find some provisions for you journey'

Kalan thanked Sunda and followed Risu and Funni down the mouth of the drey. As Kalan sat looking at his two friends he thought that it would be impossible to get to sleep. He was surprised to find, however, that it came over him almost instantly.

The wisdom of Uncle Totti

'Kalan, Kalan wake up'

Kalan opened his eyes slowly to see Sunda's red face in front of him. He stretched his tail and yawned. 'What's the time?' he mumbled.

'It's gone twelve' replied Sunda.

'What!' Kalan bolted himself upright and saw that the drey was empty. 'And the others? Where's everyone? Why didn't you wake me sooner?'

'Now don't you fret dear boy' said Sunda very calmly, 'Everyone is waiting for you outside. You were sleeping so soundly that none of us wanted to wake you up'

Kalan tutted loudly to himself and jumped up. Sunda led the way out of the drey and onto the church grounds.

As Kalan emerged he saw Risu, Funni and Tancredi all sitting together talking beneath the monument. They all smiled when then saw him, Risu waved his tail. Kalan looked up at the church clock and saw that it was already twelve thirty. 'Look at the time. Why didn't you wake me up earlier?' he said a little angrily.

'You looked so cute fast asleep all wrapped in your tail' giggled Funni.

'Yeah, plus we've been awake for a while' added Risu smiling, 'Couldn't sleep, what with thinking about everything and you snoring. We thought it best to leave you to it'

Kalan's anger at not being woken up changed to bemusement. Why had he been able to sleep so soundly before such a big event?

'Don't worry about us though' Risu carried on talking and glanced at Funni and Tancredi, 'we are raring to go'

'And Sunda has been kind enough to give us a few nuts for the road' said Funni holding out a paw full of peanuts.

Kalan stopped thinking about his sleep and turned to Sunda. 'How can we ever thank you enough?' he said looking fondly at the red squirrel.

'Oh tosh!' said Sunda, 'I'm just happy to have been of some assistance to you boys. It's been wonderful having you all as my guests, and I only hope that you'll pop in and visit me again one day'

Sunda offered his paw out to shake, but Kalan opened both of his and gave Sunda a warm, strong hug.

'Thanks for everything' he said. Risu and Funni hopped over to join in the hug as well.

If it was possible Sunda became even redder. 'Oh please, don't' he said, 'you'll have me in tears. Come on, come on, I'll see you chaps off at the railings'

He pried himself slowly out of the group hug and motioned them to follow him to the other side of the church. 'Come on fellows, race you to the other side' he shouted out and started to run towards the northern corner of the church grounds. The others were quick to follow, but Tancredi was the first to arrive.

'It's no contest for me with you squirrelys 'he laughed proudly as Sunda arrived, 'Us sparrows are as quick as you like!'

Kalan and Funni were not too far behind, with Risu bringing up the rear. As they all looked out through the railings onto Broadway it was a completely different scene than before. No people, little noise and, despite a light southerly breeze, hardly any movement at all. Sunda pointed to the scaffolding with his red tail. 'That's your easy way out of here chaps. Use it whenever you see it'

The three Battery Park squirrels looked out over to the scaffolding, but no one made a move, except Funni who turned to Sunda and hugged him again, her eyes full of tears.

'Thank you so much' she said softly, 'we will miss you'

Sunda wiggled himself from her grip and moved himself slightly backwards. 'Now then, now then,' he said, 'You're behind schedule already, and if we are going to be saying goodbyes all night it will jolly well be breakfast before you lot get going'

'Well we have had a good time here with you Sunda' said Risu

'And so have I' replied Sunda looking over Risu's head onto the sidewalk behind the railings, 'The coast is clear, so shooooo now!' Sunda started to wave his tail briskly in the general direction of the scaffolding.

Kalan sensed Sunda's uneasiness at saying goodbye as he grabbed Sunda's paw and shook it, 'Bye Sunda, look after yourself' he said quickly, then turned to Risu and the others. 'Wait for my signal then come on over'.

Kalan jumped down onto the sidewalk and ran the few feet to the first metal pole of the scaffolding. He ran up it, then waved his tail to the others from the edge of the first wooden platform.

Risu and Funni both said another quick goodbye to Sunda, and then they too ran off towards Kalan. Sunda looked at Tancredi.

'Now you take jolly good care of them Tancredi'

'Oh don't yous worry I will, see you later red squirrely pal' chirped the sparrow happily as he sped off into the air.

Sunda waited by the railings and watched until the squirrels and the fat sparrow disappeared from his sight. He turned, and looking up at the Trinity church tower began to be slightly confused by his own thoughts. Why hadn't he gone with them?

He frowned to himself, but as he gazed up at the orange – brown spire a small smile grew across his face as another thought marched into his mind. 'Why do some seek adventure, and others avoid it?

This new question pleased Sunda more and he ran off to Clermont to contemplate it in peace.

Kalan and the others found that traveling along the scaffold platform was a breeze. In no time they found themselves at the edge of the block that overlooked Albany Street. They were doubly pleased to see more scaffolding on the buildings on the other side of the street.

'Hey wow!' said Risu, 'Is it going to be this easy all the way up to Central Park?'

'Don't bet on it' replied Funni.

Tancredi flew across the street and waited for the squirrels perched on the scaffolding. They checked the small street in both directions, and quickly joined him. 'This stuff goes on for another block' said the sparrow, 'then it's finished. But I Tancredi knows the best way after'

The squirrels ran along the scaffolding until they came to the corner of Broadway and Thomas Street, and from then on Tancredi was good to his word. He used everything from potted plants to mail boxes and the squirrels quickly made their way up town. The only real problem came while they were crossing Liberty Plaza.

Funni and Kalan had already crossed and were waiting on top of a parking sign. Risu was still hiding in the potted bushes in the center of the Plaza, but would not move since two men had appeared from nowhere and were standing between him and the others. Tancredi was perched on the sign with the others and could see the men were talking quietly to each other and smoking.

'I do something, you guys stay here' he said after analyzing the situation carefully for a few moments.

'Wait!' said Kalan, but Tancredi was already flying towards Risu in the bushes.

The two men did not notice the little sparrow as he landed on the side of the plant feature and hopped his way inside to find Risu.

'Tancredi, what you doing here?' Risu whispered the moment he saw the fat sparrow.

'Come to get you squirrely' smiled Tancredi, 'I make distraction, then you take your chance and run for it. Those smoky men won't even notice you'

'What? No wait, they'll be gone in a …………'

Risu's words found no audience as Tancredi had already flown out from the bushes and started circling the two men. The sparrow then dived towards the taller of the two men and flew so close that he knocked the cigarette out of his mouth.

'What the….!' cried out the man, and both of them whirled around startled.

Risu saw his chance and bolted out from the artificial bushes and ran a straight line towards Kalan and Funni. The men paid him no attention, they were too busy waving their arms angrily in the direction of a long gone Tancredi.

'Geesh Hal' said the tall man as he stooped to pick up his still lit cigarette from the floor, 'They've even got the wildlife in on this no – smoking drive'

Risu joined the others and they ran along the edge of the sidewalk until they got to a trashcan on the corner of Courtland Street. 'That bird' said Risu panting, 'doesn't give you time to argue does he?'

Tancredi joined them shortly, puffed up with pride, and it was not long before they crossed over Fulton Street and entered the grounds of St Paul's Chapel. Risu ran up the small steps near the entrance and lay on his back on the stone floor gazing up at the tall Corinthian pillars. 'I'm whacked' he said to the world in general.

'Come on squirrelys, we is almost there. Just got to cross the big road. I'll show yous Uncle Totti's pad, you can see it from here' Tancredi flew off up into a large Elm that grew in the small cemetery.

Risu groaned as he lifted himself up and followed the others as they ran up the tree after Tancredi.

The view from thirty feet up the Elm was impressive, but daunting. To their left was a large park sitting below the white colonial style New York City Hall. Beneath them was the intersection of Broadway and Park Row, which the squirrels agreed was the widest stretch of road they had ever seen. Almost in the middle of the intersection, on a small island of its own, was a small clock tower with four large white illuminated faces telling the area it was nearly half past three in the morning.

'That's my Uncle Totti's!' shouted Tancredi excitedly and he hopped up and down making the branch the three squirrels were sitting on sway a little, 'He's got a little place on top there. He can see every comings and goings, and he likes to know the time and what's what and what's where'

'Must be really noisy' said Funni, 'what with the clock and the traffic'

'Maybe' mused Tancredi 'but Uncle Totti says the traffic keeps unwanted visitors away, plus he doesn't have to deal too much with those squirrelys from City Hall. Them guys be heavy going, especially in these days'

'What do you mean?' asked Kalan.

'Oh they decide each year who is going to be the top guy' replied Tancredi.

'I don't follow you' said Kalan

'Uncle Totti can tell yous, he knows more than me. You stays here while I is telling him we is all here' and he flew down from the Elm and off towards the clock.

'So what is it with these squirrels?' asked Risu as he and Kalan looked out over into the City Hall Park.

'Oh I am sure they're fine' said Kalan, 'we've just got to remember to be polite. They are not going to be used to traveling squirrels, and we don't want to get mixed up in anything if this is a special time for them'

'I hope they'll be as nice as Sunda' said Funni and everyone nodded in agreement. 'I think we will be very lucky if we meet anyone as nice as him again'

The smiling red face of Sunda flashed itself across Kalan's mind, then it vanished and was replaced that of Bilka. Kalan turned his attention back to the road below them. 'No let's work out how we are going to cross this' he said as a large SUV revved its engine aggressively at the stop light on the corner of Vesey Street.

Tancredi returned shortly, but was much less gassed than earlier.

'What's the problem?' asked Funni as he settled on the edge of the branch.

'Oh it's nothing' he said 'Uncle Totti's fast asleep, and he gets itchy if folks wake him. So I says we sleeps it out and wait 'til he's up'

'Yeah ok' said Risu looking around instantly for somewhere cozy to settle down' I'm having that top branch' and he pointed above his head with his tail.

'No Risu' said Kalan, 'It's best if we rest on the other side. We'll never be able to cross this road during the day,'

'Oh yeah' said Risu slowly, 'I forgot about that' and he looked gloomily down onto Broadway as two cars drove past going in opposite directions.

'It's true' said Tancredi, 'Problem here is that everything comes at yous from every direction. Yous be checking right and yous not seeing something else coming from yous left'

'There must be an easy way to cross' said Kalan, 'Humans need to cross as well' Kalan looked around him, then turned to the others. 'Give me a few minutes' he said, then ran off down the tree.

The others watched as Kalan darted across the cemetery and ran up another large Elm growing in the corner. He hurried along a branch that was growing out over the sidewalk. The end of the branch swayed uneasily as Kalan ran along it about twenty feet from the ground. As he reached the end, he made a short flying leap and landed on top of the street sign that said VESEY STREET in white letters on a blue background.

'What is he up to this time?' said Funni as she and the others watched Kalan balance himself with his tail and sit motionlessly on the sign with his back to them.

'Dunno' shrugged Risu as he delved into the pockets of his fur, 'Sunda peanut anyone?' he asked as he pulled one out.

'Sure' said Funni and Risu snapped the nut in two and offered her half.

'Tancredi?' Risu looked over at the sparrow.

'No thanks pal' smiled Tancredi 'It all goes on your waist if you eats at night' and he patted his chubby stomach with his wing.

It was over a quarter of an hour before Kalan made his way back to the others.

'We thought you had gone to sleep' quipped Risu as Kalan hopped onto their branch.

'What you see over there squirrely?' asked Tancredi.

Kalan had a very confident expression on his face, 'Crossing this road isn't going to be a problem' he said 'I think I've worked out how the humans do it. It's all done with lights'

Risu was the closest to Kalan, so Kalan grabbed his shoulder and turned him towards the corner of Broadway and Vesey, 'See that car stopped in the road?'

Risu looked down to see a small white car, its engine purring and headlights on, waiting at the crossroads. 'Yeah' he said as another larger car drove up and stopped beside the white one, 'Now there's two'

'I know' said Kalan, 'And see they are both still not moving' Kalan looked behind to make sure he had the attention of Funni and Tancredi. 'They're not moving because the lights above them are telling them not too. See?' Kalan pointed out the traffic light in front of the cars. 'When it's a red color they don't' move, buuuuuut.......' Kalan dragged out the word until the light switched to green. 'But when the light changes color the cars move'

Risu and the others watched in wonder as the cars drove off down Broadway the moment the light turned green, almost as if they had been listening to Kalan.

'That's amazing' said Funni.

'That's how they do it!' said Kalan excitedly, 'That's how humans know when to cross, because when its red one way, it's green the other'

Just as Risu had thought he had understood, Kalan's last sentence sent him back into a mild confusion. 'Red one way stops the other?' he said a little bewildered.

'When it's red for cars, it's green for us' said Funni.

'Exactly' added Kalan.

It took a few more minutes for Funni and Kalan to explain it all to Risu, but once he had understood the concept of traffic lights he was raring to go.

Uncle Totti's clock struck four am and the three squirrels ran out from St Paul's, across Vesey Street and sat panting in a doorway overlooking Broadway and the start of City Hall Park. Tancredi flew off into the park to look for somewhere safe for them to sleep until Uncle Totti woke up.

Kalan looked up at the green traffic light as Funni and Risu looked up and down the sidewalk and the road. 'On my mark, then we run as fast as we can into the park' he said without taking his eyes of the traffic light. 'Any moment now'

'There's something coming down really fast' said Funni as see watched a pair of oncoming headlamps.

'Almost there' said Kalan, not listening 'almost there'

'NOW!' he shouted as the light switched to red.

He started to run across the sidewalk as Funni cried out 'STOP!' and grabbed Kalan's tail to pull him back. Kalan reached the side of the road before Funni's tugging brought him to a halt, and as he did a car sped past the red light just a few feet in front of his face, the wind rush it created set him falling back into Funni. Shaking, he gave Funni a frightened and muddled look, and they both ran back to Risu who had not moved from the doorway.

'So let me get this straight' said Risu as they arrived back in the doorway, 'If it's red it means they go, and if it's green it means we stop?'

'It means' said Funni pulling a still shaking Kalan closer to her, 'that we have to rely on our eyes and ears and not the pretty, colorful lights'

Kalan looked sheepishly at her, then turned back to look at the road. The light was still red and there was another car humming patiently beneath it. The light turned to green, and the car slowly moved off down Broadway.

'I don't understand' said Kalan in frustration.

'Hey, what's to understand?' said Risu giving the world an almighty shrug. 'Sometimes they stop, sometimes they don't'

The squirrels sat quietly for some time and watched as the lights turned from green to red several times. Kalan's theory seemed to be sound, whenever the lights turned red any cars around slowed down and stopped.

'Maybe' suggested Risu, 'they'll only stop if no ones trying to cross the road, but if they see someone crossing then they speed up'

Funni gave Risu a stern look that helped him abandon that line of thought.

Kalan, who had regained most of his confidence, slapped his tail on the ground. This was partly out of frustration because he saw that it had gone four thirty and the traffic was slowly, but very noticeably, picking up. 'We are going to have to try and cross now. If we wait much longer there will be too many cars and people out there, lights or no lights'

'So what do you suggest?' said Funni.

'We go to the edge of the sidewalk. Risu you check left, Funni right. I'll keep my eyes on the light. When it changes to red I'll shout out ok. Then you two shout out ok if nothing is coming from your directions. Three oks and we run for the other side'

Funni nodded but Risu couldn't resist shouting out a loud 'OK!'

They hopped across the sidewalk and sat on the edge with Kalan in the middle. Funni looked down Broadway and over Park Row. Risu looked to the left up past the Woolworth building. Kalan himself checked the other side of the road, then stared up at the traffic light. It remained a defiant green for what seemed like ages. It was doubly frustrating since not one car passed by. Funni could make out some lights in the distance and saw one car turn out of Park Row and make down Broadway. Risu kept his eyes fixed on some distant, almost hypnotic, white lights.

The traffic light switched slowly to red.

'OK!' said Kalan.

Funni quickly replied with her own ok without turning her head.

Silence.

'Risu!' shouted Funni, 'What can you see? Is something coming?'

Risu snapped himself out of a little trance he had dozed into brought on by the dancing white lights.

'Oh sorry, yes... it's all clear' he said lazily.

'OK!' shouted Kalan again angrily.

'OK!' shouted Funni

'OK!' shouted Risu and all three of them dashed quickly across the road and into the City Hall Park.

'Can't you pay attention for one minute?' Funni said to Risu as the three of them looked back across the road they had just crossed.

'I'm sorry' said Risu, 'The lights got so pretty and my mind got a little lost, and I....' he paused and sniffed the air, the familiar smell of squirrel dousing was everywhere. It was a different odor to that at Battery Park, but it was unmistakably squirrel and still very fresh. 'I wonder what these guys are going to be like?' he said as his mind wandered off on a tangent yet again.

Funni huffed a little with frustration then started to look around her new surroundings. 'I wonder where Tancredi has got to,' she said.

'I been waiting on yous guys' said a familiar voice from inside a nearby bush, and Tancredi hopped into view.

'Were you watching us cross the road?' asked Funni.

'Well I was' said Tancredi, 'but I was tired and yous guys were taking so long, so I sort of napped a bit' He yawned and stretched his wings. 'I is so very tired, but I is getting yous a place. A fine squirrely place up in that tree'

The sparrow lifted himself effortlessly into the air and flapped his wings in the direction of a nearby Elm. 'It's a hollow the squirrelys here don't use so much. Come on I show yous. It's real cozy and such'

Tancredi's earlier yawn had infected all the others, and the tiredness they had been avoiding for so long began to take them over. Grabbing what last energy they had remaining the squirrels followed Tancredi into the tree.

The hollow was very similar to the ones they were accustomed to back home in Battery Park, used more for storage than living. Risu started to rummage around in one corner, while Funni yawned and sat slowly down. Kalan looked out over the park and wondered where these squirrels had their main drey. The park looked very refined and well looked after, but Kalan could not make out just how big it was or whether it carried on past the elegant white building in the middle. Looking the other way he could see Uncle Totti's. The large white clock faces showed that it was nearly five. When would Uncle Totti be up and happy to see visitors? Turning back into the hollow to ask Tancredi, he was surprised to find that the sparrow and his two friends were all fast asleep. Kalan made his way quietly inside the hollow and sat down with his back to the wall looking out at the dark night through the opening. Even though he knew he should try and sleep he didn't feel tired. He just gazed through the hole and watched as the darkness outside gradually became grayer and lighter.

After less than an hour the hollow was filled with the bright gray light of a Manhattan morning. Kalan, still looking through the opening, could feel his eyelids beginning to get heavier. As they dropped shut over his eyes he thought he saw something move on the edge of the entrance to the hollow. He lifted his eyes open again, but saw nothing, his heavy eyelids fell over his eyes again and he drifted off to sleep.

Tancredi was the first to wake, but he didn't want to disturb the others so he slowly hopped out of the hollow and flew off towards Uncle Totti's. It was late morning and the area around City Hall was very busy with people and cars everywhere. In particular Tancredi noticed two small men standing underneath his Uncle's clock. Like most city sparrows he had little fear of people and he didn't think twice as he landed on the ground below the clock and started to chirp to see if Uncle Totti was up and about. As soon as Tancredi started to sing the two men turned to look at him. Tancredi twitched his head to one side, but carried on singing. One of the men seemed to walk away, while the other bent down and held out his pinched fingers towards Tancredi. Tancredi eyed the hand carefully. He couldn't make out any food being offered between the fingers, so he hopped backwards a little and stopped singing. Something didn't feel right. Where was Uncle Totti? Tancredi thought it best to fly up to the top of the clock, but before he could take off everything went black.

'Tancredi's gone' said Risu as he woke up and looked around.

Both Funni and Kalan were also awake and stretching their tails.

'That's normal' said Kalan, 'He's probably just gone off to check with his Uncle Totti. He knows where we are, we'll just wait for him here'

'It's really busy outside' said Funni from the mouth of the hollow, 'Look I can see some other squirrels'

Kalan and Risu moved over to Funni and looked in the direction she was pointing to. They could see two gray squirrels sitting on a bench on the path that led up to the white building.

'Let's go over and say hello' suggested Risu

'No, please stay in the tree'

Risu looked at Funni and Kalan. 'What?' he asked, but the others look as confused as Risu. They all looked around to see where the voice had come from.

'You have to stay in the tree until Orav decides otherwise' said the voice again and this time Kalan turned his head upwards and saw two very large squirrels gripping the tree above the mouth of the hollow, their heads hanging down looking at him. Despite the surprise he managed to squeak out a tiny 'hello'.

The two squirrels scurried down and practically pushed Kalan, Funni and Risu back into the hollow with their tails. 'Excuse me' said Funni irately.

'Please you must stay in this tree' said one of the squirrels again.

Kalan still a little confused decided it best to try and be friendly. 'My name's Kalan, pleased to meet you' he paused and stretched out his paw. The other squirrels didn't move. 'And these are my friends Risu and Funni'

The two squirrels said nothing. Kalan pulled back his paw, took a short breath, and carried on. 'We arrived here this morning with the sparrow Tancredi' Kalan noticed that the two squirrels in front of him didn't even blink.

'I think all that hanging around upside down outside has made their heads dizzy' said Risu, but Kalan quickly gave his arm a little pinch and frowned. Risu sighed and shrugged.

'Did you two see a sparrow leave here this morning? We were supposed to be meeting up with his Uncle Totti later, do you know him?'

The burlier squirrel glanced at his colleague for a second, but both kept their stony silence. Kalan saw that they were now both standing in front of the exit and he turned slowly around to face Funni and Risu.

'I guess we will just have to be good guests and wait for this Orax then' said Kalan as he motioned to his friends to sit down.

'Orav' said one of the squirrels, 'Our elected leader and first citizen'

'Only until tomorrow' said another voice, this time from outside the tree.

The Battery Parkers watched as two more squirrels made their way into the hollow.

'You can't come in here' said the burly squirrel.

'Oh really?' replied one of the newcomers, 'Your instructions are simply to make sure these squirrels don't leave the tree. I don't believe you are in a position to add other regulations to your current mandate'

The new squirrel was much smaller than the two guarding Kalan and the others, but what he lacked for in size he more than made up for in presence.

'So if you would both like to continue fulfilling your duties from outside, I would like a few words with these newcomers'

The burly squirrel and his colleague made no reply, but moved slowly out of the hollow and back to their earlier place clinging to the tree trunk.

The new arrival watched as the two left, then turned quickly to Kalan and the others with an outstretched paw. 'Pleased to meet you all. My name is Orava and this is my personal secretary Prevost'

Kalan, Risu and Funni all took turns shaking Orava's paw. Prevost just nodded and smiled.

'You must excuse the security, but that's my brother Orav for you. He has an almost primeval fear of foreigners. He says that they eat our nuts, mate with our females and generally disrespect our home'

'So you get a lot of passing squirrels here then?' asked Kalan.

'To my knowledge none at all' said Orav as he turned to Prevost who shook his head slightly, 'You lot are the first'

'So…er.. How can he be afraid of someone he has never met?' said Kalan

'Exactly!' said Orava triumphantly raising his finger in the air, 'And it's precisely that kind of mindless scare mongering that's going to cost him the election tomorrow'

'And his ban on tree jumping' whispered Prevost.

'That as well' said Orava.

'And his new tax hike on dry fruit gambling' Prevost whispered louder.

'As well'

'And his decision to postpone February mating to March, and his proposal….'

'Yes thank you Prevost!' interrupted an irritated Orava, 'Yes indeed, there are many reasons why Orav will not be sitting out a third term as our leader'

Kalan gazed over the two squirrels that were addressing him. Orava was a small very dark gray squirrel with no obvious markings on him at all. Although smaller than Kalan, he seemed taller. Prevost sat hunched behind Orava with his head looking at the ground. His gray fur was covered with speckled white patches. As Orava continued speaking Kalan also noticed that he never looked into any ones eyes.

'Two seasons of misrule and mismanagement are soon to be ended for our so called leader who has preferred chaos to order at every turn'

Kalan started to speak but Orava had no intention of letting himself be interrupted and raised the tone of his voice. 'Only once did his administration have a moment of lucidity and clear thought, and yet it will be precisely that action, along with your assistance' Orava pointed at Kalan and the others, 'which will help to bring about his long overdue removal from office'

'Our assistance?' said Funni, her arms firmly crossed in front of her.

'Of course, my dear new friends,' Orava forced a none too convincing smile. 'As newly arrived foreigners you are therefore subject to the regulations and obligations of legislation 38' Orava could see his audience was not quite with him. 'Prevost!' he shouted, and his assistant took a couple of hops forward and lifted his head. Prevost actually looked in Kalan's eyes as he spoke.

'Legislation 38, passed as law by a two thirds majority of the governing committee of City Hall Park during the spring sitting of last years administration. Allows the right of any squirrel, resident or not, who is actually present in City Hall Park during the renewal of the governing body to express their opinion freely in that days election' Prevost finished speaking and stepped backwards.

Kalan spoke quickly before Orava could start again. 'Why would a leader who hates foreign squirrels pass a law that gives them a vote?'

'Ah ha!' said Orava, 'I can see we have a quick mind....er'

'Kalandaka'

'Kalandaka! Yes a quick mind indeed' Orava moved closer and added to his compliment by forcing his smile even wider. 'It's true that Orav has expressed his general distrust of foreigners because there is a large majority of squirrels here at City Hall who are fearful of such folk. However there is also a small, but not inconsiderable minority amongst the electorate who have more liberal views towards outsiders' He gracefully indicated himself and Prevost with the palm of his paw. 'Orav is, if nothing else, a pragmatist. He passed Bill 38 as a political move to win their consensus for other less popular proposals last year. I'm sure he never thought he would see the day when not one, but three arrive on his doorstep'

Orava chuckled to himself. 'Yes indeed. So Kalandaka, I expect that you and your colleagues here will not wish to vote tomorrow for your jailer, and I look forward to you expressing yourselves in my favor tomorrow'

Orava grabbed Kalan's paw and shook it, doing the same in turn with Funni and Risu.

'But I'd like too......' Funni began to speak but Orava waved his paw dismissively in the air.

'Prevost will answer all your questions. I'm sorry but I have a great deal to do. It's been a pleasure meeting with you. Goodbye and remember a vote for Orava is the only one that will make a difference'

Orava motioned Prevost to stay, and with one last wave of his tail, he jumped out of the hollow and down the tree.

Funni started to speak at once to Prevost, 'How long are we going to have to stay in here?' she demanded.

Prevost looked at her and gave a shrug that Risu could have called his own. 'In accordance with the City Hall Security and Well Being Act, all foreigners are to be detained until their intentions can be ascertained. So until you have been screened by security I really cannot say how long you will have to remain under observation'

'Who does the screening?' asked Kalan.

'That would undoubtedly be the responsibility of the first citizen, but in the run-up to tomorrow's election it is probable that his agenda for today is already full'

'It's outrageous that we are being held in here against our will' continued Funni, 'and I'm not having any of it' She turned to Kalan and Risu. 'Come on, let's go, they have no right to keep us in here' and she pushed Prevost aside and started to march towards the exit. Kalan ran after her and pulled her back.

'Let's not antagonize these folk Funni, wait a little longer, please. Remember we have to wait for Tancredi'

Funni tutted loudly, but moved no further.

'What about Tancredi?' asked Risu from the back of the hollow.

'I am not familiar with that name' said Prevost.

'How about Uncle Totti?' Risu asked again, 'He knows what's what and what's where'

'Uncle Totti' Prevost repeated the name to himself a couple of times as he thought. 'The sparrow who resides on the clock tower?'

'That's the chap!' said Risu who had recently taken to putting on a bad imitation of Sunda's accent.

'I have heard of him, but unfortunately have never met the sparrow in person' replied Prevost matter of factly. 'Now if you will excuse me I also must be off' and before the squirrels could reply he was already out of the hollow.

'What a weird bunch this lot are' said Risu

'Yeah well I don't want to hang around and find out if they get any weirder' said Funni who had changed her mind about waiting patiently for Tancredi. She hopped over to the edge of the hollow and called across to Kalan and Risu. 'Come on if you're coming'

'Don't make us come down there' boomed a voice from above Funni's head. She looked up to see the burly squirrel and his friend still clinging to the tree. Kalan pulled her inside.

'Funni let's think this out a bit first. We don't want to cause any trouble'

Funni allowed herself to be pulled gently back by Kalan, 'It's not right' she said

'I know' replied Kalan, 'and I promise if nothing changes soon we *are* going to get out of here, but lets be patient first and give Tancredi a little bit more time'

To get their minds off their current situation, the three squirrels talked for a long while. Subjects ranged from Tancredi and Uncle Totti, to Bilka and Sunda. They wondered how close they were to Central Park, and if the squirrels there would be like those here at City Hall Park. They discussed exactly how the 'voting' might work.

'Well I didn't care too much for Orava' said Risu, 'and I'm certainly not going to vote for the guy who left those too goons outside to guard us. Is there any one else?'

'If they are not letting us out, we are never going to know are we?' said Funni sarcastically.

Kalan too was coming to the end of his patience. They had been kept in the hollow for most of the day, Tancredi had disappeared and,

'I'm hungry' said Risu as he unwittingly filled in the last part of Kalan's thoughts.

Kalan's mind began to think of escape, and he looked out through the opening of the tree. The light was fading and some of the city lights had started to switch on. A small squirrels head popped up and looked into the hollow.

'Compliments of Orava' said the little head, and he threw some nuts into the hollow then disappeared.

Risu ran straight over to them and started to munch, 'Orava just got my vote' he said with his mouth half full.

Kalan put his thought of escape on hold for a moment and he and Funni moved over to join Risu. After only a few minutes munching several squirrels entered the hollow.

'Gentlemen, our leader Orav requests and requires your immediate presence at the main drey' said the largest of the squirrels.

'We're eating' said Funni without looking up.

'Orav has prepared a special dry fruit buffet in your honor, but insists on your attendance now!'

Kalan could sense that Funni was in no mood to be bossed about so gently grabbed her arm and whispered in her ear. 'Let's cooperate. Once we are out of this hollow it will be easier to work out an escape'

Kalan had no difficulty convincing Risu, the mere mention of dry fruit made him drop the nut he was eating and he was already on his feet ready to visit Orav.

'Please' said the large squirrel, 'this way'

The Battery Parkers followed him and the other two squirrels out of the hollow, down the tree and onto the pathway. The two squirrels that had been guarding them brought up the rear.

This large group of eight squirrels ran down the side of the pathway towards the City Hall building. Kalan enjoyed being able to stretch his legs after having been cooped up inside the tree all day.

They made a large semi-circle around a small square with a fountain and to the right there were a few small bushes that covered a small opening in the ground. Only one of the three squirrels leading the pack went down inside the drey, the other two remained outside but indicated to Kalan and the others to follow the first one down the hole.

The inside of the City Hall drey appeared at once to be very familiar to the Battery Park squirrels. In fact New York squirrels build their dreys in pretty much the same way up and down Manhattan. The height of the walls, the number of exits and the position of the main meeting hall were all similar. Even the flooring was the same tangled mix of paper and fur.

Kalan and the others had that same sense of déjà vu a human gets if he visits a Starbucks in another country. Everything looks the same, just the people are different.

After running down two or three long corridors Kalan, Risu and Funni found themselves in a large room. In front of them, as promised, lay lots of pieces of dried fruit and a large number of nuts.

'Wow!' said Risu, his mouth almost dropping open.

'Please help yourselves, Orav will be along shortly' said the squirrel they had followed. He smiled and made his way out of the main meeting hall.

Even Funni was impressed by the spread. Kalan could not even remember the last time he had had any dried fruit, and without further thought he joined Risu in the middle of the food. Funni stayed put for a few more moments, but the sight of Risu and Kalan enjoying dried raisins and apple chunks eventually got to her and she too tucked into a large piece of dried banana.

The three of them indulged themselves for a long time. Eventually Risu reached his limit, 'Ooh, my mind wants more, but my stomach says no way' he groaned as he held a dry cherry piece close to his chest.

'Save some for later' suggested Kalan, 'we don't know when we'll get offered any more'

Risu nodded and stuffed the cherry into his fur, 'But I'll tell you one thing my mind and stomach are both in agreement on,' Risu carried on talking as he tucked away other small pieces of fruit about his person, 'Orav's getting my vote now. I've never eaten this well. Ever!'

'Oh knock it off with this voting Risu' said Funni, 'We're not voting for anyone in this place. The moment we can we're getting out of here'

She turned around to start checking the best exit and gave a startled jump. Sitting in silence a few feet behind her was Orava.

'Now my friend, a non-voting citizen is a disgrace to modern democratic squirrel society'

Both Risu and Kalan turned as they heard the squirrel speak. Only it was not Orava. Funni peered closer, the squirrel looked exactly like Orava, gray with no markings and with the same slight frame. He even radiated the same presence of character, but his eyes seemed weary, tired.

Orav could see the squirrels staring at him trying to decide if he was his brother or not. Being an identical twin he was used to it.

'I am Orav. Elected leader of this community and, as you have noticed, brother of Orava'

Kalan nodded in acknowledgement but could not answer as his mouth was still full of dried banana. Orav sat up and hopped a little closer.

'I hope you have enjoyed your meal. It's my way of apologizing for keeping you in that tree for so long. I was unable to see you earlier because, as you are no doubt aware, we are having an election tomorrow and I have spent most of today canvassing the electorate'

'Are you going to keep us locked up in that hole indefinitely?' said Funni.

'You were detained merely as a precautionary measure under one of our laws, but as of this moment you are free to continue on your way or stay on with us and become useful law abiding citizens of City Hall Park'

Kalan swallowed down the last bit of banana and spoke up.

'We came to meet Uncle Totti who we were told could help us with some information about a missing friend of ours'

'Uncle Totti' Orav muttered to himself 'Yes I know him, the sparrow who lives on top of the clock on the island'

Orav looked up at Kalan and the others. Unlike his brother Orav looked in the eyes of the person he was talking to.

'He knows what's what' he added with a smile.

'And what's where!' shouted out Risu with a smile and all four squirrels relaxed into a pleasant chuckle.

'So please' continued Orav 'Tell me more about yourselves and this friend you are looking for'

The Battery Parkers took it in turns to fill Orav in on their adventure so far. As they spoke about Orav seemed genuinely interested in their quest. He had heard of Battery Park and surprised everyone when he told them that in the rest of Manhattan the Battery Park squirrels were believed to have their main drey under the water.

He had heard of Tompkins Park and although he could provide no information about Bilka or Tancredi, he promised to ask around.

'I'll do what I can, but after tomorrow' he said, 'Now I must leave you and prepare. This evening we have our last open debate before the vote tomorrow. It's in the Oak by the Old Courthouse if you would like to come and listen or ask questions'

'A debate between you and your brother? Risu asked,

'Yes we are the only two candidates left in the race. If you are thinking of voting tomorrow I suggest you come. It starts at ten pm, sharp'

'Yes we will, in the meantime perhaps we should pay Uncle Totti a visit' said Kalan turning to Risu and Funni.

'Sure' said Funni.

'That's a good idea. He'll be asleep soon and as I remember he can get quite irritable if you wake him' said Orav as he stood up to leave. 'Give him my regards and I will see you at the debate'

He bent down and picked up a piece of dried apple and hopped elegantly out of the room.

'What a splendid chap' said Risu in his best Sunda accent.

It did not take the squirrels long to find their way out of the main drey, and as soon as they were back on the pathway they could see Uncle Totti's clock illuminating the far end.

It was early evening and the park was quite full with both squirrels and people. Kalan noticed that a lot of people walking around seemed to be holding their hand to their ear and talking to themselves. He had seen this phenomenon occasionally back in Battery Park, but here it seemed like everybody that passed was talking to themselves. He remembered once that Olmaxon had explained it away as a way lonely humans can stop feeling depressed. As he ran with the others they passed many humans, some were talking to themselves as they walked, some were sat talking on the benches. None of them appeared to be enjoying their conversations.

Loneliness must be worse, thought Kalan, when you are actually living in a place where you are always surrounded by people who prefer talking to themselves than with you.

He looked ahead at Risu and Funni who had stopped under a bench. As he ran under to join them he felt very privileged to have their company.

'Do you think Tancredi's with him?' said Funni looking down the pathway to the clock.

'I don't know' said Kalan 'but I'm sure he's ok. You know Tancredi he's always disappearing then popping up later'

A short far squirrel ran past them.

'Vote for Orava!' it cried out without stopping as it made it's way towards the fountain.

'No way!' shouted Risu after him 'Orav's the one!'

'Are we going to hang around for all this?' Funni asked, looking at Kalan.

'We'll see what Uncle Totti has to say first' he replied and they all ran out from under the bench and continued down the side of the pathway towards the clock.

The pathway eventually came to an end as did the park. Uncle Totti's clock was close by, but separated by a road. The squirrels sat down by the railings and watched as a large bus maneuvered along the road and turn into Broadway.

'I've had it with roads' said Risu

'Why don't I go?' asked Funni, and Kalan had already realized that today was not the best day to argue with her, so he said nothing.

Risu looked over and saw that Funni had a very determined look on her face.

'Sounds good to me' he shrugged very diplomatically.

'Right then' she said, turned and ran to the edge of the road. After checking in both directions she darted across and made for the clock.

'What's eating her?' asked Risu as he watched Funni's progress.

'I guess she's still upset about losing that nut' Kalan replied, but he wasn't certain of his own answer.

They watched as Funni climbed up the body of the clock and eventually onto the clock face. It was not easy going as on the face there were very few parts to hold on to, but she eventually made it to the top. Kalan and Risu lost sight of her as she dipped around the other side.

'I hope she doesn't wake him up' said Risu who then had his attention diverted back towards the park as he could hear the fat squirrel from earlier shouting 'vote Orava' in the distance.

'Are we going to vote?' he asked as he peered into the park trying to pinpoint the fat squirrel.

'Maybe' replied Kalan 'Why not? We should go to that debate later, it might be interesting and we can always ask people for the best direction to take to get out of here' He then tapped Risu on the shoulder with his tail as he saw Funni reappear in the edge of the road opposite. 'She's back' he said, and Risu quickly turned around.

Funni rushed back across the road and ran up to the others out of breath. 'Nothing' she panted 'Nada. No Uncle Totti, no Tancredi, not even a bird dropping'

Kalan took a deep breath. 'Ok' he said slowly 'we'll come back later. Maybe he has gone to Tancredi's place or something. I'm sure they'll pop up sooner or later' It was obvious from the tone of his voice that he was beginning to doubt that though. 'Let's go explore this park a bit and see what else we can find out'

'So we are going to stay?' asked Funni as she slowly crossed her arms.

'Until we know the right way to take out of here, yes' said Kalan.

Funni did not look happy, and tightened her crossed arms.

'Ah come on Funni' said Kalan a little agitatedly 'don't be like that. Look around you, look at all these roads. How do we know for sure which one is the right one to take?'

'What you mean is that if I hadn't lost your precious nut we would know the way to go' Said Funni

'That is not how I'm thinking' said Kalan defensively 'I'd forgotten all about it'

'What nut?' said Risu with a smile holding his paws in the air in an attempt to diffuse Funni's growing irritation.

Nobody said anything for a few moments. Kalan sensed that Funni was itching for an argument and he had no intention of letting her have one. It was Risu who eventually broke the icy silence.

'Why don't we just explore this park a bit, ask a few of these squirrels some questions, and get some info. Then we can go to that debate. I'm looking forward to that, I've never been to one before'

'And don't forget rats' said Kalan 'There's bound to be a rat place around here. They'll know for sure the best way to go'

'Well good luck boys' said Funni, 'I intend to stay here and wait for these sparrows'

'But Funni with the ………' Kalan stopped himself in mid sentence. He had been going to explain how dangerous it was so close to the road, and how it might be better if they stuck together for the moment. However he had been reading Funni's mood correctly all day and that would have been like throwing gasoline on a burning flame. 'Ok Funni' he said instead, 'that's fine. We'll meet you back here in a few hours and see what we have been able to discover'

Funni nodded once, then turned her back to the other two and fixed a stare on Uncle Tottis.

'See you later' said Risu as he and Kalan ran off back towards the City Hall.

Funni uncrossed her arms and turned to watch them as they ran off. She slapped the ground with her tail in anger. She was angry with herself for being so stubborn, angry with Tancredi for having disappeared again, angry with Orav and all these new squirrels for having kept her locked up all day and angry for being no nearer finding her father. It was only after she had thought of all the things she was angry about that she realized that none of them involved Kalan or Risu. She sighed and slapped her tail a little less aggressively on the sidewalk. As two people ran past her the coat tails of one almost brushed in her face. She decided that it might be a better idea to keep a look out for Uncle Totti from higher up.

News of the new arrivals had spread around City Hall Park so Kalan and Risu had no difficulty finding squirrels to talk to as they ran down the main pathway.

The first time they stopped for a breather under a bench two other squirrels came up to them almost immediately. 'Hey! You are the foreigners every ones been talking about' said one of them eagerly.

'Yes that's right' said Kalan.

'Where are you guys from?' said the other squirrel his eyes wide eyes with curiosity.

'Battery Park' said Risu proudly.

'Whoa!' said the wide eyed squirrel, 'How'd you get all the way up here? Did you ride the metro?'

'Did you come all this way to help us vote?' said the other.

Kalan and Risu did their best to answer all the questions, but had little luck when asking their own. The City Hall squirrels had heard of Uncle Totti, and had a little communication with the rats, but that was about it.

'You guys should ask Prevost. He hangs out with the rats sometimes. I think they've got some digs under the west wing of City Hall'

Kalan and Risu thanked the others, but as they were leaving to head closer to the City Hall Risu couldn't resist one last question. 'Who are you guys going to vote for?'

'Aww we ain't voting' came the reply.

'Eh?' said Risu, surprised.

'It makes no difference, whoever you vote for once they take office they all act the same' said the wide eyed squirrel.

'Yeah' said his friend, 'You can vote for blue or red, green whatever, but the moment they take the pledge they all turn gray' and without further comment they both ran off.

'Is that why we never had elections in Battery Park?' Risu asked to Kalan.

'I don't know' Kalan replied, 'Well we didn't need them did we? Olmaxon was always gray long before he became our leader'

Risu smiled and the two of them darted out from under the bench and made their way towards the white, almost glowing, building.

The Debate

'Confident of winning tomorrow Orava?'

'Put me down as cautiously optimistic, remember confidence comes before a fall'

Orava and his assistant Prevost were running behind the City Hall heading towards Orava's 'office' in one of the Elms that overlook Broadway and Warren Street. He answered any questions squirrels shouted out as he passed by, but he did not stop moving.

'Orav forever!' cried out one squirrel who was rummaging in the grass as Orava passed over him.

'Forever ends tomorrow' said Orava quickly with a graceful smile. His eyes however glared as he glanced back over at the squirrel.

At the base of Orava's Elm sat the small fat squirrel Risu had seen earlier shouting out slogans. 'Come on up' said Orava as he and Prevost arrived 'And you had better have some good news'

Prevost and the fat squirrel followed Orava up the tree and onto one of the higher branches. 'Well? Well?' said Orava impatiently.

The fat squirrel needed a couple of seconds to get his breath back, and then started talking very quickly. 'Of the sixty four squirrels resident in the park, the latest figures I have are that twenty two, that includes ourselves, are committed to voting Orava. Twenty four intend to vote for Orav and eighteen are undecided or are not going to vote'

Orava slammed his tail on the tree, making the branch shake. 'That's not enough' he moaned.

'You are forgetting the three new arrivals' said Prevost calmly 'they also have the right to vote'

Orava did some quick math on his claws.

'22......25.... Yes maybe, but we still have those 18 losers. Who knows what they want or what they are going to do' said Orava raising a frustrated fist into the night sky.

'Might I suggest we activate the plan we discussed earlier?' said Prevost.

'The fire?' said Orava, but Prevost shook his head and lifted up three fingers. 'Oh you mean Momonga' Orava twitched his ears.

'Yes' replied Prevost, 'With so many undecided we need to give them an alternative to you and your brother to stop Orav from getting any last minute changes of heart. Plus if we can make Momonga critical of Orav, while basically ignoring you, it might even cause a couple of defections from the Orav camp'

Orava whirled around and shouted at the fat squirrel. 'Go get Momonga here. NOW!'

The fat squirrel nodded vigorsly and sped off down the tree.

'You sure it will work?' Orava turned back to Prevost.

'Of course. Those squirrels who are undecided or don't want to vote are like that because they are weary of the political status quo. You give them something new and apparently different and they'll jump on it, without ever realizing they are wasting their own vote while at the same time boosting your chances of success'

'And Momonga?'

'Well I'm sure initially he's not going to be happy, but we did warn him that one day he would have to pay you back'

'Ah ha yes!' Orava rubbed his paws gleefully. As well as being a contender for political office he was also one of the three most important bookies at City Hall, and Momonga had recently lost a great deal to him. 'With Momonga eating off the undecided and hopefully at the same time dragging the odd vote away from Orav,' continued Prevost 'and us making sure the foreigners give you their vote, I would certainly move from being cautiously optimistic to being quietly confident'

Not too far away from the scheming duo of Orava and Prevost, Kalan was sniffing the air near the west wing of City Hall. He and Risu were trying to pick up the rat scent and they could smell faint traces but nothing definite. As they ran along the side of the building the rat scent became even weaker, and was replaced by another familiar smell, that of rat poison.

'I think they've moved on' said Kalan with his nose in the air.

Risu started to cough violently a few feet in front of Kalan. He then jumped backwards and rubbed his nose in the grass.

'Risu!' cried Kalan and he ran over to his friend.

'I'm.........ok' coughed Risu, 'they've gone all right' and he pointed to the small dark opening he had found just under the west wall of City Hall.

Kalan took two steps towards it, and then the overwhelming stench of every rat poison ever made his head go into a spin. He reeled backwards and after helping Risu to his feet they both ran away from the building and into the middle of the lawn. 'Looks like the humans found them' said Kalan as he tried to spit the foul taste of rat poison from his mouth.

'Well they were pushing it building their digs so close to the humans' said Risu as he looked back onto the beautifully lit City Hall.

'Humans just don't expect to find rats in such a place'

Both squirrels turned away from the building when they heard the patter of other squirrels running along the lawn behind them. Risu recognized one of them as the small fat squirrel. Behind him ran a larger, darker and very sad looking squirrel. 'Excuse me!' Kalan shouted over, 'do you know where the rats have gone?'

The fat squirrel ignored Kalan and kept on running, but the larger squirrel stopped and shouted back. 'I think they moved into a new place last week. Try looking for them near the man in the box'

The small fat squirrel came back and started to tug on the larger ones tail.

'Thanks' Risu shouted back, 'But where's this man and his box?'

The larger squirrel had already started to run off, he shouted something back, but neither Kalan nor Risu could make it out. Risu coughed.

'Feeling better?' Kalan asked as he patted Risu's back with his tail.

'Yeah' replied Risu, 'Let's go look for a man in a box'

Momonga and the fat squirrel soon arrived at the base of Orava's tree office. 'Come on up, hurry!' shouted down Orava the moment he saw them.

Momonga followed the fat squirrel up onto Orava's branch and smiled weakly to them both.

'Glad you could make it Momonga' said Orava 'It's time, my friend, for you to pay back your debt to me'

Momonga hung his large dark brown head. 'What' he said morosely 'do I have to do?'

'Declare yourself last minute candidate at tonight's debate and run for office' said Prevost.

'What?' Momonga was surprised he had expected a lot of things, but not this. 'Who in their right mind is going to want to vote for me?'

'Exactly' said Orava with a chuckle.

Prevost turned his attention momentarily to the small fat squirrel. 'Go over to the main drey and declare Momonga's immediate candidacy, and be sure they make room for him at the debate' The fat squirrel nodded obediently and ran off quickly.

'I can't do this' said Momonga 'I'm not interested in politics'

'Yes you can do this' said Orava sternly, 'and you don't have to worry about politics, we will fill you in on your policies. PREVOST!'

Prevost tapped Momonga on the shoulder and looking him straight in the face told him what his politics would be. 'You have decided to unexpectedly offer your candidacy since you are tired with the current political status quo. Whereas you have no quarrel with Orava, you dislike the Orav administration and wish to offer the electorate a wider choice. With a wider choice of candidates you believe there will be a better chance of removing our current leader from office' Momonga was listening but his eyes were beginning to glaze over. 'Your platform is simply the opposite of Orav's. He says less taxation, you say more taxation for richer squirrels to help the poorer residents. He says a ban on foreigners in the park, you offer an open door policy. He says the mating season is to be delayed to March, you say February' Momonga lifted his tail to stop Prevost talking for a moment.

'I'm never going to remember all of this, and I'm not a good public speaker. What happens if people ask me why I am saying all this?'

'Well you'll have to do something' said Orava, 'You owe me, and this is the only method of payment I am willing to accept'

Momonga sighed gloomily.

'Besides' Orava continued lowering his voice a little, 'people will mistake your lack of finesse as a sign of honesty and frankness. You listen to Prevost. You've got a couple of hours before the debate starts so learn your lines' Orava pushed Prevost with his tail. 'You make sure he knows what to do and doesn't fuff it all up. I'm off to find those foreigners and make sure we have them in the bag'

'I saw two of them on the way over here, they were looking for the rats by the west wing' said Momonga

'See, you are being useful already' said Orava and after giving Prevost one last glance he ran along the branch and down the tree trunk.

'Now then, pay attention' said Prevost as Momonga watched Orava leave 'we have a lot to go over'

Momonga lifted his head slowly to look at Prevost. 'If I do this' he said gloomily 'will it square everything between me and Orava?'

Prevost thought for a moment then answered, 'If you do it well, and Orava wins tomorrow, I should think it will more than probably even everything out. Definitely likely'

'Ok' said Momonga failing to realize the number of conditionals in Prevost's answer 'Tell me what I have to do'

Kalan and Risu were moving slowly across the front of City Hall when they heard Orava calling to them from across the lawn. 'Hold up there you two!' Orava called out and they both stopped and waited as he ran over to them. 'Hello again' said Orava with a smile as he arrived 'I see our glorious leader finally listened to me for once and decided to let you out of that tree'

'Listened to you?' asked Kalan.

'Of course. After I visited you all this morning I went straight over to him and demanded that he release you. I'm so glad to see that he complied. It's just a pity that some folk around here are saying that he only did it to be sure of your votes tomorrow'

Kalan still didn't like the way Orava spoke without looking at him directly.

'He laid on a great spread for us as well' said Risu

Orava thought quickly. 'Did you enjoy all that dried fruit I had prepared for you?' he said.

'That was you?' asked Risu somewhat surprised.

'Of course. I left instructions at the drey that the moment Orav sent for you my staff were to leave a welcoming feast for my new friends. Orav is way too tight to think about such things' Orava sighed, 'But I'm sure he'll take the credit for it just the same'

Kalan was also thinking quickly. 'The hazelnuts were a nice touch Orava, where did you find so many?' he said.

'Oh think nothing of it, I offered them from my own personal supply'

'Well they were very nice, thank you very much' said Kalan.

Orava looked around and started to change the subject. 'Is there one of you missing?' he asked

'Oh Funni wanted to wait by the clock in case Uncle Totti or Tancredi came back' said Risu

'Your sparrow friends?' asked Orava, Risu nodded. 'And where are you both off to now? It's still too early for the debate'

'We're looking for a man in the box' said Kalan, 'Apparently that's where we will find the rats'

'Yes, of course' said Orava, 'they had to move home last week as the humans had one of their seasonal rat hunts. The man and the box you are looking for are just at the end of this path, behind you. It's the human entrance to the City Hall and I think the rats have an entry hole around the back of his box'

Orava beckoned to them to follow and they all ran a few feet and out onto a large gravel pathway. At the end of it was a large black box with a light on and a human standing inside. 'There you go' said Orava cheerfully 'be sure to say hello to my rat friends for me, and I'll see you both later at the debate I hope' He patted Risu and Kalan on their backs and made off down the pathway towards the south. Towards the clock, thought Kalan.

'Well I certainly misjudged him' said Risu, 'I had no idea all that food was his doing'

'You misjudged him alright' said Kalan as they both hopped towards the man in the box. 'You really enjoyed those hazelnuts didn't you?'

'They were ok, I think' replied Risu then he stopped moving. 'Hang on, there weren't any hazelnuts'

Kalan also stopped and watched Risu's face as the penny dropped.

'Ooooooh sneaky' said Risu slowly.

Funni had been sitting for a while now on the branch of the tree that had been her prison earlier that day. She was facing south looking forlornly at the clock. It chimed eight pm. For all the time she had been watching she had not seen hair nor tail of Uncle Totti or Tancredi or any bird at all for that matter.

'Much better outside the tree isn't it' came a soft voice from directly behind her. She turned startled to find Orava sitting at the beginning of the branch behind her.

'You scared me!' she said

'Please excuse me' said Orava 'I just passed by to apologize for the unforgivable way my brother treated you earlier'

'Well he did apologize and he feed us' said Funni as she folded her arms defensively, in the end I guess he isn't so bad'

Orava nodded and looked over Funni's shoulder. 'Still no luck waiting in your sparrow friends?'

Funni shook her head, 'They are probably busy someplace else' she said.

'That Uncle Totti is a good friend of mine, we were talking about the election just a few days ago' said Orava as he gazed at the clock.

'Really?' said Funni

'Of course' Orava continued, 'he agreed with so my many of my proposals and he is another one who has had enough of my brother's disastrous period in office. It's such a great pity that such a wise person can't vote'

'Why not?' asked Funni

'Well he isn't a squirrel, he's just a bird. Only squirrels have the right to vote'

'That doesn't sound very fair' said Funni 'He lives in the park like the rest of you, surely he deserves some say in how it's managed'

'Oh come now, it's always been like that. Squirrels are the only animals in the park worthy enough to vote, we understand how.........' Orava stopped in mid sentence as he caught a glimpse of Funni's adamant face. 'No wait a minute. You are quite right'

'About what?' said Funni.

'Of course Uncle Totti should have his say on the political platform, and not just him but the rats, the mice, the pigeons and all the animal residents of this park' Funni nodded in agreement with Orava as he spoke. 'Orav would never dream of proposing such a radical, yet just, action. I swear if I am elected tomorrow I'll make sure it's one of the first laws on the agenda, extending the vote to every citizen of City Hall Park' Orava hopped closer to Funni and grabbed her paw. 'Thank you for helping me see such a blinding oversight in squirrel policy here. Ah if only more squirrels were as intelligent and insightful as you this park would be a more wonderful place' Orava shook Funni's paw then turned to leave. 'I must go and prepare for the debate, and don't worry I'm sure we will win tomorrow. See you later' He waved his tail and made off down the tree.

'We?' said Funni to herself and crossed her arms again as she watched Orava leave.

Orava scurried along the side of the path and laughed to himself, 'Votes for birds, ha!'

Back at the man in the box, Kalan and Risu had found the entrance to the rat's new residence, but were sitting waiting under a tree across the way from it. This was because the man in the box was currently the man outside the box, arguing with another human who was trying to get closer to City Hall.

'I don't care what newspaper you're from sir, but if you don't have an appointment you're not going any further'

As Risu and Kalan waited patiently for the discussion to end and for the man to get back inside his box, Kalan tried hard to concentrate on what was being said.

'Besides it's gone eight, there ain't anybody worth talking too up there now anyhow'

Kalan swished his tail back and forth as he saw the man go back inside his box for a moment then remerge to give the other man something.

'Look this here's the number of the press office. You give them a call and fix an appointment for the next time'

Although Kalan could not understand what was being said he saw that the other man seemed satisfied and started to walk away. The man from the box stayed outside for a while longer watching, then he slapped and rubbed his hands together.

'Brass monkeys' he said to himself and shivered, then walked back inside his box and closed the door.

'Let's go!' said Kalan, and he and Risu ran across to the back of the box and squeezed themselves down the tiny rat hole that was directly underneath. They made their way down the almost vertical corridor, and it soon bottomed out into a largish room. Here they found about half a dozen dozing rats and another couple of corridors leading off in the opposite direction.

'Hey everyone look, we've got some visitors from the park' said one rat through half closed eyes.

'Hi squirrels' said another, 'What's it like up top? Nice and dark?'

Kalan and Risu settled in and after introductions were made, set about asking questions. To the squirrels surprise the rats knew who they were. The rat grapevine was full of stories of the Battery Park squirrels. The City Hall rats were all too happy to help out these personalities, and hopefully make themselves the subject of future tales. Although the rats had no news about Bilka, two of them – Barclay and Reade –were on their way to Columbus Park in a couple of days and offered to take the squirrels with them. This sounded good to Kalan, it was where Bilka had had the run in with the cat, and it was apparently on the way to the other place he had been spotted at Tompkins Park.

'But from Columbus to Tompkins it's a very long way' said Reade.

'And all that area's where Shokobaba holds sway' continued Barclay.

Kalan explained that they were planning on taking everything one step at a time, and thanked the rats for being so helpful. He arranged with Barclay and Reade to meet them back here in two nights when they would be ready to make the journey to Columbus.

'Sorry we can't leave sooner, but we just arrived from North Cove this morning' said Reade

'And you know we are so tired we just can't stop yawning' added Barclay.

'That's ok" said Kalan, 'You guys rest up and we'll see you here the day after tomorrow'

Kalan and Risu said their goodbyes, but as they were leaving they were advised by the rats to take another exit. They followed this tight and freshly dug corridor for several dozen feet until they popped up on the surface on the edge of the lawn on the Park Row side of the park. 'Let's go and get Funni and tell her the news' said Risu as he blinked to adjust his eyes to all the glowing lights around him. 'I hope she's found Uncle Totti' he added while rubbing his eyes.

'And I hope she has cheered up a bit' said Kalan.

Kalan need not have worried. Funni saw them coming down the pathway and greeted them with an enormous smile. 'Well I hope you two have had better luck than me. This has been a totally bird free zone'

'We've got some good news and some not so good news for you' said Kalan, 'The good news is that we found the rats, and two of them are going to take us to Columbus Park'

'The over ground route' added Risu as he saw Funni's smile waiver a little 'in the fresh air. Apparently there is no underground route from here to Columbus'

Funni immediately relaxed, 'And the bad news?' she asked. 'They just arrived and want a couple of days rest before they move on' said Kalan quickly.

To his and Risu's relief Funni seemed fine with this. They had thought she wouldn't like the idea of having to stay any more time in the park. 'Fine' she said sweetly, 'It will give us some more time to find these sparrows and...' she tiptoed up on the branch and looked for a second in the direction of City Hall, '...also give us the chance to exercise our new found voting rights to make sure that creep Orava doesn't win tomorrow'

'Eh? You don't like him either?' said Risu

'Just call it female intuition, but I think he stinks'

Risu slapped his tail in agreement and told Funni about how Kalan had tricked Orava with his story about hazelnuts. Funni also told them about Orava's earlier visit to see her.

'We can heckle him at the debate' giggled Risu

'Yeah and tell everyone what we think about him' agreed Funni.

Kalan was not having any of this. 'We will most definitely not!' he said firmly.

'Oh come on Kalan!' said Risu, 'You know he's a creep and a liar'

'That's as maybe, but we are still guests on his turf and we have no idea what other squirrels think. Lots of them here like him. We should keep our thoughts to ourselves and try to remain on friendly terms with everybody' said Kalan

'He's right Risu' sighed Funni as she realized she there was no arguing with Kalan's good sense. 'If we have to stay here for a couple of days there is no sense antagonizing folk'

'Ok, Ok' said Risu, 'but I can still vote can't I?'

'Yes, and you vote for whoever you want to' replied Kalan, 'but just keep it to yourself, don't go round telling people'

'And what if they ask me?' said Risu

'If anyone asks, just say you are undecided' said Kalan

'And what if they ask me after I vote? Hmmm?' asked Risu putting his hands on his hips.

'You tell them that it's none of their business!' said Funni.

Risu shrugged. He had never voted before and the idea interested him a great deal. 'How do they vote around here anyway?' he asked.

Kalan shook his head. 'I don't know, but I'm sure we'll find out soon enough'

Risu carried on, 'And why didn't we have a system of voting back home? I mean who said that Olmaxon should be in charge of all of us at Battery Park.

'That's just the way it worked' said Funni, 'The older squirrel just automatically takes charge of the younger ones. It's always been that way'

'But surely it's better to let us squirrels decide who should be our leader' said Risu his head awash with the idea of democracy.

'Depends' said Funni, 'Everyone doesn't always know what's best for them'

'What do you think Kalan?' Risu tapped his friend on the shoulder since he didn't seem to be paying attention. In fact Kalan was listening to them, but gazing at the illuminated City Hall.

'I think our system was ok with Olmaxon. He never actually asked for, or even wanted the job, but he did the best he could'

'He grounded us just for talking to rats, Kalan!' said Funni.

'He only did what he thought was best for everyone' replied Kalan as he turned around to face Risu and Funni, 'And after what I've seen here I think that anyone who wants power so badly is the worst type of person to be allowed to have it'

Risu and Funni thought about this for a bit, and even though neither of them liked Orava, or cared much for Orav, in the end they couldn't agree with Kalan. 'It's still fairer to be given a choice' said Funni eventually, 'rather than have decisions or people imposed on you'

The Battery Park squirrels own blossoming debate failed to get off the ground as it was soon interrupted by the arrival on the branch of another squirrel. 'Excuse me, sorry to interrupt' said the squirrel as he jumped up to join them.

'That's Ok' said Funni

'Yeah, just as long as you aren't here to tell us who you think we should vote for' shrugged Risu playfully.

'Oh no, no, no' said the squirrel, 'I've just come to ask a few questions about what you think is important'

'Finding our friend Bilka' said Kalan instantly

'Yeah' said Risu, 'also dried fruit'

'Getting to Central Park' said Funni.

'Oh no, no, no' replied the squirrel who started to scratch his back with his hind leg, 'I mean what you think is important for squirrels here in the City Hall Park. How would you improve things? What changes should be made to make life more pleasant?'

The Battery Parkers stared blankly at the new squirrel. 'We've only been here a day' said Funni, 'How can we know if things need changing or not?'

'I've just got a few questions. Maybe you could like just try and answer?' said the squirrel.

'Ok go on then' said Kalan.

'Ah, great! Ok well firstly do you think the Orav administration has done a good job this past year? You can answer with, yes a lot, yes a bit, not really, not at all, or don't know'

Kalan sighed and lifted his hands halfway into the air. Risu shrugged and Funni hopped closer to the new squirrel.

'We've only just arrived in this park. Hello!' she reminded him.

'Oh yes, yes, yes. Erm so that's three don't knows' He closed his eyes and muttered to himself as if making a mental note of the figure. 'Would you like to see more rooms added at the main drey, or should we utilize the tree hollows more?'

'Is this really necessary?' asked Risu, 'I mean surely a good leader knows what to do without having to ask'

'So is that ......erm... a yes or a no?' the squirrel scratched his back again. The Battery Parkers made no reply. 'What about gambling taxes? Do you think the new tax on dried fruit gambling is too low, too high or just about right?'

'Who are you asking these questions for?' Kalan asked.

'Oh they are just to gauge opinion, to accumulate statistics that can help formulate future strategy'

'Strategy for whom?' Kalan asked again.

'For the actual and future administration'

'You mean Orav?' said Kalan.

The squirrel hesitated, 'err......sort of...' he wasn't used to other squirrels asking him question. Most always seemed happy enough answering his, after all he made it easy for them by giving them multi choice answers.

'So Orav doesn't really make his own decisions, he bases his actions exclusively on popular feeling?' said Kalan.

'No, no, no. Not at all' replied the squirrel nervously, but was interrupted by a calm voice from behind him.

'A good administrator must always listen to the mood of the people if he hopes to lead society well'

Orav had appeared on the now very crowded branch, and was sitting behind the question asking squirrel. 'You can go now' he said to his assistant 'I've come to accompany the new arrivals to the debating tree. You go on ahead and make sure everything is prepared'

'Yes,yes,yes. Right away Orav' replied the squirrel, and after one final scratch he ran under the branch and away.

Orav turned his attention back to Kalan and the others, 'Asking questions is a wonderful way of gathering information that can help me make the correct decisions'

Kalan, Risu and Funni all felt slightly smaller in the presence of Orav. Despite his slight frame and very tired face, he gave off an almost natural aura of confidence and authority. This aura had a strange effect on Kalan, he felt as if he wanted to argue, but found himself nodding meekly instead. 'Yes I suppose so' he said softly, mentally kicking himself for not debating his point further.

'The decisions I make try to reflect the desires and aspirations of the populace,' continued Orav elegantly 'By polling the people I can understand how better to direct administrative policy'

'But do squirrels always know what's best for them?' Funni repeated her point from earlier.

'To tell the truth' replied Orav, 'Squirrels are fickle, often insensitive and always very selfish beasts' Orav's expression sunk as he spoke. The weariness on his face became more noticeable, 'Most don't even care or consider what will happen to society without good forward planning. At best a minority of squirrels might think ahead for the coming months, the vast majority don't look further than the end of the week. The future is, by its very nature, uncertain and it scares them all. It's my job and............' he sighed heavily, 'my burden to think for them. To plan ahead for them. To worry for them'

'If you don't like the job, why are you trying to get elected again?' asked Funni.

Orav blinked and raised his arms in the air in frustration, 'Because if that good for nothing, scheming brother of mine gets elected tomorrow he will turn City Hall Park into an open air casino'

'Really?' said Risu his ears twitching.

'He offers everyone quick fixes and easy answers, and that's like giving candy to a baby. Folks don't worry about the fact it will eventually rot their teeth, they just want to feel good now'

Kalan found himself nodding in agreement with Orav, 'Nobody wants to think of the future' he said

'Exactly' said Orav, almost shouting, 'Orava epitomizes the meaningless of modern day squirrel existence. So I really need your votes tomorrow, or I fear the worst' Orav calmed down a little and began to regain his poise, 'Now if you like I can take you all to the debating tree, and you can hear for yourselves how Orava charms the electorate'

The Battery Parkers were quick to agree, and soon all three of them were following Orav across the park. Orav ran in the same manner as he spoke, regal but weary. The squirrels passed by the man in the box and ran in front of City Hall, they turned right and then followed Orav as he climbed up a large Oak tree that stood between the City Hall and the Old Courthouse. The tree was packed with chattering squirrels.

Orav was accosted almost immediately by his question asking assistant and others. 'There's been a dramatic new development' said one of them

'Orav, we've got to discuss your opening lines,' said another

'Orav, we're down four votes from the last poll'

'Orav, there aren't enough places to sit'

Orav raised his tail above his head and called for silence. He turned to Kalan and the others who were still below him gripping the trunk of the tree. 'Make your way up to the top of the tree and you will find the debating area. I have to leave you now' He then let himself be engulfed by all the other squirrels and their questions.

The Battery Parkers maneuvered themselves around to the other side of the tree trunk and climbed quickly into the branches. Most of the squirrels they passed were too deep in discussion to even notice them as they passed.

The tree was very big and the higher they went, the denser the branches became. At a certain point all the branches seemed to slope downwards towards the main trunk instead of extending themselves in lots of different directions. There were squirrels sitting on top of every branch and the natural acoustics magnified every sound.

'What a racket!' cried out Risu

'This must be were they debate, but if it's going to be like this all night I'm going to get a headache' said Funni.

Kalan looked quickly around and found a small space for them to sit on a high branch with their back to the courthouse squashed between two other groups of squirrels. He tugged on Risu's tail and he and Funni followed Kalan up the branch. 'Do you mind if we squeeze in here?' Kalan asked politely to the other squirrels.

'Sure' said one of them and he and his friends obligingly edged a little to their left to make more room.

Higher up the noise was less deafening but you could still hear everything being said. 'So who are you guys going to vote for?' said the squirrel who had made space for Kalan.

'We're undecided' said Risu, winking at Kalan.

'Well if you want my advice' said the squirrel, 'You can't go wrong with Orava. He's your best bet' The squirrels sitting hunched together behind him all nodded.

'A new fresh face, for a new fresh future' said one of the nodders.

'But he looks just like Orav' said Funni 'They're twins aren't they?'

'A new fresh mind for a new fresh future' said another, but Funni couldn't make out who.

'I want to hear what this Momonga's got to say!' called across another squirrel from the other side.

'It'll be the same old Orav rhetoric recycled' shouted back the squirrel sat next to Funni.

'Momonga?' said Risu to no one in particular. No one answered him either as a hushed silence fell unexpectedly over the tree.

Kalan could see that three squirrels had arrived by the trunk below him. Orav and Orava were indistinguishable from this distance, and Kalan assumed that the darker squirrel sitting nervously between them was Momonga. An unseen squirrel voice barked out loudly.

'Welcome to this seasons last pre-election debate. Our current leader Orav, his political opponent Orava and the independent late challenger Momonga are here to explain their proposals. After they have spoken the floor will be open for your questions'

Kalan watched as the first squirrel stepped forward. The moment he started to speak, and the acoustics of the tree made it seem as if he was talking directly into Kalan's ear, it was obvious that he was Orav.

Orav spoke or, as Risu thought, droned on for a long time. He explained clearly but in a dull tone the achievements of his administration and his plans for the future. His speech was peppered with handy catchphrases for which he raised his voice and his paw from time to time to emphasize.

'We need to plan today to have a better tomorrow!'

'No pain, no gain!'

'An honest hardworking leader for an honest hardworking people!'

Occasionally little cheers of encouragement broke out, but overall the tree remained silent as he spoke.

'And in closing, I ask for your vote again tomorrow because we need to continue with the progress and stability we have had as a community here for so long. We can only expect continued success from a proven leader.

Don't be tempted to take the murky road that leads to chaos. Vote for Orav! Vote for reason! Vote for Truth! Vote for the future!'

Orav raised both his arms into the air and the tree applauded. Some squirrels cheered, and a few booed. As the applause died down, Orava stepped forward to the place vacated by Orav. They smiled at each other as they passed, but their eyes did not meet.

'A vote for Orav isn't a vote for reason, it's a vote for confusion!' Orava began his speech in an aggressive tone.

'Vote for truth? No! It's a vote for years of lies and betrayal! A vote for the future? HA! It's a vote thrown away at a shameful past' Orava continued with this aggressive, attacking tone for the duration of his speech. Kalan noticed that every time he made an important statement, Prevost was the first to cheer out praise, and that others around him followed suit.

'Don't waste your vote on another season of misrule, mismanagement and misery. Vote for Orava for a brighter future, today!'

With Prevost's goading, part of the tree broke out into cheers and applause. Orav's supporters didn't boo, but remained in stony silence. Orava bowed and waved to the tree and stepped backwards to make space for Momonga. Kalan now recognized him as the squirrel who had spoken to them on the lawn earlier that night. Momonga looked very miserable and began a very short speech in a dull monotone. 'I am Momonga,' he shrugged as if he wasn't even convinced of this fact. 'I have had enough of the same squirrels always being elected. No matter whom you vote for it always seems to be the same squirrel who gets elected. So don't. Vote for me, and he won't.

'Who is this guy?' Risu turned and asked Kalan, 'I like him'

Momonga did not speak for very long, and he spent most of his time repeating his same initial point ad nauseum. 'So vote for me, Momonga and change the status quo'

A slow applause began, but then got louder as the squirrels realized that Momonga had actually finished his boring monologue. Kalan noticed that Prevost was goading people to applaud again. The unseen voice barked out once more.

'Now we have heard the candidates. If you have a question please make your way to the question branch, and keep them short!'

A small branch that grew upwards out from one of the larger ones on the other side of the trunk appeared to be the 'question branch' since there was already a small squirrel sitting on it with his tail raised.

'Ask your question' barked the voice.

'Surely after two terms of office it's time for Orav to stand down and give someone else a chance' The squirrel's tiny voice carried all the way around the tree and into Kalan's ear. A few squirrels sitting near Prevost cheered but they were soon hushed by the unseen voice.

'Questions only! How many times do I have to tell you every time we debate, Questions only, not opinions!' it shouted.

Orav waved his arms in the air and stepped forward. 'I'll reply to this' he said and moved forward a step, 'I'll reply by saying that only someone with my proven experience can govern here. It would be folly to hand control of your lives to people who have never had any real experience of government'

The squirrel sitting next to Kalan shouted down, 'How can they, if you never give it up?'

The whole tree broke out in argument, and it took the unseen voice a while before it could bring back order. 'Just questions please' it shouted as another squirrel jumped up onto the question branch.

'I have a question for Momonga' said the squirrel on the branch. 'Would you raise the gambling tax if elected?'

Momonga shrugged and looked even more miserable than before. Kalan could see him looking over at Prevost who made some sort of signal with his arms. 'Erm......' started Momonga 'I just think that if you vote for me, I will act differently from the others. If the other candidates intend to raise the tax then I am certain your vote would depend on that' Momonga began to mumble and nobody could make out what he was saying, then he raised his voice a little, 'Because it's always the same person who gets elected no matter who you vote for'

With that it appeared as if Momonga had finished since he stepped backwards. The tree sat in silence and the squirrel who had asked the question had already been pushed off the branch by another.

'My question is for Orava! Can he tell us what will be his policy towards the mating games of next year?'

(The mating games are the City Hall equivalent of the Battery Park 'Hanky Panky Rumble')

'Yes, yes,' said Orava confidently as he moved forwards, 'excellent question. The mating games are an important, nay, essential part of City Hall squirrel tradition and I intend to maintain their integrity and passion. For two seasons we have seen these wonderful games dishonored by a rotten administration that was always more interested in filling their own coffers than providing honest entertainment and honoring the mating ritual' As Orava spoke Funni leaned over to Kalan,

'Why doesn't anyone around here answer a question directly?' she whispered in his ear. Kalan shook his head as he answered,

'I don't know Funni, I really don't know'

For almost an hour they sat and listened to Orav, Orava and occasionally Momonga repeat themselves in continuation. They ranted and raved to an audience that, in Kalan's opinion, had already decided who they would be voting for the next day. Kalan could also see that Risu had zoned out of the debate and that Funni was looking very tired. 'If you two have had enough, we can go and get some sleep' he suggested.

This bought Risu back almost instantly. 'We could kip back down in the hollow. It was, after all, quite warm plus Tancredi would know where to find us' he said enthusiastically 'I'm done here'

'Me too' agreed Funni. So the three of them made their way quietly out of the debating area, down the trunk and onto the lawn. They could still hear Momonga talking as they hit the ground,

'The same person that gets elected is bound to have the same ideas as before'

City Hall Park was completely silent and this came as a pleasant relief to the squirrels after the debating tree. It did not take them long to get back to the tree hollow and Kalan and Risu were the first to curl up and drop off to sleep. Funni instead used the last few minutes of the day gazing over at the hands on Uncle Totti's clock as they moved towards midnight. She thought about Bilka. The debating tree had reminded her of one of the things she loved most about her father, he always gave a straight answer to a straight question.

THE ELECTION DAY

All three of the Battery Park squirrels were woken by a terrific crashing sound that came from the road outside.

Funni was the first to stick her head out of the hollow. She saw that a large bus had hit a yellow cab on the corner of Broadway and the road that led to Uncle Tottis. The back of the cab was all crumpled up and there was a lot of white smoke coming out from the front of the bus. 'I guess they weren't paying attention to those pretty lights' yawned Risu as he and Kalan jumped out of the tree hollow to get a better look.

No one appeared to be hurt by the accident but a small crowd had gathered and there was a great deal of shouting and arm waving between the respective drivers. 'Looks a lot like the debating tree' mused Kalan as he viewed the scene and watched as the smoke rose lazily into the bright blue sky. He looked across at Uncle Totti's clock. All the commotion evidently hadn't woken Tancredi's mysterious relation because he obviously wasn't anywhere to be found.

'What the devil has happened to Tancredi?' Kalan asked out loud, but neither Funni nor Risu had an answer for him.

'Well you know how sparrows are' said a voice from the branch below them, 'here one day and gone the next'

Kalan looked down to see the speckled face of Prevost. 'Good morning everyone!' he said pleasantly as he hopped onto their branch. 'I just happened to be passing by and thought to myself that you three probably have no idea about voting procedure here at City Hall, or even where to go eh?'

'Well, we......' began Risu

'So I thought I'd accompany you all to the voting rooms and explain how we do it'

'That was very thoughtful of you' said Kalan.

'Well then, if you've finished watching humans hurl abuse at each other shall we go?'

'Is there a hurry?' asked Funni.

'Oh no' replied Prevost, 'Voting takes place all day long. I just thought that you might want to get it out of the way quickly so you can carry on with more important things. And I'm sure you are anxious to display your support of Orava as soon as possible'

'Hey! I'm not going to vote for.........'

The rest of Risu's sentence was muffled as Kalan blocked his friend's mouth with his tail. 'Ok Prevost we're ready, show us how the voting works' said Kalan quickly

Prevost smiled and jumped down from the tree and waited by the side of the path as the others followed him down.

'Keep your opinions to yourself' whispered Kalan to Risu as they scrambled down the tree trunk, 'at least until we are out of here'

Risu grumbled something that sounded like agreement and the three of them ran behind Prevost as he led the way to the main drey.

'It's really very simple' said Prevost as he ran. 'In the main drey you will each be given a vote. You then take this vote and place it in the room dedicated to the candidate you wish to be elected'

'What's this vote?' puffed Risu who always had great difficulty running and talking at the same time.

It's actually an old nut shell we keep for us in these elections' said Prevost.

'How do we know which room belongs to who?' asked Funni

'Good question' said Prevost and he stopped running and turned to face the others. 'And a very important question since we want to make sure we put our vote in the right room. In Orava's room eh?' he smiled charmingly at everyone.

'So?' said Funni

'By scent. Each candidate has doused a room this morning. In the main meeting hall of the main drey you can meet each candidate again and remind yourself of their scent. Then you take your vote and go to the room that smells of Orava and place your vote in complete privacy'

Once Prevost was certain they had all understood he started to run again. 'Come on, we're almost there' he shouted back and the others began to chase after him.

They followed him as he jumped down into the entrance of the main drey and along the corridors that eventually led to the main hall. Risu recognized it instantly as it was the same place where Orav had fed them the dry fruit yesterday.

Today there was a large pile of pistachio nut shells in the center. They were very old since none of them smelt of pistachio any more. Behind the pile of nutshells sat Orav, Orava and Momonga. Each of whom was wearing the most forced smile Kalan had ever seen. A couple of other squirrels who had arrived earlier were moving along the line of candidates sniffing each one in turn.

'Orava and the others are forbidden to speak to the electorate today until voting is over' Prevost whispered 'So please don't try to start a conversation, oh and don't forget that it is customary to sniff all the candidates even the ones you don't intend to vote for'

Kalan looked back over to the row of candidates and saw Orava smiling through gritted teeth as a squirrel smelled under his armpit.

'Where are the voting rooms?' asked Funni looking around the main hall.

Prevost pointed to a hole in the far right corner of the hall. As he did this one of the squirrels that had finished sniffing, picked up a nut shell and walked out of the hall and down that hole. 'At the end of that corridor you will come across three other squirrels. These are the referees, each one selected by one of the candidates. They are there to ensure fair play, to make sure it's one squirrel one vote and that sort of thing. Behind them you will find the rooms to place your vote. Orava's room is the second one on the right'

'Sounds easy enough' said Risu, 'Let's do it'

'I'll accompany you' said Prevost earnestly, 'After all it's your first time and we wouldn't want you to make any mistakes now would we?'

Kalan lent over to Prevost. 'Maybe it would be better not to. Some people might think you were showing us favoritism. We can mange on our own, don't worry'

Prevost thought for a moment and as he did he caught a very angry stare through a false smile from Orav. 'Yeeess' he whispered slowly, 'maybe you're right. But remember Orava is depending on your votes. Don't let us down, remember his room is the second on the right after the referees'

Kalan nodded and made his way over to the candidates with Risu and Funni. He moved alongside each of the squirrel hopefuls and smelled each ones odor. As he did this he couldn't help but wonder what was it that made certain squirrels desire power so much that they were prepared to go to any lengths, even ridicule, to achieve it. The candidates all nodded and smiled vainly as Kalan passed by and sniffed each one. In order to obtain power they were all prepared to lie thought Kalan as he sniffed Orava. Play on people's emotions he thought as he passed Orav or just simply cheat. This was his last thought as he passed Momonga at the end of the line.

Funni and Risu had already picked up their nutshells and were waiting for Kalan by the corridor that led down to the voting rooms. Kalan picked up a pistachio shell and turned once more to look at the three candidates. They were all still smiling and nodding at other squirrels that had entered the room. As Kalan stared closer the three of them didn't look like squirrels any more. Their smiles were forced, their eyes were blank and expressionless. The quest for power, thought Kalan, had more serious implications for a squirrels well being than his own quest for adventure. He felt a little shudder run down his spine but shook it off and hopped over to join the others.

They made their way down a very long and tight corridor until it opened up onto another large room. Here sat three very bored looking squirrels who moved over towards Kalan and the others.

'Just a quick body check' said one, 'to make sure you are only carrying one vote'

The Battery Parkers were asked to raise their arms as each one of them had their body fur and tail checked.

'Thank you. You may place your vote in one of the three rooms behind us' said one of the referees as he pointed to a small opening behind him. 'One at a time please though' he added as all three squirrels moved towards the hole.

Risu went first and emerged from the hole a minute later with, what Funni thought, was a very silly grin on his face. She went after and finally Kalan. As Kalan entered the hole he could sense instantly the three very powerfully smelling rooms. The candidates had obviously been dousing with great vigor all night.

Now although squirrels can see very well underground, this area of the drey was so pitch black that Kalan was forced to use his sense of smell to decide where to place his vote.

'Please hurry up in there' called out one of the referees 'others are waiting'

Kalan gripped his pistachio shell tightly. Vote for Orava, a proven liar? Vote for Orav, who had kept them prisoner all day? Vote for Momonga, who was probably just a stooge for Orava? Kalan turned the nut over and over in his paws.

'You took your time' said Risu as Kalan finally exited from the voting rooms. 'The smell of politics is driving me crazy' he continued, 'let's get some fresh air?'

Kalan needed no further convincing and within seconds he was racing the other two out of the drey, but as they exited into the daylight they were accosted by Prevost and another squirrel.

'Just a quick question please folks' said the other squirrel, 'May I ask which way you voted today for our exit poll?'

'A squirrels vote is his private matter' said Risu still holding onto his silly grin.

'Well you won't have to wait long until you have the facts' said Funni, then turned her attention to Prevost, 'When will the results be known?'

'Voting ends tonight at ten. If there are no recounts we should be able to know the identity of our next leader shortly thereafter. Prevost pushed the other squirrel to one side and moved closer to Kalan. 'I trust you did…………'

Kalan grabbed Prevost's paw and shook it hard, 'We all wish Orava the best of luck, but the site of all those nutshells has made me and my friends hungry, so if you'll excuse us. I'm sure you have a very busy day ahead of you'

'Yes that's right, but I really would like to…………'

Kalan never heard the rest of Prevost's sentence as he Risu and Funni were already running to the lawn in front of City Hall. Prevost watched them run off and his eyes slowly narrowed.

'So that's three down for Orava?' said the other squirrel.

'Probably' said Prevost very slowly and he shaded his eyes from the bright sun.

Tancredi knew there was daylight somewhere, but he couldn't see any. In fact he couldn't see anything because his world had been pitch black for the past twenty four hours. He was sitting on the bottom of a large golden cage. He didn't know it was golden of course, but he knew he was trapped because every time he had tried to fly anywhere he hit metal bars.

His sense of hearing had improved dramatically during the past hours spent in total darkness. Since being kidnapped yesterday he had heard many people's voices talking in many strange and different tones. He had heard cars, dogs and even sensed the presence of a cat. Tancredi also guessed correctly that he had been moved around a lot, and even now he had the sensation of being inside something that was rocking from side to side.

'PARK THE CAR HERE, WE'LL PUT HIM WITH THE OTHERS' said a human voice.

'OK'

Tancredi felt his cage rock violently and he fell against the bars for the third time this morning. The cage then started to sway from side to side and Tancredi cried out,

'You rotten brutes, let me outta here!'

'HE'S GOT SUCH A SWEET VOICE, PUT HIM IN THE FRONT ROOM'

Tancredi's cage hit the ground with a bang that vibrated through the bars. 'Hey you clumsy louts, I is dying in here!'

'LET'S GO I'M HUNGRY'

The strange human voices seemed to reply to his calls, but Tancredi couldn't understand what they were saying.

'You're wasting your time. They ain't listening buddy!'

Out of the darkness a voice spoke that Tancredi, to his relief, could understand.

'Hi, Hey! Who are you? Where am I?' Tancredi called into the blackness.

'Name's Dennis buddy, and I'm a bird stuck in a cage just like you. We all are'

Some other voices chirped up.

'I'm Frank'

'My name is Gladys and I'm here with my husband Wilberforce'

'Who cares who we all are? What's going to happen to us?' said another, very shaky, voice.

'AH quit your complaining we're all in the same boat, let's try and be sociable. I'm Totti'

'Uncle Totti?' cried out Tancredi, 'Uncle Totti it's me, Tancredi. Tancredi from the Bowling Green'

'AH Tancredi. I was wondering when you were going to pay me a visit'

The Battery Park squirrels spent most of the day avoiding the pollsters and exploring the City Hall Park, but by the evening it was impossible to avoid the election frenzy of speculation. Everyone they met would speak of nothing else. The City Hall Park bookmakers were all working overtime and the odds being offered on all the candidates rose and fell continuously depending on the latest gossip. Momonga, for instance, had started the day as a 1,000 to 1 rank outside chance. By eight pm the best you could get on him was 20 to 1. While the squirrels of City Hall Park were certainly more democratically minded than the others in Manhattan, they shared in the modern day squirrels biggest vice. Gambling. Risu had disappeared a couple of times during the day and Kalan knew why. 'I guess you don't have any of that dried fruit left from yesterday?' he said when Risu returned from one of his walkabouts.

'Erm...... no, I ...... sorry I just got hungry' replied Risu guiltily.

'What odds are they giving on Orava?' said Kalan casually.

'Oh the crooks here have got him down from 3 to 1 to evens' said Risu. Then he opened his mouth and put his paw over it. 'Oh.........'

'And who did you put your fruit on?' said Kalan.

'Umm... I couldn't resist Kalan. It's just a bit of fun'

Kalan shook his head and sighed. 'I thought you had kicked that habit?'

Risu said nothing and just shrugged. As he caught sight of the disappointment in Funni's face his head remained hunched between his shoulders.

'Is there something wrong?' Prevost had hopped over to where the squirrels were sitting. After all their exploring they had, in fact, came to rest under Orava's tree office.

'No, nothing, I'm ok' said Risu and he 'unhunched' himself.

'Hi Prevost' said Kalan, 'Voting over yet? How's Orava doing?'

'Everything is fine' said Prevost smoothly, 'still an hour or so to go until voting closes'

'Then Orava will be able to speak again?' said Funni, almost as if she cared.

'Why yes' said Prevost, 'but hopefully he won't be speaking anymore as a mere squirrel, but as our new leader'

'I bet that will sound nice' said Funni. Kalan leaned over and jabbed her slightly in the back of his ribs.

'Yes' said Prevost slyly, 'but if you will excuse me I have to attend to a few things' He nodded politely then ran up into the tree.

'Funni don't antagonize' whispered Kalan 'what happens if Orava actually wins?'

'I hope not' said Risu.

'Yeah, but only because you have probably bet on Orav' replied Funni acidly.

'Momonga actually' said Risu softly 'better odds'

'Momonga?' said Funni, 'Who is going to vote for that no-hoper?'

Risu lifted himself up and looked almost as if he was going to cry. 'He touched a chord with me,' he said almost pleadingly 'besides I bet a lot of other squirrels have ended up voting for him just to annoy those two smarmy brothers'

'He's got a point though Funni' Kalan said as he thought through Risu's reasoning. 'But I smell something else. I think Orava put that Momonga up to it for some reason'

'Why' asked Funni.

'I haven't a clue' replied Kalan, 'I don't know how politics here works, but I did see Prevost and Momonga looking at each other strangely at the debate. They are up to something'

'Why don't we go over to the main drey and find out?' suggested Risu.

'You just want to be the first to hear the result and find out if you've won' said Funni.

'Maybe,' shrugged Risu.

'Sure, let's go' said Kalan, 'Even we are talking about the result, so we may as well go there and get it over with'

Funni had no argument with this suggestion and so they set off to quench their growing curiosity.

'I suppose those crafty Chinese got you the same way they got me with that old sneaking up behind routine' Totti's deep voice broke easily through the darkness surrounding Tancredi.

'Yes. I should have been paying thems more attention' replied Tancredi.

'And you were probably calling out for me as well?'

'Yes I was'

'How many times have a told you!' Totti raised his voice, 'Don't go drawing attention to yourself. Tancredi, these Chinese devils are only interested in birds with pretty voices. You go singing off looking for me and someone's bound to hear'

'Why are they interested in us?' Another bird voice cried out, Tancredi thought it sounded like Frank.

'Are they going to eat us, serve us up plucked and fried and feed them to their kids?' Tancredi changed his mind as the other birds started to panic, it wasn't Frank the voice was too shaky.

'Shut up fool!' shouted Uncle Totti, 'If they got us for our voices, a fat lot of good it would be for them if they cook us!'

'So what's going to happen to us then smart guy?' said another nervous voice.

'Hey!' said Tancredi, 'That's my Uncle Totti and he knows what's what, so its best yous listen'

The various bird voices calmed down and once it was all silent, the deep voice of Uncle Totti boomed out into the blackness. 'What's going to happen to us is this. These Chinese guys beg, borrow or steal birds like us, then sell them to other humans. We are sort of like a lucky charm for them I think. Now if we act cool and chirp away to these guys we get bought by a family and..........' He paused to make sure it was still quiet and he had everyone's attention, 'if we are lucky and patient there will be some time when that family has to clean the cage, then we can escape. Whoosh! Outta the cage, outta the window and find our way back home. Easy. As long as we keep on chirping we'll be ok'

'What happens if we don't get lucky?' said another voice nervously.

'What do we chirp about?' called out another.

'Ah heck!' said Uncle Totti, 'Just hurl insults at 'em if you want. Talk about the weather, they don't understand. Just make sure you keep on talking 'cause you only get bought if you sing out for them'

'How do you know all this?' asked the shaky voice.

'Because' said Totti with a strong tone of growing frustration, 'Blast my tail if this isn't the second time those devious Orientals have grabbed me'

A door opened and Tancredi heard some humans come into the room, '*TURN THE LIGHT ON LETS SEE WHAT YOU'VE GOT*' and in an instant bright white light burnt into Tancredi's eyes.

There was a long moment of silence as Tancredi was trying to adjust his eyes, then Uncle Totti started hurling abuse at his captors.

'Let me outta here you thieving monsters, ya good for nothing crooks'

Uncle Totti kept this up until eventually all the others started to join in, Tancredi included. 'Hey you maggots, it stinks in this cage clean me out!'

'Hey big guy, over here! Let me out and I'll poop on your head'

'OI! Losers! Turn out that light and give me food!'

'LET ME OUTTA HEREEEEEEEE!'

'*AH THEY ALL SOUND LOVELY. WE'LL MAKE A GOOD PROFIT*'

You could feel the suspense and tension at the City Hall Park main drey long before you actually got anywhere near it. Despite each one of them pretending disinterest – as they mingled and chatted with the others waiting on the result – it was clear that even the Battery Parkers were racked with curiosity as to the outcome of the election. Each, however, had different reasons. Risu obviously had all that dried fruit riding on Momonga. He knew that even if he won he would never be able to carry it all with him to Columbus Park, but when you are addicted to the game you just don't worry about annoying little details like that. Funni had actually voted for Orav, since she viewed him as the lesser of two evils. Kalan just wanted to make sure that nobody found out that he hadn't voted.

He hadn't been able to bring himself to vote for anyone and now he was beginning to feel a little guilty that he had wasted his moment in the voting room. What if Orava won by one vote? He would be responsible. Then again, he thought, there was something about Orav that he didn't like, but then again surely either of the brothers would do a better job at leading than Momonga. Then again........., Kalan felt in his fur for the pistachio shell he had hidden there before leaving the voting rooms.

'Are you ok?' asked Funni as she saw him rubbing his stomach and looking very melancholy, 'They closed the voting room five minutes ago. I think they have started counting, we'll know soon'

'I feel a bit queasy' Kalan lied, 'I need to nip out for a bit of fresh air'

'Do you want I come with you?' said Funni concerned.

'No, no I'll be alright. I'll be back in a few minutes'

Kalan smiled as he gently pushed to one side a few of the other squirrels that were filling up the main hall of the drey waiting to be the first to hear the result. If they found out while counting that there was a vote missing and he had it? Better to get rid of the evidence Kalan thought. After a bit of gentle shoving he was able to make it to an exit. This one winded up and down and was much narrower than the main corridor he had used earlier to enter the drey. In his rush to get out of the drey Kalan just pushed on in any direction that would get him outside. He exited under a small tree near the Park Row sidewalk. Kalan ran up to the park railing and looked down onto the sidewalk.

'Best bet is to throw it in the road' he thought to himself as he jumped onto the concrete 'they'll find it in the park' As he raced across the sidewalk he thought he saw a squirrel's tail sticking out from a nearby trashcan. No matter, he had no time, he had to rid himself of that shell.

The sound of the traffic was fierce on the edge of the sidewalk. Kalan looked across the street and it was so wide that he couldn't even make out the other side through all the passing traffic. 'Perfect' he said to himself out loud as he carefully took the pistachio shell from his fur and placed it on the edge of the curb. He turned slightly sideways, and then gave the shell an almighty whack with his tail. The nutshell sailed through the air for about twenty feet, bounced a couple of times on the tarmac, and then was instantly crushed by a passing minivan. Kalan felt liberated and satisfied as he started to make his way back to the park. That tail was still there, hanging out from the top of the black trashcan, and Kalan's curiosity was back.

Whose tail was it? Was a squirrel trapped?

Kalan zigzagged his way over to the trashcan, but as he got closer he could hear voices coming from inside. Instead of jumping up inside Kalan snuck underneath and started to listen. Although the sounds coming from inside were muffled, the squirrel speaking at that moment was unmistakably Orav.

'So let's go through this one last time gentlemen. We will have 16 votes for Orava, a surprising 14 votes for Momonga and 10 undecided. This will leave me with an 8 vote margin and victory' Some other voices started to speak, but they were too soft and mumbled for Kalan to make out what hey were saying. Orav's reply to their questions was clear however,

'Of course. I've made all the necessary arrangements, just as last time. Now we really should be getting back...............'

Kalan felt something grip his tail tightly and pull him violently out into the open as Orav was speaking.

'Orav! ORAV! We've got a squirrel out here!'

The enormous squirrel who had pulled Kalan out from under the trashcan was now calling up into it. He nevertheless kept a strong hold on Kalan's tail which hurt Kalan the more he tried to struggle free.

'Let me go!' cried out Kalan

Orav and two other squirrels jumped quickly out from the trashcan and landed on the sidewalk. 'It's one of those foreigners' said the squirrel holding Kalan. 'He was under there, listening in'

Kalan watched as Orav looked around and saw the expression on his face change from shocked to worry to relaxed in the space of a few moments. Orav waved at the large squirrel to release Kalan from his grip. Free, Kalan made a large hop backwards and pulled his tail to his chest defensively. Looking harder at the three squirrels standing with Orav he now recognized them as the referees who had been in the voting room.

'Was there anyone else?' Orav asked the large squirrel who moved over and whispered something in Orav's ear. As Orav listened he nodded and stared at Kalan. 'Ok, you three get back before anyone starts getting suspicious' he said when the large squirrel had finished whispering.

'But what about this eavesdropper Orav?' asked one of the other referees.

'Leave him here with me, I'll deal with it. Tell my campaign committee that I will be waiting to know the results in my private quarters at the drey, but I'm not to be disturbed until then' He paused for a second, but never took his eyes off Kalan. 'Have a recount or two, take your time'

He waved the referees off and they obediently scurried back into the park.

'You're no better than that cheating brother of yours. I suppose deceit runs in the family' Kalan said bitterly, 'This whole election has been a farce. You've had it rigged all along'

Orav bowed his head slightly and nodded. 'It's true, you're right' he said, 'But you've got to understand what I do, I do in the best interests of every squirrel in this park'

'No way! Who are your trying to kid?' shouted Kalan, 'You've done it for your own best interests. All those squirrels believing that their vote was worth something, that it could make a difference. You lied to everyone, have you no morals?'

'Politics isn't about truth, good government has nothing to do with morality!' Orav raised his voice, 'It's about stability. It's about guarding the thin line that separates chaos from order.

'That's not true' said Kalan, 'squirrels can judge for themselves, we have more intelligence than that'

'Oh no?' replied Orav, 'Your average squirrel might think he knows what's going on around him, but you put him in a group with others and they quickly become an irrational pack. No squirrel society is more than three nuts away from anarchy. They all need a strong leadership and the stability it brings to keep their bellies full'

Kalan stood silently in front of Orav, his paws clenched together in anger at was he was hearing. Orav's tone calmed down a little. 'Democracy is a theoretical luxury promoted by well to do squirrels who have never gone a night without dinner. And you know that Kalan'

'What?' said Kalan irritated, 'What do you mean? You're not a leader, you're just a boss. I don't agree with you and your suppression of a squirrel's free will'

'I don't suppress free will Kalan, quite the opposite in fact. I provide the social stability it needs in which to flourish. Was your leader in Battery Park elected by popular will? NO. He was imposed upon society in a traditional manner and he knew his role was to maintain the status quo. The status quo Kalan. If it's working and everyone has their heads above water, why change it?'

'A repressive boss......' said Kalan, but Orav hadn't finished.

'You know the truth Kalan, deep down. That's why you threw your vote into the road' Kalan felt his stomach drop. Orav reached over and patted him in a fatherly manner on the back. 'I've been told that you and your interloping friends are leaving tomorrow with some rats. I trust you won't be creating any unnecessary chaos before you go' Orav waited a moment until Kalan turned and looked into his eyes. 'And I wish you the best of luck with your adventure' He waited again until two humans had finished walking past, then Orav ran quickly to the City Hall railings without looking back. As he ran back inside the drey he thought about what Kalan had called him, a boss. He kind of liked that, it had a certain ring to it. 'Boss Orav'.

Kalan just sat where he was, is mind in a haze, unable to think. Or maybe not wanting to think.

'Thanks for waiting everybody. I have the final results for this season's election. After three recounts we can confirm the votes cast as follows, Orava 16 votes, Orav 24 votes, Momonga 10 votes' The large referee continued to talk to the large crowd in the main drey hall even though many started cheering loudly before he could finish. 'With 10 undecided I declare Orav our leader for this season'

Funni and Risu were squashed up by one of the walls in the packed room. 'I'm sorry Risu' said Funni, 'Seems like you lost again. I hope you've learnt a lesson' To her surprise Risu didn't appear to be too upset.

'Ah well I didn't win big' he said, 'but I had a side bet on Momonga getting at least ten votes. It's not much but I'll get my stake back and maybe a little more'

He looked at Funni and smiled, 'Tomorrow we can eat dried fruit all day 'til it's time to hit the road with the rats'

The main room was beginning to empty out as the City Hall squirrels went off in different directions. Some to celebrate, some to commiserate but most just to sleep. Funni and Risu attached themselves to the end of a line of chanting Orav supporters who were heading above ground to give their good news to the rest of the park. 'We've got to find Kalan' said Funni and she and Risu exited the drey, 'he's been gone a while and he didn't look well when he left'

'I'll go check around the white building and also see if he went to visit the rats' Risu suggested. 'I'll meet you back at our tree hollow'

Funni agreed and sped off to look for Kalan near the fountain as Risu hopped over towards the man in the box. They needn't have bothered searching since Kalan was already sitting in the tree hollow with his back to the entrance staring at the dark wall inside. Having discovered the election was a sham had been bad enough, but weighing even heavier on Kalan's mind was his earlier discussion with 'boss' Orav. Most of Kalan's brain had rejected Orav's totalitarian reasoning and deception. However there was a tiny, but very vocal, part of Kalan's mind that actually agreed with Orav. Maybe squirrels need an unseen hand to guide them through life. Maybe every squirrel community is really just a few hops away from total anarchy. Maybe. Kalan began rocking himself backwards and forwards as he sat. Maybe he had been blessed with his independent strength of mind precisely because he had been born in such a stable society like Battery Park. A society built on deception and lies, how can that be a good society? The rest of Kalan's mind began a counter attack, but before it had a chance to launch another salvo it was interrupted by the arrival of Funni. 'Where have you been?' she said as she hopped into the hole and saw Kalan facing the wall. 'You've had us worried sick. Risu's still out looking for you!'

As Kalan turned, Funni's anger melted quickly into concern as she saw her friend's mental anguish.

'I......I' said Kalan stuttering nervously, 'I'm sorry I just......'

'Funni did you find him?' Risu's voice was calling out from the bottom of the tree. Funni stuck her head out of the mouth of the hollow.

'He's been here all the time!' she shouted down. Risu ran up and was as concerned as Funni with the strained expression on Kalan's face.

'What happened to you?'

Kalan took a deep breath and shook his body. He had already decided that it was best not to tell them what had happened until they were out of the park. Whereas he knew his friends would believe him, he knew no one else in the park would. 'I had a run in with a nasty animal' Kalan said eventually.

'Whoa!' said Risu, 'A cat?'

'No not a cat. But its ok nothing happened to me, just got a lot on my mind after it'

'What animal was it? Where?' said Risu with nervous excitement, but Kalan already had his head hung low.

Funni reached over and grabbed Risu's arm. 'Leave him be. He's tired and so I am. At least he's alright. Let's forget about it for tonight and get some rest. We'll talk tomorrow'

Kalan heard Funni and nodded to himself as he turned back to face the wall. This time however the arguing factions in his head were too tired to keep the debate going. Kalan curled up to sleep.

'Come on Risu, it must be really late' said Funni as she looked out through the hollow mouth at Uncle Totti's clock. Both hands were almost at twelve. The noise of Kalan gently snoring made her turn back into the hollow.

'Kalan's got the right idea. We will need all the sleep we can get before we leave this place. I'm sure he'll tell us what happened to him tomorrow'

Risu shrugged then swept the ground in front of him free of dust with his tail. He stretched his arms a little, and then settled down on the floor to sleep. As he drifted off his mind was racing with images of Kalan being chased by dark yellow eyed beasts. Funni also made herself comfortable and relaxed to let sleep come over her. While she was concerned for Kalan she felt overall quite content. She would have hated that Orava squirrel to have won the election. Orav was boring, but at least he seemed normal. Funni's last thought before she fell to sleep was happiness that her vote had helped maintain the status quo.

THE WHITE CAT

The day after the election passed without much event. Although Kalan still didn't want to talk about what had happened to him the night before, he did appear happier. The Battery Park squirrels spent the late morning making half hearted attempts to find Uncle Totti and Tancredi and passed the afternoon enjoying Risu's dried fruit winnings.

Kalan's mood improved throughout the day as their appointment with the rats drew closer. Barclay and Reade were expecting the squirrels at their hideout under the man in the box at midnight, so by early evening the Battery Parkers were already trying to get some sleep. It wasn't easy, they dozed only fitfully. Kalan kept waking up at the slightest sound, and every time he opened his eyes he saw that both Funni and Risu were doing the same.

Unable to sleep they decided to all make their way to the rat's den early. Barclay and Reade were not there when the squirrels arrived and they had to wait a few nervous hours until just before one in the morning when the rats finally showed up.

'Sorry we're late' said Barclay the moment he walked into the drey, 'but we've been out checking the route'

'I can see you guys are anxious to go' replied Reade noticing the nervous excitement on the squirrels faces, 'so we're ready to shoot'

After a few hasty goodbyes to the other rats, the squirrels were soon following Barclay and Reade down one of the long corridors that led out of the rat den. This one eventually opened out into a drain, and they moved along the wet metal surface until finally emerging out of a drain hole in the north of the park facing the Tweed Courthouse. As they climbed out of the drain they were met by a small welcoming committee.

'Just thought I would come and see you off' Orav was waiting outside flanked by two of his 'referees', 'And to wish you the best of luck in your quest'

'And to make sure that we actually leave' said Kalan dryly. Orav just smiled.

'Thanks Orav' said Risu

'Please, from now on call me 'boss'. I like all my close friends to call me that'

''Boss Orav'. It certainly rolls off the tongue' said Kalan.

'Come on guys we've got to be off' said Reade urgently pointing across Chambers Street, 'the road's clear'

'Yeah' replied Barclay, 'hurry up with the goodbyes and let's get outta here'

'Will you make sure to let Uncle Totti or Tancredi know where we've gone if they show up anytime?' said Kalan as Funni and Risu jumped onto the edge of the road with the rats.

'I will' said Orav, 'and you just make sure you keep our little secret'

Kalan made no reply and began to run towards the others.

'I'm not a monster Kalan' Orav shouted out after Kalan, 'I'm just a reality of life. Wise up and trust me, you know it makes sense'

Kalan looked back, but 'Boss Orav' was now a mere silhouette lit by the lights of the Tweed Courthouse.

'What did he say?' asked Funni as Kalan joined the others.

'Oh just goodbye' replied Kalan

'That was nice of him' said Risu, 'thoroughly decent chap'

Slowly at first, then gradually picking up speed as their confidence grew the squirrels ran along the edge of the sidewalk by the road. They followed the rats quickly across Chambers Street and down the left side of Center Street.

Kalan was impressed at how fast the rats moved, and how they were even more cautious than the squirrels. They froze at the slightest sound and were constantly stopping to sniff the air for danger. Keeping to the gutter they soon found themselves in Foley Square.

'We'll rest for a few moments in the slide' said Reade pointing to a strange looking black monument in the middle of the square.

'It's a great place to have fun and hide' added Barclay.

They all ran across the square and jumped into the base of 'The Triumph of Human Spirit'. This long tall black granite structure reached up into the sky, while another slab of rock curved downwards into the square.

'Watch this!' said Reade, and he scrambled up to the point where the curved and the straight parts of the monument meet. He sat down, feet forwards and pushed himself downwards. He slid quickly down the polished granite then launched himself into the sky as he came to the end of the curve.

'ARROOOOOO!' he squealed from the air.

Barclay laughed and went up to try for himself as Reade made his way back onto the base.

'Are you sure about this Reade?' Kalan said looking anxiously around the square, 'I mean we don't want to draw ourselves too much attention'

'It's normally full of skateboarders' said Reade as he looked around the square pleased, 'but tonight no one can see our action!'

As Barclay flew into the air Kalan looked up to see Risu climbing into the curve.

'Risu! Wait!' shouted Kalan, but Risu was already pushing himself downwards while sitting on his tail.

'Kalan, Funni, look at meeeeeeeeeeee!'

Risu soared into the air and stretched out his arms and tail. 'This must be what that lucky Tancredi feels everyday' he thought to himself as he fell down onto the square and landed on his hind legs.

'Come on Kalan, stop acting like Olmaxon with a headache. Give it a go' said Risu as he jumped back onto the monument and pushed Kalan playfully towards the black granite. Kalan looked up and saw Funni waving at him from the top of the slide. He blew his cheeks up then let the air out of them slowly.

'Ok,Ok' he shrugged and started to claw his way up. As he slid down the stone and launched himself into the air he felt a powerful rush of exhilarating energy. These rats, he thought, certainly know how to have fun.

The rats were also right about Foley Square at that time of night, it was completely empty. The five of them could enjoy the slide without worrying too much. After about half an hour, feeling a little tired but very invigorated, they all made their way down to the tiny Thomas Paine Park.

The squirrels found traveling with the rats very comforting because the rodents seemed to know exactly where they were headed. They also understood and used Kalan's system for crossing the road. Making use of the lights at the corner of Worth Street and Center Street, they crossed over in front of the Louis J Lefkowitz state office and ran into the small row of bushes that grew alongside the building. Running until they reached the end of these bushes, they turned into Baxter Street and ran across towards a children's playground.

'Welcome to Columbus Park' said Reade proudly as they ran through the wire mesh fence surrounding the playground.

'Wow!' said Risu, 'That didn't take long'

'When you know the way it's a lark' said Barclay with a look of false modesty.

'Now you guys stay here for a while, maybe get up that tree' said Reade indicating a large one that overlooked the sports court in the center of the park.

'We're going to find out if Vesey's here, we'll just look and see' said Barclay.

'We've got to play it safe now, we're in bad cat land'

'Stay safe 'cause things could start to get out of hand'

The two rats looked deadly serious as they rhymed.

'You mean Shokobaba?' asked Kalan as he remembered back to the tale Crosby and Jackson had told back in Battery Park. 'Does she live around here?'

'Yes it's her patch, but stick with us and you'll have nothing to fear' said Reade as he and his partner started to make their way to the Baxter Street entrance of the local rat den. Barclay turned around to the squirrels and pointed up to the tree that hung over a gray building that housed the park's washrooms.

'Let's go up the tree' said Kalan, 'we can see the park better from up there anyhow'

The view from the top didn't appeal much to the squirrels.

'Not much of a park is it?' said Risu as he looked down over the concrete sports ground that covered the most part of what he could see. There were a few sad looking trees with another stone building to the north of the park and the children's playground behind them, but that was about it.

'It might look better in the day' said Funni

'It doesn't matter' said Kalan, 'we won't be staying here for long anyway.

'The rats are back' said Risu as he watched three small shadows run towards the base of the tree.

(Rats are very skilled tree climbers and when sitting up high on the tops of Manhattan trees, as they often do, humans often fail to distinguish them from squirrels.)

Barclay and Reade quickly scaled up the trunk to join the three Battery Parkers. Their faces were very sullen. They had with them a third miserable looking rat with bloodshot eyes and a nasty scar on his cheek.

'This here is Vesey' said Reade, 'and things here have got very bad I'm sorry to say'

'He told us Shokobaba got his partner Bayard just the other day' Barclay put his arm round Vesey's shoulder as he spoke.

'Got?' Funni asked

Sitting behind Vesey, Reade made a silent but awful gesture as he moved his paw in a quick straight line across his throat.

'Don't you stay here' said Vesey in a frightened voice, 'come with us'

The squirrels looked at each other as the reality of what they were hearing slowly sunk in. No one spoke for a bit and neither Barclay nor Reade finished off Vesey's sentence, after all neither of them was his partner. His partner, thought Kalan remembering again the story told to him by Crosby and Jackson, was dead.

Vesey was visibly shaking as he sat between Reade and Barclay. Kalan decided to finish off his sentence in Ratspeak.

'Thanks for your concern Vesey' he said looking fondly at the disheveled rat 'but you don't have to make a fuss'

Vesey looked around nervously, 'She'll kill you, like she killed every squirrel that lived in this park, like she killed my friend'

Kalan could sense an air of rising panic in Funni and Risu.

'I'm sorry for Bayard' said Kalan trying to sound as calm as possible 'I really am, but we intend to pursue our quest to the end'

'Then you're doomed' shouted Vesey and getting hysterical he reached over to Kalan and gripped the fur on his chest tightly. 'You'll all end up as cat meat, a Shokobaba desert'

Reade and Barclay grabbed Vesey and pulled him off Kalan.

'Calm it down Vesey, you're going to give us all the frights' said Reade.

'You lot want to come?' Barclay spoke to the squirrels, 'We're taking him with us across Manhattan Bridge to Brooklyn Heights'

'Thanks but no' said Kalan finding himself shaking now, 'We have to be on our way to Tompkins Park'

'Is it on the way to Manhattan Bridge?' Risu asked also shaking.

'No it's not, and if you head up that way you are all berserk' wailed Vesey finishing off his own couplet badly, as single rats are often forced to do.

'No we're headed south east from here across East Broadway then down Market Street' Reade answered Risu ignoring Vesey.

'Tompkins is north east, through Shokobaba land. You manage that then it's no mean feat' added Barclay.

'You might make it though, as long as you travel during the day' said Reade as he gave the squirrels plan a little more thought.

'Yes and make sure you don't stay in one place for too long, make no delay' said Barclay

'They're wasting their time, before they get to Canal Street Shokobaba will have eaten them all' said Vesey

'If we move fast enough, we won't give her time to make a call' said Kalan politely finishing off the couplet for Vesey. He then turned to Reade, 'Just tell us which way to go and we will do the rest'

Despite their misgivings Barclay and Reade carefully explained the route to Tompkins to the squirrels. They would have to travel up Mulberry Street, cross Canal Street then take the first road to the left and follow it until they came to a children's playground. This playground was at the beginning of a long strip of land, which the rats called the SDR , it's official name being Sara Delano Roosevelt Parkway. This park had lots of trees that would take them half a mile or so up to a large road called Houston. Houston had to be crossed and followed east. Then they had to take the second large road to their left and this would eventually bring them out into Tompkins Park.

Now whereas Manhattan rats are practically born with a virtual map of New York City imprinted on their genetic structure, the same cannot be said of territorial squirrels. The rat's detailed route plan was way too much for Kalan to remember, but Funni came up with the solution.

'Let's divide it up. Each of us remembers one part of it'

It was the perfect solution. Kalan concentrated his memory on the route up to Hester Street, Funni the way to East Houston and Risu the last part on up to Tompkins Park. When the squirrels were sure of the trail to follow Barclay and Reade reminded them of the need to travel during the day. Shokobaba roamed free at night, but the thousands of people walking around Chinatown during the day should provide them with a cover and maybe even protection.

'You're so lucky you squirrels' said Reade, 'Humans if they see you will just oooh and sigh'

'Which is a very different reaction to what they do if they see us pass by' said Barclay lifting his paws in the air and making a scary face.

Vesey in the meantime had calmed down a little and softly wished Kalan and the others luck as he prepared to leave with Barclay and Reade.

'Don't trust anyone you three' he said, 'while two of you sleep one always stays awake' Wanting to explain his point better Vesey finished off his own rhyme again. 'One of you keeps an eye out for that cat, lest your life she'll take'

The squirrels waved goodbye as the rats made their way down the tree and disappeared into the children's playground.

'Bayard was the rat Bilka saved when he was here' said Risu as he tried to remember the rat's story from Battery Park.

'No that was Vesey' replied Funni who memory was more accurate.

'Oh' said Risu, 'we never got to ask him about that'

'I don't think it was the right time' said Kalan, 'It must have been terrible for him, we are going to have to be extra vigilant from now on'

'I don't know how I would cope if I lost one of you two' said Funni with a slight shudder.

'You won't' said Kalan firmly. He had no intention of letting fear get a grip on them.

'We'll do as the rats say, travel during daylight and make only the briefest of stops. With any luck we will be in Tompkins Park long before this Shokobaba knows we were ever here'

'I'm scared Kalan' said Funni softly

'So I am' replied Kalan, 'We all are, but we knew sooner or later we would run into a bit of danger'

'If Bilka made it' said Risu, 'then so can we!'

Kalan was relieved to find that Risu was putting on a brave face even though he could see the fear in his eyes.

'Let's rest up somewhere' said Kalan, 'The rats said that the part of Mulberry Street we have to take is over at the top of the park, so lets find somewhere up there'

The squirrels jumped from the tree onto the wire fencing that surrounded the sports ground. They scrambled along the top of it made their way around.

'What about over there on top of that building?' Risu suggested as they reached the other side.

'No' said Kalan judging the small amenities building in front of them to be too dangerous a spot to rest until first light, 'we'll be better off in one of the branches in that tree' he continued, while pointing to a tree which had branches hanging over the wire fence they were sitting on.

'There are more exits if we get an unwelcome visitor, and I don't know about you two' Kalan looked around the area as he spoke, 'but I certainly feel safer in a tree'

'Doesn't look too comfortable' shrugged Risu

'It'll do' said Funni giving Risu a shove in the direction of the tree, 'and I'll stay awake for a bit, you two make yourselves comfortable'

The squirrels climbed as high as they could and settled down in a large corner of one branch where it grew out from the main trunk.

Risu was right, it wasn't very comfortable, but they were feeling tired and each managed to find a position they could sleep in. Funni kept to her word and started to keep the first watch from further along the branch.

'You wake me up when you need to rest' said Kalan 'just an hour or two, remember you need to run with us tomorrow as well'

'Stop worrying I know' replied Funni without turning round. She was too busy looking out over Columbus Park and imagining where a cat might come from and, indeed, what it would look like.

Shokobaba was considered a very good looking cat. She was a Persian cross-breed with pure long glossy white fur. Her most unique feature was her eyes. One eye was a bright sapphire blue, the other was a deep dark brown. 'One eye sees the good in someone, the other eye sees the bad' she used to say.

Anyone else with this fortunate ability looking at Shokobaba herself would see a heart as black as her fur was white. This was a cat who reveled in the misery of others.

'I can only really enjoy life when I am taking it from others' was another of her infamous maxims.

She lived in a ground floor apartment on Hester Street. This small two room abode was directly behind her human owner's small jewelry store. Recently some human reporters had come to her home to take her photo and interview her owner because her evil had achieved some acclaim, in human circles at least.

Humans in general, and New Yorkers in particular, are always happy to hear of anyone who helps rid the city of rats and Shokobaba had recently developed a real talent for it. Over the past year she had cold bloodedly ended the lives of 99 poor souls, and she was very meticulous in keeping records – wounding never counts.

At first it had been just mice and the odd rat but as her skills improved she moved onto pigeons, sparrows and squirrels. Like most folks addicted to something her tastes changed and became more finely tuned. Just whacking the life out of a tiny mouse didn't give her a buzz anymore. Therefore, ironically, many of the animals who would have been her victims early on in her nasty career were safer now than a year ago.

What she lusted after now was a kill that gave her a challenge that tested her wits, her skills. Getting one of those rats down at Columbus Park the other day had been most satisfying. They had eluded her for far too long. Bayard had been a worthy 99th victim, but she wanted something really special to mark her 100th kill. She wanted that fat, ugly squirrel who had almost bitten off her tail in Columbus Park. A familiar dull pain in her tail started to throb as she remembered the event.

Her informants had told that he was headed uptown, apparently to Tompkins Square Park. Shokobaba was seriously thinking about making a trip up there to celebrate her 100th. It was a long way, but just the idea gave her an adrenalin rush. It would be worth it.

A tiny scratching sound caught Shokobaba's attention. She was curled up on the couch, her owner fast asleep and snoring next to her. Ms Soo Lee had dozed off in front of the TV again, the remote still in her hand. Shokobaba looked in disgust at her owner and then at the TV, and regretted that she had never learned how to turn that infernal machine off. Despite the endless repeating of the same news story on NY1 about incoming snowstorms Shokobaba could still clearly make out any unusual sound in the room.

The scratching seemed to be coming from the corner of the room behind the couch. Shokobaba stretched out her body, her legs, her paws and then, one by one in quick succession, her claws.

She jumped onto the back of the couch and then leaped silently into the corner. The scratching sound stopped the moment she landed.

'This had better be good Mirango, I've warned you once before about coming into my home' said Shokobaba looking down to where the wall met the dirty red floor carpet.

A tiny voice cleared its throat before starting to speak with a tremble. 'I......just got back........from.....erm......Columbus.........some rats came and they...they took Vesey with them'

Shokobaba flicked her claws lazily on the wall. This action only succeeded in making the voice behind the wall even more nervous.

'But.........Shoko that's not ......that's not all of it...The rats arrived with squirrels and......well....the rats left but the squirrels...sort of like still.........well they are still there. Three of them Shoko.........three'

Shokobaba stopped flicking her claws and put her face down to the tiny gap at the bottom of the wall. 'Come on out Mirango and tell me more' she purred sweetly into the opening. There was no immediate reply from the other side.

'Mirangoooooooooo...........' said Shokobaba playfully.

'You'll...... you'll hurt me again.........I've told you all I know...don't want......need to get hurt again' said the voice, so tiny now that even Shokobaba had to strain her hearing to catch the words.

'It's very true Mirango. I may well hurt you when you come out, but if you don't come out then I can promise you will be a dead mouse long before the day is out' Although Shokobaba's words were full of menace, the tone of her voice was still very playful.

Mirango didn't reply, but the sounds of movement coming from behind the wall told Shokobaba that he was coming out. At first a small paw stuck out of the gap onto the red carpet, then a nose and whiskers and eventually Mirango squeezed himself out and into Shokobaba's presence.

Instantly Shokobaba's left paw swished out and grabbed Mirango's tail. She whipped him over against the wall then held him, upside down and struggling, in front of her face.

'Mirango, Mirango, Mirango' sneered Shokobaba as the mouse stopped struggling. He knew the more he struggled the more it would hurt. 'I've told you before not to come around here. What would my dear human think if she saw your sorry face running around the house? She would think that I wasn't doing my job wouldn't she?'

Mirango looked into Shokobaba's face and found it hard to focus. Partly because of the piercing blue eye and strangely comforting brown one, but mostly because of the pain.

'If she saw you here tonight' continued Shokobaba, 'I'd have to kill you, your family and then all of your friends just to calm the old girl down'

'But Shoko…' whispered Mirango, 'I heard them talking…………they're going to Tompkins…….I heard them…… they are looking for the same squirrel you are……..they're….they're his friends..'

Shokobaba released her grip on the terrified mouse and he fell head first to the floor. The moment Mirango pulled himself together his instincts started screaming at him to run, but his brain kept them in line. Running from Shokobaba only made things worse.

'His friends you say?' said Shokobaba. Mirango nodded, trying to avoid catching the cat's eye. 'Well in the light of this interesting information I suppose I can overlook this intrusion at my home this once. You go and organize those reprobate friends of yours and make sure that if one of these squirrels so much as scratches an ear, I get to know about it'

Mirango nodded again but kept his eyes firmly fixed on the red carpet.

'In fact I want you to sort out a meet with everybody at the parking lot within an hour'

Shokobaba turned away her mind ablaze with ideas. Mirango realized that this was his invitation to leave without any further pain and he quickly disappeared under the wall. 'Hmmm' The cat murmured to herself as she walked back in front of the couch and sat with her back to her still snoring owner. NY1 was giving yet another report on the imminent snow blizzard and the bright white light from the screen lit up Shokobaba's smiling face.

'Time for a major charm offensive with three new friends'

This thought made her smile even wider and now her teeth showed and glimmered in the light from the TV.

Mirango was one of those mice who Shokobaba a year ago would have thought nothing of smacking the existence out of. Nowadays things were different and the mouse worked as an informer for the white cat. It was a humiliating experience for him, he had lost most of his friends and was in general disliked and mistrusted by his peers. Mirango reasoned that his choices had kept him alive, and at the end of a mouse's day, that was surely the most important thing.

It didn't take Mirango long to organize the other informers and hangers on at the Hester Street parking lot. Although nobody had much respect for Mirango, or each other for that matter, they knew the mouse spoke for Shokobaba and nobody wanted to get on the wrong side of her. The right side was bad enough.

The usual meeting place was under the parking lot owner's car. A 1970's Oldsmobile which he never drove, but lovingly cleaned every week. The lot was next to the China Overseas mission just across the road from Shokobaba's jewelry shop.

It was nearly dawn as everyone gathered underneath the car waiting for Shokobaba. There was another cat, a small but stocky tabby whose owner called 'Killer' but everyone else knew as Wesley. There were several mice including Mirango and two very tattered looking pigeons, Philippe and Henri. Henri had a clubbed foot, the result of a misunderstanding with Shokobaba a few months back. In fact most of this pitiful bunch waiting under the car carried physical or mental scars given to them by Shokobaba. Even Wesley had part of his left ear missing.

'I notice that we seem to be missing someone' Shokobaba's arrival took everyone by surprise. Mirango saw the cat's blue eye glint menacingly as it caught the light from one of the lamps illuminating the lot. He and everyone else shuffled a few steps backward as the cat walked slowly under the car.

'Eloise is down at Columbus' said Henri, 'She's keeping an eye on those squirrels. I thought you'd want at least one of us down there'

Shokobaba stretched her front legs in front of her and scratched the tarmac with her claws.

'Good thinking Henri' she purred gently, 'and just to think I thought you pigeons were stupid'

Henri relaxed a little and turned to Philippe with a look of relief, but the moment he took his gaze away from Shokobaba she struck out and punched him hard in the chest with a clenched up paw. He fell back winded against one of the car tires. Philippe and the others all stepped back and watched in silence. They made no more movement and didn't want to get involved as they knew Shokobaba was an impossible cat, she was also violently insane and thus beyond reasoning with. They watched in fear each one praying that they would not be next.

Henri tried to grasp for breath as Shokobaba moved closer. Through dazed eyes he could see her walking towards him, but the blow had taken his breath away and he had no energy to move. Shokobaba stretched out her clawed paw and gripped Henri's clubbed foot tightly. Henri had no air in his lungs with which to cry in pain.

'But' Shokobaba spoke in an intimidating whisper, 'when I say 'everybody' must attend a meeting you do understand that I mean E V E R Y B O D Y!'

Shokobaba raised her other paw in the air ready to strike another more lethal blow, but stopped and left it hanging there in mid air. She looked at Henri and in her minds eye saw a quivering pathetic face and the number 100. The cat retracted her claws from Henri's foot and with her other paw she patted him gently on the head.

'INITIATIVE!' she shouted and jumped around to face the others, 'If any of you showed some of Henri's initiative we'd get a hell of a lot more done around here' She strutted back towards the center and licked her paw. 'Now Mirango, tell me what you know so far. Let's have a recap'

Mirango spoke quickly repeating more or less what he had told Shokobaba back at her digs. Three squirrels had arrived with two rats. The two rats had taken Vesey and gone east while the squirrels had stayed behind and were currently sleeping in a tree near the corner of Columbus, Bayard Street and Mulberry Street. Mirango had heard them talking about their plan to go to Tompkins Park to find their friend.

Each time the mouse finished a sentence he caught Shokobaba's blue eye staring at him viscously wanting more information. By the end he was desperately padding what little information he had left with meaningless details.

'So I left them as they were sleeping to come and tell you Shoko'

Shokobaba stared at Mirango, but said nothing.

'There's three of them. Quite small'

Shokobaba rubbed her nose with her paw.

'Mulberry Street was quiet.................might rain later I think' Every time Mirango stopped the silence was so oppressive he had to break it himself.

'Canal Street was busy mind you...............took me a while to cross it...................nearly fell down a.........'

'Shut up' said Shokobaba eventually. 'Shut up all of you and listen to me. I want to know everything about these squirrels, where they came from, how they got friendly with the rats. I want to know how they intend to cross Chinatown. I want to know what they have heard about me'

'Why don't we just go and get 'em now Shoko?' said Wesley casually. Although certainly weary of Shokobaba, he was the only animal under the olds mobile who wasn't petrified into silent fear.

'Because Wesley, you fool, I don't want to kill them' said Shokobaba, 'At least not yet'

The first light at Columbus Park brought several dozen seagulls into the center sports court. Risu, who had been reluctantly woken by Kalan to take over the final watch, looked at them as they waddled around the court floor. He gazed at them fondly as they reminded him of Battery Park. He thought of running down and having a chat with them. Maybe they had flown up from Battery Park, or were on their way there. Seagulls were certainly a lot friendlier than pigeons, just much more difficult to understand.

Risu was just about to run down the tree when he remembered that he couldn't. The cat. He had to keep a lookout for a cat. A nasty white cat that had murdered Vesey's partner and whose unseen presence from now on was going to dictate how the squirrels would sleep, eat and travel. Rather than fear the cat Risu found himself simply despising it for the inconvenience it was beginning to cause.

At the same time at this border of Chinatown the humans were beginning to become active as well. Vans started to arrive and unload fish at the shops on Mulberry Street. Some old humans started to walk into the center court and they frightened the seagulls away, others started having very animated conversations on the benches near the amenities building. All this general activity eventually woke both Funni and Kalan.

'No cats to report' said Risu cheerily as he saw his friends stretching, 'Just a few old people, a bunch of seagulls and a weird pigeon who hasn't moved from that roof all morning'

Funni and Kalan both turned and strained the sleep out of their eyes to look at the park building on the edge of Bayard Street and they saw the solitary pigeon Risu was talking about. The moment the pigeon saw all three squirrels looking in her direction she fluttered her wings and flew off.

'That's odd' said Kalan, 'Was it one of those you met at Sunda's?' Kalan asked turning to Funni. She shook her head.

'No' she said firmly, 'but I don't like it here. If you two are ready to go then so am I'

Kalan looked at Risu who shrugged. 'I'm as ready as I'm ever going to be' he said 'if you remember the first part of the route let's go'

The route to Tompkins Square Park, as detailed by Barclay and Reade, was quite long and complicated. After dividing it into three easier to remember parts the squirrels had repeated their section of the route over and over in their heads. Kalan repeated the first part, which was his.

'We go up this way,' he said waving his tail in the direction of Mulberry Street 'carrying on up it crossing over another big road. Then we take the first road that leads off the left and continue down it crossing another four until we come to one that brings us to a children's playground' He turned and smiled at Funni, 'Then it's your turn'

'Well let's go before I forget my bit' she replied, 'besides this place gives me the creeps'

Looking back around Columbus Park Kalan couldn't help but agree with Funni, since they had arrived he had had the sensation that they were being watched.

'Hello squirrels' said a tiny voice from bellow. All three Battery Parkers looked down to see two nervous, ragged looking mice smiling up at them.

'You're just so beautiful aren't you?'

Shokobaba despised her owner, she also hated being stroked. Ms Soo Lee wore lots of large heavy gold rings and these scratched annoyingly on Shokobaba's scalp. 'Good morning my baby diva cat'

Shokobaba had a lot to do today and had no intention of sitting around like an ornament in the front window of Ms Soo Lee's shop.

'You keep your mommy company today?' said Ms Soo Lee, 'Everybody loves to see mommy's favorite pussycat' Soo Lee lovingly nuzzled her nose in Shokobaba's face as she spoke. The white cat seized her chance and spat out a violent cough in her owner's face. 'Oh Shoko, Shoko what's wrong baby?'

Shokobaba arched her back and threatened to vomit something as she continued with her furball act.

'Don't throw up here, come on outside baby' Ms Soo Lee picked up the retching cat and hurried to the front of the shop. Holding Shokobaba under one arm she opened the door with the other and put the cat down on the sidewalk. The moment Shokobaba's feet touched the ground she stopped coughing and strolled casually down Hester Street. 'Now you cough up that furball darling and you come back to mommy when you done' Shokobaba didn't turn around, but ran into a side alley.

Her owner disgusted her, but at least old Ms Soo Lee was as easy to manage as all the other pathetic creatures that populated her life. At the end of the alley leaning against the last rung of a fire escape Shokobaba saw one of them, Wesley the tabby. 'Why am I surrounded by pathetic losers and mind dumbingly stupid animals like my owner and you Wesley?' Shokobaba said with disdain as she arrived under the fire escape.

Wesley had long since stopped worrying about whether Shokobaba liked him or not. 'You killed anyone interesting' he said without batting an eyelid.

'Yes and look where my supremacy has left me' said Shokobaba 'awash in a sea of fools, living with an ugly hag of an owner who just has to look at me to make my every hair prickle with contempt'

'Well now you are all wised up and everything, why don't you change how you go about things a bit?'

Shokobaba moved her face into Wesley's. 'You mean kill the fools and let the interesting folk live?' Shokobaba growled as she spoke. Wesley gulped, 'Because if I do that Wesley, believe me you will be the first to know about it'

To Wesley's relief the sound of a pigeon flapping overhead grabbed Shokobaba's attention. She pushed Wesley out of her face and looked up as the pigeon came down to them. The bird made sure, however, to land just out of reach.

'Ah Eloise, Mon Cherie' said Shokobaba, 'what news from Columbus?' Eloise spoke quickly choosing her words carefully. 'Mirango and Dusi have made contact and are traveling with them now'

'Traveling?' said Shokobaba shaking her head, 'but it's morning. Where are they going with every human in Chinatown on the streets?'

'When I left they were moving up towards Canal Street running under the parked cars on Mulberry'

Shokobaba couldn't believe what she was hearing. Squirrels running across Chinatown in broad daylight? With two mice? They'd be a screaming fit if anyone spots them. 'Where are they headed?' she said slowly to the pigeon.

'I don't know. Henri is following them now. I just came to let you know they had left Columbus' Shokobaba paused and looked down the alley onto Hester Street. Constant streams of people were walking past as Chinatown was well into the start of another busy day.

'Make sure they come past here' said Shokobaba looking back at Eloise, 'you tell Mirango and Dusi to make sure of it. I don't care where their final destination is, you make sure they pass by here. This alley'

Shokobaba slammed her paw on the ground. Eloise didn't move.

'Anything else?' the pigeon asked bravely.

'GO NOW!' screamed Shokobaba and jumped towards Eloise. The pigeon shot off up into the air and flew out of the alley.

'If the humans see them they might not even make it this far' said Wesley.

'Oh I think they will' said Shokobaba 'and I intend to surprise them with your help. It's time for you to prove me wrong about how stupid you are'

By the time Eloise caught up with Henri the squirrels were hiding under a white van on the corner of Mulberry and Canal Street. Mirango and Dusi were with them.

'They've done this before' he said as Eloise perched herself beside him on a window ledge of the Chinese Amalgamated Bank that overlooked Chinatown's main drag. 'They're quick and they know how to hide from sight. It's only taken them ten minutes to get this far. I'm really wondering how they plan on crossing Canal Street'

Eloise looked down at the van, but couldn't make out any movement from underneath, 'And Mirango and Dusi? The cat has given me instructions' she asked

'Oh those two are terrified' laughed Henri, 'guess they didn't expect to be running through Chinatown this morning'

Mirango and Dusi were indeed scared stiff. Mice are considered to be almost at the same low level of social acceptability as rats in New York, and running around the busiest part of downtown during the day was tantamount to playing Russian roulette. However this fear was nothing to the one they would have if they didn't do as the white cat had asked. That would be like playing Russian roulette but with six bullets in the barrel.

Funni moved over to the mice who were huddled together near the rear left tire. 'Are you two ok? You don't have to run around with us, we appreciate the help, but I'm sure we can manage. There's no point you two risk being seen'

'No no no no no no' squeaked Mirango trying to sound as confident as he could, 'we insist because we..............we......we......' he began to stutter as he looked behind the car at the pigeon that had started to strut about near the gutter.

Funni looked as well and tutted in disgust. 'It's just a pigeon, I'll shoo it away for you'

'No no it's ok I ......erm' Mirango scratched his head as he thought, 'I know this pigeon'

Funni tilted her head to one side in curiosity.

'I'll erm... just um... go see what she wants' said Mirango as he backed away from Funni towards the edge of the car.

Funni then felt Risu's tail tap her on the shoulder.

'Kalan's worked it out Funni. It's a really busy road but we......'

Funni put her paw over Risu's mouth.

'Sssshh' she said as she strained her ears to try and pick up some of the conversation between Mirango and the pigeon. The other mouse, Dusi, just looked blankly at the squirrels with a very unconvincing smile.

Funni was able to pick up a couple of words.

'They're going that way anyhow.........no way.......oh....oh.......crazy.......'

She and Risu then watched as the pigeon flew off and Mirango ran back under the van.

'What was all that about' she said as Mirango sat down next to the still smiling Dusi, 'I didn't know mice and pigeons were friends'

'We're all friends here in Chinatown' said Mirango, 'We all look out for each other. It's a dangerous place, that's why we want to accompany you through it'

At the other end of the van Kalan was still concentrating on how to cross Canal Street. It was very wide with traffic and people passing by in both directions almost non-stop. There was also the fact that the traffic signal on the corner of Mulberry Street stayed green for only a very short time and when it did literary hundreds of people used it walking both ways. A few moments before Kalan had told Risu he had worked out how to cross and not be seen, but the more he looked the busier things seemed to be getting.

'The mice want to come with us' Funni had come over to the front of the van.

'Uh huh' said Kalan without looking around. He was busy concentrating on how fast the cars were coming down Canal Street from Confucius Plaza. Too fast.

'There's something about them that's not right' Funni carried on, 'One of them was talking to a pigeon and I'm sure it was the same bird that Risu saw earlier on the roof'

Kalan sighed and turned to Funni. He glanced over her shoulder and saw Risu still talking to the mice at the far end of the van. 'Relax Funni, they're only mice for goodness sake. It's very brave of them to put themselves at risk just to help out a bunch of strangers. What do you think they are planning?' Kalan gave a little laugh 'Luring us down into the sewer to be eaten by a gigantic two headed dog?'

'No Kalan, it's just.........I don't know I have a feeling' said Funni a little sheepishly.

'Excuse me Mr. Kalan' Dusi had scurried over and was sitting just behind Funni.

'Hello' smiled Kalan. A quick glance over Dusi's head saw that Risu was still chatting to the other mouse.

'Mr. Kalan' said Dusi, 'Me and Mirango think it's impossible to cross Canal Street during the day' As Dusi spoke Kalan caught himself nodding in total agreement. 'So we want to show you a better way to cross using the underground sewer'

Kalan's stomach almost popped and he quickly looked at Funni his eyes wide open. Funni put her hands on her hips.

'Gigantic dog eh?' she said.

If it hadn't been for Mr. Tang the squirrels would probably have stayed under his van all day. Kalan hadn't wanted to admit to the mice, his friends or even himself that he didn't trust Mirango and Dusi. He also knew that crossing Canal

Street unseen or unhurt was near impossible, yet he was averse to the idea of going underground with the mice. Mr. Tang made making a decision that much easier.

The middle aged Chinese delivery man jumped into his van and started the engine. He glanced at his order chart and bemoaned to himself the fact that he would never find as good a parking space like this on Orchard Street. Underneath his van panic broke out. Risu had been sitting close to the exhaust as it started up, vibrating and spluttering foul smelling gases into the air. The surprise had thrown him off balance and into Funni's arms.

'What the?!...' he shouted as Funni pushed him off her 'This van, it's alive!'

'Squirrels, squirrels! Hurry this van is leaving and we will be exposed!' Mirango squeaked out loudly, 'We can use this drain to get into the sewer' The mouse ran over to the drain cover just as Dusi dropped down into it.

Kalan looked out from under the van for a place to bolt to, but all he saw was a forest of moving legs on Mulberry Street. The front wheels of the van started to turn to the right, and the vehicle itself began to move backwards.

'Hurry!' shouted Mirango 'There's no time!'

Kalan saw that both Risu and Funni were both frozen with indecision. 'Alright dogs or no dogs...COME ON!' he shouted out above the drone of the engine and dived headfirst down the drain.

Risu and Mirango quickly followed, but it took a sharp blast from Mr. Tang's claxon to convince Funni.

'Come on let me out already!' shouted Mr. Tang to the driver of a black SUV while leaning out of his window and pressing down hard on his claxon 'I got work to do guy!' The SUV reluctantly let Mr. Tang out into the road as Funni's tail disappeared down into the drain.

'Erg! Its wet!' was Funni's first impression as she fell into the drain. This was almost instantly replaced with a 'My god the smell!'

The stench of rotting fish and food was overpowering to the squirrels sensitive noses. Funni had to cover her mouth with her tail to stop herself from retching. 'It takes a little getting used to' said Mirango, 'but follow us and we will be out and on the other side of Canal Street in a few minutes'

Funni glanced nervously at Kalan, who lent over and whispered, 'No dog could live down here in this smell' Reluctantly, but nonetheless keeping a safe distance behind the mice, the squirrels followed Mirango and Dusi along the sewer drain.

'Keep up!' shouted Mirango looking back over his shoulder, 'stick to the sides so as you won't get wet'

This was advice the squirrels didn't need. They were already gripping desperately to the sides of the drain as they moved along. The idea of falling in the gooey liquid filth that ran through the center of the sewer worried them as much as the prospect of being ambushed by a two-headed dog.

Despite Funni's misgivings, there was no dog or ambush. The mice and the squirrels traveled along a couple of drains that vibrated with the weight of the moving traffic above them without incident. Within minutes Mirango was already sticking his tiny head out from the top of another drain hole. 'We'll have to run a few yards before we have any cover' he squeaked down to the others.

Kalan pushed past Risu and Dusi to join Mirango looking out onto the busy street. He saw that they had indeed crossed that impossibly busy road and were now on the north east corner of Mulberry Street and Canal Street. The nearest cover was a blue Ford parked about ten yards further up. Kalan could see that there were less people walking about, but still far too many for all five of them to run around unseen. 'Let's do this one at a time' he said.

Kalan as usual went first and one by one squirrels and mice followed. As they regrouped under cover of the Ford the squirrels found that this part of Mulberry Street smelt and sounded completely different from that just a few hundred feet across Canal Street.

The Battery Parkers had entered into what remained of downtown's 'Little Italy', an island of surreal Italian restaurants and bars surrounded by an encroaching Chinatown. They didn't stay around for long to take in the sights. In fact by the time they had turned right into Hester Street and crossed over Mott Street the squirrels found themselves already back in Chinatown and unknown to them, little more than a block away from Shokobaba.

Mirango and Dusi couldn't believe their luck up to this point. Eloise the pigeon had told Mirango to make sure the squirrels passed into Shokobaba's alley, and up to now the mice hadn't had to manipulate or deceive the Battery Parkers since the route they themselves had decided on would take them past it. The only problem that now presented itself to Mirango was that the white cat's alley was on the opposite side of Hester Street. As the group reached the corner of Hester Street and Elizabeth Street Mirango knew he had to think of something.

The five of them had been running along Hester Street using the abundant parked cars as cover. They were now sitting under another large delivery van parked near the corner with Elizabeth Street.

As Kalan and the other two squirrels looked out across Elizabeth wondering how best to cross it Mirango pulled Dusi to one side, out of earshot of the squirrels. 'We've got to make them cross over to the other side if we're going to make it to that alley'

'Do we have to Mirango?' Dusi whispered back, 'They are nice folk, you know what's going to happen to them in that alley'

'And you know what will happen to us if we don't deliver them' replied Mirango coldly.

'Let's run off with them' said Dusi, 'I can't go through with this. I've enough guilt already without having to add three squirrels to it Mirango'

Mirango moved his head closer to Dusi's ear.

'You fool!' the tone of his whisper becoming a little aggressive 'you think it's that easy? You really think Shoko won't hunt us down? That evil monster won't give up. Ever'

'I'll run. I can hide, bring her on' Dusi was beginning to raise his voice.

'Keep it together Dusi' Mirango put his paw on Dusi's shoulder and pushed down hard, 'that cat will come after you alright, but only after she's killed me and everyone else you leave behind'

Dusi looked at Mirango in defeat, then started to twitch his whiskers and opened his eyes wider looking over Mirango's shoulder.

'Are you two alright?' asked Risu who had made his way over to see if they were ready to cross the road.

Mirango whirled around to give Risu an almost frightening grin. 'Oh yes, yes, yes' he said through teeth gritted into a smile 'we were just coming over to tell you. It's just that the car park you see over on the other side is full of cats'

'Really?' said Risu his ears pricking up.

'Yes, yes' replied Mirango, 'In fact myself and Dusi were just talking about it. We think it's much better if we travel on the other side of Hester Street'

'Hey Kalan!' Risu turned and shouted across to the other two squirrels. 'The mice say that the car park you want to run through is cat city!'

Kalan and Funni hopped over and looked inquisitively at Risu and the two mice. Dusi hung is head, while Mirango kept up his grin.

'Yes Mr. Kalan it's full of cats. In fact this whole part of Chinatown is crawling with predatory felines'

'And Shokobaba?' said Funni.

Dusi looked up, 'You know her?' he asked quietly.

Mirango, unseen by the squirrels, moved his paw behind his back, grabbed Dusi's tail and squeezed hard. As Dusi grimaced in pain, Mirango rose his voice a notch and continued,

'Oh yes, her as well. In fact I suggest we go and visit my cousin Borut. He lives in an alley just up on the left there. He can tell us the safest way through this part of town 'cause he'll know the whereabouts of all the cats today'

The squirrels looked at each other.

'In fact' Mirango continued, 'Dusi was just suggesting that he runs on ahead to let my cousin know we are coming'

Kalan glanced back at the mice, then at Risu who shrugged his agreement. He then turned to Funni who, although she still felt a little uneasy with the mice even after the safe passage under Canal Street, didn't want to come across as being too paranoid.

'Yeah ok' she said thinking that it was time to give the mice the benefit of the doubt.

'Ok Mirango' said Kalan, 'let's do it your way'

Mirango pushed at Dusi, 'Go on then' he said, 'run and tell Borut we are on our way'

Without picking his eyes up from the ground Dusi ran back along the edge of the road and sidewalk until he came to the first drain hole, then jumped down inside.

'We're staying above ground right?' said Funni as she watched Dusi disappear, her mistrust of the mice beginning to surface again slightly.

'Of course' said Kalan, 'as long as we've got all these cars to hide under we're ok' He then turned to Mirango, 'So where's this alley then?'

Dusi knew where the alley was, and for a few minutes he sat in the drain arguing with himself whether to go there or not. As usual in the end his fear of Shokobaba was too great and he resigned himself to getting the whole thing over and done with as soon as possible. It didn't take him long to negotiate the labyrinth of drains that led to the one that brought him out almost next to the entrance to the alley. He popped his head out for a few seconds, saw no one was coming, and then ran quickly over the sidewalk and along the edge of the alley wall. The alley seemed empty to Dusi. He sniffed around and felt the air with his whiskers, but the alley was too full of conflicting odors for Dusi to make out Shokobaba's scent.

'Looking for me?'

The mouse heard the familiar menacing but smooth tone of Shokobaba's voice. He spun around but still couldn't make out where it had come from. 'Shoko?' he said shivering with fear.

The white cat pounced down onto the mouse from where she had been hiding a couple of rungs up the fire escape ladder. With one paw she pushed Dusi head first into the ground. 'What are you doing here? Where are Mirango and those squirrels?'

Dusi picked his face up from the ground but found he couldn't move the rest of his body under Shokobaba's weight. He could however see the tabby cat Wesley moving slowly towards him.

'Shoko' squeaked Dusi, 'Shoko, they're coming. They'll be here in moments. Mirango sent me on ahead to tell you to get ready'

Shokobaba lifted her paw from Dusi's back, and then flicked the mouse roughly across the ground in the direction of Wesley. 'Here you go Wesley, we'll use him instead of the other mouse'

Wesley nodded and grabbed Dusi's tail

'You know what to do' said Shokobaba, then jumped back up to her hiding place to wait for the squirrels' arrival.

'What's going to happen to me Wesley?' stuttered Dusi.

'Just act scared and keep your mouth shut when those squirrels get here' said Wesley. Dusi had no problem with this. Being terrified was something he didn't have to act at being, he just hoped he wouldn't have to feel like this for long.

Dusi's prayer was answered. As Shokobaba looked down the alley onto Hester Street she saw Mirango turn the corner and run down into the alley. He was followed by three small but fast moving squirrels. Shokobaba smiled to herself as she saw all four stop halfway the moment they caught sight of Wesley. The tabby had seen them arrive out of the corner of his eye and began to hiss loudly at Dusi. He lifted the trembling mouse by his tail and shook him from side to side.

Shokobaba watched the squirrels' reactions intently. One of them seemed to be getting ready to try and help Dusi, but Mirango was trying to hold him back. With a grand scream Shokobaba jumped down next to Wesley and smacked him hard in the face. The tabby let go of Dusi who fell to the ground. Shokobaba wailed at Wesley as she struck him hard again, he had not expected such a realistic attack. Shokobaba then kicked Dusi with her hind leg in the direction of Mirango and the squirrels. 'Run friend' she said loudly.

Dusi, although in a state of scared confusion, picked himself up and hurried down the alley to Mirango and the others.

'What the??' Mirango said as his terrified friend got himself over to him and a safe distance away from the fighting cats.

'Are you ok?' said Funni and she pushed past Mirango and caressed the shaking Dusi with her tail.

'What is going on?' Kalan said as he watched Wesley cry out in pain and run away, his face bleeding profusely.

Mirango, as he too watched the scene unfold with eyes wide open, gave an honest answer. 'I have no idea'

Shokobaba turned to face the squirrels and sensed them ready to run, so she didn't move any closer. 'Are you ok Dusi?' she called out in a sweet yet concerned voice, 'Dusi?'

Dusi stuck his head out from under Funni's tail and shouted that he was fine. He then hid himself back behind the tail.

'That's a relief' Shokobaba called back down the alley, 'That tabby is nothing but trouble but he'll think twice before trying to hurt any of my friends again' Shokobaba sat down and started to lick the blood off her paws, 'Mirango' she said, 'Is that you? You not going to introduce me to your friends?'

Mirango wasn't a hundred percent sure how he should play things, but decided to answer the cat as best as he could. 'Yes Shoko it's me.........erm......these are some squirrel friends of mine. I'm sorta like helping them find their way to the SDR'

'Well stop being so shy and come down here and tell me more about it. You don't have to worry about that tabby anymore' Shokobaba waited to see if Mirango was coming. The mouse stayed put quite confused as to what to do. 'You know you are safe with me' she added, Mirango understanding at once the menace behind her sweet tone.

'That's Shokobaba?' Risu whispered more fascinated than scared, 'What's she doing saving mice from other cats......I thought......' Risu stopped in mid sentence as he watched Mirango run towards the white cat.

'What's happening Kalan? What are we going to do?' Funni said still cuddling the shaking Dusi in her tail.

'I don't know Funni......I don't know what to think' replied Kalan. He then bent down to Dusi. 'You didn't tell us you knew Shokobaba. What's going on?'

Dusi didn't look up. He didn't speak and just prayed to himself that it would all be over soon.

'Dusi?' said Kalan again.

'Can't you see he's scared out of his wits, leave him be for the moment' said Funni protectively.

Kalan backed off. As he did he looked briefly upwards and thought he saw the same pigeon from Columbus Park and Mulberry Street watching them from a window ledge. 'Risu you keep your eyes out for trouble behind us' he said, 'I'm going to talk to that cat'

'Are you crazy?' said Risu, 'That's Shokobaba!'

'I know that' replied Kalan, 'and I just saw her save Dusi's life, so you two stay here and let me find out what this all means'

'But......' said Funni, but Kalan was resolute.

'The first sign of trouble' he continued, 'and you run'. He hopped down the side of the alley towards Mirango and the great white cat.

'Ok here he comes now' whispered Shokobaba as she saw Kalan leave the group, 'Keep it up Mirango you're doing well' As he drew closer she raised her voice, 'I won't have that cat causing trouble Mirango. How could I live with myself if something happened to you or Dusi, or any of my friends for that matter?'

Shokobaba looked up and smiled as Kalan edged closer. 'Hello there' she said sweetly. Kalan stopped in his tracks. 'Don't be scared. I know, I know I'm a big bad cat, but please, I won't hurt you little squirrel'

'You're Shokobaba' said Kalan almost as if the name itself was a condemnation.

'Yes that's right, but please, call me Shoko. Mirango has already told me that you are Kalandaka' Kalan nodded. 'Well that's almost as much of a mouthful as Shokobaba' Shokobaba gave a little laugh then nodded in the direction of the others, 'Your friends don't want to come down and introduce themselves?'

'They're fine where they are' said Kalan as he tried to asses the situation. Even though he was scared and quite intimidated by her large blue and brown eyes he tried not to show it. 'Is it true that you killed Delancy the rat up at Columbus Park?'

Shokobaba sighed and looked down at Mirango. 'You see what I was talking about?' she said in frustration, 'That murderous Tabby has been at it again and I get the blame. Shokobaba did this. Shokobaba did that. Just because I'm white and stick out from the crowd I get the blame for everything'

'So you didn't do it?' asked Kalan.

'Of course not!' said Shokobaba mocking offense, 'I turned up on the scene too late to help out. I warned everybody about that tabby, but no one ever listens, eh Mirango?'

Mirango turned around to face Kalan with that alarming toothy grin on his face again. 'It's true Kalan, Shoko has been helping us out for some time'

Kalan was trying to understand things as best he could. 'So all these stories we've heard about the evil white cat are lies? Every rat we have on the way here has been lying to us?' The confusion in Kalan's mind was clearly discernable from the tone of his voice.

'Kalan' said Shokobaba soothingly, 'I cannot deny that in my misspent youth I have done some terrible things. I am a cat for heavens sake, it's in our genetic structure!' She patted Mirango affectionately on the head as she continued talking, 'But as I've gotten older, and hopefully wiser, I've discovered that friendship is such a beautiful thing. I've been trying to mend my ways by helping out instead of causing trouble. I realize the rats hate me because of my past, and they have every right to do so because forgiveness can't change what I have done in the past. My hope now is that my actions can at least make a difference to the future'

Mirango continued to smile at Kalan, 'She's a changed cat' he said enthusiastically.

'And what about the story of you fighting a squirrel in Columbus Park? Was that all made up by the rats as well?' Kalan asked.

Shokobaba put her paw to her eye as if wiping away a tear. 'It was that brave squirrel who made me realize how hollow my life had been. I only wish one day I could meet him again and show him how he changed me' Shokobaba was trying hard to induce some tears and carried on preaching. 'I forgive the rats for their anger towards me. You should forgive many things in others but nothing in yourself. I hate myself for what I've done, and won't stop hating.........' Mirango looked up in amazement as Shokobaba started to weep, '.........until I've repaid my debt to everyone I've ever hurt'

Kalan moved over until he stood between the cat and the mouse. He held out his paw. 'Well, let us at least set off on the right foot' he said.

Shokobaba, as she gazed at Kalan's face through her crocodile tears, felt an almost uncontrollable urge to bite and slash. She managed however to maintain control over these compulsions and shook Kalan's paw with her own.

A few yards further down the alley both Risu and Funni watched the unfolding events with their mouths wide open. 'What on earth is he doing?' said Funni, 'Oh my gosh, they're coming down here. What do we do?'

'Stay calm Funni' said Risu, 'Kalan looks relaxed enough'

Dusi wanted to scream 'RUN' to everyone, but bit his tongue. Kalan walked slowly down towards Risu and Funni with Mirango at his side. Shokobaba kept her distance a few feet behind.

'What's going on Kalan?' Funni demanded as Kalan arrived. Both she and Risu took a few steps backwards. Shokobaba saw this and stopped moving forwards.

'Look' said Kalan, 'I know this is going to sound odd, but I think Shokobaba is on the level'

'What?' Funni shouted 'Have you gone mad?'

'I think we can trust him' replied Kalan.

Shokobaba moved backwards as the three squirrels started to argue. Mirango found himself moving closer to Shokobaba. He had no idea what she was planning but a quick glance into her eyes confirmed to him that whatever it was, it was going to turn nasty sooner or later.

Funni pushed Kalan and Risu to one side and pointed her tail at Shokobaba. 'You tried to kill my father!' she shouted.

Shokobaba took another step backward and bowed her head. 'And that day' said the cat sniffing slightly 'your courageous father made a nasty old cat realize how much better life could be if I changed my ways. I owe him my very soul'

'Well I don't believe you, and I'm not going to forgive you either!' Funni cried out angrily as Risu pulled her back towards him and Kalan.

'I know its hard little squirrel' replied Shokobaba 'but if you can't find it in your heart to forgive then life just becomes one long meaningless existence full of resentment. Believe me I know. It eats away at a person. Since I've made a fresh start I live a life full of satisfaction and purpose' Funni didn't interrupt as Shokobaba continued talking. 'And my purpose today, apart from saving dear Dusi, is to make sure the three of you get to the SDR unmolested'

Funni crossed her arms, and kept silent. Shokobaba took one step closer and the squirrels did not move.

'I ask only one thing in return from you' she said softly 'once you get out of Chinatown let the world know that Shokobaba is a changed cat. A humble cat, trying to make amends for all the wrong I've done' Shokobaba's eyes filled with tears again. Funni shrugged and turned her back to the cat.

'I suppose' she said quietly.

Forgiveness is an emotion that comes quite easily to squirrels. They never hold a grievance for very long. Back at Battery Park Skudzo used to sum up squirrel thinking on the subject by saying,

'Grudges are like empty nut shells. You go around collecting them 'because you think they might come in useful one day. Yet before you know it you find your stash full of worthless shells and you go hungry 'cause you wasted your time on them and not on the things that really matter'

Cats, on the other hand, carry grudges around as if their lives depended on it. They almost hardly ever forget, and they certainly never forgive.

Wesley had managed to drag himself back to his owner's apartment on Grand Street with his face streaming with blood from where Shokobaba had cut deep into his skin. He had spent the whole painful journey planning revenge. This time she had gone too far. He remembered how Shokobaba had told him that it would just be a 'pretend fight' to fool the squirrels.

'Killer! Oh my Gawd! Killer!' His owner went into a fit the moment Wesley stumbled through the open window of the second floor apartment. 'Oh my! You've been fighting again. Harry! Harry!'

The old white haired lady shouted out to her husband in the other room 'Come quickly, we've got to get Killer to the vet'

Wesley had amassed a large collection of grievances with Shokobaba over the years. As his panicked owners dabbed his face with a cloth that stung and put him into his pet carrier for the trip to the vet the tabby decided it was time to cash in the grudges he had been collecting. He would of course have to act and think alone because, like most of the animals who had thrown their lot in with Shokobaba, he had no friends.

Back at the alley Shokobaba was well on her way to convincing the squirrels that any stories they had heard about her were exaggerated. Kalan, for one, had apparently let himself be persuaded that the cat he saw before him had changed her ways and was genuinely repentant. Risu had also decided to give Shokobaba the benefit of the doubt. He, in particular, was just so plain excited to see and hear a cat up close for the first time.

The jury was still out for Funni. She didn't trust the mice, and the mice were friends of Shokobaba. She kept her misgivings to herself though as she did trust Kalan's judgment. She listened as the white cat continued her successful charm offensive.

'Well the playground isn't too far from here, plus there are lots of trees for you to rest in when you arrive. Then it's about a half mile straight up to Houston' Shokobaba paused for a moment, then decided that her charm was beginning to have enough effect enough, so added another thought, 'You know, now I come to think about it, it's been such a long time since I went on a trip anywhere. Would you guys mind if I tagged along?'

The squirrels looked at each other, not really knowing how to react.

'Oh come on,' said Shokobaba jokingly, 'I could act as your honoree bodyguard. The SDR is full of cats that haven't seen the error of their ways like me and I'm sure Mirango and Dusi don't want to travel that far away from home'

Mirango instantly shook his head in agreement with the cat, but Dusi spoke up, 'I don't mind' he said unexpectedly. Dusi had been listening to Shokobaba smooth talk the squirrels into her confidence and he had grown determined to do something to help them. He hadn't worked out how or when yet, but he intended to stay with them until he had worked out a way to warn everyone. His morals had finally triumphed over his survival instincts.

For a split second Shokobaba's blue eye glared menacingly at Dusi, almost as if she had read his mind, but then her face broke into a beautiful smile.

'Of course the more the merrier' she said looking back at the squirrels, 'what do you say?'

'Ok Shokobaba' said Kalan

'Wonderful!' replied the cat excitedly, 'now Mirango will lead you safely down to the SDR. I've a few loose ends to tie up here, then I'll meet you down there this evening'

Mirango couldn't believe Shokobaba was letting the squirrels go, but he certainly had no intention of arguing. 'Come on then guys' he said to Kalan and the others, 'It's just a couple more blocks'

Dusi unwrapped himself from Funni's tail. 'Are you fit to travel?' Funni asked with a very motherly look in her eyes.

Dusi nodded eagerly anxious to get as far away from Shokobaba as possible, but the cat had no intention of letting him go.

'Dusi' she said sweetly, 'After all that business with the tabby I really think you should rest up here for a bit. I wouldn't want you getting hurt again'

'Yeah' said Risu oblivious to Shokobaba's real motives, 'Maybe the cat's right, you look wasted'

'I'll be ok' said Dusi defiantly, 'I want to go with you all' He stood up and as if to prove his point he hopped a few feet down the alley ahead of the others. 'Come on' he shouted back to everyone.

Shokobaba's tail started to wag angrily, but she kept her smile intact. 'Dusi, Dusi, Dusi' she said, 'I tried to tell you earlier, before I had to save you from that cat. I have some bad news for you' Dusi's whiskers twitched, but he didn't speak. 'I don't really want to say this in front of everybody' said Shokobaba soothingly 'but as you are so determined to leave now I guess I'll have to. It's your mother Dusi' Dusi gulped hard. 'That tabby has sworn to get her, we have to find the old girl together. If you leave now she'll be in great danger, you know she still doesn't trust me'

Mirango understood instantly the implication of Shokobaba's words. As he looked at Dusi's tearful face he realized that his friend had understood them as well.

'Your mother?' Risu said 'maybe we should stay around and help?'

'Oh no' said Shokobaba as Dusi slowly made his way towards her, 'myself and Dusi will be able to work things out won't we?' She wrapped her paw around the dejected mouse as he came closer.

'Now Mirango,' she said, 'get these squirrels up to the playground and I'll join you all in a couple of hours'

'And Dusi?' said Mirango as he looked forlornly at his doomed friend.

'Well I think Dusi will have to stay and take care of his mother' said Shokobaba 'you've only got one mother'

Mirango nodded and his eyes filled with tears as he looked at Dusi with Shokobaba's giant paw resting gently on his shoulder. Dusi didn't look up. Kalan saw the worry written over Mirango's face, but Mirango knew the squirrels didn't understand the situation. Shokobaba had successfully charmed them all. 'Yeah' said Mirango as he turned his back on his friend for surely the last time 'you've only got the one' He ran up the alley and the squirrels followed him. Shokobaba and Dusi watched in silence as they got to the end of the alley and turned the corner back into Hester Street.

'Well that went well didn't it Dusi?' Shokobaba pressed her paw harder onto Dusi's shoulder as she spoke 'Those squirrels are even more gullible than I thought. Not half as clever as you little mouse, are they?'

Dusi started to whimper. He hoped that the end would mercifully quick. Shokobaba dug a nail into Dusi's back and he squealed with pain. She threw him against the alley wall and he fell lifeless to the ground.

'Thought you could get the better of me, didn't you? You forgot that you are a guest in my world Dusi......and a polite guest never leaves the party early. In fact my guests never leave at all' All the sweetness of the voice the cat had put on for the squirrels long gone, she moved her head closer to Dusi's. 'You're lucky though as I don't want a meaningless rodent as my 100th victim' Shokobaba's voice was little more than a malicious whisper in Dusi's ear, 'But I don't think you will be walking again any time soon' She raised a paw to deliver another blow.

'SHOKOBABA!'

A voice shouted from the beginning of the alley. The cat turned around to see Kalan running back towards her. She sat down hiding Dusi's body from the squirrel. If he had seen anything she would kill him now.

'Sorry Shoko' said Kalan a little out of breath 'I forgot to tell you something'

'What's that then?' the cat replied.

'You can call me Kalan' He said with a smile.

Shokobaba gave a tiny sigh of relief, the fool hadn't seen a thing she thought. 'That's very sweet of you...... Kalan' she said.

'I trust you Shokobaba, but you must understand my two friends will need a bit more time'

'Well I hope I'll live up to the faith you have put in me'

Kalan nodded, 'I hope so too' he said as he looked around, 'Dusi?' he said almost absent mindedly.

'Oh he's already gone on ahead to find his poor mother'

'I hope she's ok, I had better be getting back to the others' said Kalan and turned to leave, 'I just wanted you to know that I believe everyone deserves a second chance'

'I promise I won't let you down' said the cat and waved a paw at the squirrel as he ran back down to Hester Street, She watched him hop around the corner with her eyes squinted with malice. 'Idiot' she said to herself. 'Did you hear that fool Dusi? He's not going to be as lucky as you. At least I'm going to let you live, albeit as a cripple. Hahaha!' She turned around to finish her business with the mouse, but the laughing stopped the moment she saw that Dusi had gone.

'Dusi?' she shouted 'DUSI!' She turned her head in every direction looking for a sign of the mouse. 'Dusi where are you? Get back here you little piece of......' She ran along the alley wall sniffing, she was beginning to panic, 'You come back here now or I'll rip out your eyes'

Shokobaba cursed herself for letting Dusi slip away. Then another thought struck her.

Kalandaka.

It was his fault Dusi had gotten away, if he hadn't distracted her. Maybe he wasn't as stupid as she thought.

In the meantime Kalandaka and the others had crossed the Bowery, but had been spotted by some schoolchildren who had started to chase them.They were hiding under a beat up Fiat near the corner of Hester Street and the Bowery, but the children had followed them and some were kneeling on the sidewalk trying to coax the animals out.

'Hey! Squirrel! I've got something for ya' said one of them, a twelve year old girl with large yellow glasses.

'Let me see Ade…How many of them are there? They must be scared' said her friend. Two more were calling to others to come and see the squirrels. A crowd was beginning to form.

'This is bad' said Risu, 'I've heard stories of these little humans kidnapping animals and keeping them in cages'

'We'll have to get to the park using the drains' said Mirango, 'but the nearest drain hole is about twenty feet further up'

Risu jumped with shock as one of the children swept a stick under the car. All of them jumped to avoid getting hit. Some of the kids started laughing.

'No   Paul'   one   of   them   cried   out,   'you'll   hurt   them'
'Aw shut up and help me find something longer'

A couple of the children were poking their faces under the car and looking directly at the squirrels huddled together. It was too dark for them to make out that one of them was actually a mouse.

'There's a whole bunch of them' shouted one girl as Kalan stared at her face.

'This is going to get out of control real soon' said Funni beginning to feel very uneasy, 'let's just make a run for that drain cover'

The way ahead was however blocked by children's feet and legs. There were now nearly a dozen of them surrounding the vehicle.

'Hey! You kids, get away from my car'

As if things couldn't get any worse, the owner of the Fiat had heard all the commotion and ran out of a nearby shop.

'Hey Mister! There's a family of squirrels under your car' said the large girl with glasses.

'Well they had better find another place to sit under 'cause I'm leaving' he said as he stuck his key into the door.

'Ok, ok don't panic' said Risu, directing his speech more to himself than to anyone else 'but our cover is about to drive off'

Kalan thought quickly. 'You three make a dash for the drain hole, I'm going to run out and get everyone's attention'

'No wait' said Mirango, 'let me do it, I'm good at scaring little kids 'cause they all think I'm a rat' The car motor started up and Mirango shouted out his last sentence. 'GO! I'll catch up with you in the drain'

With that he ran straight out from under the car onto the sidewalk. He ran over one of the kids hands as she was kneeling on the sidewalk, then made a couple of circles around some of the others. All the kids started screaming, some ran off down the street while one of the boys tried to hit Mirango with his rucksack.

A gap opened up for the squirrels in front of the car and Funni was the first to see the drain hole in front of them and she led the other two squirrels as they sprinted out from under the Fiat, along the gutter and into the drain hole. They were joined a few seconds later by an exhausted, but strangely exhilarated Mirango.

'Ha!' Mirango laughed as he fell feet first into the drain, 'If they think I'm a squirrel they love me. If they think I'm a rat they have a heart attack!'

'You ok?' asked Kalan as the mouse dusted himself off, 'Thanks for helping us out, that was neat'

'I'm fine' replied Mirango, 'I just don't get it though. What is it about you guys that humans love? I mean we are all rodents aren't we?'

This was to be the topic of conversation for the rest of their journey along the drains to Roosevelt Park. Funni believed humans loved the squirrels' fluffy tail. Risu was under the impression that humans hated nuts. That was why they liked squirrels because they were the only animal that was happy to take them.

'They must hate them, I mean they are always throwing all sorts of nuts at us'

'Well I don't know why' said Mirango, 'all I know is that us mice and the rats get a raw deal in this city'

They soon found themselves walking along another drain that was much noisier than the others. Funni began to feel a little nervous with the sounds of cars thundering overhead.

'That's Chrystie Street' said Mirango, 'We've arrived'

The squirrels followed as the mouse ran excitedly up the slippery side of the drain and all four of them popped their heads out of the drain hole on the edge of the park and Chrystie Street. They saw the colorful shapes of the children's playground and several large trees.

With Mirango hiding in the middle, the four of them ran out from the drain and up the nearest and tallest Elm.

'I hope we won't have to wait too long for that cat' said Risu as he looked down over all the plastic and concrete that formed the start of Roosevelt Park. 'I'm getting sick of all this gray. Will Tompkins Park be green? I miss the grass'

'I hope so too' said Funni, 'it all looks so bleak. No wonder we haven't met any other squirrels since City Hall'

Mirango too was looking down thoughtfully over the park. Now that they had arrived his mind had returned to thinking about Dusi. What was that cat going to do with his friend?

'Mirango, how long do you think we will have to wait for Shokobaba?'

The mouse looked back along the branch to see Kalan was talking to him. 'She'll be here around dusk' he guessed.

Dusk came and went. Night fell, and there was still no sign of Shokobaba. The squirrels managed to sleep and rest a little while they waited, but all were anxious to get moving.

As midnight approached Mirango started to hope that something had happened to Shokobaba. Maybe her owner had locked her in the apartment. Maybe, joy of joys, she had been run over by a car. This last thought made Mirango smile and he hopped over to where the squirrels were sitting huddled together. Only Funni was awake, well half awake at least.

'Maybe you should go without Shokobaba' he said, for once actually thinking of the squirrel's well-being 'you'll be safer'

'Safer?' Funni yawned, 'What do you mean?'

'PSSSSSST'

A hissing sound came from under the tree. In the distance a clock started to strike midnight.

'PSSSSSST'

Mirango and Funni looked down and saw the bright white form of Shokobaba.

The hellos and the goodbyes

Funni woke the others with the news of Shokobaba's arrival. The white cat stayed below, circling the base of the tree, so Mirango climbed down to get instructions.

'You took a long time' said Mirango as he jumped to the ground in front of the cat.

'Shut up' whispered Shokobaba aggressively, 'and follow me'

Mirango dutifully followed after the cat as she ran under one of the climbing frames in the playground.

'What have those squirrels said about me?' Shokobaba demanded making sure she could still see them waiting in the tree while looking over Mirango's shoulder.

'They believed you' said Mirango honestly.

'And that little runt Kalan?'

'Nothing Shoko. They have only been wondering where you had got too, that's all' Shokobaba said nothing. She sat staring up at the three small dark figures in the tree. 'Look Shoko' continued Mirango, 'if they had any doubts they would have run off already wouldn't they?'

'Maybe' said Shokobaba, 'maybe not'

The mouse took a deep breath to build himself up to his next question. 'Is Dusi ok?' Mirango asked meekly.

'You worry about yourself Mirango' replied Shokobaba 'and go get those squirrels down here NOW!'

Shokobaba had, in fact, spent all of the afternoon hunting for Dusi, but the mouse had successfully gone to ground. The cat had threatened, bullied and knocked about lots of Chinatown residents today, but no one knew where he had got to. No matter, thought Shokobaba, it wasn't that important for the moment, but the second she got back from her bloody trip to Tompkins Square Park Dusi would be the first item on her agenda.

'Where have you been all day?' Funni was the first to speak as the squirrels arrived under the play frame with Mirango.

'I'm sorry I got here so late' said Shokobaba reverting back to her honey sweet voice, 'it took me ages longer than I thought to help out Dusi and his family, and then my good for nothing owner found me and locked me up in the front room. I only just managed to get out not twenty minutes ago' The cat gazed at the three squirrels sitting in front of her and she winked her brown eye at Kalan. 'So Kalan' she said, 'are we all ready to go?'

'Why yes' he replied cheerily, 'If you feel up to it. Apparently this park is quite long and we will have to cross a couple of roads, but we hope to get to Houston before the dawn'

'Are you coming with us Mirango?' asked Risu.

The mouse glanced at Shokobaba for a second, he didn't know what to say. 'I err...... I'

'It's a long way up to Houston' Shokobaba cut in, but addressed herself to the squirrels. 'I don't think his little legs will carry him all that way and back again'

'Yes that's right' said Mirango sounding almost grateful, 'I'm not coming any further. You all have a safe trip'

'Well you make sure to say 'hi' to Dusi from us' said Funni. She was secretly pleased to see the back of Mirango, after all she had never trusted him. Kalan and Risu also made quick goodbyes, but made it clear that they were anxious to get a move on.

'Lets see how fast you squirrels can really run' said Shokobaba, 'I'll race you to the edge of Grand Street'

'You're on' said Risu and he led the other two off across the concrete playground.

Shokobaba turned her face to Mirango as the squirrels scurried off. 'You find Dusi by the time I get back' she said threateningly, 'or you'll take his place impaled on my claw. Now get lost, I'll be in touch via the pigeons' She pushed Mirango to one side and chased off after the squirrels.

Mirango watched the white cat disappear into the night and his spirits lifted a little. Dusi had gotten away, good for him.

As Mirango slowly made his way back down the drain that would take him home to Hester Street his high spirits fell down the drain with him. It sunk in deep that Shokobaba had decided on getting rid of him or Dusi.

Dusi had chosen to hide himself in the last place he felt Shokobaba would come looking for him. He was under the floorboards in Ms Soo Lee's apartment, and had been there all day nursing his back wound. Fortunately for Dusi Shokobaba's nail had caused only a shallow flesh wound in his lower back, so he had been able to lick it clean.

Like Wesley the Tabby, Dusi had spent the day contemplating a mixture of survival and revenge and he decided the best way to start would be scaring Shokobaba's owner. Feeling better, but still sore, he decided to make his way into the bedroom and cause a little mayhem. Wesley hadn't been as lucky as Dusi with his wounds. The cut on his cheek had needed three stitches and would no doubt leave a nasty scar – or another permanent 'kiss' as Shokobaba liked to call the disfigurements she left on folk. He was back in his apartment on Grand Street after the visit to the vet and he was still awake but drowsy thanks to the anesthetic the vet had given him. Wesley had the usual irritating urge to scratch his injury but knew that would only make things worse. To take his mind off things he spent most of the night sharpening his claws on the wooden leg of the dining room table imagining it was the white devil herself.

Not too far away from Wesley's apartment Kalan, Risu and Funni were waiting by the trashcan on the sidewalk in front of Grand Street as Shokobaba arrived.

'Wow! You guys are quick' she said as she bounded up to them, 'I wont race you lot again or I'll lose every time'

Grand Street was the first of several roads which cut through Sara Delano Roosevelt Park and it was fairly quiet so the animals had little problem crossing over it. Apart from a few shadowy human figures, who in any case paid the travelers no attention, the SDR was empty and the Battery Parkers were able to run quickly along the ground.

Shokobaba tagged along behind them and was impressed at the way they traveled, it was obvious to her that they had spent their time on the road perfecting the technique. They always checked their destination before running to it. Generally one of them went first, and then when sure it was safe, would beckon the others to follow. Any strange noises they stopped, any unfamiliar smells, they stopped. Sometimes one of the squirrels would run up a tree or onto a fence to check that everything was safe ahead. Shokobaba congratulated herself on not having gone after them at Columbus Park. They would have spotted her coming from a mile away.

As the four of them made their way across a large basketball court Risu, who was leading the group at that point, whacked his tail and the squirrels darted to the safety of a tree on the Chrystie Street side. Shokobaba ran after them,

'What's the panic' she asked as she watched the squirrels climb up the tree trunk. She, as usual stayed firmly on the ground.

'There are people ahead, lots of people' Risu shouted down, and he pointed out to Kalan and Funni the large group of shadows he had heard from the basketball court.

Shokobaba couldn't see anything, but from the top of the tree the squirrels could clearly make out around twenty people talking, haggling and arguing around a tiny enclosed park on the edge of Broome Street. Inside this miniature park - known to local residents as the 'Hua Mei Bird Garden' - the subject of all the haggling appeared to be several large cages filled with birds of different shapes and sizes.

'We'll have to cross the road and go around them' suggested Risu.

'You insensitive brute' said Funni, 'just look at those poor birds, what's going to happen to them?'

Although they couldn't understand the Chinese with which the bird traders were talking, the squirrels could understand a few fragments coming from the birds,

'I can't stand it any more, get me out of here!'

'Quit your gripping!'

'Remember just keep talking, that's what Totti said to do'

'Yeah, right! And a fat lot of good it did him, on his way to who knows where!'

'Don't yous go bad mouthing my Uncle Totti. He knows what's what and he'll think of something'

The squirrels all turned and looked at each other,

'TANCREDI!' They all cried out in unison.

'What?' Shokobaba shouted up the tree trunk, 'What's going on?'

'Keep Shoko busy' Kalan whispered to the others, 'While I go over there to find out what's happening'

Kalan leapt from the tree to another, and then scurried down and over to the crowd at the Hua Mei Bird Garden. Risu and Funni climbed down their tree trunk to Shokobaba.

'We think we've found an old friend of ours up ahead' said Risu.

'Another squirrel?' Shokobaba asked, 'Your friend from Columbus Park?' The cat didn't realize that she was licking her lips as she spoke.

'Bilka?' Risu replied absent mindedly, 'Oh no, not him, not a squirrel. A sparrow. Some men up there have got him locked up in a cage'

Risu turned to Funni, 'You see, I told you these humans lock up animals in cages'

Funni shrugged unconcerned 'So what's to know?'

'Birds in cages' said Shokobaba and shook her head 'such a terrible tragedy'

She thought back to one of her earliest victims, Ms Fay Fat's budgerigar. How easy it had been to get her claws inside the cage, and to think her owners just thought she had flown away. Shokobaba smiled to herself. Birds in cages, mice in cages what a wonderful way of serving up dinner.

'Is there anything I can do to help?' she said

'I don't know' said Funni 'We'll see what Kalan says when he gets back'

Kalan had slipped unseen through the crowds and was inside the bird garden. Despite the lack of light it didn't take him long to home in on Tancredi's cage, his voice was so unique.

'Yous guys gotta understand my Uncle Totti's been through all this before. Is telling yous don't be............ KALAN!'

'Hey Tancredi' said Kalan smiling broadly, 'how did you ever end up in there?'

'Oh Kalan you got no idea' Tancredi began speaking in an excited hurry, his words banging into each other, 'These humans are crazy, they go catching birds that talk nice – like me – and sells 'em. They gots me and Uncle Totti back at the City Hall. They just sold him, but I think the humans that bought him are leaving town and taking him with 'em. Kalan yous gotta get me outta here, we's gotta help him'

Tancredi fell back against the side of his cage. The emotion of seeing Kalan again, and the worry he had for his Uncle Totti, made the tiny sparrow's head spin.

'Ok Tancredi, don't worry we'll get you out of here' said Kalan and gripping the bars of the cage searched around for a way to do just that.

'There's like a door thing down front' said Tancredi, 'but I don't knows how to open it'

Kalan quickly found the part of the cage Tancredi was talking about. There was a small gold chain linking the door with the rest of the cage. Kalan thought, correctly, that a strong enough bite would break the chain and fling the door open. Unfortunately the moment he tried to put the chain in his mouth, the other birds went crazy.

'ME NEXT!'

'Look Tancredi's breaking out!'

'ME! ME! ME AS WELL!'

'HEY SQUIRREL! When you're done with the sparrow get your furry backside over here, I want out too!'

This high pitched commotion brought the unwanted attention of one of the Chinese vendors who spotted Kalan hanging on the cage.

'HEY! SHOOO!' The man shouted out, and jumped over the small park gate. 'YOU GET OUTTA HERE SQUIRREL!'

'I'll be back!' said Kalan as he jumped down onto the ground and ran through the man's legs and back towards the basketball court.

'HEY! Where did he go?'

'YO Tancredi! What happened? You ain't free fella? Squirrel got marshmallow teeth?'

Tancredi didn't reply instead he flew excitedly around his cage. He knew Kalan would think of something. He just hoped it would be in time to save Uncle Totti.

Uncle Totti himself was also hoping for some luck. He had been sold earlier on that evening after chirping away louder than all the others. His idea had been a simple one, that the sooner he was sold the sooner he could escape. Everything had seemed to be so right. His new owners had three small kids, and he knew that if he charmed them it would only be a matter of time before they opened his cage and then............... Freedom!

He hadn't counted on the fact that this family were in the middle of moving house. They were leaving New York's Chinatown and headed to Wichita, Kansas to set up a restaurant with some relations who had recently arrived from Shanghai. Uncle Totti had no idea where Wichita was or where they were headed. All he knew, as he sat in his cage in the darkness of the removals van, was that he was leaving town. Maybe tonight, maybe in the morning, but he knew that once he left New York it would be an almost impossible task to ever find his way back. Totti rocked himself back and forth on his perch hoping for some sort of miracle.

'You'll need a miracle to set all those birds free' said Shokobaba as Kalan explained the situation to everybody, 'If those men are anything like my owner they'll be keeping a close eye on those birds until they've finished doing business'

'We won't need any divine intervention, just a good distraction' said Kalan confidently.

'What do you have in mind?' Shokobaba asked. She was getting a little annoyed by this hold up.

'If you could get those men's attention Shoko' said Kalan, 'while we squirrels bite the chains on the cages. There are about nine cages so that's like three apiece. We'll need a minute or two'

'I've got very sensitive teeth' said Risu, not warming to the idea of having to bite metal.

'Oh it's not strong' said Kalan, 'It's quite supple, one good snap with your molars should do it'

'And what do you want me to do? A song and dance?' Shokobaba was being to show her irritation, 'If one of those men knows my owner and recognizes me, he'll take me back and demand a reward! I can't risk that'

'Please Shoko' said Funni, 'Tancredi is our friend. He's helped so much in the past flying around for us'

Shokobaba shook her head adamantly. 'I'm sorry squirrels, but those men scare me' she lied, 'they may lock me up in a cage as well, or worse, take me back to my terrible ogre of an owner. She'll be looking for me now, and she'll beat me if she ever found out I was this far from home' Shokobaba decided it was time to turn on the waterworks. She hung her head. 'She's always beating me. That's why I wanted to get away'

She sobbed a little with her head held low to the ground and hoped that this would be enough to get the squirrels to change their minds. The idea of freeing a sparrow that could fly on ahead and warn folks obviously didn't appeal to the cat at all.

'Well we can't leave Tancredi' said Risu, 'We've got to do something. Maybe I can cause a distraction? We might not have the time to release them all, but at least we can get Tancredi out of there'

'No Risu' said Kalan, 'We're going to get them all' Kalan looked back at the cat who still had her head close to the ground. 'It's a pity Shoko doesn't want to help' he said coolly 'I guess all the stories I've heard about cats being fearless were made up by the same rats who told us how evil you were Shoko'

Shokobaba raised her eyes and dug her claws into the ground.

'Well I'm certainly not going to believe another word a rat tells me", continued Kalan, "cats are fearless ha! As if that were true!'

Shokobaba started to visibly shake. She could barely control her growing anger. This little squirrel was deliberately provoking her. 'Why you little.........' she said in a high pitched hysterical tone, but instantly regained her self control mid sentence '......you little tease' She turned her back to Kalan however as if she was offended. The reality was that if she looked him in the eye she would want to hit him.

'I'm sorry if I upset you Shoko' said Kalan cooly

'Yeah it's ok Shoko,' added Risu, 'you stay here we'll think of something'

Shokobaba was weighing things up quickly in her mind. She had made friends with the squirrels and had gone to great lengths to convince them to lead her to the one squirrel she desired to meet again more than any other. Why throw all that hard work away over a stupid bird rescue now that she was so close?

'No, no squirrels I'm the one who should be sorry not you' the words almost hurt as Shokobaba forced them sweetly out of her mouth, 'You're quite right we should help them all, not just your friend' The cat turned around slowly with a smile glued to her face. 'I'm just being selfish. Of course I'll help. I'll 'cause such a distraction it will wake the whole neighborhood'

'That's the spirit' said Risu

'Well done Shoko!' Kalan smiled broadly at the cat, who smiled just as broadly back.

'What are you going to do?' asked Funni.

'Never mind that' replied Shokobaba, 'you three just hide yourself in that garden and wait until you hear me. You free your friend and those birds and then I'll meet you on the other side of Delancy Street when we're done, ok?'

'Sounds great' said Kalan.

The squirrels spread out and divided the Hua Mei Bird Garden between them, three cages each. Shokobaba watched as they ran off and growled angrily to herself. Her charade was getting more and more difficult to maintain. Whereas Bilka was earmarked as her 100th victim, Kalandaka was most certainly going to be number one o one. She took a deep breath and put thoughts of murder to one side as she made her way purposely to the crowd of haggling Chinese.

The squirrels were soon hiding near their allotted cages, and they didn't have to wait long for a signal from Shokobaba. They heard a long low wailing sound that started to rise higher and higher until it sounded almost like an ambulance siren.

'mmmMMMMMMEEEEEEEEOOOOOOOOOOOOOOOOOOOOWWWWW'

It reached such a pitch that it almost hurt.

Shokobaba jumped into the middle of the largest group of men and started hissing and wailing surprising them all. The men standing near the bird cages turned around and made their way over to the commotion.

'MAD CAT!'

'SOMEONE GET A STICK'

'PICK IT UP!'

The moment the men moved out of the bird garden the Battery Parkers leapt into action.

Kalan ran straight to Tancredi's cage door, gripped the chain between his teeth and bit hard. The chain was even more supple than he thought and it snapped in two instantly. Kalan pulled the cage door open and stuck his head inside.

'Meet you on the other side of Delancy Street' he said to Tancredi, then jumped across to the next cage. The sparrow hopped across from his perch and out through the open door.

'Freeeee!' he chirped as he flew up into the night sky.

It took the three squirrels less than a minute to free all the birds.

'Wha hey!'

'Thanks pal!'

'Yu shi ju jin'

The men watching or trying to catch Shokobaba didn't notice the birds flying free overhead, but the cat did. She lashed out and scratched one man's hand as he tried to grab her and then ran off back towards the basketball court. As she left a couple of the men started to laugh.

'THAT CRAZY CAT MIGHT BRING US LUCK TONIGHT'

'LOOKED LIKE THE ONE SOO LEE GOT'

Their laughter quickly stopped when they saw the empty cages in the bird garden. The men started to make even more noise than Shokobaba, screaming and shouting in anger and at each other. It was just as well that a patrol car passed along Chrystie Street and flashed its lights. Instead of a fight breaking out, the men just all ran off in different directions.

The squirrels regrouped on the other side of Delancy Street. It was a large road to cross but there was little traffic. Shokobaba joined them soon afterwards.

'Where's Tancredi?' Risu asked as he watched the scene of chaos unfold on the other side of the Street.

All the commotion had woken up a good number of the local residents who were shouting down at the police who had got out of their car and were looking around the bird garden with flashlights.

'He got out of the cage all right' said Kalan, 'I guess he's just a little scared they might catch him again'

'What were those birds doing in those cages anyhow?' Funni asked.

'Because,' said Shokobaba 'humans like to keep them locked up in their homes and listen to them. It's very cruel and in fact this is not the first time I have helped to free birds. I liberated a budgerigar from her cage once'

'Well you did very well tonight' said Risu, 'I've never heard such a racket'

'I call it my 'mad cat shout. Gets humans to open doors for me. Those birds should try and learn the technique' Shokobaba nodded towards the sky as she spoke. 'Humans only like having animals in their homes if we look cute and keep our mouths either shut or singing sweetly. The moment we start wailing or foaming at the mouth, they lose it and will do anything to distance themselves from us'

'Well I think we should distance ourselves from them now' said Kalan, 'I'm sure Tancredi will find us sooner or later. He knows we're headed up to Tompkins Park'

'I guess so' said Risu, 'after all that time cooped up in a cage I reckon he wants a bit of time to stretch his wings'

The squirrels headed off along the Forsyth Street side of the SDR with Shokobaba bringing up the rear as usual. As she followed the cat hoped that there would be no more interruptions on the journey as her patience was now wafer thin, but luck wasn't traveling with her tonight.

As the group made its way slowly up the SDR Shokobaba heard a low flying whooshing sound. She looked up to see a screaming sparrow dive just centimeters from her face. She lashed out instinctively with her paws, but missed the bird completely.

'RUN SQUIRRELYS!' Tancredi screamed out as he flew back into the air, 'BAD CAT BEHIND YOUS!'

As Tancredi prepared another dive, Kalan ran back towards the cat. The sparrow launched himself towards Shokobaba, who this time was ready for him. As he flew in close she lashed out with her paw. She would have got Tancredi had Kalan not jumped onto her paw a split second before it made contact with Tancredi's head.

'NO!' he shouted as his weight pushed Shokobaba's paw back to the ground. 'Cut it out Tancredi! The cat's ok. She's helping us!'

Shokobaba jumped backwards as memories of the last squirrel who had dared to touch her came flooding back. She bit her tongue and flicked her claws in and out of her paws. She watched as the tiny sparrow landed on the ground and sneered to herself as he was surrounded by the three squirrels. She imagined various scenarios of her jumping into the group biting and slashing, but held herself back. 'Kalan I need to......... get a sip of water ' she said coldly without looking anyone in the eye, 'I'll be back in a minute. You just remind that sparrow I helped him to escape'

Without waiting for a reply, certain that if she heard a squirrel say one word she would bite their head off, Shokobaba turned around and ran off in the direction of Chrystie Street to calm herself down.

Tancredi watched the cat leave, 'I thought that cat was stalking yous' he said

'No she's been helping us' said Funni

'That cat don't want to helps no one pal' scoffed Tancredi, 'she just wants to kill squirrelys. You guys are crazy'

'She's a bit strange' said Kalan, 'but don't worry about her, tell us how you got in that cage'

'Yeah' said Risu, 'How'd they get you?'

'No time for that' said Tancredi, 'I has found Uncle Totti. Yous guys gotta help or they going to take him a long ways away'

Tancredi explained as quickly as he could about the apartment on Eldridge Street where all the birds had been kept. He started getting agitated as he spoke about the large white removals van parked outside that the family of humans had been filling earlier with everything they had in their apartment, including Uncle Totti in his cage. 'He's inside that van and we've got to get him out'

'Where are they going to take him?' Funni asked

'That's just it' said Tancredi,, 'I don't know! But Uncle Totti he says the bigger the van the further you go… and, well, this one is huge!'

The sparrow explained where the van was parked. They would have to cross over Forsyth Street and go back down to find it near the corner of Broome and Eldridge Street. 'I just hope it's still there' said Tancredi, then froze as he saw Shokobaba was back.

'Another rescue?' Shokobaba sighed, 'At this rate it will take us months to get uptown'

Kalan twitched his head to one side and looked curiously at Shokobaba.

'Maybe' he said, 'but just think of how many birds we will have made happy'

Shokobaba face showed that she failed to see any humor in the situation. Kalan carried on regardless, 'Don't worry Shoko. I think I'll be able to handle this one'

Kalan turned himself towards Risu and Funni, 'Let's do it this way. You guys keep on traveling up the SDR and wait for me when you get to Houston. I'll go with Tancredi and see if I can help find Totti'

'Are you sure?' said Funni

'Look, if he's in a cage like the others it only needs one of us to bite the chain. Tancredi can keep lookout' replied Kalan, then he turned to Shokobaba, 'And I know you are anxious to keep on uptown Shoko, so you go with the others. I won't be long'

Shokobaba's mind pushed itself into a faster gear. She didn't like the idea of the group splitting up, and she was certain Kalan was up to something. 'I'll come with you and the sparrow' she purred, 'I feel bad about the scene I made earlier, and want to show you I can be a helper rather than a whiner'

As Shokobaba spoke she finalized her nasty plan of action. She didn't need all three squirrels to lead her to Bilka. Funni and Risu would be more than sufficient. Alone with Kalan it would be easy to maim him and the bird, not kill, not kill – that was going to be difficult, go on uptown with the others and then after creating hell in Tompkins finish Kalan off on her way back home.

Perfect.

Tancredi looked nervously at Kalan. It was clear to Shokobaba that the sparrow didn't fancy the idea of the cat tagging along. Kalan on the other hand seemed very enthusiastic.

'That's great Shoko, we may need your 'mad cat' routine again' Sensing Tancredi's nerves Kalan spoke to him directly, 'Don't worry Tancredi, Shoko is on our side'

The sparrow certainly wasn't convinced, but he had no time to argue. Uncle Totti needed his help now, or it might be too late. 'Ok, ok' he said, 'but let's go before that van leaves.

Kalan nodded to Risu and Funni.

'You be careful' said Funni. 'We'll be waiting for you at the end of this park' She gave Risu a slap on his back and the two of them continued on their way up the SDR.

The police car and its occupants were still milling around the Hua Mei Bird Garden, so Kalan, Tancredi and the cat ran first across Forsyth Street before crossing back over Delancy Street. As usual Shokobaba brought up the rear, but this time an evil smile was fixed on her face. She wouldn't have to pretend to be nice to Kalan for much longer.

With Tancredi leading the way in a mix of hops and short flights, it wasn't long before they found the van. It was parked on Eldridge Street, around a hundred feet down from the corner with Broome Street. It was, as Tancredi had warned them, very large. On the dirty side of it was written:

'*Wonderful Wichita Removals. To Kansas and be yonder*'

Kalan and Shokobaba sat under a blue mailbox watching the van from a safe distance, as they could see there were two humans moving around near the back of the van.

'The door's open' said Tancredi from his perch on top of the mail box, 'now's our chance!'

Without waiting for a reply he flew towards the van. He landed silently on the roof of the van, just above the open door and flapped his wings at Kalan. The moment Tancredi saw that Kalan was running towards the van along the gutter, he hovered for a few seconds by the open van door, and then flew inside.

Luckily for Kalan the two men had moved away from the back of the van and had walked over to the building, and so he climbed unseen up the side of the van and jumped inside.

Shokobaba kept herself under the blue mailbox. Her mind was now made up. Let Kalan make his pathetic rescue, then she would slice up all three of them. The thought of at long last letting vent to her blood lust excited her immensely.

'He's not here! The cage is empty!'

Inside the van Tancredi and Kalan were sat together in the seat of a large leather chair. The door of the van was only slightly ajar, but it let in enough twilight to illuminate the worry on Tancredi's face. 'What's happened to Uncle Totti?' The sparrow looked down on the empty bird cage that was lying by the easy chair.

'He must have got away' said Kalan cheerily, you always said he was smart'

'Yeah' said Tancredi, 'He knows what's what. He knew they was leaving town' The sparrow turned around to Kalan with an earnest look on his face. 'We'd better get out of here pal, those men come back and shut that door, it ain't opening again in New York City'

As Tancredi spoke Kalan had a flash of inspiration.

Shokobaba was ready. No more small talk. The first chance she got she was going to dish out a lot of pain to that squirrel and his friends. The mere thought of finally maiming some animal made her giggle with an almost childlike pleasure. The more sensible, but just as nasty, part of her mind urged for caution. She had to strike when they were all together. If one of those sparrows escaped and warned the other two squirrels on the SDR all her careful planning up to now would be shot.

She looked carefully over the scene in front of her. The van still had is door slightly open, but there was no sign of the squirrel or the sparrow. She thought she saw something fly quickly out from the top of the door, but eventually decided it was a mere trick of the light. The two men were leaning against the door of the building talking softly and smoking. The cat looked under the van, and it seemed to her the perfect place for her crime. The birds couldn't fly out easily, it was nice and dark, perfect. As her eyes mover slowly up the side of the van again she saw the unmistakable head of the squirrel. He was gripping the side of the door with his paws and waving his tail, beckoning her to come over. Shokobaba scratched her claws one last time on the sidewalk under the mailbox and trotted stealthily towards the van. The moment Kalan saw that she was coming over he disappeared back inside.

Making a quick glance to make sure the men were still occupied n their late night conversation, Shokobaba jumped up onto the edge of the door and called inside softly. 'Kalan? What's up? Where are you?'

There was no reply. Shokobaba moved slowly inside the van. 'Kalan have you rescued the bird? We really should go. I've found something really interesting under the van. You should come and take a look with me….. Kalan?'

Shokobaba flicked her claws out. Under the van, in the van, what the heck. 'Kalan?'

'I'm over here' Kalan's tiny voice seemed to be coming from the very back of the van. Shokobaba crouched down and moved slowly towards it.

'Kalan are you ok?' Shokobaba tone of voice was very sweet but there was a bitter aftertaste in the air after she had spoken. 'Are you playing some sort of game with me Kalan? Don't be silly, now's not the time, we've got to get out of here'

'It's not a game Shoko'

Shokobaba sensed she was getting closer to the voice. Her claws tingled in anticipation. 'Where are your sparrow friends? Where's Uncle Totti?'

Shokobaba started to circle around the area where she thought Kalan's voice was coming from. Her eyes were gradually getting used to the darkness at the back of the van and she could easily make out shapes.

'Uncle Totti wasn't here Shoko'

The white cat started to grit her teeth. 'Well, is he safe?'

Kalan moved out from under the box he had been hiding behind and jumped silently atop of a large cabinet. He could see Shokobaba moving slowly towards his earlier hiding place. 'Is Totti safe?' Shokobaba pricked up her ears for Kalan's reply.

'I'm sure he is. He knows what's what'

Shokobaba looked upwards. The squirrel had moved. Kalan caught sight of her bright evil blue eye lit by the light coming in from the open door, but she hadn't spotted him. 'You're starting to scare me' she said trying to sound playful 'stop this game and come out'

From the top of the cabinet, Kalan skillfully jumped onto the underside of the roof. There were several metal rails stretching lengthways along it and Kalan gripped one of these. Moving upside down he made his way silently towards the door, at the back of the van Shokobaba was still rummaging around the boxes near the cabinet.

As Kalan arrived at the door he could hear Tancredi chirping loudly outside. That was the signal. Kalan slipped out of the door and onto the roof just a second before one of the two men slammed the door firmly shut. At almost the same instance the engine started up and the whole van vibrated beneath him.

'Jump, squirrelly, jump!' Tancredi shouted out loud as he buzzed around Kalan.

The man who had closed the door had gotten into the passenger seat at the front and the van started to move. Kalan lost his balance and fell backwards as the van jerked forward. The driver then slammed the vehicle noisily into reverse and started to make a three point turn. Kalan sat himself back up and as the rear of the van came up to the sidewalk he launched himself onto a small tree. He flew through the air and grabbed the tree trunk with a strong hug. Tancredi continued to hover around the squirrel as he slid slowly down to the ground, and they both watched as the van from 'Wonderful Wichita Removals' headed east towards the Holland Tunnel, New Jersey and be yonder.

'Bad cat?' Tancredi asked as the van turned the corner.

'Bad cat's in the van' replied Kalan with a satisfied smirk.

'Sweet pal, sweet' said Tancredi admiringly.

The moment the van door slammed shut Shokobaba made a mad dash towards it. Even though her eyes had become accustomed to the dim light of earlier, now everything was pitch black. She stared blankly in the direction of the door. Her eyes not blinking once. As the inside of the van started to rock she realized she was moving, but the expression on her face remained unchanged. She knew Kalan was no longer in the van with her, and she also knew she had no idea where she was going. Her stare became more intense and she started to tap her nails on the van floor. Lightly at first, but gradually with more pressure, digging each nail hard into the floor. By the time the van was in the Holland Tunnel the little nail on her right paw snapped in two. The pain gave her an excuse to let out an almighty wail, but her scream had more to do with frustration than pain. That squirrel had been on to her all the time. That squirrel had trapped her. That squirrel had made her break her nail. That squirrel. That squirrel. That squirrel.

That squirrel was making his way back to his friends with Tancredi. Of course Kalan had known all along that Shokobaba was not to be trusted. He had spotted the pigeons watching the action back in the Hester Street alley, the same ones that had been following them all around Chinatown and talking to the mice. He had guessed correctly that they were all working for the cat. Kalan had also realized that they were mainly doing it out of fear. This became more than apparent after he had sneaked back to the alley and caught Shokobaba threatening Dusi. Kalan had thought it better not to let on his suspicions to the other Battery Parkers, he had opted just to wait until an opportunity presented itself to ditch the cat without getting anyone hurt. Tancredi's van had been a godsend.

'You what?' said Risu as Kalan told him and Funni what had happened when he and Tancredi caught up with them on the edge of SDR Park and West Houston.

'Well I guess that might explain why I didn't like the mice' said Funni.

'But we saw her save Dusi!' said Risu a little frustrated, he was having a hard time taking it all in.

'Yeah' replied Kalan, 'and then I saw her trying to kill him when she thought we had gone'

'And why didn't you tell us?' Funni asked pushing her tail near Kalan's face.

'If that cat had suspected for one second that we were on to her, we'd all have been in danger. We were safe as long as she thought she had us all fooled'

'So why go to all that work' said Funni, 'to make friends with us and follow us all the way up here?' As she spoke the answer came to her and she answered her own question. 'Bilka! She wanted us to lead her to Bilka!'

'Wow' said Risu as he absorbed all the details, 'That's one sneaky cat' The others nodded at him in agreement, 'So I guess if we ever bump into her again there will be a lot less chit chat and a lot more biting'

'Hopefully we've seen the last of her' said Kalan, 'that van was pretty big and Tancredi's Uncle says they travel the longest distances'

'And what about this mysterious Uncle Totti?' asked Funni looking over to Tancredi, 'Has *anyone* actually seen him yet? How did he get away?'

Tancredi shook his head. 'I don't know. He wasn't in the van. I is going to help yous get to Tompkins then I is gonna look for my Uncle Totti. He's probably back at his clock............ I least I pray he is'

With Tancredi lending a hand it wasn't long before they had crossed Houston and First Avenue and were making their way up Avenue A towards Tompkins Square Park. Their progress had been made a lot easier by the 'Green streets' project set up by the City Council. Many of the unused spaces between roads and crossings had been transformed into tiny gardens and shrub filled spaces. In fact most of the central strip that separated the bi directional traffic on West Houston was made up of tiny trees and grass, and this made traveling a breeze for the squirrels.

It was still dark when the squirrels got their first site of the large trees of Tompkins Park as they sat on a mailbox on the corner of 7th Street.

'I don't see any buildings at all over there' said Funni excitedly as she gazed over the street into the darkness of the park.

'We're going to give Bilka a surprise' said Kalan

'Yeah not half as big as if we had turned up with that cat in tow' said Risu with a laugh.

'Shut up you' said Funni nudging Risu, 'He won't be awake for a long while yet. He's probably just snoring peacefully in a warm drey'

The squirrels had been traveling for several hours and had covered more than a mile. As Funni spoke the idea of sleeping in a comfortable, safe place made all of them unconsciously yawn at the same time.

'Well he's got the right idea' said Risu, 'Let's get over there and join him'

The three of them had not smelt the familiar odor of other squirrels since City Hall, and it comfortingly wafted over them as they ran across 7th Street and into the park.

Tancredi had found for them an old unused Parks Department wooden drey box around twenty feet up an oak facing the street. Once inside it became obvious that the Tompkins park squirrels used the box for storage space as it was filled with loose twigs, leaves and various pieces of paper and card.

'These guys have got a bit of everything in here' said Risu as he tried to shift things around and make himself a comfortable spot. 'Hey Kalan!' he said as he rolled himself backwards into a pile of newspaper scraps, 'Do you think these squirrels are going to be having an election while we're here?'

'I sincerely hope not' replied Kalan dryly, 'I think I'd like that about as much I'd like bumping into Shokobaba again'

'Bad cat' said Tancredi listening in from the edge of the box. 'You squirrelys got lucky that she wanted your pal, else she'd of got yous as soon as she sees yous'

'Yeah' said Kalan, 'I suppose we've got to hand it to Bilka. He must have riled her something rotten'

'And you are certainly not in her good books either now' said Funni, 'She's probably cursing your name in the back of the van right now'

'Maybe' said Kalan acting unconcerned, 'I just hope she learns a lesson on her way to wherever she's going and treats whoever she meets down there more respectfully'

'Fat chance' chirped Tancredi, 'The moments theys open the doors, she's gonna jump out and cause all manner o pain to the poor souls she runs into'

'Don't be so certain Tancredi' said Kalan as he laid back comfortably in Risu's pile of paper, 'Thought expands the mind, and locked up in the dark she is going to have a lot of opportunity for extending her mental horizons'

In fact Kalan was half right. As her van spend south along the New Jersey Turnpike Shokobaba was thinking hard about Kalandaka. Not of what she had done to him, but of what she would do to him. She imagined scratching him, and each time she struck she took a letter of his name.

'Kalandaka' *WHACK!*

'Kalandak' *SRATCH!*

Unfortunately with this time passing mantra, once she had eliminated his name letter by letter his smirky, know it all face reappeared in Shokobaba's minds eye and she had to start all over again.

'Ka' *SWIPE!*

'K' *SMASH!*

'KALANDAKA!'

Shokobaba found herself, for the umpteenth time, screeching out the squirrel's name and shaking her head. This time however it wasn't only her who was screeching. The driver of the van hit the brakes hard and the van came to a noisy stop. The cat was flung violently towards the back of the van, and just avoided being squashed by a large bookcase as it – and the rest of the furniture that hadn't been tied done well – went flying everywhere.

The driver had slammed into an emergency stop to avoid hitting another car that had burst one of its back tires. Both vehicles had come to a halt on the hard shoulder and although everyone was a bit shaky, no one was hurt.

'I don't know what could have happened' said the driver of the car as he analyzed his tire with the driver of the van, 'must have hit some glass or a stone or something'

'You got a spare?' asked the driver of the van

'Yeah I got one in the back' As he said this, the car driver looked over at the van and a thought came to him, 'I hope you Fellas had everything strapped down good back there'

The two men from the van looked at each other. 'You go check' said the driver to his colleague, 'while I help out here'

Back inside the van Shokobaba was licking her paw to get her mind off the pain the broken nail was giving her. However the spilt second she heard noises coming from the van door she sprung up and leaped towards it. As it slowly opened she flung herself towards the human figure behind it. With her claws stretched out she managed to scratch his face before she hit the ground.

As the man screamed out in a combination of shock and pain Shokobaba looked quickly around to get her bearings. She saw the direction the van was facing. That wasn't a route she wanted to continue, so she turned and ran quickly off in the opposite direction. She moved quickly off the road and into a green hedge that ran along the side of the highway. Soon the sounds of the men shouting were long behind her.

Shokobaba didn't have any idea where she was, or even if she was headed in the right direction. She was, however, out of the van. That was the first step to getting back to New York, and getting back to New York would be the first step to having a reunion with............ that squirrel.

The Afternoon at Tompkins Sq Park

Funni was the first to wake up. It had only just gone midday, but it seemed a lot later because of the heavy dark clouds covering most of Manhattan. She hopped over to the box entrance and looked out over Tompkins Park. It certainly wasn't as elegant looking as the City Hall Park had been, but there was a great deal more grass and lots of large welcoming trees. She sensed Risu close behind her and edged to one side to let him peer outside as well. 'It's really nice' he said, 'I wondered how long it was going to be before we saw grass like home again. There's so much of it'

'What's up? What can you see?' Kalan mumbled loudly from the back of the box, as he too woke up.

'This looks like a great place Kalan,' said Risu, 'come and have a look'

Kalan crawled over to the others and putting one paw on Risu's shoulder and the other on Funni's he pushed himself up to get a better view.

Despite the gloomy weather the sight of the large green open spaces and plenty of large trees was very satisfying for all of the squirrels. Kalan looked and smiled. 'What are we waiting for?' he said, 'let's get down there and make some friends' He led the way out of the wooden box and down the trunk. 'Tancredi told us that these squirrels were a friendlier bunch than the City Hall lot' Kalan and the other two ran across a pathway, through an iron fence and onto the main central lawn of Tompkins Square Park.

'I hope he hooks up with his Uncle Totti' said Risu, 'and then keeps his promise to come back up here after. I kind of miss the guy when he's not around'

'Well when we find Bilka I certainly won't mind hanging around here to wait for him' said Kalan as he sat on his hind legs and looked around the lawn, 'All that running around on concrete has made my feet sore'

Kalan spotted what he had been looking for. 'Let's start by introducing ourselves to those guys' and he pointed over towards two light brown squirrels he had spotted sitting near the base of a tree to the edge of the lawn.

The two Tompkins Park squirrels were too wrapped up in their own argument to even notice the arrival of the squirrels from Battery Park.

'Don't you go there, I'm telling you I know what happened'

'Ah shove it where the sun don't shine. I saw it with these my own eyes'

One of the two pointed to his eyes with his paws outstretched. 'Those eyes couldn't make out the difference between a walnut and doggy do-da. Come to think of it, that would explain the smell around here'

'And just what are you trying to suggest? If there's a problem with personal hygiene I'd take a long sniff of the air around your tail before I began accusing others'

'You want to make something of it? You want a piece of me?'

'Bring it on'

'Erm excuse me......' Kalan decided it better to interrupt the discussion before it got worse. The two Tompkins Park squirrels turned around and realized they had visitors. 'Sorry to interrupt' Kalan cleared his throat as the two watched him in curious silence. 'But we're new to the Park and we just wanted to know where your main drey is. We're looking for a friend of ours you see'

'You guys are friends of Bilka?' said the squirrel with the smelly tail.

'Yes. Yes!' said Funni, 'Where is he? Is he here?'

The two squirrels looked at each other briefly, 'He went off down 9th Street just a few days ago. Said all his goodbyes and everything'

'No he didn't' said the other Tompkins Park squirrel, 'I swear I saw him just yesterday hanging out at the Pagoda'

'You know when you see something with your eyes closed it's called a dream'

'Oh really? Well when I look at you with my eyes open I call it a nightmare!'

This time it was Funni who broke up the two. 'Where's this Pagoda? Maybe we should start looking there?'

Even the arguing squirrels could sense the strength of urgency in Funni's tone of voice. 'The Pagoda is half way up the large Elm in the lawn just behind this one'

The squirrel turned his body half away around and pointed in the direction of Avenue B, 'It's the home of Shin, our leader' He turned back towards his competitive colleague, 'Did I get that right at least?'

'Well the sun may shine occasionally on fools, but they still remain suntanned fools'

'Are you calling me an idiot?'

'Do you need me to spell it out for you? Sign language perhaps?'

'Well I can see you guys have a lot to talk about,' said Kalan interrupting again, 'so thanks for the help and see you around'

'Yeah anytime, happy to have been of help'

'You didn't help them, I did'

'You couldn't help yourself down a tree'

'Oh is that so? Why don't I help you to a whack from my tail?'

'Go ahead, I'm trembling here, you got me real frightened now. No really you have'

The squirrel took a few steps backward, 'It's not from any feeble force you could muster of course... but the smell your tail will leave in its wake. Man, *that's* scary'

The other one ignored the sarcasm and spoke to Kalan while trying to stare out his tormentor. 'Hey, new guy! Did I help you out or what?' Getting no reply he turned around to find that they had gone.

'See I told you' answered the other squirrel, 'You gotta do something about that smelly tail or you'll never make any friends'

'So what does a Pagoda look like?' asked Risu as he and the others crossed through another fence and onto a smaller lawn.

'Like that' said Funni looking upwards.

Risu looked up and saw a large wooden object balancing between the trunk of a tree and its thickest branch. It appeared as if bits of triangular boxes had been placed one on top of the other, each becoming smaller the higher up they went. 'There's a squirrel sitting outside' said Risu straining his neck upwards, 'Do you reckon that's Shin?'

'Only one way to find out' replied Kalan and he ran towards the base of the tree. The others followed and all of them climbed quickly up.

The squirrel sitting alone outside the wooden Pagoda gave the Battery Parkers a tiny smile by way of a welcome as they jumped onto his branch. 'Hello' he said softly, 'Our little Park seems very popular with foreign squirrels these days. One last week, three of you now'

'We're Bilka's friends. I'm Kalan and this is Funni and Risu. We've been looking for him'

The squirrel nodded as if he already knew who the squirrels were.

'Well I'm sorry but Bilka left us a few days ago, but maybe Shin knows where he went'

'Could we ask him?' Funni's tone of voice was as earnest as ever, and she looked over to the small dark entrance of the Pagoda as she spoke.

'Shin isn't in' said the squirrel quite flatly.

'Can we wait for him then?' asked Kalan.

'Of course' said the squirrel reverting back to a friendly tone, 'Please step inside and make yourselves comfortable. I'm sure he won't be long'

Muttering an array of various thanks yous, the Battery Parkers squeezed themselves through the narrow entrance hole into the Pagoda. The inside seemed much larger than they had expected so they spread out a little and found places to sit down. There was a strong, but not unpleasant smell of musty incense, and small circular window like holes in the Pagoda walls let in quite a lot of the gray light from outside. The squirrels sat in silence and waited, each one wrapped in their own thoughts. They didn't have much time to dwell on them though as after only a few moments the squirrel who they had been talking to outside pushed himself through the entrance and gave them another tiny smile.

'Is Shin on his way?' asked Funni

'Shin is in' replied the squirrel.

Risu's 'Weirdo Alert' started to sound off in the back of his mind and he edged a little closer to Kalan.

'I am he' said the squirrel and sat down in the center of the room. He took a deep breath and raised his arms up into the air, hummed a little chant, then lowered them to his sides. 'And I welcome you all to my humble home' He closed his eyes.

'Thank you' said Kalan 'Thank you for your welcome and let me just say that we are.........'

'Why didn't you say who you were outside?' Funni cut into Kalan's attempted diplomacy and asked what all of them were thinking.

'Funni' muttered Kalan under his breath.

'I am Shin when I am here in the Pagoda. Shin the moral guide, Shin the key to inner wisdom, Shin the leader of our community' Shin did not open his eyes as he spoke. 'When I am outside of these wooden walls of enlightenment I am merely a humble squirrel. Argumentative, impulsive, foolish'

The alarm bells in Risu's head were going ape, but he kept it quiet. Funni also didn't know what to make of Shin and looked hopefully over to Risu who shrugged. Kalan began to realize why Bilka hadn't hung around for long.

'I see' he said tentatively, 'So as Shin, could you tell us something about Bilka's stay here? Did he mention where he was headed?'

With his eyes still firmly shut, Shin started to hum.

Kalan tried again. 'We'll be on our way very soon. We just need to know which direction he took'

Shin lifted his paw to his lips to indicate he wanted silence, but kept on humming. In fact the volume of the humming was slowly rising.

'This is useless' said Funni, 'Let's get out of here and find someone else'

Risu was all for this and he got up to leave with Funni, but Kalan pulled them both back.

'Wait a minute, let him finish for goodness sake'

They reluctantly sat down and waited. And waited. And waited.

For nearly twenty minutes Shin hummed in a constant low tone and then, just when Risu was about to drop off to sleep, he stopped humming and opened his eyes. 'Aaaah' he said in that pleasurable way you do after a drinking a glass of cold water on a hot summers day. 'My mind is clear and my body is pure'

'Well that's wonderful' said Funni sarcastically, 'I instead have a headache'

Kalan punched her slightly on the arm, but she punched him back harder. Risu stepped in and pulled them apart. 'Don't you two go starting up like those squirrels we met earlier. Cut it out'

Kalan felt a little ashamed, but Funni was only just beginning to get angry. 'Why do we always have to be polite to every lunatic we meet?' She said, her voice quavering with frustration.

'Because everybody is different' said Kalan, 'and we have to respect those differences'

Shin appeared to not notice the argument his guests were having and he just smiled blandly at the wall.

'Please Shin' said Risu, 'Is there anything at all you can tell us about Bilka?'

'He decided to leave us' said Shin 'he felt that he had not yet achieved the purest state of mind, and therefore was not ready to join our community. He left us about three days ago. His final destination was unclear to him, but I knew' Shin stopped talking and turned his smile from the wall to the squirrels.

'And?' said Funni

'I knew and I told him. His final destination would be his inner fulfillment'

Shin, apparently satisfied with himself, crossed his arms and began to hum.

'Again with the humming' said Risu

Funni turned angrily on Kalan. 'Are you satisfied now? Can we go please?'

Kalan nodded meekly. 'We'll be off now Shin, see you around.........or something' said Risu as the three of them edged their way around Shin and exited the Pagoda.

Shin looked straight ahead fixing his stare on the back wall of his wooden sanctuary, but if anyone had been paying attention they would have noticed his humming had become a fraction louder. The moment they got outside Kalan launched into an uncharacteristic tirade of frustration.

'Geesh Funni, how could you call someone a lunatic to their face? We're guests in his house and you insult him? Just what do you think you were playing at?'

Funni had no intention of taking any criticism from Kalan. 'Because I'm a normal squirrel, and I'm sick to the back teeth of having to politely put up with all these crazies we are meeting. I just want to find my dad'

'We all want to find Bilka' replied Kalan, 'and see if he wants to come with us to Central Park. That's why we're here'

'I'm not sure I want to go that far anymore' said Funni, 'I haven't met anyone normal since we left home, so I reckon Central Park will be full of humming squirrels'

'Don't talk like that Funni' said Risu, 'We've met some cool folks, what about Sunda? You liked him'

Funni crossed her arms and just huffed.

'And how do you think Sunda would have acted back there in the Pagoda?' said Kalan

'I'm not talking about it any more' replied Funni and she started to climb down the tree trunk, 'We're wasting time, and we've got to find out where Bilka is'

'No wait, let's sort this thing out first' said Kalan and he made after her.

'Let her be' said Risu following 'let her run if off'

'No Risu, she's wrong. She can't go around judging people by her own standards'

'You do pick on her sometimes' said Risu

'No I don't'

'Oh come on, admit it you are always on her case a bit'

'What do you mean by that? I'm just trying to keep us all together' replied Kalan ruffling his fur indignantly.

By the time Risu and Kalan got to the bottom of the tree a full blown argument had erupted between the two. 'She's just being herself and you can't handle that' said Risu raising his voice.

'If being herself means being rude to everybody she meets then she's got to change' Kalan was also beginning to shout.

'And who are you to tell anyone that they've got to change?' Risu began pointing at Kalan, 'What about you and all your secrets? Not telling us about the cat or keeping us in the dark back at City Hall. Is that fair?'

'There's no similarity between the two. One concerned our safety, the other is just about good manners'

'And it's good manners to always pick on Funni?'

'Guys, Guys!' Funni stepped in between them.

'Look!' she said and both Kalan and Risu looked with her around the lawn beneath the Pagoda tree. There were maybe twenty or so squirrels dotted around. Some foraging, some hiding or recovering their stashes, some eating, but all of them arguing. The squirrels closest to their right were already in full swing.

'Who's moved my stash?'

'Your mother. You needed to lose weight anyhow'

'Well I'd need to lose weight if I wanted to become a skinny good for nothing like you'

'Dream on fat boy'

'What is going on here?' said Kalan as he and the others looked and listened to the multitude of fighting squirrels. To his left another squirrel couple were at it as well

'Don't stand so close, you're bugging me'

'It's you that's standing too close to me......... back off!'

'I was here first! You moved'

'Every squirrel here is arguing about anything and everything' said Funni. She looked at Risu and Kalan with an ironic grin, 'It's infectious isn't it?'

Kalan and Risu realized that they had been arguing since leaving the Pagoda and shook their heads.

Two squirrels came up to the Battery Parkers as they sat under the pagoda tree trying to get a grasp on the situation.

'Hey guys, is Shin up there?' asked one of them. He seemed to be sporting a black eye.

'Shin is in' said Risu trying to be friendly yet subtly sarcastic ar the same time.

'Great' replied the squirrel, 'well if you'll excuse me, me and my friend here want a word with him'

'I'm not your friend' said the other squirrel in a surly voice.

'Sure, sure' said Risu and he moved aside to let the squirrels pass, 'but can I ask you something though?'

'What?' said the squirrel with the black eye.

'Why is everyone arguing?'

'No we're not' replied the other squirrel.

'He wasn't asking you' said black eye, 'and yes in fact we do argue, and I'll tell you why'

'Well go on then genius, tell him'

'I will'

'When? Next winter?'

'I mean I would tell him if I could,' black eye sounded a little confused, 'I mean.......... Er..... Well I don't know exactly, but I know we do'

'Typical' said the other squirrel tutting loudly.

'I mean I don't know why we argue, but I would be happy to tell you if I knew. It's just that I don't'

'Ah quit your confusion and get up the tree'

'Don't push me around, I'm going'

'Yeah not fast enough. Get on up the trunk I don't want to look at your backside all day'

'Trust me it's better than looking at your face'

The two squirrels took the rest of their argument up the tree trunk with them and left the Battery Parkers on the ground very perplexed.

'There is something very wrong with this place' said Risu.

'It's like some sort of bug' said Funni 'an arguing bug'

'Everyone is so aggressive and it's starting to rub off on all of us' said Kalan.

Risu and Funni agreed, but no one had any suggestions and all around them the air was heavy with verbal argument.

'You think you're so smart'

'I don't think, I know'

'What you know wouldn't keep a banana peel green'

'What are you talking about?'

'You're so dumb'

'Banana peels green? You've got no ideas, you've got no clue...and somehow that doesn't surprise me'

'It's as if' said Kalan, as they all listened to the increasingly ludicrous discussions 'they are arguing for the sake of it. Like it's the only type of conversation they've got'

'What say we split up and have a look around? We can't argue with each other that way' suggested Funni.

'I'll stay here' said Kalan, 'I want to try and talk to Shin again'

'Good luck' said Risu then he pointed in the direction of Avenue A, 'I'll go that way and see what I can come up with'

'Good' said Funni, 'We can all meet back at the wooden box we slept in when we're done. And let's try not to argue with anyone ok?'

Kalan watched as his friends sped off in different directions and felt a little guilty for having argued with both of them. However he wasn't able to contemplate on this for long as soon another two arguing squirrels were making their way towards him.

'Seeing as how you couldn't work out how to use your legs if you hadn't seen how everyone else uses theirs, I'm going to ask this guy' said one of the squirrels as they approached Kalan. He had dark orange fur and a bright white chest.

'At least my legs don't have to wake up every morning to find they've got to carry your fat belly around! The other squirrel shouted out from behind,

'And besides, what makes you think that guys gonna know jack?

'Anyone in this park is going to have a better idea than you'

'Really? I think my idea that you are a fat, lazy bozo is pretty universally accepted round these parts'

'How would you like to universally accept my paw up your nose?'

'Great, do it. Anything that would stop me having to smell your breath'

'What's up?' interrupted Kalan, 'What's the problem with you guys?'

'It's like this' said the squirrel with the bright white chest, 'My colleague here thinks that its going to rain and that it'll wash away all the nuts from our stash we've got hidden in the middle of this lawn'

'Uh huh' nodded Kalan as he listened

'But I say it ain't' continued the squirrel, 'and even if it does they're buried too deep for rainwater to wash them up'

Both squirrels looked at Kalan eager for his reply.

'Well.....' Kalan started off slowly, 'you both have good points, but even deep stashes can get washed up if the rain is heavy enough' Kalan looked up to the dark gray sky, 'It's difficult to say what the rain will be like'

'He can't answer us' said one of the squirrels impatiently, 'Typical. Let's go ask Shin'

'Yeah, right, and get an earful of humming and 'find the answer within you' talk' said White Chest.

'Why don't you just bury your stash in a place where even if it does rain, it's still going to be safe?'

The two squirrels looked first at Kalan and then at themselves.

'Hey, now that's clever'

'He's got a point there'

'We could put it all in the old bolt holes on the creaky oak tree'

'Or how about in between the stones near the edge of the dog run. That place always stays dry, plus not too many other squirrels like hanging out there'

'Yeah I like that idea' White Chest smiled and pulled his friend closer to him, 'Let's go dig it up and move it before the rain starts'

He turned and patted Kalan on the shoulder. 'Thanks pal' White Chest then chased into the middle of the lawn after his friend.

Kalan watched them leave and felt pleased with himself for having broken up the argument, but as he started to make his way up the tree to Shin's Pagoda, he could hear another one in full swing.

'And I say humming or no we go in. I don't want to stand outside here looking at your ugly face all day'

'For crying out loud how many times? He doesn't like being disturbed when he's meditating, we have to wait outside till he's done'

'Still humming huh?' said Kalan casually as he reached the Pagoda branch.

The squirrel with the black eye nodded, 'He's been at it since we got here'

Still feeling confident from his earlier success at diffusing verbal warfare, Kalan decided to give it another try. 'So what do you guys want to talk to Shin about?'

'It's his problem' said Black Eye pointing an accusing paw at the other squirrel. 'He wants to hang out near the children's playground on Avenue A'

'Too right I do' interrupted the other squirrel, 'There's rich pickings over there'

'OK ok' said Black Eye, 'but I'm telling you that the kids over on the Avenue B end are far more generous'

'Oh professor Dumb you are so misguided. Those kids are so tight they keep their hands clenched even when they fall over'

'Yeah sure, sure, and I bet the mini humans on Avenue A are just giving it out 24/7'

'Well I don't know if they would give a thick head like you the time of day, but........'

The arguing squirrels suddenly became silent and twitched their ears. 'He's finished humming'

'...... let's do it'

Black Eye pushed his way past the other squirrel and squeezed himself into the Pagoda.

'Come on' he called out from inside, 'before he starts up again'

After letting out a small sigh the other squirrel also made his way inside.

Kalan looked out over Tompkins Park. There were lots of squirrels about now, and although he couldn't hear too much from up in the tree, it was clear from their body language that they were all arguing. It was a pretty depressing sight, so Kalan turned his attention back to the Pagoda and moved closer. He lent his ear against the side of the wall until he could make out what was being said inside.

'The answer is always closer than you think, but it is often hidden under the flimsiest of disguises'

Kalan recognized Shin's calm and melodic voice, 'So you need to open all your eyes to see the answer'

'All my eyes? I've only got two'

'You forget that it is your inner eye that can see around the corner, that can look over a mountain. Use it to uncover the solution to your problem. Try to see over the mountain, try to look around the corner'

'Sure, Shin inner eye, right. But what we want to know is whether the kids on Avenue A are.......'

'HUMMMMMMMMMMMM'

'Shin?'

'Aw shoot, he's off again. HEY! Shin!'

'HUMMMMMMMMM'

'Forget it, it's over. Total waste of time. Should have used my inner eye and saved myself the bother of coming up here'

Kalan listened as the argument grew while Shin hummed away in the background. As he listened he began to understand just why all the squirrels at Tompkins Park could never agree on anything.

'Let's go ask Shin, Let's go see Shin. He'll know what to do. Geesh. Who is the real meat head? The loon or the loons who waste their time listening to him?'

'Aw quit your whining. If you spent less time moaning and more time thinking you might actually not give everyone you meet a headache'

As the squirrels emerged from the Pagoda Kalan was ready for them.

'Have you ever actually been to the Avenue A playground?' he said to the black eyed squirrel.

'Well, err... no, not as such'

Kalan quickly turned to the other squirrel. 'And I guess you've never hung out much at the Avenue B one have you?' The squirrel shook his head, 'So neither of you really know which park could have the best pickings do you?'

The squirrels looked at each other and shrugged while muttering a variety of 'wells', 'I's', and 'maybes'.

'So here's my suggestion' said Kalan excitedly. He pointed his tail at Black Eye. 'You don't argue and go with him to the Avenue A playground tomorrow. Stay the day without arguing and see what pickings you get'

'But.'

'No buts' said Kalan waving his paw. 'The following day you go with your friend to the Avenue B playground and do the same' Kalan was now staring squarely at the other squirrel, but he stepped back a bit to look at them both. 'Do this for a week or so, alternating days, and by the end you'll have a good idea as to which playground has the most generous kids'

The two squirrels looked blankly at Kalan's confident face, but their blank looks soon turned into small smiles as the idea sunk in. 'That's not a bad notion' said Black Eye.

'Yeah, I like it' said the other squirrel, 'we could start right now at your playground if you like' He patted Black Eye on the shoulder.

'Great' said Black Eye who in turn gave Kalan a friendly pat 'Thanks for that'

The other squirrel was already making plans. 'I'll go and round up a few of my cousins and tell them, if we are going to hit the playgrounds we should hit 'em big'

He glanced up from his thoughts and smiled at Kalan. 'You want to come as well?'

'I might pop by tomorrow and see how you're all getting on, but right now I want to try and have a word with Shin'

'Good luck with that' smiled the other squirrel, then pulled on his friend's tail. 'Let's go round up the cousins and practice a few cutie stares, you know how kids can't resist them'

'Ok' said Black Eye, 'see you around' he said to Kalan and ran down the trunk with his friend. Kalan watched them hit the ground and gave a final wave goodbye with his tail then moved back towards the Pagoda.

The humming from inside had stopped, but as Kalan took a step towards the entrance he was pushed backwards as Shin came out through the tiny hole and onto the branch.

'Shin' said Kalan, 'I was just coming in to speak to you'

'Sorry' replied Shin keeping his eyes fixed on the ground, 'but that will have to wait. Shin isn't in'

'Yes he is' said Kalan, 'I'm talking to him.... I mean...you'

'No, sorry' replied Shin slouching, 'You must be confused. I'm not in the Pagoda'

'Yes I can see that' said Kalan refusing to allow himself to get drawn into anything other than a normal conversation, 'You are not inside the Pagoda, but you are still Shin'

'Please little squirrel, come back later when Shin is in' Shin turned his back to Kalan and looked down over Tompkins Park. The presence of this newcomer was irritating him. He thought of trying to hum and concentrate his mind on somewhere else, but he found that difficult to do outside the Pagoda. Maybe if he just ignored him the squirrel would eventually get bored and go and annoy someone else.

'A fine leader you are' said Kalan to Shin's back, 'Look down there below you. All those squirrels you should be helping through life are wasting their time in futile arguments because they have no guidance from you'

Shin didn't reply. He lifted his shoulders and rubbed the back of his head on them.

'A good leader should help end arguments, or at least try and solve them'

Shin listened as Kalan continued talking then without turning muttered under his breath, 'Shin does what he can'

'No he doesn't' said Kalan, 'he sits in that Pagoda and blanks out the problems he hears by humming'

'It concentrates the mind'

'It concentrates your mind, but it doesn't solve anything. You may well have found your inner peace for a while but every time you come back to reality all the problems you were running away from are all still here waiting for you'

'But if everyone could follow Shin's lead, then they could all find inner calm'

'And never get anything done!' Kalan noticed that he was raising his voice, so lowered it a bit. 'Shin' Kalan said trying to sound comforting and confident at the same time. 'Squirrels are practical animals, we need practical advice. Don't get me wrong, I'm all in favor of expanding your mind, in fact I wish I had your ability to find a peaceful place in my thoughts sometimes' Kalan hopped over and sat beside Shin, 'But just look down there' he said, pointing to the groups of squabbling squirrels. 'Those poor guys need some leadership. They come up here hoping to get some guidance and maybe a decision. They then end up running back down without a clue and finally just take it out on each other'

'You sound like your friend' said Shin sullenly, 'Shin told him that squirrels must find inner balance and understand the significance of their existence in the greater sense'

'And what did Bilka say to you Shin?'

Shin took a deep breath, 'He said that squirrels don't care about any hidden meanings in their lives. They only want to know how to get through the day, the week at best, without any undue stress'

'Well I think he's right' said Kalan, 'The majority of squirrels I know don't think about why they are here, they want to know when they are going to eat next or if someone has found their stash or if they are going to have to go on douse patrol in the rain. These are all things that you, as their leader, can help them out with'

Shin shook his head slightly and edged away from Kalan, he didn't like what he was hearing, but Kalan carried on. 'Maybe when a squirrel has no other worries or thoughts on his mind he can spend time pondering his greater meaning' While speaking Kalan thought back to his own sessions gazing out over the Hudson from Battery Park. Since he had been on the road he really hadn't had the time to sit back and think clearly as he had often liked to do. 'But it's a luxury most of us don't get around to having' he added.

'Yes well you should take this up with Shin, the next time he is in' said Shin, and without looking at Kalan – he had avoided Kalan's eyes the whole time – he edged his way quickly along the branch away from the annoying newcomer.

Kalan didn't want to give up, but the sensation that it would be a futile exercise was greater than that of rising to the challenge. He looked again at the lonely and confused figure of Shin out on the edge of the branch and then silently started to make his way down the tree trunk.

Two arguing squirrels were scrambling their way up.

'He'll know what to do, not like you'

'Garbage! He'll just hum us out of the room as usual'

'Forget it guys' Kalan said as he passed them halfway down the trunk, 'Shin isn't in'

It had been threatening to rain for most of the morning, and the second Kalan's feet hit the ground the weather made good on those threats. The first drops were large and heavy and almost hurt as they hit Kalan's fur. Kalan, ever the optimist, realized that the rain would send all the squirrels diving for cover so he would only have to follow them to find their main Drey. He chased behind a group of a half dozen squirrels who were running towards the large stump of a dead Oak tree on the East 7th Street side of the park. More squirrels were arriving from other ends of the park. Kalan followed one particular couple who jumped into an opening a few feet up the stump. The pair were, of course, arguing.

'I told you it was going to rain, but do you ever listen? Do you heck!'

'Oh for Pete's sake I don't know what's wetter, you or the weather'

Kalan followed them down the hole as it sloped gently out into what was clearly the main corridor of the Tompkins Park Drey.

The rain was coming down hard now, and the sound of it rumbled above the Drey as Kalan looked around. It came as no surprise to him that every squirrel pair he passed was still involved in a heated argument of one type or another. The noise of squabbling squirrels got louder and louder as Kalan approached the main meeting area of the Drey, and as he came out from the corridor into the large open space he was met by complete pandemonium. Kalan saw squirrels shouting at each other, others waving their arms in the air in animated arguments. The two squirrels to Kalan's immediate right sounded as if they were going to fight.

'Come on then, come on give me your best shot!'

'My best shot is going to knock you right into the middle of next week!'

'Dream on, you couldn't punch your way out of a wet paper bag'

Kalan found himself intervening and spoke to the squirrel closest to him who had his paws raised in front of his chest, 'Why do you two want to fight? What's this all about?'

'It's his fault' said the squirrel making a feeble swing at the other one, 'This bozo has been drilling holes in the wall between our rooms'

'I only did one. I need more air, I can't breath at night'

'Yeah and now I can't sleep because I've got this great big hole by my feet'

'This is ridiculous' said Kalan shouting above the din in the meeting room, 'Let me see'

The squirrel lowered his paws and seemed to relax a little. He looked over to the other squirrel who nodded. 'Yeah ok. It's not far, just down this corridor on the left'

Thankful to leave the main hall Kalan let the other squirrels lead him down the corridor for about twenty feet, then they turned left into a small cul du sac that contained a dozen small squirrel sleep holes.

'See' said one of the squirrels as Kalan followed him into his room. He was pointing to a two inch hole in the wall near the ground, 'Could you sleep with that by your feet?'

'And the other room?' said Kalan looking at the other squirrel who was already beckoning him to come over. Kalan popped his head into the much smaller and narrower room.

'I couldn't breath, I needed an air hole'

'Only an air head would make one like this' said the other squirrel. He was still in his room, but was poking his head through the hole.

Kalan looked quickly around the narrow room as a thought came to him. 'You're both right' he said, 'This room is very stuffy and needs extra ventilation, but on the other hand a hole so low to the ground is very inconvenient' Kalan pointed to the ceiling with his tail, 'Why not make a hole at the top of the wall? That way air still gets to circulate in here, while it shouldn't disturb your friend in his room'

There was a short moment of silence, then the squirrel who had his head poking out of the hole spoke up, 'Sounds good to me. I mean you need to breathe in here after all'

'And you can't sleep with a hole blowing air over your feet' said the other, 'I'll go find some stuff to plug it up for you'

'And I'll start digging a new hole for you up at the top'

'No, wait till I get back, I'll be able to give you a boost up so we can make it as high away from you as possible'

Listening to the two squirrels agreeing with each other gave Kalan a lot of satisfaction, but another thought crossed his mind, 'Did you guys go to Shin with this problem?'

'Oh sure' said the squirrel in the room with Kalan, 'We told him about it a week ago, but he told us some stuff about the answer was hidden behind how we conceive the problem'

'Yeah that's right' added the other squirrel, 'Something like the solution could be simply a variation of the problem' As he spoke his eyes widened, 'And now I come to think about it' he continued slowly giving his thoughts time to form into words, 'he was exactly right' He looked up from the hole to the other squirrel a little shocked at his moment of enlightenment.

'Why couldn't he have told us without all the mumbo jumbo' said the other squirrel with a frustrated tone, 'he didn't use to be like this, playing around with fancy words' He turned his gaze from his friend to Kalan, 'He used to give us a straight answer to a straight question'

Kalan couldn't resist asking the obvious question, 'What happened to him?'

'Well about three months ago Shin lost his partner in a nasty accident with a Doberman that had gotten away from its owner'

The other squirrel had pulled his head from out of the hole and joined the other two in the smaller room.

'That's right' he said continuing the story, 'She was minding her own business and this brute just ran past, picked her up in his jaws and .... Well...... that was that'

Kalan shuddered to himself as he imagined the terrible scene.

'Anyway Shin was devastated, as you'd expect completely inconsolable, but like the next day the P.D stuck that wooden Pagoda up on that tree. Shin was convinced it was a sign from his partner and every time he went inside he said he felt close to her.... Calm like. And every time he was outside he'd just lose it again' The squirrel shook his head and pierced his lips, 'That's when he changed and started giving us all this 'inner-meaning' stuff'

Kalan reminded himself of the lonely figure of Shin with his back towards him on the branch and felt very guilty. He had been so critical before, just jumping to conclusions. Poor Shin.

'Hey Kalan!' The sound of Risu's voice stopped Kalan's thoughts instantly. 'Hey Kalan, you down there?'

Kalan moved out of the room and shouted back to Risu who was running along the corridor. Risu ran down to greet him, 'A couple of folk said they'd seen you go down this way' said Risu with a smirk as he reached Kalan 'Its complete chaos in this place' Risu's smirk fell off his face when he saw that Kalan was near to tears.

Kalan saw Risu's concern but waved his paw in front of Risu's eyes. 'It's nothing Risu, don't worry about me it's ...erm ... all this noise that's all, where's Funni?'

'She found these two squirrels that weren't arguing and is helping them move their stash before the rain washes it away'

'Moving it to the stones near the dog run?' said Kalan, a sly smile coming back onto his face.

'Yes' said Risu a little taken aback, 'How did you know?'

'Because the squirrels here are starved of any practical advice. I just listened to their grievance and then gave the first logical solution that came into my head'

'Hmmm' said Risu with a shrug, 'I don't do logic. I'm pretty confused most of the time'

'You are one of the most practical, down to earth squirrels I know. Watch me and you'll see that it comes naturally'

'Watch you what?' Risu was perplexed.

'Let's go and break up a few arguments,' said Kalan and he grabbed Risu's paw and pulled him gently back towards the main hall.

'I'm not going in their again, my head hurts' wailed Risu

'Come on, let's make it into a game. How many disputes can we settle in ten minutes?'

'Kalan I understand your words, just can't work out what the heck you are talking about'

'Watch and listen' shouted Kalan so he could make himself heard in the main hall. He went straight up to the first squirrel couple that was arguing by the entrance.

'Give it up. You have no, no, no, no, no chance'

'My no, no, no, no, no chance is a thousand times better than any chance I would have if I had *your* body'

'What? Are you telling me you she'd prefer your flab to my muscle tone?'

'What's the problem guys?' shouted out Kalan

As usual the Tompkins Park squirrels were only too eager to extend their debate. 'This excuse for a squirrel reckons that Akka fancies him over me. I mean just look at him, that face could kill a fly'

'Akka?' shouted back Kalan.

'Akka is that wonderful girl arguing with her friend over there' said the flabby squirrel pointing towards a small pretty squirrel sitting a few feet from them, 'And besides' he continued, 'What I lack in physical features I more than make up for with my personality'

'HA!' shouted out his colleague, 'Your personality has the toughest job in this place'

'I'll take you out right now if you want'

'Wait here!' said Kalan and walked straight over to Akka.

'Excuse me interrupting, but are you Akka?'

'Maybe' replied the tiny squirrel, 'Who wants to know?'

'My name is Kalandaka and I was just wondering if you would be kind enough to solve a little problem for me?'

'Sure' replied Akka warming to this new face, 'anything to give me a break from this queen of pain' She glared at the other female she had been squabbling with.

'That makes two of us' replied her friend icily.

Kalan gently took Akka's arm and guided her to where Risu and the other two squirrels were waiting. She let herself be pulled over, but looked bewildered., 'What's this all about?' she asked

'Akka' said Kalan, 'These two guys would like to know which of them you like, as they both think you prefer the other one'

The squirrels went bright red.

'You must be joking. I'm not interested in either of them' scoffed Akka with that tone familiar to generations of male squirrels. It was the one you get when you know you have a snowball's chance on the beach in July. 'If you must know I'm holding out for Shin. He's a bit mixed up at the moment, but single and good looking'

Without any further comment, and not even a glance at her two potential suitors, Akka turned and went back to her own argument. Kalan looked at the two rejected squirrels and held up his paws defensively, 'Sorry, but you heard it from the girl herself'

'Shin told us that a squirrel shouldn't always be searching for truth if he is not prepared to accept that often that which is discovered may be unpalatable'

One of the two squirrels was talking to Kalan with that same wide eyed look of revelation the others had had in their rooms' minutes earlier. 'Sounded dumb at the time, but I guess I know what he was on about now' He turned to his rival and put a friendly paw on the other squirrels shoulder, 'I never really liked her anyhow. She's got a stocky tail'

'Ha, Ha' laughed his friend, 'Yeah and I always thought her eyes were too close together....but ...er.. I think we ought to go and apologize to Shin now that we know what he was on about. Remember you called him a loon'

The other squirrel looked a little sheepish, 'I know, I know you're right. I just wish he'd have told us straight without all that beating about the bush'

Both of them turned to face Kalan and took it in turns to shake his paw. 'Thanks for clearing that up'

'Yeah, thanks. We're going to go off and say sorry to the boss'

'He'll appreciate that I think' said Kalan as they hopped away, 'You see Risu' he went on, turning to look at his friend 'The squirrels here aren't so bad, they just need a little plain talking'

'I think I follow you' said Risu, 'ask them what's wrong and then offer a bit of practical advice'

'Just the first idea that comes into your head will probably help them out' Kalan replied nodding.

'But why can't they work it out for themselves?' said Risu

'I guess' said Kalan, 'that frustration and arguing go hand in hand most of the time and it can get a bit habit forming when everyone you know is at it. Look at us earlier today, we all slipped into the verbal aggression soon enough didn't we?'

'You are so right' said Risu after he had given the subject moments thought, 'Look how the pigeons and the humans living in this city have ended up'

Risu clasped his paws together and gave them a vigorous rub, 'Come on then, let's go break 'em up'

The rain continued to thunder down onto the grass above the main drey at Tompkins Square Park, and the sound of it echoed louder and louder as Risu and Kalan broke up one argument after another. It took them about an hour, but the main hall was transformed from an infernal screaming chaos into an oasis of mild mannered discussion.

'I solved more problems than you' said Risu triumphantly as he eventually caught up with Kalan near the center of the room.

'I was getting some of them to solve other squirrels problems as well' said Kalan

'Nah. I'm the best, you're always wrong. I win'

For a moment Kalan stared in confusion then as he caught a glimpse of a smile from Risu he playfully swished his tail in front of his friend's face, 'Stop that' he smiled,

'You know I'm kidding with you' laughed Risu 'Just wanted to see if you were still up for an argument after all this mediation'

'I think we should go and find Funni' said Kalan, and Risu had no argument with that.

After braving the downpour and getting very wet looking for her, Kalan and Risu eventually found Funni waiting for them in the Parks Department wooden drey they had originally agreed to meet up in. The squirrels whose stash she had been helping to move had given her a few nuts as way of thanking her and she laid them out on the floor. Kalan and Risu hungrily tucked in as she offered them around.

The Battery Parkers spent a long time in the drey discussing what they had all seen and done at Tompkins Park. Funni wanted to leave that same evening, but Risu reminded her that they still hadn't gotten any information about which direction Bilka had taken. Kalan in any case had another reason for wanting to stay on a while longer.

'We've got to help these squirrels and Shin understand one another' Kalan said earnestly, 'Shin has got to start talking to them and not over their heads, and they've all got to start thinking more for themselves'

'And how long do you think that's going to take?' replied Funni.

'Who knows?' said Kalan, 'But we've got to do something or in a week they are going to be at each others throats again'

'I'm in' said Risu, 'This is a nice place, lots of grass. I don't mind hanging around a while'

'But why should we care?' said Funni

'Caring comes naturally to me' said Kalan, 'And let me tell you a secret. It comes naturally to you as well' Funni had her arms crossed but her mind open as Kalan carried on talking. 'Funni, you helped those squirrels move their stash, they were nice folk weren't they?' asked Kalan

'Simple folk' replied Funni, 'and let me tell you a secret. We girls get irritated by people who can't work things out for themselves'

'You get on fine enough with Risu' said Kalan smiling. Funni relaxed a little and laughed with Kalan.

'Hey!' said Risu, but he didn't have time to complain because Funni came straight over to him and hugged him playfully.

'Ok ok' she said, 'You've convinced me, but I'm doing nothing in this rain'

'You're right about that' replied Kalan looking out onto a Tompkins Park that was becoming water logged in parts of the lawn. It was only late afternoon but the dark clouds made it seem like night. Those same clouds also showed no signs of letting up on the waterworks any time soon. The sky lit up as the first lightening bolt stretched itself across the lower Manhattan sky. It was followed moments later by a loud, low, rumbling clap of thunder that almost shook the tree they were in.

'Maybe we should adjourn to the main drey gentlemen' suggested Risu hiding his fear by putting on Sunda's accent.

Kalan stuck his tail outside of the wooden box for a few seconds. When he pulled it back inside it was drenched, 'We'll need a week to dry off after only a couple of seconds in that rain' He started to squeeze the water out of his tail.

'Let's try and make ourselves comfortable here 'til it's passed' said Funni looking at Risu. She moved away from the entrance and made herself a space in the pile of paper scraps. Risu moved over to join her and Kalan, flicking his still wet tail around came over as well.

Kalan and Risu talked some more about how they had solved the various arguments back at the main drey, but Funni kept quiet. As the thunder and lightening danced with the rain overhead, Risu's silly accent had made her think about Sunda. Her thoughts took her back to imagine the little red squirrel quivering with fear in Clermont. She remembered how he had confessed to her that thunderstorms were his biggest nightmare and she wished she could be there to comfort him. As she thought she smiled to herself. Maybe Kalan was right, maybe caring after folk did come naturally to them all.

Recent events had also turned Shokobaba into a more caring animal.

She cared a lot as she sat shivering and wet under a water tower on the West bound side of the New Jersey Turnpike.

She cared about getting wet, about catching a cold.

She cared about how tired she was and of how much her feet hurt.

She cared about if she would ever get home, if she would ever she Chinatown again.

But most of all she cared about the squirrels. The squirrel that had bit hard into her tail, and the other, smaller one that had trapped her in the van.

Kalandaka.

Oh yes, how she cared about him. He had tricked her, made her break a nail, got her wet, left her for lost goodness knows where and had foiled her plan of catching up with the one who had bit her tail. All this caring made Shokobaba let out a high pitched wail of frustration, but even this didn't help her feel any better as it was instantly drowned out by a deafening clap of thunder. Half of her – the more caring half – wanted to keep on walking despite the rain. The other, more sensible, half told her to stay under the relatively dry cover of the water tower until the storm had finished. As Shokobaba sat debating which half of her mind to listen to, a small white van came to a halt on the hard shoulder on the road in front of her. She squinted her eyes to try and make out the writing on the side of the van. She couldn't understand much but she recognized a series of symbols she saw all the time back home,

'NY 10010'

'NY NY'

NY, this was plastered over everything human back home. It was on store fronts, signs, papers. It meant home, and that vehicle was pointed in the opposite direction to the one she had been traveling while in the removals van. Shokobaba put two and two together and decided that that white van could take her home, what was she waiting for? She raced out from under her shelter into the heavy rain and down the grass verge towards her ride home. A human figure with an umbrella was kneeling by the side of the van, running a hand along the edge of the passenger door. Shokobaba looked desperately around for a way in, but all the doors were shut. The figure called out to another person still sat inside the van.

'I can't see anything, it looks normal. I think it was just your imagination'

Shokobaba couldn't understand what was being said, but she did recognize the voice of a woman when she heard it, and to cats females humans were play putty. Shokobaba jumped in front of the female figure and started to wail mournfully.

'Oh my lord' said the woman holding the umbrella.

The soaked white cat moved in for the killer punch. She rubbed her drenched head and back along the woman's legs, looking up and meowing for all she was worth.

'You poor, poor thing. What on earth are you doing out here?' The woman opened the van door and Shokobaba jumped straight inside.

'WHAT THE!?'

Another woman was sitting inside and the flash of white cat leaping inside gave her a start. 'Alison, it's a cat. Look the poor thing is scared out of its wits'

'What is a cat doing on the New Jersey Turnpike?'

'You know Alison, I reckon it must be one of those stories we hear of people getting rid of unwanted pets on the freeway. Don't you remember that Larry King program about it the other month? We can't leave it here'

Shokobaba sat meowing on the floor in front of the passenger seat. Two women. Two middle aged women. String puppets for a cat like Shokobaba. She knew she would be calling the shots from here on in.

'Pass me that blanket before it gets hypothermia. What evil twisted mind could abandon such a beautiful creature on a night like this?'

'I guess it was providence that made you stop to check if we had hit something back there. Other wise we'd never have found this cat. Alison, she might have died'

'Oh don't say that Nancy. Wrap it up warm and let's get going. You know my mother is going to worry if we aren't home soon in this weather'

The engine started up and the van with its three female occupants sped off down the freeway. The writing on the side of the van said:

'Gramercy Park Florists.

'From the garden state to your door'

65 East 20th Street

NY 10010 NY'

Shokobaba was indeed heading back home. She relaxed in her warm, damp blanket. For the first time in ages she felt comfortable, but her mind couldn't stop thinking about the squirrels. She cared too much.

The Old Woman, Cha'ly and Tibbles

Whereas the storm had long since passed on up into Canada, it had nonetheless been raining constantly over Manhattan for three days. It was a great relief therefore when Risu woke up the other two Battery Parkers on the fourth day of their stay at Tompkins Park. 'The sun!' he shouted excitedly, 'I thought I was never going to see it again' The others were quick to jump up and join him on the edge of the wooden box they had been calling home since they arrived.

'Can we go now?' asked Funni

'Yes' replied Kalan as eager as she was to be off, 'we're done here'

The Battery Parkers had spent the past few days trying to put things straight at Tompkins Park. The last remaining arguments had been settled and, more importantly, many of the park residents had begun sorting out their disagreements and problems on their own.

Kalan had not been so successful with Shin. Outside the pagoda he wouldn't listen to anyone and denied his own identity. Inside the pagoda he spoke very little and spent most of the time in deep meditation. Nonetheless the Tompkins Park squirrels still looked to him as their leader despite all the difficulty they had had in understanding his philosophical wisdom. It had been Funni who had come up with way for them to understand the advice Shin gave out,

'Debate it' she had said one evening at the main drey. 'Whenever he tells you what to think or do and you don't understand at first, come back here and tell everyone else. If you all pitch in ideas you'll come up with the answer eventually'

It worked. Even if the Tompkins Park squirrels didn't always hit on perhaps the best interpretation of Shin's advice, it didn't matter. The important thing was that they were at last working out their problems, however mundane - and believe me most squirrel problems are extremely mundane - for themselves.

Shin had spoken to one pair who had been arguing over who had the strongest tail. Shin said, 'The challenge of developing an inner strength of mind is the most fundamental of squirrel objectives. Have faith in the squirrel within, don't get distracted by physical irrelevances'

The general opinion back at the drey after a lengthy debate was that Shin wanted to see who could hang the longest from a branch with their tail. Kalan started to argue with the Tompkins Park squirrels that this was not what Shin had meant, but Funni pulled him to one side and told him that as long as they were happy with their own interpretation of the advice, they wouldn't be arguing.

'What does it matter so long as everyone is getting along'

Kalan found that he couldn't argue with her logic.

They had also found out that Bilka had left the park crossing over Avenue A and had gone along St Marks Street to a place called Union Square. The Tompkins Park squirrels had heard of Union Square, but didn't have any clue as to how to reach it. Now whereas Funni and Kalan didn't seem to mind the lack of direction, Risu had voiced his concern. He had made it clear that he thought they should stay until they had got a route in mind, but no one seemed to have paid him much attention.

This sunny morning Kalan was very anxious to leave. His trip through Chinatown had emboldened him, and to some extent the others, so that the idea of traveling across town during the day no longer held too much fear for the squirrels. However he also wanted to see Shin one last time and at the very least apologize for jumping to conclusions and criticizing him the first time they had spoken. He made arrangements to meet up with Funni and Risu at the children's playground on Avenue A. It would be their set off point for St Marks Street which was directly opposite.

Although the day was getting quite warm under the bright sun, the grass was still very damp and muddy from three days of rain. Kalan kept to the side of the path and then climbed up a large fat Elm tree. He planned to use the higher branches to swing over to the tree with Shin's pagoda, thus avoiding the grass altogether. As he grabbed the trunk and started to pull himself up he surprised two squirrels who were hanging from their tails from the lowest branch.

'Whoa! Careful' said one of them loudly as Kalan climbed past. His body started to swing ever so slightly.

'You get swinging and you're going down' whispered the other one through gritted teeth.

'I'll be alright' replied the slightly swinging squirrel, and he clenched his teeth and tried desperately to concentrate all his weight to his head.

'Sorry' Kalan shouted down to them, 'I didn't see you there'

He now recognized them as the squirrels who had totally misinterpreted Shin's advice into a tail hanging contest. 'How long have you two been hanging there?' said Kalan remembering them from the debate the night before.

'UGgggggggH' said the squirrel as he tried not to swing.

'He can't talk' said the other squirrel very slowly in a gruff voice, 'talking will make him swing more'

'Well...erm...good luck then' said Kalan and he carried on up the tree trunk.

About half way up he pushed himself into the air and grabbed onto another branch, this one stretching out from Shin's pagoda tree. Kalan landed safely and carried on up the new tree. However the branch from which he had launched himself from swung up and down and vibrated violently for a few seconds. These vibrations flowed back into the main trunk of the tree and, although imperceptible to the human eye, moved downwards to the lower branches.

'Oh for the love of.........' shouted out the hanging squirrel with the gruff voice as the gentle tremors worked their way onto his branch and he too, ever so slightly, started to swing.

Kalan climbed down onto the branch of the Elm with the pagoda. As he approached he could hear the familiar humming sounds of meditation coming from inside. Shin was in. Kalan peered inside and saw Shin had his back to the entrance. He was sitting with his arms outstretched and his paws open flat. Kalan squeezed his way inside and moved around the side of the room and eventually sat himself down in front of Shin. Surprisingly Shin stopped humming immediately and opened his eyes.

'I've come to say goodbye' said Kalan, 'and also to apologize for the way I talked to you the other day'

As he spoke Kalan thought he caught the glimmer of a smile in Shin's eye. 'I was out of order and didn't realize what a trauma you had been through, although even that is no excuse for the way I acted'

'Life never really ends' said Shin, 'It merely takes on different forms or you just perceive it to have a different meaning'

Kalan sat silently waiting for Shin to continue, but he did not say anything else. Shin was, however, looking Kalan in the eyes and Kalan noticed that they were large, friendly and brown, but filled with tears. 'We've got the squirrels here discussing your words of advice' Kalan said cheerily, 'They are having a bit of difficulty, but I guess the change in you was a bit of a trauma for them as well'

'There is no need to hurry in the quest for enlightenment. It comes to us all sooner or later. And even if one squirrel arrives at his enlightenment and inner peace many years before his friend it makes not a difference. The enlightenment is the same for both no matter at what time they discover it'

Kalan smiled and bowed his head. The two squirrels sat in a relatively comfortable silence for about five minutes, then Kalan started to edge his way around the wall and towards the exit.

'Well so long Shin. I hope your inner peace is infectious' said Kalan as he slipped out of the pagoda. He waved his paw, but Shin didn't turn around, so he jumped down onto the branch and began to make his way down the tree.

'KALAN!' Shin's voice cried out from inside the Pagoda. Kalan, caught by surprise, whirled back and onto the branch. He popped his head back inside the pagoda and came face to face with Shin. 'Don't you be in too much of a hurry to live your ambitions and dreams Kalan. Sometimes the journey is often more rewarding than the destination' Shin smiled at Kalan for the first time.

'Thank you' replied Kalan 'I'll remember that'

Shin turned himself around and got back into his favorite position to meditate.

'And you remember something Shin' said Kalan calling back after the Tompkins Park leader, 'remember that a pagoda doesn't make a squirrel who he is. In or out you are always Shin'

'Thank you' replied Shin without turning around, 'I'll remember that'

Feeling a lot better Kalan jumped back into the branches and launched himself with added vigor into the next tree. He landed heavily on the tip of another branch and let himself enjoy the swaying sensation it gave him. As the branch stopped moving Kalan continued along it to the trunk and started to scurry headfirst down it. He remembered the two squirrels who had been hanging by their tails and realized that his swaying around had probably made matters a lot worse for them. He wasn't wrong. As he got to the lowest branch he could see and hear both squirrels struggling to stop themselves from swinging.

'UggggH'

'Can't .... hold....... on' said the one closest to the trunk as the subtle tremors from Kalan's swinging flowed down through the tree.

His friend was also struggling, but the more Kalan watched the more he couldn't see any swinging at all. They seemed perfectly still to him. He decided it best not to say anything, in fact best not to be seen at all, so he moved around to the other side of the trunk and jumped down. On reaching the ground he heard a small cry followed by two dull thuds on the ground. Kalan ran around the tree to see what had happened and found both squirrels lying on the floor.

'Are you ok?' Kalan said as he ran over to them.

'I can't feel my tail' called out one of them.

'Oh Geesh, neither can I' said the other.

'What do you expect?' said Kalan, 'You've been hanging from it for hours, you've got to give time for the blood to get back circulating'

One of the squirrels sat up and put his hand on his waist, 'Did you see which one of us fell first?' he said looking hopefully at Kalan.

'No sorry I was looking the other way,' replied Kalan.

The other squirrel also sat up and started rubbing his tail, 'Well that was a waste of time then' he said looking over at his friend.

'Pretty pointless wasn't it?' Both squirrels were now trying to massage some life back into their numb tails.

'If you ask me' said Kalan, 'I think you've both got strong tails. It's pretty much even I reckon'

The two squirrels looked at each other and nodded. 'Yeah I guess so' said one of them

'You're right' said the other, 'Let's call it a draw and go and do something useful for a change'

They both tried standing up and jumped from foot to foot as the blood rushed back into their legs and tails.

'You guys take care now' said Kalan and he started to run off down the pathway towards the Avenue A side playground.

One of the squirrels waved feebly to him with his tail. 'Hey, I can feel it coming back to life'

Approaching the playground from the pathway, Kalan was spotted by Risu who started waving his tail at him from a small bush near the swings. It was around ten in the morning and the park was already quite full with kids and their parents. The children were screaming with excitement since the rain had kept them all indoors for the past couple of days. Swings were being swung vigorously and slides were being slid down with gusto.

'What a racket' said Kalan as he joined Risu and Funni under the bush.

'Ha yeah, these little humans are full of something' said Risu above the din.

'Adrenalin I think' replied Kalan, 'and I hope you've both remembered to bring your supply 'cause we are going to need it today'

'I'm ready' said Funni

'You know I'm actually sorry to be leaving' said Risu, 'So much green, so many trees. The idea of running over all that concrete again......... I don't know. How about staying another day or two and enjoy the sun?'

'Risu!' Funni found herself shouting. She hadn't been expecting this.

'Hey, I'm sorry. Can't I say how I feel anymore?' Risu shrugged.

'Risu's right Funni' said Kalan, 'it would be nice to hang around and explore the park more, it's the nicest one we've been in since we left home......but,'

Kalan moved closer to Risu, 'We're getting closer to Bilka and Central Park. Tompkins Park is cool but Central Park Risu...... don't you remember? Why settle for second best?'

Risu looked up at Kalan and tried to explain himself better, 'I know all this, and I don't want to stay here forever, just a few more days, that's all'

Funni threw her arms in the air, 'Risu' she said angrily, 'I have no intention of staying here a minute longer and neither does Kalan. So what are you going to do?' She paused to let Risu reply, but he said nothing so she carried on, 'Are you going to stay here on your own? Catch up with us later?'

Risu was shrugging in continuation now, but he was sticking to his guns. 'We don't even really know where we are going' he said, 'we run off down some road, but we don't know where it leads. The squirrels here don't know where Union Square is, so how are we going to find it? Tancredi's gone, there are no rats to ask directions to. I say we stay a little longer and plan things better. Ok?'

Risu's unexpected rebellion took Kalan and Funni by surprise. Funni felt angry and Kalan frustrated because he knew that Risu's argument was, in fact, a completely valid one. Kalan's plan – for what it was worth – had been to head down St Marks Street and, at a certain point, ask the first animal they met for directions. He hadn't thought too much of it, but now, confronted by Risu's second thoughts, he wished he had.

As the kids in the playground screamed and laughed with the sun in their faces, the three Battery Parkers sat in the shade in a silent, gloomy semi-circle close to the rubber tire swings.

'Well you can just catch up with us later' said Funni eventually, 'We'll go without you'

'No we won't' said Kalan, 'We all go together'

'Then I'll go on my own' huffed Funni.

'Oh for goodness sake' said Kalan finding it increasingly difficult to disguise his own growing frustration at the situation, 'We've just spent the past few days solving everyone else's problems and here we are again starting another of our own'

Risu gave an almighty shrug and rolled his eyes upward, 'My feet have only just stopped being sore after that run through Chinatown' Funni continued huffing and turned her back on Risu, 'Do you know how long it will be 'til we feel grass under our feet again Funni?' said Risu.

'It doesn't matter' she replied without turning around.

The gloomy silence came back. Funni faced Avenue A, Risu gazed longingly into the park and Kalan was sat between the two lost for a solution.

'You guys don't want to take St Marks to get to Union Square'

A friendly voice came from within the bushes. 'Go up to the corner of the park and take 10th Street to the church of St Marks. The rats have got a place there and it's just a hop and a jump from Union Square'

Funni turned around in time to see a familiar face emerge slowly from the bush.

'Shin!' said Kalan as surprised as the others to see the Tompkins Park guru out of his pagoda tree.

Shin nodded and smiled at Kalan, but made his way directly over to Risu and placed his tail on the small squirrel's shoulder. 'I know how you feel Risu' Shin spoke softly, 'Tompkins Square Park is one of the best and one of the greenest and one of the friendliest in Manhattan. If you want to stay on I don't believe there is a single squirrel in town who could argue with you' Risu felt emboldened by Shin's words and stopped slouching. 'But' continued Shin shifting the tone of his voice downwards slightly, 'there is not a squirrel in town who has two friends like these' Shin's tail dropped gracefully from Risu's shoulder and waved itself in the direction of Funni and Kalan, 'The most beautiful, green, tree filled paradise in the world is nothing but a barren wasteland if you have no friends to enjoy it with'

Risu sighed, he knew where Shin was headed. 'And I guess' Risu said meekly, 'you're going to tell me that the bottom of a trash can could be the greatest place in Manhattan if I'm in it with my friends'

Shin nodded, 'It might be a bit smelly, but you'll have more fun'

Risu formed a frown by pushing his bottom lip up towards his top one and pushed them both outwards.

'Don't turn your back on friendship Risu. It enriches everyone's lives. Just look at me' Shin glanced over towards Kalan as he carried on speaking, 'I've spent the past few months wrapped up in myself and look at all the unhappiness I caused myself and my friends'

Risu began shuffling his feet. Funni smiled as this was a sure sign that he was in the process of changing his mind. 'The church of St Marks you say?'

'Yes' said Shin, 'It's a ten minute run up 10th Street, and you'll be over halfway to Union Square'

Kalan looked at both Risu and Shin standing next to each other and didn't know what he felt happier about. The fact that Risu was finally coming around to leaving the park or Shin's almost miraculous change of character.

'And there is a rat place at this church?' Risu was still asking questions to give himself the confidence to leave.

'Union Square has the largest rat community in Manhattan. It's so big in fact that I believe you can get there directly from St Marks using the rat's underground network'

Risu looked down at his shuffling feet. He could sense that all eyes were on him.

'Also' continued Shin, 'If you leave now you could all be in Union Square before the evening'

Risu shrugged and sighed at the same time and finally looked up to Kalan and Funni, 'Can we at least stay a while at Union Square?'

'YES!' Funni and Kalan shouted out in unison.

'Great' said Risu slapping his paws together, 'Let's be on our way then'

Kalan hopped over to Shin with a look of gratitude and confusion in his eyes. How had Shin known about their problem?

'Come and follow me' said Shin sensing Kalan's curiosity, 'I'll accompany you guys to St Nicks' Shin pointed to a small church that was standing on the corner of 10th Street overlooking the park, 'I haven't been there in a while, and it's on the way'

Shin and Kalan started to run, while Risu hopped over to Funni who was still standing with her arms folded and grabbed her arm. 'Are you planning on staying? Race you there'

Funni pushed Risu playfully and started to run with him along the edge of the park towards the North East corner.

Ahead of them Shin and Kalan were running together. 'How does it feel to be out of the pagoda tree Shin?' asked Kalan as they ran in and out of the park fence.

'Very liberating' replied Shin, 'but also a little terrifying'

Shin and Kalan reached the far corner of the park and sat down to wait for the other two. Kalan still had a lot of questions. 'The world outside your pagoda scares you?'

'Not as much as I was beginning to scare myself' said Shin, 'And I've got you and your friends to thank for helping me realize what was wrong'

'Please' said Kalan, 'We are all looking to find an inner peace, and not everyone is lucky enough to find it. Plus I am sure each squirrel has their own way'

'You think your journey is yours?'

'I think that it could be' said Kalan as Risu and Funni arrived.

Risu had cheered up visibly and turned to face the park, 'So long grass, I'm going to miss you'. Risu then looked down at his feet and waved them in Funni's face, 'Ready for more concrete guys?'

'Cut that out' said Funni waving them away with her tail.

Risu looked up to her smiling, 'Come on let's go before I change my mind again'

Shin led them to the edge of Avenue A, and once the road was clear they raced across and onto the front steps of the church of St Nicholas. 'Whoosh! That was a rush' said Shin as he panted a little out of breath on the lower step, 'It's been ages since I've crossed a road' Beckoning the others to follow he ran around the side of the church onto 10th Street and pointed up along it. 'Look guys, St Marks is on your left after you cross 2nd Avenue. The rats have a large place somewhere near the entrance. It shouldn't be hard to locate'

Kalan peered carefully up 10th Street. There were a few people walking along the sidewalk and the road was filled with lots of the usual parked cars. It seemed safe enough.

'Now do take care' Shin said, 'and remember if you are ever passing by the finest park on the Lower East Side you know you are always guests of honor' The Battery Parkers all said thank you and Shin began to back away from them towards Avenue A, 'No, no' he said waving his paws, 'It is I who has to thank you all. And I do, I do from the bottom of my heart' Shin gave them all one last tooth filled grin and then turned the corner and disappeared.

The short trip down 10th Street passed without any incident. The Battery Parkers were quite expert by now at using parked cars for cover, and the humans they passed were – as usual – wrapped up in their own mysterious thoughts to even notice the squirrels.

When the squirrels reached 2nd Avenue they saw St Marks on the opposite side of the busy Street. Risu made the point that the trees in front of the church seemed to be growing out of concrete. They quickly ran across 10th Street and then waited and studied the traffic on 2nd Avenue from underneath a green Volvo parked near the corner. It was a very busy road and the cars were moving along it extremely quickly.

'They are all traveling in the same direction though' said Kalan with his usual optimism and waved his tail downtown.

The main problem they discovered was the lights at the crossing. They went green for the cross town traffic at very sporadic intervals and never with the same intervals.

'26, 27…' counted Funni as the lights turned back to red 'Hey! Last time they changed after 39!'

The solution presented itself however in the form of a large group of schoolchildren from PS 34 (The Franklin D Roosevelt School on 12th Street).

'Let's cross with this lot' suggested Risu as he saw the large group of ten year olds and their two stressed our teachers preparing to cross 2nd Avenue.

'Steven keep on the sidewalk. Dolores! Stop pushing'

'Good idea' said Kalan and the Battery Parkers got themselves ready to run.

Unlike the majority of adult New Yorkers the squirrels had passed over the days, the children of PS 34 spotted them instantly as they ran out from under the Volvo. The kids started shouting and pointing at the three squirrels as they crossed the road and this was just another strain on their teachers.

'Oh my goodness!....... Keep together kids....... Dolores!!... Don't run after them, keep your eyes on the road....... DANNY DON'T!'

The squirrels hurried onto the small, concrete open space in front of St Marks and straight up the largest tree. Below them the children were shouting and pointing upwards and the teachers were having a hard time convincing them of getting back on course for the planned trip to the Ukrainian Museum.

'It's always those little humans who spot us' said Funni looking down to a ground full of excited kids, 'Why is that?'

'I reckon it's 'cause they're closer to the ground than the others' said Risu.

'Oh little squirrel, the other humans, they see you too'

'It's just their brains don't pass the information through'

The unmistakable sound of Ratspeak came from a branch above. The squirrels looked up to see two large rats sitting and smiling above them.

'When you are young you see everything. I mean it's all new and it's all important'

'You get older and squirrels – hey, they ain't a novelty, they're mundane, insignificant'

The two rats looked at each other as they carried on expressing their theory to the squirrels, 'So you see the adults they see you, be really they don't'

'Their brains are jaded, so of you they make no mental note'

The rats grabbed the trunk of the tree and slid elegantly down to the squirrels' branch, 'I mean look at us two rats in a tree in broad daylight'

'Normally that would send humans crazy, give them a fright'

'But up here they think we are squirrels, its all on the level'

'They don't see us as some rodent incarnation of the devil'

'Because they are not really looking!' said Risu excitedly to Funni and Kalan. He found Ratspeak so much easier to follow sometimes

'Exactly little squirrel' said the darker of the two rats and held out his arm, 'This here's Desbrosses and my name is Moore'

The other rat also moved forward to greet the squirrels, 'But you can call me Des, it's easier I'm sure'

Presentations over, the five of them looked back down over 2nd Avenue.

'Nice crossing squirrels' said Moore gazing back at the kids as they made their way reluctantly to the museum on the corner of 12th street, 'it certainly was a good 'un'

'Yeah' said Desbrosses, 'and crossing 2nd Avenue ain't my idea of fun'

'Thanks' replied Funni, and without any further pleasantries got straight to the point, 'We're headed up to Union Square, could you guys lend us a hand?'

The rats were, as New York rats almost always are, more than happy to help out.

Shin had been right about the rats having a den under St Marks Church and he had also been right about it being linked all the way to Union Square. The Union Square rat community was indeed Manhattans largest and it had an underground network of tunnels, sewers and bolt holes that stretched as far as 2nd Avenue to the East and 6th Avenue to the West. Desbrosses and Moore explained to the squirrels that they would be happy to accompany them to Union Square, but asked that they wait until it got dark. Even in the relative safety of an underground sewer Manhattan's rats still feel safer moving around at night. The squirrels understood and were content to pass the afternoon people watching on 2nd Avenue and exchanging stories with the rats.

The rats knew of Shokobaba but hadn't heard of Bilka or the Battery Parkers, 'We've been out of the loop for a while hanging out with family on Avenue D' said Moore as way of explanation.

'This will be our first trip to Union Square in months' added Desbrosses, 'perhaps as many as three'

Despite this the rats had traveled the length and breadth of Manhattan during their short lives. They had been to Battery Park once and City Hall a few times. However it was when they started talking about Central Park that Kalan and the others listened in mouth wide open silence.

'Uncountable trees and fields of grass as far as your eye can see' Desbrosses said.

'It's the only place in Manhattan where we've ever felt truly free'

'The park is full of friendly locals and there's not a car to be seen' 'Guys' said Moore earnestly, 'Its wonders are hard to describe if you've never been'

After all their recent ups and downs the three squirrels remembered their conversations back at Battery Park. Central Park was still after all one of their motivations for leaving home in the first place. Listening to the rats bought this fact back home to them.

'How far away are we?' asked Funni, 'We've already traveled so far'

'No, no' said Moore, 'It's still a hell of a long way from where we all are'

Funni turned and looked despondently at Risu.

'We'll hang out with your dad for a bit at Union Square. It sounds like a fun place' Risu said cheerily. Even though he liked the idea of getting to Central Park the fact that they had traveled so far and were still, apparently, no closer didn't go down too well with him either. In any case talk of Central Park helped time fly by, and it was in fact the rats and not the squirrels who pointed out that it was dark enough to make their way to the den under St Marks.

With Desbrosses leading the way and going one at a time, so as not to draw too much attention to themselves, they all ran down the tree. Next a quick dash across the tiny square to the entrance to St Marks, and from there they kept to the edge of the building until coming to a small circular hole in the ground. It could not have been more than two inches in diameter but, nonetheless, Desbrosses then Funni, Risu, Moore and finally Kalan all squeezed themselves down through it. The hole remained as narrow as it's opening at first, but as Kalan allowed gravity to pull him slowly downwards, it soon opened up and eventually he found himself falling. Before his fall got too hairy he landed with a tiny splash on the ground in a pool of pungent water. He jumped instantly out and onto the side of the drain where he started to shake the smelly liquid from his body.

'Gross' he said looking over to the others who were sitting nearby.

'I got lucky' said Risu, looking smugly dry,' Funni broke my fall'

'Hey squirrels!' Desbrosses was calling to them from further along the drain, 'Come and follow me when you've dried your hair'

'For all the adventure and excitement that's Union Square' said Moore, who was still sitting beside the squirrels.

Kalan shook the last drops of water from his tail and pushed himself into the others. 'How long is it going to take?' he asked Moore as they all started to run after Desbrosses.

'Half an hour' replied the rat confidently, 'It'll be a piece of cake'

'Come on Tibbles, you take a piece now, its lovely lovely'

Shokobaba gazed with distain at the outstretched, wrinkled old hand in front of her. Held limply between a bony thumb and index finger was a crumbling piece of fruit cake. Shokobaba couldn't help but notice that the black raisins sticking out of the cake were exactly the same color as the dirt under the old woman's nails. The white cat hissed in disgust and stepped backwards.

'Oh don't be like that Tibbles, it's so tasty you know' The old woman pushed the cake into her mouth and smiled as she chewed. Shokobaba turned her back in repulsion as crumbs and a raisin fell from the old woman's mouth on the floor.

Ms Winifred Armstrong lived at 68b Gramercy Square, and had been doing so for as long as anyone local could remember. Her daughter ran a florists nearby and was one of the two women Shokobaba had hitched a lift with back to New York. She was also the woman who had left Shokobaba with her elderly mother 'to keep her company'.

The white cat had, of course, been trying to get out of the old woman's apartment from the moment she had arrived, but it was proving to be very difficult. Winifred kept all the windows and doors tightly shut and never left the building. There was only one occasion when she would allow the stagnant air to be ventilated and that was when she would open a French window in her front room – the one that overlooked Gramercy Park - to let in her friend 'Cha'ly'. However whenever she was about to do this, she would violently poke Shokobaba with her walking stick and force the cat into the back room and then shut the door. Shokobaba hated that back room more than any other in the old woman's apartment but by trying to avoid Winifred's fruit cake the white cat had in fact backed her way into it. This did not go unnoticed.

'Hmmmmm' said Winifred, 'Well if you don't want none I bet Cha'ly will fancy a bite'

The old woman turned and with an almost frightening burst of speed walked into the front room and shut Shokobaba behind her. 'You be a good cat and stay in there' she said from behind the door, 'We don't want you to go scaring Cha'ly now do we...eh?'

Shokobaba leapt towards the door and stuck her head down to the tiny gap between it and the floor. She couldn't see anything, but she could hear the old woman struggling to open the French window.

'Oh Cha'ly! You been waiting long out there?'

The window creaked open and Shokobaba heard the 'pit a pat' of tiny feet running onto the carpet in the front room. 'Oh my, you've brought some friends Cha'ly......my goodness so many of you'

Shokobaba kept her ear to the ground. She counted eight, maybe nine. 'Oh my, oh my, Cha'ly, those nasty people at the park aren't feeding you are they....eh? You try my fruit cake Cha'ly, and your friends too, you all look so famished'

Shokobaba banged her head lightly against the door. 'Think cat, think' she muttered to herself. In the next room was an open window to New York and freedom, while in this room............ Shokobaba shuddered slightly and turned to look at the rest of the back room.

In the far corner was a rancid cat litter which hadn't been changed since Shokobaba had arrived. She had in any case started doing her 'business' on the settee and carpets in the hope that the old woman would kick her out, but it had made no difference as Winifred's sense of smell had gone south years ago.

In the center of the far wall was a fire place. Shokobaba had tried climbing up the chimney, but it had been blocked up. Her eyes moved further along the far wall and then suddenly she stopped and turned back towards the door. The white cat couldn't bring herself to look again at the tiny group of horrors that decorated the area between the wall and the long green settee. She banged her head against the door again. 'If you don't get out of here girl you'll end up staying permanently like them'

The 'them' Shokobaba was referring to was also the group of things she couldn't bear to look at – Winifred Armstrong's small collection of stuffed animals. Her late brother had been a taxidermist and she had had her last three pets stuffed. A black haired Yorkshire terrier and two white Scotties. Forming the rest of this motley crew was a stuffed Owl, a viscous looking stoat and a squirrel. The thought of ending up like those things with their black, lifeless eyes gazing forever at the green settee made Shokobaba cringe and a cold shiver ran through her body.

'Oh Iplo pleeeease, stop taking food from her fingers, you have no idea where they've been'

'You speak for yourself. You're quite happy to delve around in that bowl of nuts that smell like cat's pee'

Another squirrel also spoke up from the front room and gave Shokobaba a jolt as she realized that he was standing right by her door. 'I don't know if you guys have noticed, but this whole dump smells of cat lately. Take a whiff near here'

Shokobaba shifted herself away from the door slightly as she heard some more squirrels run over towards it.

'You're right Ketor….. Do you think the old girl has got a cat next door?'

'I don't know but it smells very strong'

'CHA'LY! CHA'LY! Get away from there now'

Winifred stood up and shooed the squirrels away from the door to the back room, 'Don't you go baiting Tibbles now Cha'ly. You know what cats are like'

The squirrels jumped away from the door, and a couple started to make their way out of the window.

'Oh my Cha'ly, don't go. It's perfectly safe, old Tibbles can't get you. Come over here and have some more cake.

Despite Winifred's attempts the squirrels had decided to leave. Not because of the potential cat, but simply because they had filled their cheeks and fur with all the cake and nuts they could manage for the night. One of them was so laden down with nuts he couldn't jump up to the window.

'For goodness sake Iplo! Leave a few behind, we'll be back tomorrow'

Reluctantly Iplo dropped a few nuts on the floor and managed to jump up and join the others on the balcony. 'Just as long as you lot remember that those are mine' he said pointing back to the nuts he had been forced to leave behind.

'Yeah, yeah sure' one of the others said unconvincingly. Iplo joined him and they ran across the edge of the iron balcony, down the front steps that led to the front door of 68b, across the road and back into Gramercy Park.

Some of the other squirrels who were carrying lighter loads jumped from the balcony onto the overhanging branches and swung back into the Park using them. When Winifred was certain all the squirrels had gone she stood up and, very shakily, closed the window. After what seemed like an eternity for Shokobaba, the old woman hobbled over to the back door and opened it. The cat rushed out into the front room.

'You missed Cha'ly and his little friends. Naughty Tibbles' Winifred started to giggle, 'I know what you'd like to do. You cats are all the same.........eh?'

Shokobaba looked forlornly at the tightly shut French window. What she would like to do would have to wait. What she had to do was plan an escape from little old lady land.

Just six streets below the brooding Shokobaba, Kalan and the others were making very good progress. They were traveling in a sewer that ran directly under 14th Street. The only problem was the smell, it was getting to be too much for the squirrels.

'I can't stand this stench any longer' said Funni who already had enough issues to cope with being underground, 'I've got to get some fresh air'

For the first time in a while Kalan found himself completely agreeing with her instantly. 'Yes, it's really unbearable' he said, then called on ahead to the rats, 'Hey Moore, Des, we need to get out of here and back up top'

The rats were about ten yards ahead of the squirrels and looked at each other a little bewildered.

'We're almost there, now's not the time to stop' Moore shouted back at Kalan

Funni started to make wrenching noises and had to put her paw to her mouth.

Risu called back to the rats, 'Got to go up top, it's an emergency!'

The rats ran back to the squirrels and saw instantly Funni's sickly expression.

'OK, let me think' said Desbrosses and he looked upwards, 'That grate up there, can you see?'

Funni looked up and almost instantly started to climb up the side of the drain.

'Where will it bring us out?' said Kalan as he and Risu followed Funni upwards.

'On a little grass island' replied Moore 'at the end of 4th Avenue'

'It'll do' said Risu quickly.

As usual the rats were right. The squirrels emerged onto the small traffic island that marks the end of Park Avenue on 14th Street. It's so large that it is, in fact, a mini park with a few trees and even a couple of benches. Funni filled her lungs with the comparatively fresh air of 14th Street and the desire to throw up soon left her. She and Risu made their way over to the nearest tree and ran up. Kalan waited by the grate until he was convinced the coast was clear for the rats.

'Hurry guys' he called down to them, 'it's safe to come up now. It's all clear'

'No thanks Kalan, we'll keep on going from down here'

'You are almost there' The voice of Desbrosses came up from the sewer, 'Union Square is just across the road you know'

'We'll see you later' said Moore, 'just run across the street and go'

Kalan looked up and across the busy street. Of course, there it was, an oasis of trees surrounded by very heavy traffic. 'It's just over there!' Kalan called over to Funni and Risu.

'We know we can see it!'

Kalan looked back down the drain, 'Thanks guys, we'll see you there' There was no reply. Moore and Desbrosses had already gone.

Kalan ran over to join his friends and from the top of the small tree they surveyed the area in front of them. The small island they were on was in the middle of 14th Street and marked the end of Park Avenue South and the start of 4th Avenue. The squirrels peered over the road at Union Square Park. Although it was nearly 10pm the whole square was bustling. Cars were rushing along 14th Street in both directions, people were walking in and out of the metro and many others were still strolling around.

'Whoa!' said Risu as he took in the array of lights and sounds, 'How do the guys who live here get any shut eye?'

'It must take a little getting used to I reckon' said Kalan, having to shout over the siren of an ambulance that came screaming along 14th Street, then made a sharp left onto Broadway.

'Do you think he's over there?' said Funni as the sound of the ambulance faded.

'Bilka?' said Kalan, who didn't really know what reply to give 'I….'

Risu spoke instead. 'I'm sure he is' he said confidently. 'There is so much going on around here. His curiosity wouldn't have let him go already'

Funni smiled at Risu, 'That's what I think' she said slowly, impressed that Risu was on her wavelength.

'Well after you then young lady' said Risu in his post Sunda accent, 'lead the way if you please' and he waved his tail in the direction of Union Square Park.

Needing no further encouragement, Funni happily led the other two down the tree trunk and quickly but carefully across the last stretch of Park Avenue.

As the Battery Parkers ran onto the sidewalk that encircled the park other events were occurring at that same time downtown. At the very bottom of Manhattan Skudzo was sitting alone on top of the telescope that Kalan used to sit on and contemplate life while gazing out over the Hudson Bay.

In fact Kalan's old 'thinking place' had, over the past few weeks, become Skudzo's favorite location to hang. Partly to get away from all the commotion down in the main drey under Clinton castle, but mostly to think about Kalan and the others. He was, of course, worried about them and he missed them too, but tonight his thoughts were uncharacteristically well organized and clear. As Skudzo let himself be seduced by the ripples of light reflected from the downtown skyscrapers on the surface of the Hudson he came to an important realization.

He was curious.

For the first time in his life Skudzo actually had a burning desire to explore further than the end of his nose. He blinked and turned his gaze away from the hypnotic rippling water and back into Battery Park.

'Are you ok Skudzo?' Ardilla was sitting on the pathway below the telescopes.

'Yeah, yeah of course' said Skudzo. He shook his head, as if trying to dislodge the thoughts he wasn't used to having, and in one mighty leap jumped down to Ardilla. 'What are you doing round these parts anyhow?' he asked as he straightened himself out after his jump.

'Well I heard there are a couple of new rats in the park today and rumor has it they've got news of Bilka, Kalan and the others'

Skudzo was a little surprised at the tone of excitement in Ardilla's voice. 'You know Olmaxon doesn't want any of us hanging around the rats until everyone's forgotten about all that business' said Skudzo trying to sound serious.

'Yes' said a straight faced Ardilla, 'you coming with or not?'

'Yeah, come on'

Skudzo smiled broadly and pushed Ardilla off in the direction of the rat's place. He did, however, take a good look around to make sure they weren't being followed.

As Skudzo and Ardilla were dropping in on the Battery Park rats further up the road at Trinity church Sunda sat atop the church steeple letting a light breeze blow into his face as he gazed up Broadway. Unlike Skudzo curiosity was not an alien emotion to the red squirrel, but Sunda had realized a long time ago that once you open the lid of the curiosity box it is not easy to close it again.

The peace and serenity he had discovered in his short time at Trinity church had helped calm his own rampant curiosity for life. The church had transformed it into a more reflective, analytical and mind expanding study that could easily be satisfied by sitting on the church steeple. His mind could wander freely, but his body stayed firmly put.

Sunda had liked it that way until recently. The visit from the Battery Parkers had shaken up his personal curiosity box, and the past few nights he had found himself spending more and more time coming to the top of the steeple and gazing downtown. Looking at the city and thinking about having one last adventure. And why not? He could head off right now and catch up with them in no time. There was so much more to be seen, to be discovered and he could do it with squirrels who were as thirsty for knowledge as he was.

The commotion in his mind calmed down for a moment and he sat in mental silence just feeling the breeze blow softly over his red fur. After a while a single thought popped into his head. Surely Sunda old boy, he wondered to himself, when the silence in your brain is one you are comfortable with surely that is the sign of true peace of mind? Why go starting fires when one is perfectly warm enough as it is? Sunda took in a deep breath from the breeze. The Trinity Church clock struck 10pm, but Sunda barely noticed. How nice the lights look at this time of night he thought.

Less than a mile away 10pm marked the start of a very important meeting in Chinatown. At the back of an alley just off Mott Street a strange collection of animals were discussing their immediate future. Wesley had convened this meeting and Dusi, Mirango, several members of Dusi's extended family plus a handful of pigeons were in attendance.

'We cant' find out anything about her whereabouts' said Mirango, 'The rats don't trust us and won't tell us anything'

'You can't blame them' said Dusi 'They know we work for her'

'Worked' said Wesley correcting Dusi's grammar, 'Worked. It's over. She ever comes back here and she'll find it's a whole new ballgame. Look how things have been lately without her. Peaceful, friendly. I don't even remember a time when it's been so pleasant living in Chinatown'

'Maybe she'll never come back' said one of Dusi's cousins hopefully.

'Don't bet on it' said Mirango, 'The moment we let down our guard, or stop worrying about her...... that's when she'll jump on you from behind and..............' Mirango slammed his paws together creating a slapping sound that made everyone jump.

'In any case' said Dusi 'Shoko's owner has been running all over Chinatown in a blind panic, and that cat's face is plastered everywhere. Even if she's not physically here, it's like she's still watching us'

Dusi was referring to the 'lost' posters that Ms Soo Lee had had printed out and stuck on every road sign and telephone kiosk she could find. It was a small letter sized bill which had a black and white photo of Shokobaba staring blankly into the camera. Below the photograph Ms Soo Lee had written:

Lost. Beloved white Persian called Shokobaba.

Reward $100 for safe return.

Contact Soo LEE 212 555 6354

Please Help.

'Yeah I've seen them. Those bills are all over the place believe me. I saw one as far up as Houston' said one of the pigeons, 'It's only a matter of time 'til those humans find her'

'Maybe' said Wesley, 'but no one has actually seen her, and you guys have been flying all over the place. Not a peek, not a whistle'

'You know who would tell us,' said Dusi, and everyone turned their attention to him, 'Those squirrels. Don't forget that Kalan one saved my life. They were smart'

'Yeah right on genius' said one of the pigeons sarcastically, 'Shokobaba left with those guys, so you want to know where they are? They are probably searching for nuts in the afterlife now'

'NO, no wait, hold on' said Wesley, 'What was the name of the park they were all headed to?'

'Tompkins' said Mirango, 'It's on the other side of Houston'

'Well I think the simple answer would be for the pigeons to fly up there and ask around' said Wesley nodding to himself.

'Get outta here' replied one of the pigeons rudely, 'we ain't flying that far up'

'Fine' said Wesley calmly. He knew how to deal with pigeons. 'Then let's just all have nervous breakdowns here not knowing if Shokobaba is going to wake us up in our sleep tomorrow or the next day' Wesley paused and looked and the pigeons, 'I least I know I won't be the first person she visits when she gets back'

'And what is that supposed to mean?' said one of the pigeons ruffling her feathers.

'Well I distinctly remember her saying that she would keep in touch with us all via the pigeons. And then you guys lose track of her half way up the SDR. If

she got into trouble and was desperately looking around for you lot.......'
Wesley closed his eyes and hung his head 'Well let's just say I wouldn't want to
be in your feathers when she gets back home'

The pigeons started to move about a little agitated. They hated helping out
other animals, but became more well - disposed when their own skins were on
the line. 'OK, ok, we'll go looking' said one of them after they had had a mini
conference between themselves.

'No time like the present' said Mirango, looking first at the pigeons and then up
into the night sky.

'Aw shut yours, we're going'

'Just remember' said Wesley, 'to be nicer. People talk more when you are
pleasant'

'You shut it and all'

The pigeons made a lot of noise and commotion, but eventually all four of
them flew off uptown. As the birds flew high over Grand Street and then over
The Bowery they argued amongst themselves as to who should do the talking
when they arrived at Tompkins Park. Eventually Eloise was chosen since being
the only female in the group she was considered to be the politest one of them
all.

'I'll do it, but those filthy scags had better have some good answers or I'll spit in
their faces' she said as they flew together uptown, proving yet again that New
York pigeons a different perspective on polite conversation to everyone else.

Sparrows are altogether a lot more pleasant. Inquisitive, but friendly, they are
always eager to help out and make firm friends.

Tancredi was an excellent example. The pigeons flew high over him as he sat
having a little rest on top of 'No parking' sign on the corner of Prince Street.
He had flown all the way up from his home and was also on his way to
Tompkins Park. He had had no luck in locating Uncle Totti and was very
concerned about his uncle. His sparrow relative hadn't been seen back at his
clock near the City Hall, but Tancredi had found a small pile of dry cookie
crumbs back at his home at Bowling Green Park. Uncle Totti always left dry
cookies whenever he came visiting and Tancredi was convinced it was a sure
sign his Uncle was around.

It was after he had polished off the cookies that Tancredi had decided to visit
Tompkins Park and see how his squirrely friends were doing. He also had a
sneaking suspicion that Uncle Totti was uptown somewhere anyhow. The
sparrow had popped in on Sunda at Trinity Church on his way up, but they
hadn't met. Tancredi had been hovering around Clermont and hadn't seen
Sunda high up on the church steeple.

It was taking Tancredi longer than usual to fly anywhere tonight. He wasn't that svelte on any normal day and the cookies he had so eagerly devoured weighed him down even more. The 'No parking' sign break was almost his tenth stop in the past mile.

'I has gotta eat less' he said to himself and rubbed his protruding belly, 'I is gotta get me a diet, for my health. Find the squirrelys, find Uncle Totti, and then find a diet. Good times are over for you pal. You is a mess'

Tancredi's stomach seemed to growl its disagreement at this plan, but the fat sparrow ignored it. He began flapping his wings furiously and he pushed himself back into the air.

Back at Union Square the first thing the Battery Parkers noticed was just how much of a mess the place was. There were cans, paper, cardboard boxes and the odd person or two dotted about everywhere on the grass or the pathways and under the benches. The trashcans were so full that people had started throwing their garbage just about anywhere. Despite the late hour there were still a few local squirrel residents running around and the Battery Parkers soon introduced themselves to the first tiny squirrel they met. She was leaning against the base of a tree close to the 4th Avenue exit of the Union Square metro.

'Helloooooo' Risu shouted across to her from the path where he and the others were walking. The tiny squirrel waved an even tinnier paw at him.

Risu, Kalan and Funni made their way towards her and when they got closer they could see she wasn't leaning against the tree, but scratching her back on the bark.

'Ahhhh man, that's the spot' she said as she rubbed her back up and down on the tree. Once she felt satisfied she smiled broadly, 'What's up guys?' She acknowledged the arrival of the Battery Parkers with a very chilled and easy going manner. 'You want to join me? Scratch that stress away man'

'I don't have an itch' said Funni coolly.

The tiny squirrel blinked in what seemed like slow motion, 'Don't know what you're missing sister'

Before Funni could reply Kalan managed to get in first. 'We're looking for our friend Bilka. We've come all the way from Battery Park. Do you know anything about him?'

The tiny squirrel stopped scratching and leant against the tree. 'No kidding? You guys know Bilka? That's crazy man, totally cool'

'Is he here?' asked Funni her natural impatience coming out, 'Have you seen him? Where is he?'

The Union square squirrel bent over towards Funni and drew an invisible line in the air in front of Funni with her paw.

'Chill out sister. Bilka is crackin', he's cool. If you guys are friends of his then that's like total man'

There was a long pause as the tiny squirrel slowly leant back against her tree. She smiled across and could see Kalan and Risu looking back at her in anticipation and Funni with her arms folded staring at her impatiently. 'Oh yeah, yeah..... Sorry man' she said laughing a little, 'Your friend Bilka? He's set himself up over at the Gandhi Garden. It's an awesome place and you can really get yourself around his good vibes down there man'

She jumped over into the middle of the Battery Parkers and grabbing Risu and Funni's shoulder she turned them around, with her in the middle, to face the park. 'Gandhi Garden is directly opposite people. You've got to go out the park a little, it's on the sidewalk next to Broadway. He's probably still awake too man, he likes that sweet stuff those humans leave around a little too much lately. That juice won't let you sleep man, keeps you awake. It ain't cool'

The Union Square squirrel was referring to Bilka's weakness for soft drinks. Back at Battery Park, Bilka could often find half filled cans or plastic cups with still a little drop of soda pop still swilling around inside. Here at Union Square though he had found that it flowed in and around the trashcans like water.

Funni pulled her head out from under the tiny squirrel's arm and started to run towards the Gandhi Garden.

'What's the rush sister?' The tiny squirrel pulled Risu closer, 'That girl got itchy fur man'

Risu smiled back at her, 'Sorry about our friend, but Bilka is her dad you see. Thanks a lot though'

Risu pulled himself away and turned to run as well, 'Wait up Funni!' he shouted and ran after her.

The tiny squirrel turned to the last squirrel left by her, 'Her pop has got to teach her to chill man'

'That wouldn't be a bad thing' said Kalan with a smile, 'Thanks again and see you around' He hopped towards the path, but turned to wave at the miniature squirrel before running after the others.

'Stay cool man' she said and waved back as Kalan disappeared across the main lawn of Union Square Park.

He soon caught up with Risu and Funni. They were sat under a bench off the Broadway edge of the park.

'Look' said Risu in a whisper as Kalan arrived by his side. He was pointing his tail across the sidewalk to a small garden by the side of the road. Kalan peered across and could make out another of those metal statues humans like making of themselves. This one was a little different as the metal human was wearing strange simple clothes and seemed to be supporting himself with a stick. Kalan's eyes moved downwards and he saw a large squirrel sitting comfortably between the human's feet. The squirrel appeared to be in a very relaxed state, maybe even asleep. One thing was certain though as Kalan's heart missed a beat. It was Bilka.

Bilka wasn't asleep, he was thinking. Here in Union Square he had discovered a place and a community that he could really relate to. In particular he found sitting under this human's statue very peaceful. Ideas came to him quicker and he could analyze his sometimes wayward thoughts in a strange kind of calm. He was also fond of the hidden grin on the human's face.

Although he appeared physically motionless, inside his head, Bilka was spinning from side to side – the effect of finishing off a half drunken cup of Coke someone had left by a bench earlier that evening. Tonight Bilka also could feel another sensation. There was more grinning going on close by. He focused his eyes and saw three squirrels sitting in a little row on the sidewalk directly in front of him. Their faces were beaming and formed one long smile.

'What took you so long?' he shouted across to them.

Before he could say anything else he was engulfed in a sea of hugs. Bilka was safe and the first part of their journey was complete.

FINE.

The Apartment at 68/b Gramercy Square

Iplo and Ketor were sniffing under the door to Winifred Armstrong's back room.

'It's a cat I tell you, she's got a freaking cat back there' said Ketor earnestly

'Oh I don't know. She's got a lot of smelly things back there, it could be anything' replied Iplo.

The two Gramercy Park squirrels were the only guests that morning at 68b Gramercy Park. The old woman, who had been up since six, had let them in the moment she had seen them on her balcony.

'Come ere Cha'ly, away from that door now' She threw a nut on the floor, but the curious squirrels stayed put.

'Here pussy, pussy, pussy' laughed Ketor under the door and he scratched the white paint slightly with his paw.

On the other side of the firmly closed door Shokobaba sat facing it. Her face was stuck in a sort of fixed grimace, but she said nothing as the two squirrels continued to torment her from the other room.

'Don't talk like that' said Iplo, 'It would surely be more appropriate to say, 'here smelly, smelly, smelly''

'You know Iplo, I don't understand why we come here every day' Ketor was giggling 'The old woman's breath stinks, the nuts are stale and now there is the stinky smell of cat's pee everywhere'

'We're just gluttons for punishment I reckon'

Iplo laughed back as he chewed on a cashew.

'Hey pussy cat!' Iplo pounded his paw on the door, 'Tell your owner to eat some mints!'

'Cha'ly! Cha'ly! You stop that'

Winifred rose from her chair and moved slowly towards the squirrels who, by now, were laughing uncontrollably. They hopped away from the door, but called back 'We can still smell you from here stinky cat' shouted Ketor, 'How can anyone who drinks milk all the time make pee this pungent?'

The squirrels continued laughing as they made their way out through the French windows and back into the park.

Shokobaba gritted her teeth and dug her claws deep into the old woman's light green carpet.

'Keep laughing squirrels' Shokobaba said to herself, 'Keep it cheerful, because believe me you are going to need a sense of humor when I get out of here.

Printed in the United States
217768BV00001B/173/A

9 781847 281319